MURDER on Charity Lane

By Jo Nichols

The Marigold Cottages Murder Collective
Murder on Charity Lane

MURDER on Charity Lane

JO NICHOLS

Allison & Busby Limited
11 Wardour Mews
London W1F 8AN
allisonandbusby.com

First published in Great Britain by Allison & Busby in 2026.

Published by arrangement with Minotaur Books, an imprint of St. Martin's Publishing Group.

A CIP catalogue record for this book is available from the British Library.

First Edition

ISBN 978-0-7490-3480-1

By choosing this product, you help take care of the world's forests. Learn more: www.fsc.org.

MIX
Paper | Supporting responsible forestry
FSC® C018072

Printed and bound in Great Britain by Clays Ltd. Elcograf S.p.A

EU GPSR Authorised Representative
LOGOS EUROPE, 9 rue Nicolas Poussin, 17000, LA ROCHELLE, France
E-mail: Contact@logoseurope.eu

1

MRS B

Wednesday morning found Mrs B of Marigold Cottages at her kitchen table, filling her weekly pill organizer. She ticked in the white ovals, the peach oblongs, the pink circles, then the golden flaxseed that Ocean insisted she take. Finally, she added the squooshy vitamin Ds, which delighted her for some reason. She enjoyed the process in a juvenile way, like a toddler with a match-the-shapes toy.

Of course, when you got older, young people tended to treat you as a child whether you liked it or not.

Mrs B kept her edibles in a different case, the embroidered Peruvian pouch that her husband had brought back from a business trip. She adored shopping in the marijuana dispensaries that had sprung up around Santa Barbara like, well, psychedelic mushrooms after a purple rain. The clerks loved a woman of her age asking about pot gummies, and their surprised pleasure amused her.

She closed the pill bottles, then said, 'Oh, shit,' because she was trying to swear more often. At her age, you needed to try new things.

'What's wrong?' Ocean asked, from the stove.

'Nothing, just practicing.'

Ocean glanced at her. 'You just took them.'

'I know that!' she said, though actually she'd forgotten if she'd taken her pills before she filled the organizer.

When she thought back, she distinctly remembered swallowing them – but she didn't distinctly remember when. She wouldn't admit that to Ocean, though. Ocean was like a daughter to her, which meant she wasn't obliged to tell the actual truth, just the emotional truth.

'I was just thinking about my Little Free Library.' She snapped a pill compartment closed for emphasis. 'I haven't added new books in weeks.'

Ocean ignored her and added beans to the chili simmering on the stove. Her own range was acting up so she borrowed Mrs B's every day or two to make dinner for her kids – though she'd leave an extra bowl on the counter, naturally. Mrs B looked forward to it as she went into the foyer to rummage for books. She'd asked the other tenants for copies of recent favorites, and had them stacked on the sideboard.

She put three of them in her mesh bag along with a few rags, then headed outside and surveyed the property. Her haven and her heart. Six cottages encircled the drought-resistant courtyard of gravel paths, decorated with succulents, lavender, and puffy white fountain grass. The petunias in the clay pots were beginning to look ragged, though. Time to replace them with marigolds for the fall. She'd send Anthony to the nursery. He didn't know the first thing about flowers, but he appreciated when she asked him to learn.

As she walked down the steps to the sidewalk, a raven watched from the roof of her Little Free Library.

'Just a few new books,' she told the raven. 'There's no Poe, I'm afraid. Or are you a crow? I never can tell.'

The bird took flight, soaring above the parked cars before landing in a sycamore down the block.

Her street library looked like a two-story dollhouse version of one of the Cottages. She cleaned the roof with her rags, then added a picture book called *The Baby Who Stayed Awake Forever*, which made her laugh, and a couple of fantasy novels. One was called *Asunder* and one was called *Foul Days*. Hamilton had raved about them, but together the two titles felt a little foreboding.

Or maybe that was just her.

Six months after the murders at Marigold Cottages, life had returned to normal. Which was lovely, of course. Still, a teensy part of her thought back fondly to those terrifying, fascinating days of everyone working together.

Obviously she wasn't hoping for another death. Of course not! Yet she couldn't deny that she missed the solidarity and camaraderie of a shared goal – to keep herself and everyone she loved out of jail. She missed the Murder Collective.

2

SOPHIE

I was leaving work when Nicholas texted me to stop at his place before I went home. Which was weird, because we spent 90 percent of our time at his cottage anyway. Of course I was going to stop there.

So I texted, What's your address again?

I'm still at the corner of Love and U.

Yeah, he'd become the kind of person who texted me cringey love messages. Fortunately, I'd always been the kind of person who found them adorable. Yet as I walked the ten blocks home from work, I wondered if Nicholas wanted to have a Serious Talk. What if this was bad news?

I would've made myself sick about that, but c'mon. You don't break up with someone after telling them you live on the corner of Love and U. Not after six glorious months together.

Things were different now. *I* was different now though I still hadn't sold the play I'd written based on the murders. Well, *loosely* based on the murders. In my play, James 'Dead Rick' Dedrick and Gregory Ybarra are both killed in a community of cottages in Santa Barbara. That much was true. Yet somehow I'd neglected to mention that we'd framed Lily-Ann's ex for the killings because he'd assaulted her. And I definitely hadn't pointed any fingers at the real culprits, as both were my beloved neighbors.

Anyway, I'd sent copies to contests and production companies but never heard back. I did, however, get a better job. When the New Vic Theatre's director of development moved to Serbia, I took her position. My parents were thrilled. There was a quiet dignity in planned giving that they could brag to their friends about: *Oh Sophie? She's working in development.*

And to be fair, raising funds for a professional theatre company was a serious job. Well, except for the pay, which was more tragicomic.

Still, some things hadn't changed, such as my ability to worry needlessly. So when I reached the Marigold Cottages, I bustled up the stairs from the sidewalk, ignored my cottage, and crossed the full length of the courtyard to Nicholas's bigger, better cottage at the far end of the property.

He swept the door open, kissed me perfunctorily, then ushered me to the comfy chair in his living room, where he poured me a glass of sparkling Martinelli's and presented me with a plate of mini-cupcakes.

'What is going on?' I demanded.

'Pick a cupcake,' he said. 'Any cupcake.'

'Tell me the flavors.'

He pointed to each one in turn. 'Red velvet, strawberry, bananas Foster, and *tiramisu*.'

'Ooh, yum,' I said, and reached for the bananas Foster.

He shifted the plate away. 'Not that one!'

'You said pick any cupcake!'

'Yeah, and you were supposed to pick tiramisu. It's your favorite.'

I snorted and picked the tiramisu. 'Happy now?'

'Very. Except, uh . . . just nibble. Don't down the whole thing.'

For the record, I was not in the habit of shoving an entire cupcake into my face hole, even a small one. Still, I did as instructed until my lips closed on something metallic. A moment later, I spat a tiny brass key onto my palm.

Then Nicholas said, 'Sophie Gilman, I am stupid for you. Will you move in with me?'

Also, for the record, Nicholas used to act cold and aloof around me. Around everyone, but mostly me. He was the least-friendly person at the Cottages. He'd been a little intimidating, to tell the truth. He'd put on a front that was cooler than the rest of us. And because he and Mrs B had history, it took forever to drag him into the Murder Collective.

But now? Now he was stupidly in love with me and wanted me to share his apartment.

I said yes, energetically. By which I mean we had the kind of sex that required a bananas Foster mini-cupcake afterward.

I floated through the next few weeks, spinning dreams of cozy dinners, sleepy mornings, and paying half as much rent. Still, one tiny part of me worried: What if we broke up? We wouldn't stay friends. We loved each other too much to downgrade to friendship. We'd never speak again. That was just the way we were. Not like Lily-Ann and her ex-husband, Piotr, who'd stayed in touch until he tried to kill her.

I pushed those thoughts aside, knowing that negativity got me nowhere. I'd learned that the hard way, after losing too much of myself to the creep who'd stalked me. But that was the past, and I was ready for a bright new future.

I focused on work, organizing my donor lists and honing my pitches. And learning from the Givemore Girls, a chat group of women who raised funds for local nonprofits. We networked about donors, venues, and vendors. And we invited each other to events, because you never knew if one rich old couple might support the symphony in addition to the pet shelter. In fact, I'd already connected a retired oral surgeon with a group that harvested backyard fruit trees for soup kitchens.

That had been my biggest triumph so far, but I hadn't made a penny for the New Vic. Still, Mrs B was thrilled that I'd helped deliver fresh oranges to people in need, so I took the win.

My friend Angela, who'd invited me to the Givemore Girls, kept the chat alive with her accomplishments at Bright

California, an after-school STEAM program. Well, that and trite motivational quotes from her mentor: 'My goal is to live my life in such a way that when I die they'll say, she cared.'

I probably needed a mentor, only I didn't know any rich women except for Lily-Ann, and she'd suck at motivational phrases. The thought made me laugh. She'd say things like, *When I die, check Excel for my instructions,* and *You are loading your dishwasher wrong.*

I adored Lily-Ann. She was the only person who could say, *That color isn't flattering*, and I knew without any doubt that she meant it with love. She was practical, loyal, brilliant, and terribly honest. I was going to miss living next door to her, even though I was only moving across the courtyard.

So I focused on worrying about the new tenant in my old apartment. Would they fit in with the rest of us? I wanted to rely on Mrs B's taste, but she'd collected such a strange cast of characters that I'd written a play about us. Who would she find next?

3

LILY-ANN

The Bianco Carrara marble pleased Lily-Ann every time she stepped into her remodeled bathroom. She reveled in its pristine smoothness. Also, the faint gray veins interlaced within the stone matched the shade of her deep, luxuriant bathtub.

Even Anthony fit in that tub.

Better yet, he cleaned it afterward. She suspected that his

tidiness was a consequence of his years in prison, which she'd told him made his assault conviction worthwhile. Perhaps other men would've recoiled at that, but Anthony had simply looked at her with his grave face and smiling eyes. He understood her. And she trusted him to know what she meant despite how she sounded.

She opened the linen closet, the interior of which she'd redesigned for her makeup and hair supplies. Her skin routine centered around the newest line from Shiseido, her makeup was mostly Chanel, and her thick auburn bob would be a stringy mess without her Augustinus Bader haircare. Which reminded her to gift a bottle to Ocean's daughter, Riley, for her upcoming birthday. She knew Riley would appreciate the indulgence. Most of the Marigold residents preferred Ocean's son, Miles, but Lily-Ann clicked with Riley's abrasiveness. Sometimes you wanted so desperately to connect with people that instead you pushed them away.

She dabbed Clive Christian No1 behind her ear and reveled in the scent of floral lime before shutting the closet door. A much better use of space, now that she kept her linens in the antique French chest at the end of her bed.

Speaking of bed . . . she found Anthony lounging on hers, watching her with one arm behind his head, his bicep bulging and his chest bare. His torso was decorated with a tattoo of what she'd first thought was a lighthouse with seagulls but was actually a prison tower with doves. She refused to admit that she liked his tattoos, but she found herself extremely fond of the skin beneath them.

'Morning, Lil,' he said in his rumbling voice.

That was how he always greeted her the mornings he woke up in her bed, like a ritual. She liked that. Routine comforted her. Anthony worked until two or three in the morning, washing dishes at the Sidecar tavern downtown. He usually slept in his studio apartment across the courtyard because he didn't like messing up her cottage with the scent of stale bar and industrial soap. Then he'd join her for lunch, stay through dinner, and leave for work at seven or eight.

She also liked him calling her Lil, despite a lifetime of insisting upon the full Lily-Ann. Because she knew Anthony wasn't shortening her name, he was calling her 'li'l', which she was to him. Everyone else saw her as big and unfeeling, and treated her that way, but not Anthony. He treated her gently, even when she struggled to return the favor.

She'd considered asking him to move in with her – largely because Sophie was so delighted about moving into Nicholas's cottage – but she didn't. She liked her own space. Also, since her ex-husband had betrayed her, she loathed the idea that she *needed* a man, a housemate, a partner.

On the other hand, she never minded having Anthony around; he was one of the few people she could say that about. Despite being so large, Anthony knew how to make himself small. He'd sit in her living room, gazing out the window while listening to his audiobooks and fading into the furniture. He'd found a list of 'The One Hundred Best Books of the Twenty-First Century,' but he'd been too intimidated to start until Hamilton narrowed it down to 'The Twenty Least Boring of the One Hundred Best Books of the Twenty-First Century.'

So far, he loved Claire Keegan and Cormac McCarthy. Anthony wasn't stupid, though he certainly wasn't intellectual. But then, neither was Lily-Ann. She didn't care much for music or literature. What she enjoyed were data, rules, and puzzles. And, increasingly, Anthony.

She crossed to the bed and kissed him. She liked his big hands on her waist, tugging her lightly toward him, but she resisted the urge to join him. She had a database waiting and she despised being late for work – even though she worked from home. Come 8:45, she expected to be at her laptop with a coffee to her right and a notepad to her left.

She spent the first hour of work responding to unnecessary emails from coworkers, then began compiling the stats she'd received from other work teams. She enjoyed that. Well, she didn't care about the stats, but she liked the process, imposing order upon the chaos.

She mostly ignored Anthony while working, though she smiled when she heard the shower running: the image of Anthony in her dainty shower reminded her of a bull in a china shop. Her gentle, painted bull.

He brought her a fresh coffee, then headed home to change and lift weights and whatever else he did at his own place.

At lunchtime, Lily-Ann heard Sophie and Nicholas laughing outside. She brought her salad to the front porch and watched them happily debate whose blender to keep after they moved in together: they had a lot of redundant housewares.

Sophie had begun dressing more formally for her job at the New Vic. Wearing dresses and blazers. With her petite runner's body – by which Lily-Ann meant petite *Asian* body, though she wasn't sure if that was appropriate to even think – she looked cute in everything she thrifted. Glossy black hair, brilliant clear eyes, sweet warm smile. Lily-Ann adored her. And she appreciated her commitment to sustainable dressing; still, she mentally added 'well-cut black blazer (new and expensive)' to the list of Christmas gifts she'd already started. Maybe she'd tell Sophie she got it off a resale site, just to make her happier.

But it wasn't her wardrobe that made Sophie look different these days. It was her confidence. Her gaze was steadier, her chin higher. Hell, even her ponytails were tighter. Lily-Ann toyed with the idea of charting the relationship between Sophie's moods and her ponytails. Maybe that would make a good Christmas gift, too. She'd ask Ocean.

For Sophie, what happened six months ago wasn't about the murders, it was about her standing up to her stalker and rescuing Lily-Ann from Piotr. She saw herself differently now. In fact, on one of her nights out with Lily-Ann and Ocean, she'd even said, 'I mean, maybe, y'know, I'm sort of, I guess, like a totally bad bitch?'

'An absolute monster,' Ocean said, while Lily-Ann chipped in with, 'The *worst* bitch.'

Being in love also helped. Sophie glowed as she sang the praises of her old, cheap blender to Nicholas.

'I will not subject him to a garage sale,' she insisted.

'Maybe he's ready to move on, to find another partner now that you're taken.'

Sophie gasped. 'He would never betray me.'

Lily-Ann watched them spend another five minutes flirting as they stacked kitchen goods willy-nilly into boxes. Which made her teeth ache. They put half the cloth napkins in with the silverware and the other half with the flour and sugar.

She grew increasingly tense until Anthony stepped onto the porch and put his hand on her hip. For a big man, he moved pretty quietly. He smelled of the mint bodywash she'd given him, and when she glanced up at him she saw laughter in his eyes.

'Don't,' he said.

'But they're doing it wrong!'

'They'll figure it out, Lil. She's only moving across the courtyard.'

She didn't see how that mattered. 'The distance isn't the issue. You can't—'

'Let me know if you need help moving furniture,' Anthony called to them.

'Oh!' Sophie said, not having noticed them. 'Hey.'

'Will do,' Nicholas said. 'Thanks.'

'And I'm happy to help label boxes,' Lily-Ann told them.

'Oh, Lily-Ann, go inside,' Sophie said. 'The chaos will only make you crazy.'

'Not if you—'

'Speaking of chaos,' Anthony murmured into her ear before she could finish. 'We've got ten minutes before you're due back at your laptop.'

By which he meant there was time for rushed sex. Lily-Ann felt her body warm up. She liked rushed sex.

'Take a picture of the back of your TV so you know where the cables go,' she called to Nicholas and Sophie, before Anthony dragged her back inside.

4

OCEAN

On the surface, Ocean's new painting didn't look like anything special. It was an almost photorealistic depiction of a hedge. Glossy green leaves filled the canvas, freckled with white ovals of sunlight and a cluster of salmon-colored berries. Ocean liked the composition, but what interested her most was what the hedge concealed. What the viewer *couldn't* see.

Which is a lot to ask of a painting, she said to herself.

She stared at the canvas until she heard laughter ringing across the courtyard. She smiled at the happiness in Sophie's voice. The freedom. She remembered when she'd first arrived at the Cottages, how she'd struck Ocean as timid and brittle.

Not anymore. There was more to her than met the eye. Just like this painting, if Ocean ever managed to make it work.

She frowned at the berries for a few seconds before she remembered that Mrs B had asked her to pass along a message. She wiped her hands on a rag, even though they were clean already. She hadn't touched paint today; after teaching her morning sculpture class, she'd just stood in front of the half-finished project and pondered.

Thinking about art, naturally, but also about the woman she'd been dating. The woman who, with crowing delight, Mrs B had introduced her to.

'*I'm a proper yenta now*!' Mrs B had crowed, after years of quizzing every single woman – every single *single* woman – she'd met about their sexuality.

She'd never developed the slightest hint of gaydar, either, so nobody had been safe: not young women with yoga mats, not middle-aged women with BMWs, not new mothers with strollers. But most of all, not medical professionals. At this point she'd charted the sexuality of every podiatrist, ENT, and medical transcriptionist in Santa Barbara. All in the vain hope she would find someone for Ocean.

Then she met CJ in the YMCA locker room and demanded to know if she was gay. Apparently CJ had said, 'Well, I'm not *not* gay,' which resulted in Mrs B immediately blurting, 'Oh!

Finally! I can't wait for you to meet Ocean!'

CJ was almost ten years younger than Ocean, with auburn hair and winged eyeliner and a sunshine smile. She was vivacious and femme, and wore bright dresses and big earrings. She enjoyed crystals, journaling, and chatting with her pet birds. Riley called her a 'flower-crown lesbian,' which Ocean had never heard before but sounded exactly right.

After her divorce from Zoe, between raising the kids and feeling like the world's premier romantic failure, Ocean had shied away from meeting people. But after three dates with CJ she was starting to feel a terrifying sensation of hope. Maybe it wasn't too late for her.

She tossed her rag aside and headed for the courtyard, where she found Sophie and Nicholas messing around with boxes, while Anthony dragged Lily-Ann back into her cottage.

'Wait, Anthony!' Sophie called. 'Do you need a blender?'

'Yes,' he told her.

'Promise you'll take good care of him!'

'He likes moonlight walks on the beach,' Nicholas said. 'And electrical sockets.'

Anthony swept Lily-Ann inside and closed the door behind them.

'Did I miss the big giveaway?' Ocean asked, crossing the courtyard.

'Yeah, I'm sacrificing my hard-won independence over here,' Sophie said.

'Also, her twenty-year-old blender,' Nicholas added.

'There's a joke here about blended families . . .' Ocean looked at Sophie. 'Speaking of which, Mrs B wants you to check in with her before you go back to work.'

'Is she okay?' Sophie asked.

'Other than humiliating me at her dermatologist appointment? Yeah, she's fine. She, uh, browbeat CJ into getting you an invite to a party in Hope Ranch.'

'Who's CJ?' Nicholas asked. 'Her friend at the Y?'

Sophie elbowed him. 'And Ocean's new squeeze. What party? Why invite me? Are you going?'

'I'm not going, but apparently you are.' Ocean raised her hands before Sophie could ask. 'I have no idea.'

Nicholas popped the blender lid into place. 'Mrs B works in mysterious ways.'

'So mysterious that she rarely knows what she's doing,' Ocean said.

'Ha!' Sophie added more books to the stack on the porch. 'I'll talk to her.'

Ocean considered offering to help them move, but she had an appointment downtown – and also she needed to emotionally recover from Mrs B interfering with her not-yet-girlfriend's life like this. CJ worked as the housekeeper for a superrich couple in Hope Ranch, and the old biddy had arranged the invitation to give Sophie a chance to fundraise or network. Not that Ocean was going to admit that. Let Mrs B justify her own meddling.

The whole thing made Ocean uncomfortable; plus, CJ was picking her up at home for their fourth date tonight, which meant the kids would meet her for the first time. That felt like a serious step. To Ocean, at least. She suspected that nobody else cared.

She retreated back to the art studio behind her cottage, then heard the front door slam, which was how Riley announced her return from high school. She'd started tenth grade this year and announced she was going to 'crush it.' Ocean had to bite her lip to keep from suggesting that Riley not set her sights *too* high. She wanted to be her daughter's cheerleader, but couldn't bear when she got disappointed or hurt.

She went inside and yelled, 'Do you want popcorn?'

'With too many chili flakes!' Riley yelled back.

The kernels were popping when the front door opened again. Miles slipped inside, dropped his backpack, said, 'Popcorn? Don't mind if I do,' then lay in the corner of the living room with his basket of Lego pieces. He'd grown out of them for a while, but since starting fifth grade he began using them again to decompress after school.

She listened to him mumble about ninjas as he settled a motorcycle on top of his Lego ramen shop. She kissed his brown head, thinking he needed a haircut, and handed him a bowl of popcorn. Mixed with nutritional yeast, because she was still her hippie parents' daughter. She made Riley come to the kitchen to get her bowl with added Korean chili flakes, then asked about math class, which was safe because Riley enjoyed being so much better than Ocean at math.

She chattered about logarithmic equations until Ocean said, 'Some musicians write a beat but others logarithm.'

Riley groaned. 'Thanks, Dad.'

'Log a rhythm!' Miles said. 'Instead of write a beat!'

'Thanks, mini-Dad,' Riley said.

'You're welcome, my child,' Miles said.

Riley threw a popcorn kernel at him, and Ocean didn't snap about making a mess. She and Riley were getting along better than usual, as long as Ocean stepped carefully. She wasn't entirely sure if 'stepping carefully' meant 'parenting badly' but she was willing to give it a shot.

She helped Miles with his world map flashcards, then went

downtown for a meeting with the owner of a gallery in La Arcada. He was a charming gent who'd made a living as an artist in Santa Barbara for forty years, which spoke to his talent, his business acumen, and his willingness to sacrifice his soul to the Hungry God of Pretty Seascapes.

They'd known each other forever, so he loudly admired the photos of her work, which was frankly why she'd made the appointment: they both knew her art wasn't right for his gallery. Still, he offered to make a few calls, which left her sufficiently flattered and hopeful.

When she got home, Riley was in her room while Miles was with Anthony, whom he'd adopted as a babysitter. Well, without the pay or responsibility. When Anthony wanted Miles to leave – usually because he was heading to Lily-Ann's house – he just gruffly told him to get lost. They were such an odd couple, sweet, small, chattering Miles and big, looming, silent Anthony. Ocean refused to think that a boy needed a male role model, considering the state of most male role models in the world, but Miles certainly enjoyed Anthony's company.

She felt like she needed a role model of her own, as she wondered what to wear for her date. Lily-Ann had impeccable taste, but Ocean did not have an impeccable wardrobe. Sophie was too young to suggest anything workable – Ocean's fashion sense was geared more toward covering the rough patches than exposing the smooth ones.

She eventually went with black jeans and a navy button-down. Then she added her grandmother's gold ring, to show she'd gone to some effort, and knocked on Riley's door to ask her opinion.

'You look great,' Riley said. 'For a waiter at a barbecue restaurant.'

Ocean felt herself flush. 'Should I wear my cowboy boots?'

'Only if you put on a skirt.'

'I don't have a skirt.'

Riley turned back to her phone. 'Well, that answers that question.'

'C'mon, Riley. You know I'm not good at this.'

Riley sighed, but glanced up. 'Those jeans, your knit black tank top, and your burgundy Adidas.'

'What if I get cold?' Ocean asked.

'Then suffer. You have nice arms. They're doing all the work here.'

'The literal heavy lifting?'

Riley ignored her, so Ocean went back to her room and changed into the tank top. She enjoyed the idea that she had nice arms. Thank you, Rock Sculpture 101, which some days felt like chain gang labor. She added a chunky belt, then felt stupid for caring so much, so she went into the kitchen for a slug of whiskey and felt better.

CJ wasn't due for another half hour. Instead of pacing nervously, Ocean headed for Mrs B's house to check in with her. She found Miles and Anthony in the living room with Mrs B, eating rugelach and watching a show about cuttlefish.

'What're you doing watching TV?' she said, because Mrs B had claimed she hated 'the boob tube.'

'Waiting for something dramatic to happen,' Mrs B told her.

'Do cuttlefish lead lives of drama?'

'Oh, not to them, dear. To *us*.'

As if on cue, the doorbell rang. Ocean made a face, then stepped into the entryway, expecting Well, she didn't know what to expect. She still dreaded surprise visitors after the murders last spring. But when she opened the door, she found

CJ, looking too young in a short cotton dress that showed off her perfect legs and sandals revealing a turquoise pedicure.

'I'm a little early?' CJ said, with a sweet uncertainty.

Her eyes shone under her sap-green winged liquid eyeliner, and her sienna lipstick enhanced the tawniness of her skin. Ocean wanted to paint her. She wanted to stand there and admire her, to walk in a circle around her like a sculpture in a museum.

Instead, she resisted the urge to flex her arms and kissed CJ hello. 'Early, gorgeous, and at the wrong cottage.'

'I am?'

'Yes. Stunning.'

CJ flushed. 'I mean at the wrong cottage!'

'That, too. This is Mrs B's.'

'And *this* is Mrs B!' Mrs B said, swanning in from the living room, her rust-brown caftan billowing behind her. 'Look at you all dressed up! And look at me, dressed at all. I'm usually naked when you see me in the locker room. Oh! I've been meaning to ask, does CJ stand for anything? Catherine Julia, that's my guess. Or Complete Joy.'

Mrs B swooped in to hug CJ before she could answer, and Ocean spotted Miles in the archway, looking uncharacteristically shy, half-hidden behind Anthony.

'This is my son, Miles,' she said. 'And our friend Anthony.'

'Miles is the one in the back,' Mrs B informed CJ, perfectly straight-faced.

CJ giggled, and Miles said hello, and Anthony looked at CJ – which was a lot coming from Anthony.

'I'm glad to meet you,' CJ said, with an impish little smile.

'We should go,' Ocean said.

'CJ said she was early,' Mrs B reminded her. 'Should I make

cocktails? I pour a mean gin and tonic, by which I mean an extremely friendly one. Positively convivial. I'll squeeze in too much lemon, shall I?'

'Aren't you helping with my map project tonight?' Miles asked Ocean. 'I need to memorize them by next week.'

'I thought Anthony was helping you,' Ocean said.

Anthony glared at Miles. 'I am.'

'You can't even find Chile!'

'So show me again.'

Ha. Anthony was asking Miles to help *him* memorize the countries, so Miles would learn them. Typical Anthony. Clever in his understated way.

'Once the show is done.' Miles dragged Anthony toward the living room. 'We're going to miss the cuddly fish.'

Anthony gave Ocean a look, either amused that Miles called them 'cuddly fish' or impressed that Ocean's date was so hot. It was hard to tell with Anthony. Then Ocean said thanks but no thanks to the gin and tonics, and Mrs B said don't you mean gins and tonic, and Ocean said, why not gins and tonics, and CJ sort of looked at them until Mrs B patted Ocean's arm and said, 'Have a lovely time. I'll keep an eye on the kids.'

Ocean ushered CJ outside, then said, 'Well, I'm glad she announced that you see her naked.'

'Miles is so cute. And Anthony is exactly like you described.'

'I could take him in a fight.'

CJ laughed. 'Do I get to meet Riley?'

Ocean had done the dating math and figured that CJ was physically old enough to be Riley's mother. Just barely, but still, that made the age gap feel okay. Except CJ *seemed* so much younger, like a generation closer to Riley, which made her a little uncomfortable. So she sputtered for a moment, before spotting Sophie heading across the courtyard to Nicholas's cottage.

'Oh! That's Sophie, who you're inviting to the party. I told her to expect a call from the kindly woman who helps Mrs B with her bra in the YMCA locker room.'

'Is that really how you described me?'

'Sure. The undergarment fairy.'

'Undergarments,' CJ said, her eyes gleaming with teasing laughter.

'That's what we called them in my day! Your bloomers.'

'And Sophie knew what you meant?'

'Sure, after I explained that Mrs B flutters around the locker room after water aerobics until someone helps with her bra clasp. Though on second thought I'm not sure 'flutters' is the best description.'

CJ laughed. 'Mrs B is who I want to be when I grow up.'

'I'm still waiting to see who *Mrs B* becomes when she grows up,' Ocean said.

'You can't fool me. You adore her.'

'Yeah.' Ocean gave CJ a lingering look. 'I'm not great at hiding my admiration.'

CJ took her hand and led her away.

5

CJ

After she finished swimming her laps the next morning, CJ Moore flip-flopped across the YMCA locker room, listening to the old ladies from the water aerobics class chatter about 'polyps' and 'Pedro Pascal's posterior.' In the shower stall, she stripped off her swimsuit, which made her think of Frank. Not that nakedness reminded her of her elderly boss. No, but he'd given her the far-too-expensive designer one-piece a few birthdays ago, along with a note insisting that she swim laps at the Y pool every morning instead of coming to work so early.

He would've preferred that she use his pool, but she didn't like mooching off him too much. Also, despite the size of the mansion, Frank's pool was a bit small for laps. He claimed that she'd earned job flexibility after years of managing his house, his music, his prescriptions, and his money. And for tolerating – though he'd never say this aloud – his wife.

She'd accepted the gift and secretly worked the extra hours anyway. He needed the help. And she adored him. She'd started working for him directly out of college and he'd grown to become her mentor and friend and, yeah, a father figure.

By the time she was dressed, most of the old ladies were gone – though not Mrs B. For reasons CJ didn't understand, Mrs B didn't like towels at the Y. She preferred to use the hair dryer to wick water from her body. Her loose skin fluttered in the breeze like fleshy prayer flags. Maybe not the most beautiful sight, but there was something liberating about an old lady who simply didn't give a crap.

After Mrs B shrugged her bra onto her bony shoulders, she peered around the locker room looking for help. She eyed the remaining two older women before she turned to CJ and tutted. 'You didn't have to wait for me!'

'I'm not sure Santa Barbara can handle you unleashed.'

'Ha! True!' Mrs B turned around. 'Be a dear, won't you?'

CJ straightened the straps and worked the clasp. 'There you go.'

'I am decent once more,' Mrs B announced. 'How tedious decency is. Don't you find it boring?'

'Hmm. Not real decency, no.'

'Feh! I bet you preheat your oven.'

'Of course I preheat my oven. Who doesn't?'

'This is your mission, my dear. See what happens if you don't.'

'I know what'll happen, Mrs B. My cakes will be raw.'

'You don't know that, you only suspect. What's that old saying? Life is short, eat dessert raw.'

'Eat dessert *first*,' CJ corrected.

'Oh! Oh, yes, that makes more sense. Well, now *that's* settled, is everything still set for tonight? With Sophie at the party?'

'You can stop worrying. Nothing changed since last night.'

Mrs B huffed at her, then said, 'I don't know why they call it development. It's just a fancy way of saying fundraising. Trying to make it sound more professional than a bake sale. Not that Sophie can cook. Well, she makes a fine shortbread, but that is all.'

'I hope she preheats.'

'Ha!' Mrs B slipped her purple caftan over her head. 'Mark my words, young lady. One must eat the raw cookie dough of life.'

'Who said that, Aristotle?'

'That's why you and Ocean get along so well. You both like mocking old ladies. Now Sophie, on the other hand, is sweet. And her new job is all about connections, so . . .'

'You're hoping she'll connect with Frank?'

'To the tune of thousands of dollars!' Mrs B's eyes sparkled. 'Is he interested in the theatre?'

'Not really,' CJ told her. 'He's more about music.'

'Well, Sophie's office is in the same building as the symphony.' Mrs B shut her locker. 'So that's settled. Oh, except, can she bring a friend?'

'You're always welcome.'

'Not *me*. There's no telling what I might say. Nicholas.'

'Which one is he?'

'Sophie's boyfriend. He's not quite my stepson, which is a pity because I'd fancy myself as the wicked stepmother. Why *are* they so reviled? It's typical, don't you think, that nobody blames the father? What were you saying? Oh! Yes, Nicholas.'

'Is he looking for connections, too?'

'No, no, he works for the city. When I was a girl, there was no higher dream.'

CJ slipped into her navy linen button-up over knit pants. Frank's wife liked her to wear dark blue when she was working, to make clear that she was an employee. She'd once shown up in an exuberantly tacky sundress just to watch Karina side-eye her all day.

'I'm sure it's fine,' she said, 'but I'll check and text Ocean.'

Mrs B rattled off her number, then said, 'Oh, I must fly! For some reason, Ocean gets cranky if I make her wait. She doesn't mind if it's a minute or two but after half an hour she starts chewing nails and spitting horseshoes.'

'Baffling,' CJ agreed, as Mrs B wafted from the locker room. She considered running outside to say hello – that's where she'd first spotted Ocean after all, during pickup after swim. She looked a mess though, and didn't want to be struck by passing horseshoes, so she went to the mirror instead. She applied elaborate eyeliner and fuchsia lipstick. They were the only things that kept her from looking middle-aged in her dumb navy blue outfits. Also, she knew they pissed off Karina as much as they amused Frank, and what was life without a little pettiness?

Twenty minutes later, she parked in her usual spot outside Frank's mansion on Charity Lane. Hope Ranch, Charity Lane. Some developer had really enjoyed themselves. At least there wasn't Do-Gooder Drive or Saintly Street.

She let herself through the side door, then sorted the mail at the kitchen desk. Largely into recycling, because after a ten-year battle she'd finally established most of Frank's accounts online. She checked in with the gardeners and confirmed an appointment with the cardiologist, then slunk around the house until she spotted Frank in his office in the west wing.

She smiled, but didn't disturb him.

Instead she continued past, then checked the clock on the double Viking range, which squatted like a spaceship in the otherwise-retro kitchen. Frank had bought the mansion in the late 1970s and to his wife's dismay he hadn't done much updating. Even his music production gear never advanced past the 1990s: He still adored his Roland synth and Cheetah sampler, unless it was the other way around. CJ never could remember.

She shifted Karina's unused, two-thousand-dollar health-shake mixer aside to reveal the ornate brass Italian espresso maker, then put her college-era barista training to the test. Soon steam hissed over Frank's double cappuccino, a treat that neither she nor Frank mentioned to Karina.

Frank didn't have many pleasures left.

At ten-thirty on the dot, she poured the espresso over the

foam in the navy and gold Wedgwood cup and headed for Frank's office. He'd insisted that it wasn't her job to wait on him, but she insisted that it was her pleasure. The old man had put up a good fight, but she'd won that one.

The curtains were closed and Frank lounged on a leather couch listening to Stevie Wonder on his old turntable. His eyes half-closed, his skinny frame a little tense. For the past few years, he never seemed completely comfortable, like his body didn't know how to fully relax anymore. And he'd been shutting himself in and listening to vinyl more often recently: Bach and Mozart and the disco and funk bands he'd produced in the 1970s and 80s.

As she set his saucer on the coffee table, he focused on her and sang along with the record. She gave him a look. 'I'm glad we're not listening to Sir Mix-a-Lot this morning.'

Frank's laugh turned into a coughing fit, which made her nervous until he caught his breath. He was declining again, and she didn't think he had one more rebound in him. At least his mind was still sharp. Sharpish. And he enjoyed his caffeine in the morning, and his two or three cocktails in the evening. CJ had come to work for him back when he'd been a spry sixty-seven. She'd graduated from UC Santa Barbara with a degree in sociology, so she had found herself burned out on food-service work when she had met Frank at a long-closed French bistro that served perfect quiche and baguettes.

When she'd handed Frank his third glass of wine, he'd handed her his card. 'Come work for me. I'll pay you better than this.'

At the time, she hadn't realized how sketchy the offer had sounded. Especially after he offered an impressive salary and a free place to live in one of the most beautiful corners of the world, a mansion in Hope Ranch perched over the ocean cliffs.

In retrospect, in a shocking violation of every story about an old music producer and an innocent young girl, he'd treated her like family from day one. And she'd returned the favor. She'd coordinated his spending with his accountant, arranged regular medical care, updated his haircut, and organized his vinyl records so logically that he'd almost fired her. She'd even encouraged him to donate a fat sum to World of Goods after a big tsunami. As a tax incentive, she'd said, though they'd both known he'd needed to feel like he was still contributing to the world despite retirement. And part of that, she realized years later, was helping her. She didn't have parents worth the name, so he'd become a rock in her life. Whatever happened, she knew he'd support her. She'd never had that before.

Then Karina entered the picture and changed things.

After Frank caught his breath, he said, 'You're going to be the death of me.'

'At least you'll die with a smile on your face,' she told him.

'That's the dream.' He sipped his coffee. 'Go out on a high note.'

She talked him through his day as she tidied the room then parted the drapes. 'Oh, Sunny's here. On the patio with Karina.'

'I should count my blessings he ever leaves,' Frank grumbled. 'That freeloader.'

'Yeah, you hate him hanging around.'

Sunny's real name was Jonathan Wheeler, and he was Frank's oldest friend. They'd grown up together in the Fairfax neighborhood of Los Angeles, then both retired rich in Santa Barbara. CJ didn't quite understand what Sunny did for a living. He invested, he said, but he never explained in what, and Frank just said that Sunny made money make money.

She was browsing through the events page of the *Independent*, trying to convince Frank to visit the gorgeous grounds and cactus gardens of Lotusland by listing the less attractive options first, when the office door opened.

'Are you holed up in here again?' Karina asked, stepping inside wearing a shapeless white linen dress.

CJ appreciated that Karina was an unlikely wife for a retired music mogul. No fake boobs or Pilates body. She looked like a normal, attractive woman in her early sixties with no desire for nips or tucks, despite years of sun worshiping. CJ admired that. If only Karina didn't have such a terrible personality.

Yet Frank loved her. CJ watched his eyes soften as she entered the room and swung the heavy velvet drapes open.

Sunny shuffled in behind Karina, wearing a green button-down over navy board shorts, with age spots on his bald dome, gold chains on his turkey neck, and flip-flops on his regrettable feet.

'It's gorgeous outside, Frank, you need sunshine.' Karina made a bowling gesture. 'Come play bocce.'

'Are you and CJ plotting against me? She's trying to trick me into visiting Lotusland.'

Karina tsked. 'Honestly, CJ. Lotusland? What are you thinking?'

'That it's gorgeous outside and Frank needs sunshine.'

Karina's gaze sharpened on the Wedgwood cup. 'Is that decaf?'

'Of course.'

'I should hope so.' Karina sat beside Frank. 'Sunny wants you to get a transfusion. There's a new procedure that boosts muscle regeneration and, um, neuron growth?'

'Young blood!' Sunny rasped, lowering his sunglasses. 'I'm telling you, Frankie, this is like parabiosis two-point-oh. Even the goddamn Mayo Clinic is admitting that sweet young plasma will rejuvenate you. You'll be a new man in no time. Bouncing Karina off the California king like the old days.'

Karina rolled her eyes. 'You should look into this, Frank. I know Sunny is Sunny, but he showed me some articles.'

'I'm finally getting used to being an old man,' Frank said. 'Now I want to be young again?'

'Do it for me! You know I want you to live forever.'

'That sounds exhausting.'

Karina took his hand. 'Please?'

'Well, I . . .' His voice turned watery. 'For you, anything.'

'I'll make an appointment! Oh, and don't forget our massages later. We'll have them by the pool, after lunch.'

'Would you like to add that transfusion appointment to the schedule?' CJ asked Karina, keeping her voice bland and professional. 'The cardiologist called to confirm, but the rheumatologist is still playing hard to get. There's Pax's massages, and do you want the nutritionist to stop back in?'

'Yes,' Karina said. 'As I mentioned several times.'

'So we'll need to schedule this around her. Hmm. Isn't the urologist also on the list? Why don't I email you the schedule and you can add the transfusion people?'

'Why don't *you* make the appointment?' Karina said. 'As that's your job.'

'Oh.' CJ attempted to look unhappy. 'Yes, of course.'

She didn't glance at Frank again, but she knew there'd be a flash of appreciation in his eyes. Now she could delay the transfusion appointment forever, without him having to hurt Karina's feelings with a refusal. Karina really did love him and really did want him to live forever. Frank loved her, too, for whatever reasons. But in private he'd admitted to CJ that he was tired, sore, and ready for a long sleep.

6

SOPHIE

As Nicholas drove, I gazed out the passenger window and gathered my courage. Fundraising events still scared me a little, and Hope Ranch didn't feel like Santa Barbara: the streets were too lush, too private, too dimly lit. I'd only lived in town for a few years, but I'd learned to expect Spanish architecture and dry lawns pebbled with succulents. Also, streetlights.

On the other side of the ornate HOPE RANCH sign, mansions started appearing with well-watered gardens and expansive lawns. There was an actual lagoon – currently covered in algae, sure, but I'd thought lagoons only appeared in horror movies.

'Like Swamp Thing,' I said aloud.

'Except we're in Hope Ranch,' Nicholas told me, 'so he'd be Hope Thing. He rises from the muck, black eyes gleaming, and is quite optimistic about all this.'

I laughed. 'His catchphrase is "Everything is fine." Which is true if you never leave this neighborhood. Oooh, look at *that* house. Maybe we should move here instead of into your cottage.'

'What would Mrs B do without us?'

'What would we do without her?' I asked.

'Right? Look at her, making connections for you in a public gym.'

'Me? She found Ocean a *girlfriend* in a locker room! We should've brought her along. She loves a party – and any chance to spend time with you.'

'I'm trying,' he said.

'You're doing great.'

'I just can't stand the idea that she thinks she owes me anything. The idea of taking advantage of her because I'm her husband's son . . .'

'You know that "debt" doesn't exist in Mrs B's vocabulary. And you love spending time with her, too.'

'Yeah, she's just so her.'

'She's the her-est,' I agreed. 'Okay, Charity Lane is coming up.'

He took a left onto a narrow road, then pulled into a drive that snaked through olive trees and ended at a mansion that faced the bluffs overlooking the Pacific. I'd searched the address on a real estate website, and the description mentioned a saltwater pool, bocce court, sunken rose garden, and a calf-high hedge maze surrounding a fountain. In addition to the expansive main residence, there was a guesthouse, a pool cabana, a music studio, and a dining pavilion – whatever that was.

A dozen high-end cars were parked beside the four-car garage. Nicholas pulled his Honda next to a white Mercedes as I checked myself in the mirror. I'd started cutting my own bangs using a YouTube tutorial then made Nicholas fix them. I'd never seen him so nervous, but he managed to minimize the damage. At least they'd finally grown long enough to touch my eyebrows. I'd pulled the rest of my hair in a low ponytail. Forget the cool-girl no-makeup trend, I needed loads of black mascara and burgundy lipstick.

'You are gorgeous,' Nicholas told me. 'All you have to do is introduce yourself and hand out your cards.'

'Oh, god! I forgot my new business cards! They're—'

'In the back seat,' he said.

'Aw. You remembered.'

'We're a good team.' He looked at the mansion. 'I just hope they're expecting us.'

'I hope they're expecting *just* us,' I told him. 'I love Mrs B, but for all we know she promised the DeYoungs I'd give a ukulele recital.'

Nicholas reached into the back for my cards. 'Ukulele?'

'I strummed the one Mrs B keeps on her shelf, and now she thinks I'm a savant.'

I stepped from the car and took a slow, steadying breath of salt air and jasmine. My outlook on life had changed a lot in the last six months, but I was still nervous about showing up at a Hope Ranch party I'd barely been invited to. So I grabbed Nicholas's arm for moral support. He felt solid, in his navy suit and matching shirt, with his silver rings and bracelet keeping him from looking uptight. CJ had been vague about the dress code, so I'd scanned a copy of *Santa Barbara Magazine* for photos of wealthy parties. Brightly colored dresses seemed to be the consensus, so I'd worn the red floral midi-dress I'd thrifted, along with my best pair of heels. At least Nicholas and I were dressed for the same event.

Floodlights illuminated the drive and the nearest wing of the house, which was a sprawling two-story building that reminded me a little of a Frank Lloyd Wright, sort of blocky and layered, teetering on the line between stunning and ugly.

CJ opened the door when Nicholas knocked. She was a tall woman with a beautiful head of wavy auburn hair and absolutely on-point makeup that made her look younger than me, even though she was probably five or so years older.

'Sophie!' She gave me a hug. 'I almost didn't recognize you outside of the parking lot.'

She meant the lot at the YMCA, where we exchanged polite greetings when I dropped off Mrs B. And I was so nervous that I said, 'Ha! If I had a nickel for every time I heard *that*.'

CJ's smile widened. 'And this must be Nicholas?'

'Thanks so much for, uh . . .' He gave one of his self-deprecating looks. 'Squeezing us in.'

'Oh, of course. Although, I don't know what Mrs B told you?'

'Just to come.' My nerves jangled again. 'I hope it's all right. She didn't put you in an awkward position, did she? She said the DeYoungs were hosting an event for World of Goods and I should mingle?'

'Oh, no, that's perfect.' She looked relieved. 'I was afraid you were expecting something bigger. It's only an informal get-together – not a proper networking event.'

'That's perfect. As long as we're actually invited. I know it's tough to say no to Mrs B.'

'It's tough to *want* to say no to her.' CJ brushed a lock of auburn hair off her face. 'She's so lovely. She just shines. Don't worry, Frank is the same. Well, he's slowing down, but he's got the same big heart. And the New Vic is great, so – good causes all around!'

I felt myself wrinkle my nose. 'I mean, I love the theatre, but it's not World of Goods.'

'What do they do?' Nicholas asked.

'Deliver emergency supplies to disaster zones,' I told him. 'Mostly medical goods. They save thousands of lives every year. They're amazing.'

'Frank's been a big supporter for many years. Although recently . . .' CJ hesitated. 'Well, he's a friend of Jane Sheffield's, I don't know if you know her?'

'I don't think so,' I said, an instant before I remembered she was my friend Angela's mentor.

'She's in charge of development for World of Goods.' She gave me a sidelong smile. 'She's here tonight. You can't miss her.'

When we stepped inside, I gaped at the foyer. A wide staircase swept upward to the second floor, drawing my eye toward the arched ceiling that lofted high overhead. Across the glazed concrete floor in an oversized fireplace, a stack of logs burned merrily, warming the room too much for early September. Mission-style furniture provided accents here and there, along with an oval table with an enormous vase holding sunflowers, wild grasses, and eucalyptus.

Everything looked a little too old-school, but also extremely grand.

CJ ushered us along a corridor toward the murmur of conversation and I said, 'I've been meaning to thank you for helping Mrs B at the Y.'

'Well, I owe *her* now, for introducing me to Ocean.'

'Ocean's the best,' Nicholas said. 'She's so . . . *there*.'

I shot him a look, as his usual eloquence abandoned him. 'Yeah, in addition to being kind, loving, beautiful, brilliant, funny, and strong, she is in fact often present.'

'Like I said.'

CJ laughed. 'Did Mrs B mention she challenged Bettina to an arm wrestle?'

'Oh, god, who's Bettina? Is she the one she calls her "frenemy"?'

'She doesn't say frenemy,' Nicholas told me.

'She does! I've heard her.'

'She says "funemy," and she has no idea what it means. She called me her "fun-in-law" once.'

I snort-laughed. 'So Bettina is her funemy?'

'And also the water aerobics instructor,' CJ said.

'She challenged the *teacher* to an arm wrestle?'

'Oh, god, I can't wait to tell Ocean,' Nicholas said.

'Don't do that,' I said. 'She'll make Mrs B write "I will not arm wrestle the teacher" a hundred times.'

At the end of the hall, a great room stretched in front of us. Sofas faced each other in the center of the room, while geometrical chairs and clunky side tables formed conversation nooks illuminated by track lighting. Everything looked expensive and about fifty years out of date. Still, even now, the room had the swanky-cool vibe of a bygone era, like there was a hint of cigarettes and martini lunches lingering in the air.

In the lawn beyond a wall of windows, floodlights illuminated the sweep of a fountain, a sculptural tree, the silhouette of a gazebo. During the day, the windows must've framed the even-more-extraordinary view of the ocean and Channel Islands.

There were fewer people than I expected. About twenty guests sipped wine, nibbled hors d'oeuvres, and chatted. One caterer circulated with trays while another stood behind a white-clothed buffet table. Most of the guests appeared to be in their seventies, and all of them were burnished with the unmistakable gloss of wealth, which was good news in terms of networking for fundraising opportunities.

CJ ushered us through the murmur of conversation toward an elderly gentleman sitting in a nook with a few others. Frank DeYoung looked old even for this crowd, with a fringe of hair like a monk's tonsure and a Band-Aid on the side of his neck. He wore a black velour tracksuit and thick glasses that didn't conceal his warm brown eyes and white eyebrows. The woman beside him looked closer to sixty than mid-eighties. She had short, tousled bleached hair and a lot of wrinkles, like she'd spent her youth on the beach, which was a real Santa Barbara type. She wore a pink sequined top over stretchy black pants, but the friendliness of her outfit didn't match her peevish mouth.

Frank raised his empty glass to CJ and greeted her with, 'Stiff nut.'

Not the greeting I'd expected, and I guess my surprise showed on my face.

'His favorite drink,' CJ explained to me. 'Amaretto and Maker's Mark. Frank, this is Sophie and her boyfriend, Nicholas. She works with the New Vic.'

'And *I* am Karina DeYoung,' the pink-bedecked woman said, 'since CJ didn't introduce me. I suppose you're another World of Goods superfan?'

I nodded. 'Yes, of course, very much so.'

'Of course,' she repeated, sipping her white wine. 'Though if you work in the arts, you must wish that some of that funding trickled your direction?'

'Trickled? Hmm . . .' I pretended to ponder. 'Not exactly, no. As long as I'm wishing, I'll wish for a whole monsoon.'

When Karina laughed, I saw the beauty in her. 'Yes, wealth should be *enjoyed*. You'll go far with that attitude. Now! Why don't you grab a glass of wine. If you prefer red, I recommend the Andremily Mourvèdre.'

I didn't know what either of those words meant, but I said, 'I'll try that, thank you.'

CJ put her hand on Frank's shoulder. 'Another stiff nut?'

'You know he's had enough,' Karina told her.

That sounded like our cue to retreat, so I pulled Nicholas toward the buffet. I asked the caterer for two glasses of 'Andromeda Moorsomething,' and she didn't bat an eye before uncorking a new bottle and pouring us glasses.

7

OCEAN

Ocean smiled at the inside of the fridge. She smiled at the eggs and the yogurt and the blueberries. Standing there like a love-struck child, the cool air on her face, thinking about CJ texting to say she'd miss her at the party tonight.

She really liked CJ. Sure, she was too young and bright, but she lightened her world. The older Ocean got, the more she understood why men chased younger women. She still didn't approve, but she understood.

When a knock sounded at the door, she stopped smiling and turned to find Mrs B stepping into her cottage.

'There you are!' Mrs B said, pointing her phone at Ocean.

'Shockingly in my own house?'

'I need you to text CJ for me.'

'She's at that party you sent Sophie to.'

'Exactly!'

Ocean took Mrs B's phone. 'Why do you need me to do it? I know you know how to text.'

'Texting is undignified.' Mrs B sat at the counter wearing a jade-green caftan with layers of gold jewelry she'd collected over the years. 'Tap tap tapping away.'

'Oh, so *I* should do it?'

'Exactly.'

'Have you been in your gummies again?'

'Absolutely not! And I resent the implication.'

'Uh-huh. So can I interest you in a snack?'

'My gummies *are* a snack! My favorite is boysenberry.' She gave Ocean a loopy smile. 'You'd prefer girlsenberry. Speaking of which, how are things with CJ?'

'She's okay.'

'Ha! Ha-ha! I see that smile in your eyes! Good for you, you should be happy after *that woman*.'

'You can say my ex-wife's name.'

'Yes, but why bother? Now, then. I'm Golda Bakofsky's daughter.'

Ocean blinked at her. 'What're you babbling about, you mad old woman?'

'I mean text that to CJ! Text her the words "I'm Golda Bakofsky's daughter."'

'Why?'

'So she knows who you are.'

Ocean gave Mrs B a look, then sat beside her and tapped at her phone.

Mrs B

Hello! I'm Golda Bakofsky's daughter.

You may also know me as Ocean.
Mrs B is dictating this to me while stoned, for some reason
I can only apologize for whatever happens next.

'Good! Now ask if she met Nicholas at the party.'

Ocean did as instructed, and a minute later, CJ responded.

CJ

Hello! I am CJ. I believe I remember you from such occasions as our first kiss.
Yes, I met Nicholas. Nice guy.

'Text her "And handsome." Oh, wait, no, she's already dating! I wonder how she stumbled into romance? We will never know! Surely, no angel of loving insight introduced her to the perfect girl!'

'Girl?' Ocean said.

'Crabby woman,' Mrs B amended. 'Let's see, what do I want to say? Well, you know Nicholas is absolutely determined to get Sophie's play produced? Ask CJ if anyone at the party likes to fund the dramatic arts?'

Mrs B

The interfering old woman wants to know if anyone at the party ever funds local playwrights

Mrs B

She's looking over my shoulder and saying she is not interfering
she is
Nurturing
She is a back-door texter
Now she's saying she is not
A back-door texter

CJ

She is a nurturing texter and if anyone knows about plays, it's Frank's friends George and Helene Kagant

Mrs B

She is very politely asking you to point Nicholas in their direction

CJ

He's talking to them as we type

Mrs B chortled. 'What a mensch.'

'Yeah, Nicholas is great,' Ocean told her. 'He's probably not even stoned right now. Is that all?'

'Yes. Wait, no! Ask for a selfie.'

'A selfie?'

'Do it!'

Mrs B

Now she wants a selfie

CJ didn't respond immediately, so Mrs B told Ocean about her top five favorite fruits, then told her that Hamilton claimed strawberries weren't *real* berries, then a photo popped onto the screen. A selfie of CJ making a funny face with the party in the background.

Ocean's heart gave a little hop and Mrs B said, 'Ooh, her hair is dry. I so rarely see her with entirely dry hair. Such a pretty color. But that's just CJ, I want to see the whole party.'

'Do you know what a selfie is?'

'Of course I do! It's a picture you take *yourself*.'

So Ocean asked CJ to take pictures of the whole party, including Sophie and Nicholas. Photos began to pop onto the screen a minute later, and Mrs B snatched her phone back.

'Look at all that food,' Mrs B said. 'What was that you said about snacks?'

8

SOPHIE

The red wine tasted almost smoky, which made me feel oh-so-sophisticated. I sipped again as I surveyed the party, trying to decide where – and how – to insert myself. Or if I could simply hide in the corner drinking fancy wine.

Then a woman called my name from across the room. As I turned, she swooped in for an air-kiss on the cheek. She looked a little smoky, too, draped in a slinky black dress and stiletto heels. She sort of fit with the décor: classy and old-fashioned, though usually she was extremely on-trend.

'Angela!' I said, raising my glass.

'*C'est moi.*' Angela had lived in France for a year and never let you forget it. Still, she was a cornerstone of the Givemore Girls, and always took the time to give me a little help and guidance. 'What are you doing here? I thought this was my private hunting ground.'

'The DeYoungs support Bright California?' I asked.

'Not yet, but give me a few days. You've got to stay sharp, Sophie. The old donors don't have long lifespans. And Frank's got such deep, delicious pockets. I want to crawl into them and live there.'

She clinked glasses with me and I pointed out Nicholas, who was perusing the catered food across the room. Angela had a habit of fixating on wealthy people – so somehow I'd never told her that Nicholas was going to inherit the Marigold Cottages.

'How'd you get invited?' Angela asked me.

'I'm a friend of a friend of Frank's personal assistant.'

'Oh, CJ? The word is that she's more than an assistant to Frank.'

I made a face. 'No way.'

'Not like that! Don't be gross, he's a thousand years old. She's just his . . . *confidant*. She's like his work wife, except she works here.'

I glanced toward Frank and Karina. 'His real wife doesn't mind?'

'She's not what you expected, right? He's worth ninety million bucks, you'd think he'd marry a twenty-four-year-old gold digger with blonde hair and a bouncy personality who raises funds for Bright California, but *non*.'

'Karina doesn't seem like the biggest fan of World of Goods.'

'She's not the biggest fan of *any* giving. Look at this place! It hasn't been redecorated since the seventies. Karina wants to remodel for the low-low price of four million and change.'

'Ah,' I said.

'Right? But CJ doesn't want the work to disturb Frank in his, like, final years.'

'How do you know all this?' I asked.

'Jane, of course.'

'Your mentor.'

'The one, the only, Jane Sheffield.' Angela sipped her wine.

'This year's shoo-in for the Millerbrandt Award.'

'What's that?'

'Big fancy prize for the best human on earth. Jane's officially the VP of engagement at World of Goods, which means she raises all the money.'

I made fake appreciative noises, then sipped my wine and made genuine ones. 'Mm. This is ambrosia.'

'You're in the big leagues now, Sophie.' Angela nodded toward Frank's group. 'See the bald guy sitting across from Frank, draped in gold chains? That's Frank's best friend, Sunny Wheeler. He only gives to, like, niche anti-aging organizations and he *will* pat your ass. Across from him, with the beard and the bangs, are George and Helene Kagant. They're into the symphony and the art museum and maybe cats?'

'Sounds promising,' I said.

'Music, Frank!' a woman called from across the room. 'We need music!'

Frank shifted in his seat, looking vaguely alarmed. Karina patted his arm, and he relaxed back into the cushions.

'And *that* is Jane,' Angela said, nodding toward the woman who'd yelled.

'I wonder why she likes you,' I said, because Jane looked exactly like a more-polished, middle-aged version of Angela. 'You're even dressed alike.'

Well, Jane's black dress, stilettos, and statement gold earrings looked like money while Angela's looked like dupes, but still it was like a young Goldie Hawn and Kate Hudson.

'They're going to need a new VP of engagement at some point,' Angela said, with a slightly wolfish smile. 'Once she wins the coveted Millerbrandt Award for nonprofits, she'll take over as CEO. She brought in like eight hundred million last year. Most of it in medication, equipment, and PPE – not cash – but still. She's headed for the top and I'm right there with her.'

9

NICHOLAS

Nicholas grabbed a fresh bottle of the Mourvèdre and approached the concentration of gray-haired wealth gathered on the long, low-slung beige velvet couches in the center of the room. He wasn't here to fade into the background as Sophie networked. No, he and Mrs B had a plan. She'd encouraged him to come to raise money for Sophie's play. Tonight's guests could fund a production with pocket change. They just needed someone to sell them on it.

So Nicholas gestured with the wine bottle, offering a top-up. 'Anyone?'

'Please,' the bald guy with the chains said. 'You're the theatre girl's boyfriend?'

'Nicholas,' he said.

'I'm Sunny Wheeler. So bright they named me after a star.'

'Also, you're always emitting hot air.' The small woman across from him paused in her demolition of a plate of fruit and cheese. 'I'm Helene, this is my husband, George.'

'I've heard of you,' Nicholas told her, pouring the wine. 'You're the other theatre people.'

Helene peered at him with bright, curious eyes. 'Have we met?'

'I don't think so,' he said, though she did look a little familiar. 'Hmm. Unless we went to the same plays?'

'Perhaps your eyes met across the crowded theatre?' George stroked his full white beard. 'As the orchestra played a lively tune, the curtains opened wide, replete with possibility. Then tragedy struck! The moment passed unremarked.'

Helene batted at her husband. 'Ignore him, Nicholas! So do you work at the theatre, as well?'

'Only as an audience member,' he said. 'Although Sophie is a—'

'So what *do* you do?' Sunny Wheeler interrupted.

Nicholas evaded the question, mostly because he wanted to talk about Sophie, but also because work had been so draining lately. He didn't want to hear any opinions on turning the downtown blocks of State Street into a car-free zone for pedestrians or how e-bikes were out of control. He'd hoped the city would've agreed on a comprehensive redevelopment plan by now. Instead they were struggling with a budget shortfall that kept him awake at night.

Though perhaps covering up two murders with the other residents of Marigold Cottages six months earlier was responsible for most of his sleeplessness. He still felt vulnerable over how they'd framed Lily-Ann's husband for murders he hadn't committed, even if he did deserve incarceration. Though this wasn't the time to worry about it.

'Sophie is a playwright,' he blurted, apropos of nothing. 'She's just finishing a play based in Santa Barbara.'

To his surprise, George lit up and started talking. The guy was clearly an eccentric – his bushy beard and non sequiturs proved that – but he was also clearly a lover of art. He launched into a speech about contemporary playwrights that was so knowledgeable Nicholas suspected he'd been a professor of drama.

'I'll tell you what would make a good play,' Sunny Wheeler interrupted, resting his half-empty tumbler on his belly. 'My seventy-fifth birthday party.'

'Why is that?' Nicholas asked.

'Picture this, Nicky. A hundred and sixty guests in a ballroom. Black tie, absolute mounds of funeral bouquets. A big photo of yours truly on the dais. Then six of my friends carry my coffin to the front of the room. My wife, God rest her soul, comes out wearing a mourning veil and weeping. How's that for drama?'

'That . . . happened?'

'You betcha.'

Nicholas didn't know whether to be awed or appalled. 'You had a fake funeral for your birthday?'

'No reason to miss an event that's all about me,' Sunny said. 'And men in my demographic – the ones who haven't prepared – have been dropping like flies for years.'

'Ah,' Nicholas said, instead of *Prepared for what?*

'The coffin was comfy, too. Snug as a bug.'

'It was open casket,' Helene said, with a quick roll of her eyes. 'He looked like a bald vampire.'

Sunny leaned toward Nicholas. 'I listened to the eulogies, and I don't mind saying that it turns out I am *quite* the fellow. "Beloved," that's the word.'

'Either that,' Helene said, 'or everyone prefers you dead.'

Nicholas found Helene charming and approachable, but he didn't want to push too hard so he drifted away. He figured he'd planted the seed, mentioning Sophie's play. He didn't want to scare anyone off. Though Mrs B would wonder why he wasn't carrying a sack full of cash when he reported back.

He checked on Sophie, who was still chatting with her awful blonde friend, then slipped into the corner to enjoy his second glass of spectacular wine. Another guy was already there: he looked five or ten years older than Nicholas, with dirty-blond hair and impressive forearms, one of which sported a tattoo of a mermaid reaching for a crescent moon.

Nicholas was about to introduce himself when a woman across the room started yelling about music. A middle-aged woman with a lot of blonde hair and a tight dress that she completely pulled off. She pointed at him and shouted. Why was she talking to *him*? Then her gaze shifted to the guy beside him and she called, 'Oh, *Pecs*! I didn't see you there. Be a dear and get the soundtrack started? And none of your new age nonsense.'

The guy opened a cabinet, synched his phone, then glanced at Nicholas. 'What do you think for this crowd, Adele or Billie Eilish?'

'Uh,' Nicholas said.

'Oh, here we go!' the guy said, tapping at his phone. 'Frank Sinatra.'

As the music started, Nicholas said, 'Perfect. Fits the décor.'

'They like the oldies. Frank – I mean, our Frank – was a big-time music producer back in the day. Some of the stars jammed in his studio as recently as five, six years ago. Like Matty Almond, a few guys from True Blue.'

Nicholas didn't know either of those names, but he said, 'Neat.'

'His studio's amazing. Serene. Great place to meditate.' The guy considered him. 'Are you from World of Goods?'

'Just tagging along with my girlfriend. I'm Nicholas.'

'Pecs.'

That was a little too on the nose. 'Pecs?'

'No, no. Pax.'

'Oh, Pax! Like peace.'

Pax flashed his perfect white teeth. 'Exactly like peace.'

'So you're a friend of, uh . . .' Nicholas gestured toward the woman who'd yelled for music. 'Hers?'

'Jane? Not really. I'm closer to the DeYoungs. I'm their bodyworker, I see them four times a week. Karina asked me to come tonight. She said that way she's not the youngest person here, but I think it's really so if anyone falls over, I can pick them up.'

'A new spin on "pickup artist,"' Nicholas said, then cringed internally at the terrible joke. On the bright side, when he told Sophie later, she'd giggle.

Pax gave him a pity smile. 'Yeah.'

The pause lasted a few seconds before Nicholas raised his empty wineglass in explanation, then headed for the bar.

10

CJ

CJ added another splash of Amaretto to Frank's cocktail. No matter what Karina said, she wasn't going to deny him one of his few daily pleasures. She occasionally joined him for a stiff nut when Karina spent the evening out. They were strong and sweet, just like Frank. And unique, too. She'd searched online but still didn't know where he'd found the recipe. She got a little misty-eyed when she realized that she'd miss mixing him cocktails. She took pleasure in the ritual, like with his cappuccinos, getting everything just right so Frank relaxed when he took that first sip.

When the music started, she watched him rise unsteadily and head for the deck. He used to host raucous listening parties for his albums, but background music made him uncomfortable now, because he couldn't concentrate on either the music or the conversation. She started to follow him, to keep him company, but that was so daughterly that it would make Karina sour for a week.

She scanned the crowd for Pax, to ask him to go, but she spotted Sophie instead, looking slightly overwhelmed, so she drifted over and said, 'Any luck?'

'Not yet,' Sophie told her. 'The truth is, I don't even know how to start. Do you ever wonder if you're not cut out for your job?'

'Well, I never saw myself as a personal assistant slash housekeeper slash wrinkle-wrangler, but here I am, almost fifteen years later.'

Sophie gave a charming snort. 'Wrinkle-wrangler?'

'That's what Frank called me once. How long have you been doing development?'

'A month and a half.'

CJ pretended shock. 'And you're not an expert yet? What is wrong with you?'

'I know, I know! I just can't stand being useless.'

'You know what would be useful?' She gave Sophie the stiff nut and a plate of empanadas. 'Bring these to Frank on the veranda. And, uh, would you mind asking him for advice about fundraising? He loves playing the wise old man.'

'Sure, as a favor to you, I'm happy to ask the rich guy about fundraising.'

CJ nodded solemnly. 'Thanks. And ask about playwriting, too. He worked with creative people for decades, he might have a tip or two.'

'I can see why Mrs B introduced you to Ocean,' Sophie said. 'All this,' she said, 'and bra straps, too.'

11

SOPHIE

When I stepped through the sliding glass doors, an ocean breeze cooled my face. The night smelled of jasmine with a distant tang of seaweed.

Frank was sitting on a cushioned bench, gazing into the darkness, his shoulders stooped. He seemed deep in thought, maybe brooding. I felt awkward disturbing him, but when he turned, his big-framed glasses couldn't disguise the warmth in his eyes. He had a character actor's face, the likable fixer in a 1970s mobster movie. Dream casting: Joe Pesci.

'You're not CJ,' he said.

'No, but she did send me with food and drink.'

He patted the bench beside himself. 'Then you'd best deliver it. She's a harsh taskmaster, that one. What's your name again?'

'Sophie.'

'I'm Frank.'

I took a seat. 'This is such a beautiful spot.'

'It is. I'm so spoiled.' He gazed at the ocean. 'You know how, back in the day, elderly Eskimos would climb onto an ice floe and float away?'

I didn't mention that I thought they were called Inuit and also that I wasn't sure if that was a myth. I just nodded.

'Me personally, I don't like the cold. But put me on a canoe in the Pacific, with the sun shining down and the waves bobbing?' He raised his glass. 'I'll drift away on an endless supply of stiff nuts.'

'Don't forget the empanadas.'

'CJ just had you bring those to soak up the alcohol. That girl is such a mother hen. Did she send you out here to ask me for money?'

'Well, she *claims* she sent me out here to ask you for advice.'

His laugh surprised me, low and easy. 'She can't help trying to help. It's like a reflex for her. Advice about what?'

'I want to be a playwright.'

'Have you written any plays?'

'Oh, sure. Though only my most recent is any good.'

'Then you *are* a playwright.'

'Well, I want to be a better one?'

He took a bite of empanada. 'Do you believe in your work?'

'I think so?'

'Creatives are always the last to know. Does *anyone* believe in your work?'

I nodded, thinking about Nicholas. 'More than he should.'

'Good. Here's my secret. All I ever really did for my artists was pretend to be in a position to validate their art. Take them seriously. The only person who could truly validate them was themselves, but creatives live in a fun house. They need other people to see them straight.'

'Huh. I think of art as being solitary.'

'That's a hard road. Artists need people, often fairly desperately. And they need to connect their self-image to the work itself, not the reception it gets. That's the win, right there.'

'So follow your passion and the money will follow?' I asked.

'Hah! No, for money you need to get lucky. Look at me. Luck is what paid for this view. The point is, you're already an artist. A playwright. You crossed that threshold. At your age, you think you have forever, but I promise you, it's over in a heartbeat. And that's okay, as long as you stick to your art. Spend your life writing jingles for radio ads, that's fine. There is no small art. You want to be a playwright? You are one. I'm sorry to tell you, but you've already won.'

'Well,' I said. 'That's a new way to look at it.'

He gave me a twinkling look. 'Now, then. You're raising money for who again?'

12

NICHOLAS

When Nicholas found Sophie standing alone on the deck, she turned and gave him a smile that made his breath catch. It was embarrassing how much he loved her. He almost didn't notice the spectacular grounds unspooling toward the cliffs and the sea. There was an elegant pool, lined with old-world Spanish tiles, and scattered plantings of garden roses, lavender, and parsley.

'You just missed Frank,' she said.

'Did you ask him about your play?'

'A little,' she said. 'But guess what? He's going to become a Gateway Donor at the theatre!'

'That's amazing! That's like six figures! You actually asked him?'

'Well, he sort of dragged it out of me.'

'Even better. But don't forget to promote my favorite young playwright, too. You need to be a little selfish.'

'What I need,' she said, 'is to meditate on Frank's wisdom. Let's do the maze.'

She took his hand and led him past the bocce court. Happy party noise spilled from an open window as they approached the box hedges that formed a swirling labyrinth. With the walls at calf height, Nicholas could easily see over the curving lanes and dead ends.

'This is like a maze for toddlers. Hmm. Does Frank have kids who are going to inherit all this?'

'Nope. My friend Angela told me that's why he's such a beloved . . . Well, she said "target." But, you know, donor. He's got nobody to leave his wealth to except his wife, Karina.'

When Nicholas tried to step over the hedge, she stopped him, claiming it was bad luck. So they walked around until they reached the exit on the ocean side of the maze. There was a gazebo at the edge of the bluffs, and they paused and watched glimmers where waves caught the moonlight. The wind played with Sophie's new bangs, and he brushed them into place just for the excuse to touch her.

'You know who else is beloved?' he asked, before telling her about Sunny's funeral party.

She laughed tipsily, and gave a shiver, so he held her closer.

'Thanks for coming tonight.' She snuggled against him. 'Everything is easy when you're here.'

'I wanted to come,' he told her.

She drew back a few inches. 'Wait, you weren't pushing my play in there, were you?'

'No! No.'

'Oh, thank god.'

'Not *pushing*.'

'Nicholas . . .'

He nuzzled her neck. 'They happened to ask if I knew any young unproduced playwrights, and after racking my brain—'

'*I'll* rack your brain,' she said, grabbing his head and shaking it in her hands.

When they finished kissing, she led him back toward the house on a flagstone path that curved past a bungalow-type building with olive trees in terracotta planters.

'Must be Frank's music studio,' Sophie said, peering closer. 'What a life. He says he got lucky.'

'Huh. Usually rich people ascribe one hundred percent of their success to hard work and brilliance.'

'Frank's different. I like him.' She fell silent as they neared the main house. 'He reminds me of Mrs B a little. He's so comfortable in his own skin.'

Nicholas heard a car door slam in the front driveway, then caught sight of the catering van being packed up, along with a few cars leaving. 'Oh. People are heading home already.'

Sophie's hand tightened in his. 'C'mon, we need to say goodbye.'

They followed the path around the side of the house. Across the drive, Angela stood with one hand on her open car door while saying goodbye to Pax.

'Did you notice she's dressed exactly like that Jane lady?' Nicholas said.

'She knows how to flatter her mentor. Who's that with her?'

'Pecs. You'll never guess why.'

'His name is not Pecs!'

'Well, Pax. He's their massage therapist.'

'Huh.' Sophie peered closer. 'That explains Jane's "new age music" comment.'

'Yeah.'

'We should go thank CJ,' she said, leading him around the front of the house. 'And Frank, too. He gave me some great advice.'

'Not to mention that wine.' He squeezed her hand. 'You did really well, Soph.'

'All I did was lurk.'

'You were *you*. That's all anyone needs.'

She pulled Nicholas closer. 'It's possible I've fallen in love with you.'

'Huh. Weird. There's an off chance that I love you back. Now we—'

A scream sounded from inside the house.

13

SOPHIE

I grabbed Nicholas's arm, my pulse roaring in my ears. I recognized that scream. Not the voice, but the shock of terror. I was all too familiar with fear: from my stalker, from finding a corpse outside my window, from seeing a masked man attack Lily-Ann.

Blurred shapes moved inside the windows of the house. My hand tightened on Nicholas as I heard a man's voice rising and falling. A woman shouted for an ambulance, and my vision started to darken at the edges.

'Soph,' Nicholas said. 'Sophie.'

I took a deep breath. 'I'm okay.'

'Did you hear that?' Angela asked from behind us.

Nicholas held me close. 'Should I take you home or—'

'Someone must've had a heart attack,' I told him. 'We should help.'

I dragged him to the front of the house, then stopped at the open door. Frank's friend George, the erudite man with the bushy white beard, stood in the foyer, murmuring into his phone. His wife, Helene, was bustling upstairs, followed closely by Jane.

And CJ knelt at the base of the staircase beside Frank DeYoung.

Well, beside Frank DeYoung's *body*, which was sprawled on the polished concrete floor. One of his pant legs had hiked up to reveal his blue-veined pale calf. His hands were too white and too still, and his neck was bent wrong.

I froze in place as Pax the masseuse crouched beside CJ. I shifted my gaze away, focusing instead on the ice cubes scattered along the stairs from a dropped drink. I didn't want to acknowledge the ugliness of a broken body, so my gaze fixated on the ice cubes like nothing mattered more.

Karina stood on the second floor, at the top of the stairs, far above Frank, looking pale and unsteady, about three inches from fainting. Then Helene gathered her into her arms, and my gaze fell to where Frank's best friend Sunny watched stricken from the other side of the foyer, his sunglasses skewed on his face, grasping one of the mission-style benches for support.

'What happened?' Angela asked, entering behind me and Nicholas.

'Ambulance is on the way,' George announced.

'Is he – breathing?' CJ asked Pax.

Pax felt Frank's neck for a pulse, then shook his head. He might've whispered 'no' too quietly for anyone to hear.

Sunny gave three wrenching sobs, then sank onto the wooden bench.

Karina didn't move. She looked like a statue of a woman suddenly widowed as CJ took Frank's hand with a tremulous smile, tears on her face while George kept talking to 911 dispatch.

'What happened?' Angela asked again.

'He tripped,' Pax told her.

'No,' Karina said, barely loud enough for me to hear.

'He fell,' Helene said. 'Oh, god, Karina, I'm so sorry.'

Karina pointed downstairs toward us. 'She pushed him. I saw it. She pushed him.'

14

VERNON

On the bright side, the Hope Ranch call wasn't for a robbery. Detective Sergeant Vernon Enible hated burglary calls to wealthy neighborhoods: the homeowners always expected the police to track down their stolen goods, and it was his job to disappoint them.

On the dimmer side, while the accidental death of a tottering eighty-one-year-old didn't require the expertise of the Crimes Against Persons Unit, it still required Vernon's presence. So he needed to show up.

And on the positively bleak side, while parts of Hope Ranch were merely rich, the DeYoungs were wealthy. The truly wealthy were untouchable. Even if you knew they were guilty, you couldn't work the system effectively, because their lawyers were already working it against you. Hell, you often couldn't even confront them directly. Instead, high-end criminal attorneys turned the justice system into a goddamn book club. You talked and talked and talked.

Still, 'Old Man Falls Down Stairs' shouldn't take much time. Vernon would tut somberly, say a few comforting words, then return to the station.

At least that's what he thought before he arrived at the scene. The mansion looked like a fancy apartment building from the 1970s, all concrete and stained wood, though the water features were a nice touch. And you couldn't beat the expansive garden and ocean bluffs. Unlike some of the mansions he'd responded to, he actually liked the DeYoung place.

Maybe he'd start saving his pennies.

He stepped from his car and glanced toward the three patrol cars. The tension in the air – or in the postures of the officers at the door – struck him as edgier than an accidental death deserved.

'What's the issue?' he said as he approached.

'The wife – the widow – says the decedent was pushed,' Officer Aldwell told him.

He paused outside the grand front door. '"Decedent"?'

'What in your day was known as "the dead guy,"' Aldwell explained, while glancing at her notepad. 'Mrs Karina DeYoung, sixty-four, has been married to the decedent for about ten years. Hosted a party tonight. The last guests were gathering in the foyer before heading out. As per usual.'

'As per usual?'

'They always said goodbye there, it was a kind of tradition.'

'And you already found that out?'

'I did,' Aldwell said.

'Huh,' he said, impressed despite himself. Aldwell was just a kid, but already thinking ahead. 'Now tell me the good stuff.'

'Karina DeYoung saw the housekeeper push her husband down the stairs.'

'The housekeeper?'

'CJ Moore, thirty-five. She started working for Frank DeYoung soon after graduating college.'

'Good,' Vernon said.

'Why's that good?'

'A housekeeper can't afford the kind of high-powered crime attorney who makes my life miserable. Where is she?'

'Separated into the downstairs library, waiting for you. Eight guests were on the premises at the time of death. The two members of the catering staff stayed behind to clean up. They're in the kitchen, they didn't know anything happened till the ambulance arrived.'

He listened while Aldwell continued briefing him, then he perked up at a familiar name. 'Sophie Gilman, the half-Chinese girl?'

'I didn't ask about her ancestry.'

'You know what I mean. And Nicholas Perez, too?'

'You know them?'

'They live at the Marigold Cottages.'

Aldwell whistled. Everyone on the force knew the site of a double homicide. 'You want to talk to them first?'

'Nah, I'll start with Mrs DeYoung. She's the one making the allegation.'

After glancing into the party room, Vernon paused at the door to a den on the second floor. Officer Aldwell indicated Karina DeYoung, huddled on a couch, her eyes red with grief. She struck Vernon as unglamorous and middle-aged, which surprised him. He figured music producers married women who looked like the dancers in videos. Two other women, whom the officer identified as Jane Sheffield and Helene Kagant, were comforting her while two men, George Kagant and Jonathan 'Sunny' Wheeler, murmured into their phones, apparently spreading the news.

'Mrs DeYoung,' he said, stepping into the room. 'I'm Detective Sergeant Vernon Enible. I hate to intrude but I need to clarify a few things.'

He said 'clarify' instead of 'question' because wealthy people got squirrelly about being 'questioned' but were highly confident that they saw things clearly. Karina DeYoung tearfully said that of course she'd help, and he reiterated his condolences before asking her to tell him exactly what she saw.

Karina sniffled. 'I saw *her*. CJ. I saw her push Frank.'

'You're referring to CJ Moore?'

'She just reached out and . . . oh, God.'

'I'm sorry, ma'am. Could you set the scene a little?'

She smoothed her black pants with trembling fingers. 'We were – we were at the top of the stairs. Most of the guests had left, but the rest of us . . . we're the kind of people who, once someone says, "I should be heading home," it's thirty minutes before anyone actually leaves.'

'You'd all been in the, uh, room with the buffet table?'

'The great room, yes. Then George said they should be going.' She attempted a watery smile. 'Well, he said, "Time to pretend we're leaving," because he's George. Then Pax left with . . . what's her name?'

'Sophie Gilman?' Vernon suggested.

'No, the blonde one.'

'Angela,' Jane Sheffield said.

'Right. Pax walked her out, and we, the rest of us, followed as far as the foyer. Frank is used to – *was* used to our long goodbyes, so he headed upstairs.'

'We stood around chatting,' Jane said. 'I think maybe CJ brought Helene's coat?'

'She did.' Helene tugged at the collar of her black embroidered jacket. 'I was talking with Sunny and George about local theatre. One of the guests is a playwright.'

'Oh, is she?' Vernon asked.

Helene nodded. 'She wrote a murder-mystery play set in Santa Barbara.'

'I'll have to give that a read.' He looked back to Karina, who was blank-eyed and pale. 'So they were in the foyer and you were where?'

'Upstairs with Frank,' Karina said. 'CJ was already with him because she thinks she's his daughter, even though he'd rather that *I* help him, so I ran upstairs. Then we were saying goodbye and – and . . .'

She waved her manicured hand, telling him she couldn't speak, so he said, 'Maybe Ms Sheffield can take over?'

Jane Sheffield straightened as everyone's gazes turned to

her. She was the type of glamorous middle-aged woman who still turned heads. Looked like she should've been the wife, but instead she raised funds for international relief.

'Sunny was talking about life extension,' she said in a throaty voice. 'His favorite subject. Then what happened? Pax hadn't returned from the driveway yet, which I remember because I was going to have him help Sunny to his car, and then – we were laughing, we'd had a few drinks. There was a noise in the great room, a sort of crash.'

'A crash?' Vernon asked.

'When I looked later, I saw broken glass. I guess a wine bottle rolled off a shelf and smashed on the floor.'

Vernon took note of that, because you needed to exert serious force to shatter a wine bottle. 'And then?'

Jane opened her mouth to continue but Karina spoke first: 'That's when it happened. I was at the top of the stairs with CJ and Frank. Everyone turned to look at the noise, but I looked at Frank instead and that's when I saw her.'

'What exactly did you see?' Vernon asked.

'CJ. I saw CJ, standing behind Frank. Her face, that stupid winged eyeliner . . . I can't forget her expression, she looked *eager*. She reached out with both hands and shoved him and – he *fell*, and I heard . . . the sound and – it was awful. I keep hearing the sound.'

Vernon murmured sympathetically, then considered the men in the room as the other women comforted Karina. He doubted they had anything useful to add. Men tended not to notice details that didn't affect them personally. So he thanked the widow and went to find the suspect.

Officer Aldwell pointed him to a long rectangular room packed floor to ceiling with vinyl records on built-in shelves.

At the far end of the room, fifty or so bottles of expensive booze were displayed behind an impressive bar. A massive stereo covered the other wall, behind gold velvet low-slung couches centered around a black Asian-looking coffee table.

It was Vernon's perfect living room.

A pale figure huddled miserably on one of the couches. CJ Moore, a tall woman shrinking into herself. Her face looked bloodless and her eyes sunken despite her almost-calligraphic makeup. Sitting there pulling tissues from a box and shredding them. She didn't seem to notice him; she kept staring at a square window that looked out over the garden. Or that would have, in the daytime. At night, with the room bright, it had turned into a mirror, so maybe she was staring at herself.

She tore a tissue into strips, then pulled out another. She ripped that one – then startled when he approached. She stood suddenly, gawkily, like she wasn't sure how her body worked. He asked her to sit, then sank into the velvet couch across from her. Made him want to light a joint.

He talked her through the events of the night, which agreed with everyone else's right until the only moment that mattered.

'I heard glass break in the great room,' CJ Moore said. 'I was at the top of the stairs, I guess helicoptering a little?'

'I don't know what that means, helicoptering.'

'Being a mother hen? That's what Frank called me. His balance isn't great, and he'd had a few drinks, um, so standing at the top of the stairs made me nervous. Then the bottle smashed in the great room.'

'The wine bottle?'

'I mean, I don't know at the time but everyone turned, including Frank. Except he turned too fast and I saw him stumble so I reached out to catch him. I tried to catch him. I swear. That's what Karina saw. She saw my arm out, grabbing for him.'

Vernon talked her through the events once more, then asked, 'Why is Karina so sure you pushed him?'

'She was drinking. She's in shock.'

'Is that all?'

CJ took a breath. 'I don't know. Yeah, I think so.'

'Do you get along?'

'Sure. Sort of. She – Karina doesn't like me.'

'Why is that?'

'She's jealous.'

'Of you and her husband?'

CJ took a breath. 'I'm closer to Frank than she is. I was. In some ways. In a lot of ways.'

'Did you have a sexual relationship?'

She shot him a look of perfect disgust. 'He's fifty years older than me.'

'And worth a hundred million dollars more.'

'Eighty-six million,' she said. 'No, we didn't have a sexual relationship. He was my friend and my boss and . . .'

She started crying, so Vernon stood to leave. Fortunately, she didn't catch him struggling to lever himself out of the couch. He turned things over in his head as he left the room. He had an accusation but no proof. Aside from the widow, no one saw CJ push the victim. Then there was the question of the sudden crash that had immediately preceded the fall.

Vernon beckoned Officer Aldwell to him and said, 'Wine bottles don't shatter so easy.'

'That's true,' she said.

'So how did this one break falling off a counter?'

'It didn't. It's not a wine bottle. It was Amaretto. And I

already googled. The square bottles are known for breaking.'

'Damn, Aldwell. I'll be working for you soon.'

She turned away, but not quite fast enough to hide her smile. He jotted down the additional information in his notepad, then moved back to the foyer to watch the crime scene unit working. He thought about Nicholas Perez and Sophie Gilman. Most people never came across *one* murder in their lives, but look at them: the third corpse in six months. Was that just a coincidence? Or were they here for some unspoken reason?

He left the blood spatter to forensics and went to find out.

15

SOPHIE

When Detective Enible stepped into view, my stomach clenched. I never thought I'd see him again. He was the cop who'd arrested Anthony and Mrs B – and eventually Lily-Ann's ex-husband, Piotr. The cop who *still* suspected that I, along with everyone else at Marigold Cottages, was complicit in a murder, or guilty of a cover-up.

Which wouldn't be so bad, if it weren't so true.

I'd felt sorry for James Dedrick when I'd found his body outside my cottage. I hadn't known that he'd planned to assault me. I hadn't known that's why he'd died. And Gregory Ybarra, well, he attacked Mrs B – not physically, but still. And that's why *he'd* died.

Yet in the end we'd shifted the blame to Piotr, because justice mattered more than law.

I doubted that Detective Enible agreed, though, and I dreaded the possibility of him poking around in our lives. I guess that's why I recognized him instantly, viscerally. A middle-aged man with a friendly, jowly face. I hated that he looked like a SoCal Columbo, rumpled and approachable. I knew better than to trust cops – because I read the news – but I tended to crumble under authority. I was terrified that if Enible talked to me, I'd blurt dangerous secrets.

After getting initial statements, and taking a thousand photographs of the house, the uniformed cops had asked me, Nicholas, Angela, and Pax to wait in the great room. Angela chatted to Pax and Nicholas, who would forever be Pecs in my mind. Seriously, he had bigger boobs than I did.

'Frank was a big funder of World of Goods,' Angela told Pax, stretching out on the couch and kicking off her heels. 'That's his major cause. Though Jane says he puts a lot of money into support for migrant workers, too.'

'Sounds like a great guy,' Nicholas said. 'I remember my dad listening to some of the bands he produced.'

I wanted to hear more about his dad. He didn't talk about him much and he *had* been married to Mrs B. However, my curiosity would have to wait because my phone was blowing up with Marigold Cottages Murder Collective texts after I'd explained what happened to Frank DeYoung.

Ocean

How are you holding up?

Sophie

Fine, but that detective is here

The same one as last year

Edible

Sophie
Not Edible.
Edible

Sophie
Gah!
Enible!
Vernon Enible

Hamilton
Don't talk to him.

Sophie
We're just witnesses. Not suspects

On the couch across from me, Angela was telling Pax, 'Sunny says Frank wanted to die penniless. To give it all away and keel over the next day. At least before he married Karina.'

'I don't know how much you can trust what Sunny says,' Pax said.

Angela tucked her stockinged feet beneath her. 'Jane says the same, though.'

'Was she angling to get World of Goods in his will?' Nicholas asked.

'Of course she was. She's good at her job. Also, she thrives on public acclaim. Eats awards for breakfast. She was due to win the Millerbrandt, which would've rocketed her into the fundraising stratosphere.'

I heard Nicholas's phone buzz in his pocket, but he ignored it while I texted on mine.

Lily-Ann
Anthony says, and I quote, 'No.'

Sophie

There's nothing to say. We were outside
We heard a scream we went inside. That's all

Hamilton

There is no word for dentists who give away candy. There is no word for teachers who claim the alphabet starts with F. But there is a word for a cop lying under oath.

Hamilton

Testilying.
It's so common there's a word for it.
Don't trust them.

I adored Hamilton, but he didn't trust anyone who lived outside of Marigold Cottages.

Ocean

Nobody mention this to Mrs B or she'll buy a deerstalker cap and start Marpling

Hamilton

Those are two very different intellectual properties.

Ocean

How's CJ? Is she okay?
Should I come be with her? Is it too early for that?

Hamilton

One is Sherlock Holmes by Sir Arthur Conan Doyle.

Lily-Ann

Yes, if you hadn't slept together yet.

Hamilton

The other is considered the pinnacle of cozy mysteries.

Ocean

We KNOW Hamilton!

Sophie

CJ's upset but okay

I wasn't sure if that was true, but I texted Ocean privately to reassure her, then Detective Enible entered the room and closed the door behind himself, a little harder than necessary.

'Sophie Gilman,' he said.

'I gave my statement to the police officer,' I told him, 'and have nothing to add.'

'Whoa,' Enible said. 'This hostility is new.'

'I gave my statement,' I repeated. 'But it's nice to see you again.'

He chuckled. 'And you're looking lovelier than ever. I just want to check your statement is correct. You were outside with Mr Perez until you heard a scream. You entered to find CJ Moore and then Pax Heron checking Mr DeYoung's condition.' He flipped through his notepad. 'At that point Karina DeYoung was at the top of the stairs, and moments later Jane Sheffield and Helene Kagant joined her?'

'That's right.'

'Do you know where they were at the time of Frank DeYoung's death?'

'I don't, sorry.'

'Great, thanks. That's a big help.' He lowered his notepad, like we were just chatting. 'So what are you doing in Hope Ranch? It's a long way from the Marigold Cottages.'

I stood from the couch. 'Okay, then. It's time to head home.'

'Throw me a bone, Sophie,' Enible said. 'That's not—'

'Nicholas?' I prompted.

'Right!' He rose beside me, his hand touching my lower back. 'Let's go.'

'Oh! Are we leaving?' Angela shoved her feet into her heels. 'Me, too! I don't have anything to add to what Sophie said.'

Enible considered me from beneath his shaggy brows. 'Of course, Ms Gilman. Say hello to Anthony Lambert for me.'

I almost said, 'Okay!' but Nicholas steered me toward the door.

'If you'd indulge me one more minute, Mr Heron?' Enible asked Pax.

Pax swallowed. 'Oh, sure. No problem.'

I almost told him he didn't have to stay behind, but Nicholas was already ushering me away from the foyer and the crime scene. If it was a crime scene, and Frank DeYoung hadn't simply stumbled. Which he had, given his age and drinking and the fact that of *course* CJ hadn't shoved him and – and I found myself blinking away tears, remembering his easy, confident warmth as he'd assured me that I already was a playwright. I didn't need to prove myself to anyone.

When we stepped outside, the comfortable cool night air chilled me to the bone. I found myself trembling, so Nicholas wrapped his jacket around me. I calmed as I caught his familiar scent in the collar.

'Sophie, you're such a *femme forte*!' Angela said, trotting after us. 'First you ignore the detective's questions, then you walk out on him. I need strength like that.'

I flushed. 'I, um, wanted to go home?'

'I thought you were soft, but damn you are a boss bitch.' She unlocked her car with a *twee-toot*. 'See you next time.'

After she pulled away, we climbed into Nicholas's car. His

headlights swept across the olive trees as the pavers wobbled under his tires.

'Boss bitch,' he said.

'Oh, shut up,' I told him, but I couldn't help smiling.

16

VERNON

Vernon tapped his pen on his notepad. He didn't know what to make of Sophie Gilman's refusal to speak with him, except that it was suspicious. She was the kind of woman who used to be called neurotic, the kind who now wandered around with a support chihuahua. That wasn't the type who refused to talk to the authorities. Somehow, her meekness had disappeared.

Possibly because she felt guilty about the lies she'd told him last time.

Vernon had never unpicked those lies, but he knew they existed. He knew she and her friends had covered for Mrs B and Anthony. Still, he'd gotten his arrest back then, and he'd get another one now. He just needed to question the right people.

He allowed his gaze to linger on Pax Heron for an intentionally uncomfortable moment, then said, 'Wait here, sir.'

The guy looked nervous enough to share *all* the gossip if Vernon rattled him a little. So he returned upstairs and separated the gorgeous Jane Sheffield from the others. He led her to an alcove with two chairs and a round table. Jane had the husky voice and sultry demeanor of a woman from the era when they could make you weak in the knees with a glance.

When he quizzed her about Mrs DeYoung, she said, 'Poor Karina takes all this' – she gestured vaguely – 'far more seriously than Frank ever did.'

'I don't know what that means.'

'No, darling,' she purred, 'you wouldn't.'

'Hmm. How would you describe their relationship?'

'Better than it appeared,' she said. 'He loved her.'

'What did she think of him?'

'Despite how Karina looks,' Jane told him, 'she's all woman.'

He didn't know what that meant, either, but he suspected she was playing with him. Jane understood power dynamics, and she wasn't impressed by a badge. So he focused on the facts: how much money had the dead guy given to World of Goods, how long had she known him, and could she think of any reason CJ would've wanted him dead.

'Do you know what they were to each other?' she asked. 'Frank and CJ?'

He could imagine, but he said, 'What?'

'Best friends,' she told him, which was not in fact what he'd expected.

He moved on to Sunny Wheeler, Frank's oldest friend, who was the archetypal rich weirdo. Happy to chat about his investments in life-extending therapy: cryogenics, blood transfusions, weekly IV packs. Vernon got less out of him than Jane, mostly because the poor guy couldn't stop crying.

Finally, Vernon spoke with Helene and George Kagant. She was a chatty woman whose flustered air couldn't conceal her intelligence, and he was what happened if a mad scientist got his doctorate in literature. They claimed they hadn't seen anything suspicious, but they filled in the blanks of some of the relationships. George had known Jane back in the mists of time. They'd even gone on a few dates before losing touch – he claimed – for twenty or so years. And Helene wanted Frank to invest in a nationwide initiative to convert all pet shelters into no-kill shelters with long-term care for unadopted animals.

He left the Kagants consoling Karina and headed back downstairs to question the massage therapist, Pax Heron, who to Vernon's dismay seemed less nervous after waiting. Which wasn't ideal, but he played along, giving a smile and asking about his work.

'I specialize in bodywork for seniors,' Pax told him.

'Massage for old people?' Vernon asked.

'Also palliative and hospice care. I often focus on craniosacral therapy and lymphatic drainage – though some clients respond even better to a simple head rub or applying lotion to their hands and feet. Often we just do guided breathing.'

As far as Vernon knew, the only kind of guidance that breath needed was in and out, but he took a few notes, then asked the guy what he'd seen in the moments before Frank DeYoung fell.

'Nothing,' Pax said. 'I was coming back inside to make sure no one needed a ride. They'd all been drinking.'

'And?'

'I saw Frank lying in the foyer. At the base of the stairs.'

'Then what happened.'

'I checked his pulse?'

'Who else was there?'

'Right beside him? CJ, of course. She ran downstairs when he fell. Sunny and George, I think? Everyone was milling around, calling for an ambulance. Jane and Helene went upstairs to Karina who, uh, said that CJ pushed him.'

Vernon tapped his pen on his notepad. 'You think that's what happened?'

Pax shook his head. 'No way. She loved him.'

'CJ did?'

'Yeah, like a father.'

Vernon wondered if Frank DeYoung loved CJ like a daughter, or something else. 'What about this noise in the great room?'

'Oh, yeah. That came before the scream. There was a pop of glass shattering. I thought a caterer dropped a stack of plates but someone said it was a wine bottle?'

The sudden distraction of a loud noise struck Vernon as a little too convenient. 'How'd it break?'

'No idea.'

'And you definitely heard the sound before the scream?'

'I think so.' Pax scratched the tattoo on his arm. 'Yeah, I heard the crash from outside. I mean, the windows were open in the great room.'

'Quite the coincidence,' Vernon said, trying to draw him out.

'There's no such thing,' Pax told him, with complete assurance. 'We simply overweight unlikely events when we attach meaning to them.'

'Oh, is that what we do? So you massaged Frank four times a week. Talk to me about his physical condition.'

'He's been getting shakier,' Pax said. 'The past two months in particular. Between you and me, I'm surprised he hadn't already had a fall. It's just a tragedy he was at the top of the stairs.'

'Tragic coincidence,' Vernon said aloud, as he wrote the words. And he would've believed them, too, if not for the eyewitness.

17

OCEAN

The third time Mrs B returned from errands with a dent in her Prius, Ocean realized she needed to step in. She'd geared herself up for a fight. She hadn't wanted Mrs B to stop driving completely, just . . . mostly. Frankly she hadn't trusted Mrs B behind the wheel in years, not since she'd admitted that she didn't look over her shoulder before switching lanes anymore.

'I listen to the beeps!' she'd said. 'That car is always beeping at me for something. I just never know what.'

'That's not as reassuring as you think,' Ocean told her.

She hadn't taken Mrs B's keys, but she'd insisted on driving her anywhere farther than the local co-op. Everyone else helped, too, including Anthony after he got his license. Well, except for Hamilton, of course. And to her relief Mrs B hadn't felt infantilized; instead she enjoyed the extra time with her favorite people.

Ocean felt like a caricature of 'Mom's Taxi,' though, as she drove Mrs B around more than her kids. At least she'd gotten in the habit of handling her emails while waiting in the pickup area outside the YMCA. At the moment she was rereading CJ's email for the third time – the reply to the voice message and texts Ocean had left her.

> I'm shaken up. I don't know. He was my rock and now he's gone. There's this empty space. I'm all unbalanced, I don't know where to put my feet. Does that make sense? I'm afraid I'm not good for anything right now.

I'm too shaken up. Thank you. Thank you for wanting to take care of me. You're wonderful, but I'm a little terrified of becoming needy? A burden. You take care of so many already, Ocean. I don't want to be one of them. I want to be something else to you.

I don't know what I'm saying so I'm just going to send this and tell you that you'd better keep texting me and leaving me messages! I love hearing your voice. And please tell me normal things! I just might not be great at replying?

Everything feels off. The house isn't the house without Frank. Karina hates me. I don't know. I'm okay, though. Just shaken up.

Ocean sent her a voice message, saying that she understood, then shared her favorite new fact: while doing geographic flash cards with Anthony, Miles had fallen in love with Montevideo, Uruguay. She said she hoped that was normal enough, because she'd kind of lost track of 'normal,' then Mrs B flung the passenger door open.

'I have news!' she announced, plopping into her seat.

A drop of water splashed Ocean's face. Mrs B was wearing her cotton navy sailor-suit maxi-dress, to match the marine theme of the YMCA swim classes. She must've raced from the locker room to share the gossip, because her white pixie cut was still soaking wet.

'You set a new record for the over-eighties women's bench press?'

'Even better.'

Ocean pulled away from the curb. 'You managed your bra without CJ?'

'The other women are happy to help.'

'You don't need help.'

'No, but it's mitzvah to let them do a mitzvah.'

'How convenient for you.'

'Would you hush?' Mrs B said. 'There's been a death!'

Well, shit. Apparently someone had told Mrs B about Frank DeYoung. That didn't bode well. Still, Ocean played ignorant. 'Oh, no. At the Y?'

'In Hope Ranch! At the party Sophie and Nicholas went to! It must've happened after they left. I can't believe CJ didn't call me. I had to learn about it through the water aerobics grapevine.'

Ocean could imagine how that went. A lot of whisper-yelling and meaningful splashing. 'Did anyone know the dead guy?'

'Aha!' Mrs B stacked her silver bangles on her wrist from the dashboard where she kept them during class. 'So you already knew.'

'Knew what?'

'That CJ's boss tumbled to his death.'

'No, I had no idea.'

'You're a terrible liar. Did she text you?'

Ocean sighed. 'Sophie and Nicholas were still there when it happened.'

'And *they* didn't tell me?'

'They wanted to, but I wouldn't let them. I didn't want you to worry.'

'Worry? Why would I worry? This is wonderful news!'

'What are you talking about, you mad old woman?'

'Well, not for CJ. Poor girl. Have you seen her? You should give her a shoulder to cry on.'

'I offered, but she's kind of turtling at the moment.'

Mrs B huffed. 'Turtling is for reptiles. Or amphibians, I never could tell the difference. In any case! The good news is that CJ doesn't like Karina, did you know that?'

'I don't even know who Karina is.'

'She's Frank DeYoung's much-de-younger wife.'

'I see what you did there.'

Mrs B looked pleased. 'So I'm pretty sure that she killed him.'

'You think Frank's wife killed him because CJ doesn't like her?'

'No! Because *she* doesn't like CJ. What kind of person wouldn't like CJ? A monster!'

'While I can't disagree with you there—'

'I know!' Mrs B crowed. 'Another murder is exactly what we need.'

Ocean didn't answer; she just drove along upper State Street, past the post office and the liquor outlet where Mrs B bought her Drambuie.

'Because,' Mrs B continued, after a minute of silence, 'we've never been closer than when we solved the previous murders.'

'We didn't exactly solve them,' Ocean reminded her. 'We framed Piotr while two of us got away with murder.'

'We *handled* them,' Mrs B said, like some kind of old lady mob boss. 'We need to convene a meeting. We have to clear CJ's name.'

'There's no way she's a real suspect. The guy just fell.'

'Well, wouldn't *that* be convenient.'

Ocean turned left at the Presbyterian church. 'Old people fall.'

'Bah!' Mrs B's bracelets jingled with accusation. 'Did Sophie and Nicholas see it happen?'

'No, they were outside.'

'Hmph. At least they met all the guests, so we're already a step ahead.'

'Of what?'

'The police! Do you trust them to investigate CJ?'

Ocean frowned at the cross traffic. 'Okay, good point.'

'And you know CJ's innocent. She's lovely.'

'Sometimes,' Ocean said, giving Mrs B a quick meaningful look, 'the loveliest person you've ever met is also completely whackadoo.'

Mrs B shook her bracelets again. 'Tease all you want, Ocean. This is clearly a case for the Marigold Cottages Murder Collective.'

18

LILY-ANN

Lily-Ann stood in her walk-in closet and tried to enjoy the well-ordered shelves. 'Walk-in' made it sound bigger than it was. Sure, she'd had it customized with Farrow & Ball Peignoir paint and space-saving racks, but it was still nothing grand. Especially when she didn't even *want* to dress for this particular event.

'I don't wear leggings,' she called to Anthony. 'I don't even own a pair.'

'How about your tracksuit?' he asked from the bedroom.

'No one wears cashmere to yoga class.'

'Mm. The way you look in that, you'd start a riot.'

She stepped from the closet and closed the door decisively.

'I'm not going. I don't know why you want to. You have your kettlebells.'

Anthony shrugged. 'I like trying new things.'

She had to admit she loved that about him. Piotr had been terrified to try anything he wouldn't instantly ace, but Anthony didn't mind looking silly or incompetent. He was so comfortable in his skin that he didn't get embarrassed. She wasn't exactly shy herself, but that didn't mean she wanted to *om* through a sea of twenty-year-olds with tight asses encased in Lycra.

'What if we do it here?' she asked him.

His forehead creased. 'The yoga class?'

'I'll find an instructor online.'

'And?'

She felt herself blush. 'I'll wear my tracksuit.'

'Now that is a deal.'

She showed him where to move the furniture, then she found a beginner's yoga class on YouTube. She changed into her cashmere sweats, enjoyed Anthony's supportive leering, and grumbled through the first few poses. Then she started enjoying herself. Strict poses and regimented breathing techniques were right up her alley. Meditation was more difficult, but she managed to ignore the buzzing of her phone until after the final namaste.

Ocean

Mrs B heard about the death in Hope Ranch.

Is everyone free at two this afternoon?

Marigold Cottages Murder Collective at Hamilton's house

'Oh, lovely,' she murmured, feeling a lightness in her chest.

Anthony glanced at her.

'Another murder mystery.'

'The dead guy from that party?' he asked.

She nodded. 'Ocean's girlfriend's boss.'

'You're afraid of leggings, but murder doesn't scare you.'

'Murder does scare me,' she told him. 'But no other puzzle has so many moving pieces. I like the challenge. And leggings have no dignity.'

'Neither does death,' Anthony said.

'Surely that depends on the death?'

'You're sexy when you're wrong,' he said, putting a hand on her cashmere hip.

She felt herself color. 'That makes no sense.'

He gave her one of his blank looks. She didn't like expressions she couldn't unravel, so she turned back to her phone.

Hamilton

MCMC!

Marigold Cottages Murder Collective.

MC squared. Which means we equal E.

Because E=MC2.

Sophie

It's weird that nothing's faster than the speed of light, which is our primary sense

Too convenient!

Nicholas

Flat earther

Hamilton

All electromagnetic radiation moves at C.

Not just light.

Sophie

Oh

Hamilton

In a vacuum.

Ocean

Well, I'm glad we answered my question

Nicholas

Two o'clock at Hamilton's

We'll be there

Hamilton

I have a new batch of kombucha.

Just started the second fermentation.

Lily-Ann

We will also attend the meeting.

Lily-Ann turned to tell Anthony to replace the furniture, but didn't say anything because he was wrestling with his phone. She didn't want to interrupt him. He stayed busy with his phone. In the end, she watched him tap his screen for two full minutes before he finished.

Anthony

See you there

'You're adorable,' she said.

He clearly didn't know what she was talking about, but he said, 'You should see me in cashmere.'

'I *should* see you in cashmere.' She mentally added a charcoal sweater to her Christmas list. 'Will you move the furniture back? Um, to the exact same—'

'I know, Lil,' he said.

Lily-Ann ducked her head and checked the time. Then she removed her hair from a bun, changed into a cranberry silk blouse and black trousers and went into the kitchen. She opened the fridge and called to Anthony, 'If we don't bring an appetizer, Hamilton will pass around candied salmon again.'

'I liked his candied salmon.'

She gave a shudder. 'We have feta. Did you buy the olives?'

'Yes.'

'Castelvetrano?'

'In the door.' There was a pause. 'Miles calls them Castlevania olives, after a vampire show.'

'We can make wooden stakes from toothpicks,' she said. 'You took him shopping?'

'He likes errands.'

'You'd make a great father.'

He appeared in the doorway. 'Yeah?'

She suddenly didn't know what to do with her hands or how her face was supposed to look. She bent into the fridge to hide her expression. Then she took a breath and calmed herself and cooked garlic and lemon peel in olive oil to pour over the feta and olives. She set Anthony to slicing a baguette for crostini. As they worked, she talked through the guests at the DeYoungs' party – at least the ones that Sophie and Nicholas mentioned – and felt a shiver of anticipation. She loved finding order in chaos. Riddles and spreadsheets satisfied her on a fundamental level.

After the Marigold murders last spring, she'd missed investigating a crime.

She didn't much care about guilt or innocence; it was the process that interested her. Unfortunately, she knew that intruding on a family's grief for her own gratification wasn't kind – so she dearly hoped that *Mrs B* would insist upon an investigation.

19

SOPHIE

Hamilton left his front door unlocked, so I knocked once and let myself in. Every time I visited his cottage, the neatness surprised me. His brain was cluttered and idiosyncratic, but his living room was serene. The walls were a neutral cream color, the couch was white and unstained, and his birch bookshelves were organized with game boxes and fantasy novels.

The living room was empty so I crossed toward the kitchen, listening to Hamilton in mid-conversation: '. . . my current theory is that we're going to find levels of toxicity in the Mississippi River that mimic the effects of lead on the brain that we've—'

'Interesting,' Lily-Ann interrupted. 'But I asked if you have soda.'

'Oh, right. To drink?'

'Yes,' Anthony said.

'No.'

'Tap water's fine,' Lily-Ann told him. 'We'll cut up lemon wedges.'

I smiled to myself and called, 'What smells so good?'

Anthony appeared in the kitchen doorway, holding a plate of toasted baguette slices. 'Salty cheese in garlic and olives.'

'Feta,' Lily-Ann said.

'My kombucha won't be ready for another week,' Hamilton announced.

'Good thing I brought iced tea.'

I set the pitcher on the coffee table, then separated the bread onto two plates so nobody would have to reach. As I finished, Nicholas came in with Ocean and Mrs B, who pointed a small wooden hammer at me.

'I brought a gavel!' she told me. 'Will you take notes? Not notes, what do I mean? Moments?'

'Minutes?' Ocean suggested.

'Minutes! What an odd term.' She peered at me. 'Do you have your computer?'

I didn't, so I ran home. By the time I returned with my laptop, everyone was settled in a half circle with plates on their laps, as Mrs B presided from her place of honor in Hamilton's gaming chair. She wore a full-sleeve black caftan embroidered with off-white thread. Classy of her to put on mourning clothes as we discussed the recent death.

She banged her gavel on the chair's plastic armrest and announced, 'The Marigold Cottages Murder Collective is now in session! So. I've spoken, despite all of you turncoats and backbiters, to my friend CJ who told me—'

'She doesn't want to talk about this,' Ocean interrupted.

'Yes! That's *exactly* what she told me.'

Ocean pinched the bridge of her nose. 'Naturally, you backed off immediately.'

'She also told me she is suspected of pushing her boss down the stairs. Which is seven flavors of nonsense. Still, she's terrified they're going to arrest her, so she asked me to look into the case and—'

'Except she didn't ask, did she?' Ocean said.

'Not in so many words. However, in order to compensate for not being entirely honest about the previous murders, we should—'

'Don't even think that,' Nicholas snapped.

'Especially not aloud,' Hamilton added, while Lily-Ann said, 'Mrs B! We don't discuss that case.'

Mrs B blinked. 'Oh, yes. Right. Sorry.'

I didn't transcribe any of that, naturally, though I was a little relieved that I wasn't the only person still affected by the murders earlier in the year. Or by how we'd hidden the truth.

'That – *not* said, does anyone have any questions?' Mrs B continued.

'What's CJ's last name?' Ocean asked.

Mrs B glared at her. 'I'm sorry?'

'Her surname. The surname of this close friend of yours.'

'I don't know, Ocean. And you know I don't know.'

'Yet you're nibbing in—'

'However, I know that *you* know her surname, which is just as good as me knowing it.'

'Uninvited,' Ocean finished.

'Because that poor detective has another innocent person in his sights . . .'

I took a breath to remind her that the 'poor detective' had, in fact, had guilty people in his sights, too. But I decided not to mention that.

'And CJ helps with my bra straps!'

'And as we all know,' Ocean said, 'in the *People v. Maidenform*, the courts ruled that as proof of innocence.'

Mrs B slammed her gavel again. 'It's like you want her to be guilty!'

'Of course, I don't.'

'Does anyone *other* than Ocean have questions?'

'What's sweet in this?' Nicholas asked, dipping his bread in the feta and olives. 'It's so good.'

'Nicholas!' Mrs B said.

'Honey,' Anthony told him.

'All right,' Lily-Ann called us to order. 'Before we begin, Mrs B, Ocean, can we agree on one thing? If CJ is guilty, we *will* turn her in to the police.'

'What level of guilty?' Mrs B asked.

'That's a good question,' Ocean said.

'How are there levels?' Nicholas asked.

'Manslaughter, murder one, murder two,' Hamilton said, gesturing with a crostini for emphasis. 'Then there are mitigating circumstances and *mens rea*. That is, state of mind.'

'Malice,' Anthony said. 'Aforethought.'

Silence fell. Partly because Anthony rarely said anything like that, but mostly because he knew more about crime and punishment than the rest of us. Well, punishment, at least.

'It's not murder,' I said. 'CJ says he tripped.'

Lily-Ann stood from her chair in an elegant swirl of burgundy silk. She never missed. I wondered if she'd let me borrow any of her jewelry for fundraising events. Never mind, that ruby and gold bracelet probably cost more than my rent.

'Sophie is correct. The most likely case is that Frank DeYoung simply fell down the stairs. The second most likely case is—'

'Wait!' Hamilton said, springing to his feet. 'Wait, wait. Whiteboard!'

He dashed into the other room, his Birkenstocks slapping the floor, then returned rolling a whiteboard. He tossed the dry erase marker to me. I wasn't sure how I was supposed to take notes and also write on the board, so I gave it to Nicholas, who listed Lily-Ann's points as she said them:

1) Accidental death. Old man falls down stairs. Why is wife/ Karina so sure CJ pushed him?

2) If CJ did shove him, why?

3) Ocean says shut up, she didn't. Mrs B seconds that motion.

4) If Karina is guilty, that's why she's pointing a finger at CJ.

5) Bottle breaking distraction. Did several people collude? Planned in advance?

6) If so, what's the motivation for collusion?

'I can't tell if numbers five and six are the same,' Nicholas said, looking un-thrilled with his own list.

'Each of the guests who were in the house at the time of death deserves their own number,' Lily-Ann said. 'And there's another possibility, as well.'

Ocean squinted at her. 'I can't think of one.'

'There's a remote chance that someone who wasn't present at the time set this up.'

'A *remote* chance!' Hamilton crowed. 'Ha! Like a trip wire or similar.'

'I'm not writing down trip wire,' Nicholas told him. 'Or any other Wile E. Coyote–style causes of death. I'm all out of anvils.'

Lily-Ann said, 'I was thinking more along the lines of someone tampering with his medications.'

'That's a good point,' I said. 'But shouldn't we start with the motive?'

Ocean scrubbed her short hair. 'Which I guess means finding out about the will and beneficiaries.'

'CJ might know,' Mrs B suggested.

'Oooh,' I said, 'I wonder if she's expecting to inherit.'

Mrs B gave me a prim look. 'Somehow that never came up in the YMCA locker room.'

'As if you wouldn't have asked!' Ocean chimed in. 'Don't think I've forgotten the dermatologist! And you ask complete strangers how much they paid for their house!'

'That's different, everyone cares about property values. In any case, what motivations should we look for? I mean, other than money?'

'Love, hate, fear, guilt,' Lily-Ann said.

Anthony grunted. 'If Frank DeYoung spilled his drink on someone's shoe.'

'I don't follow,' Nicholas told him.

'People kill for small reasons,' Anthony said. 'So small you can't see them.'

'So motivation is too vague to focus on?' I asked.

Lily-Ann gazed at Anthony for a moment, then said, 'Where does that leave us?'

'I'll talk to my cop friend,' Hamilton said.

'The one from your online game? Will he help again?'

'He will if Miles asks him.'

'Miles, my son?' Ocean asked. 'My son, Miles?'

'Yeah, Miles plays a healer in *Realm of Rangers*, and those are rare. They're excluded from a lot of experience points, which is bad game design unless the player understands how to leverage their rarity into access to more powerful parties. Miles is happy to help anyone, so he gets invited to everything. There are a few late-game raids that require a healer.'

Nicholas drew the nerd-face emoji on the whiteboard.

'I'll talk to my friend Angela,' I said. 'She's a fiend for gossip, and she's got an in with Jane Sheffield, who's her mentor.'

'I'll pretend you're all normal,' Nicholas said.

Ocean huffed a laugh. 'I'd like to help with that, but I won't be able to pull it off.'

'I'll talk to CJ!' Mrs B said.

'Please don't,' Ocean said.

'You can come along.'

'Oh, thank you.'

'Can you talk to your artsy friends, Ocean?' Lily-Ann asked. 'It's a small town and art galleries rely on wealthy philanthropists. Someone might have a connection to the DeYoungs.'

'Sure,' Ocean told her. 'And what're you going to do?'

'Puzzle it all out,' Lily-Ann said.

20

OCEAN

Ocean was surprised by how much she'd enjoyed the Marigold murder investigation. She found the whole thing laughable, of course. She knew how ridiculous they were, playing detectives. Still, Mrs B seemed to shed years as they walked back together across the courtyard. Her eyes were bright and her stride was strong. Her caftan flowed behind her like Batman's cape and Ocean couldn't keep herself from smiling.

'Are you free tonight?' Mrs B asked. 'For dinner with CJ?

Will you yell at me if I invite her on such short notice? Should I make goulash? I don't have mushrooms. Why don't I have mushrooms?'

'You're happy,' Ocean said, at the door to Mrs B's cottage.

'I'm not happy, I'm *pleased*,' she said, then lowered her voice. 'Lily-Ann is glowing, did you see her? And Hamilton is thrilled we're meeting at his house again. It makes him feel like a member of the community. Like a central member of the community, which of course he is. You all are.'

'That's a lot of centers.'

'That's what love is, my dear. A cornucopia of centers.'

That stopped Ocean. 'Huh. I like that.'

'I am very wise.'

'Right. So you're just happy for everyone else, huh?'

'Of course. And for myself. I needed this. A new investigation because . . .' She glanced around as if checking they were alone. 'The way things ended last time didn't feel like an untarnished victory, if you know what I mean?'

'I do.'

'So solving a crime in which, well' – she lowered her voice even more – 'none of *us* are guilty? That's what I need. It's what we all need. That and mushrooms.'

Ocean laughed. 'Ask CJ to dinner some other time. She can't tonight.'

'Oh, are you taking her out?' Mrs B stepped inside her cottage, then turned with the door still open. 'What is this, the fifth date?'

'It would be, but—'

'That's lovely! Is the sex good?'

Ocean felt herself flush. 'Why would you ask me that?'

'It's more interesting than asking if she makes you laugh.'

'Well, she does. She does make me laugh. And I'm not seeing her tonight. She needs more alone time. I think losing Frank for her is like what losing you would be to me.'

'Are you sure dragging her out of the house wouldn't make her feel better?'

'I'm not sure about anything. Dating at this age. A younger woman. And now she's been accused of murder. What will the kids think?'

'You're worried about Riley?'

'A little.'

Mrs B pressed her lips together. 'First, we know she didn't kill Frank. Just like you would never kill me.'

'As much as I might want to, sometimes.'

'Ha! And second, you're not worried about Riley. You're hung up about your ex-wife. Things fell apart with you and Zoe, so you think you're bad at relationships. You're afraid you're not lovable.'

'Don't be stupid,' Ocean grumbled, because *you're right* would've been too painful.

'In this cornucopia of centers, Ocean, you're the one that holds everything together.' Her sweet, wrinkled face was aglow with earnestness. '*Nobody* here doesn't love you. You're wonderful, you're a treasure and beloved and—'

Ocean closed the door in the old biddy's face, flushing with embarrassment. Mrs B cackled from inside, and despite her mortification, Ocean couldn't help smiling along. What a monster.

On the way to her own place, she snipped a few blooms from the pink and orange floribunda rosebush between their cottages. She folded her pocketknife away – along with her thoughts about CJ – and went into her kitchen for a vase.

She loved this time of year. Only a couple more months of heat – September and October were often hotter than July and August in Santa Barbara – before the seventy-degree days returned. Plus, the kids were back in school, but not yet jaded, just like her own art students at City College.

Miles was already preparing for his school trip to Catalina Island, where the kids spend a full week away from home. Well, he was deciding which baseball hat to bring. Meanwhile, Riley was agitating for a tattoo, though Ocean wasn't sure if she really wanted one or was just testing the waters. Which meant Ocean didn't know if she should put her foot down or start sketching ideas.

If she really *did* want a tattoo, what better than a design created by her mother? Surely, that was every teenager's dream.

Ocean smiled again as she stepped into her cottage and heard the kids talking. Mrs B was right about her fear of romantic failure: she'd been so certain that Zoe was the love of her lifetime . . . right until everything burst into flames. Still, there was so much love in her life. For her friends and family, true, and maybe, just maybe, she'd get romance right this time.

21

HAMILTON

The now-quiet cottage smelled of feta and olives, half his furniture was in the wrong place, and Hamilton closed his eyes and reveled in the moment. Replaying the last few hours in his mind: everyone talking and bickering and laughing.

He swept crostini crumbs from the couch cushions and moved the furniture back. He washed Lily-Ann's serving dish, then crossed to the window and watched the courtyard as he sipped a soothing glass of buttermilk.

Nobody was there, not even Sophie or Nicholas, who'd been busily moving her boxes into his cottage – the biggest one on the property. A pair of Sophie's boots stood among the succulents, forgotten for the moment. They looked like rain boots to Hamilton, which didn't make sense for Santa Barbara. Maybe they were in fashion, though he wouldn't know about that.

After he finished tidying the kitchen, he went to his office and opened a window into his game. *Realm of Rangers* wasn't the most popular MMORPG; it wasn't even in the top ten, but there were still fifty thousand players online at any particular time – and they were as fanatically devoted as any *World of Warcraft* addict. And one of them was a local cop with access to the station computers, who was frothing at the mouth to raid the Voidlands. So Hamilton sent Miles an in-game message: We need information from pb Cyntria. For Mrs B. Can I offer your healing services on his voidlands raid?

Two hours later, when Ocean allowed him online after homework or chores, Miles responded with, Sure! I'm loaded with mana and ready to reincarnate! Is it true that oil is made of dinosaurs?

Hamilton explained fossil fuels, then Miles sent him links to adoptable cats in the area. Hamilton had mentioned that he was considering adoption and Miles had run with it. The two of them messaged about an orange cat named Gouda and a three-legged cat named Quatro.

Finally, Hamilton chatted with the cop, the 'player behind'

Cyntria, who was a warrior woman from the frozen desert of the eastern plateaus. He shared Miles's character stats and the cop messaged: Damn, son. We can take this all the way to the vault.

Perfect, Hamilton said. Next Thursday night, 7 PST?

I'll tell my team. With a healer in the party, we're going to kill this.

Hamilton waited an hour, then messaged him, Oh, hey. Did you hear about that Hope Ranch death? Old guy fell down the stairs?

Yeah.

Making a false assertion always elicited more information than asking a question, so Hamilton typed, Have you arrested the wife yet? She's totally guilty.

Wrong. She's not even a suspect.

She's going to inherit $80 million.

She already had access to the money. Joint accounts. No motive.

So he tripped? Boring. Sucks to be a cop in SB. Nothing good ever happens.

Unless his housekeeper pushed him. Word is the wife blames her.

Oh! Well, that was interesting. Still, Hamilton decided to leave things there. He'd ask for actual evidence after the cop playing Cyntria started depending on Miles to keep his party alive. Once they entered the Voidlands, there was nothing the guy wouldn't hand over.

22

LILY-ANN

The painting in the entryway of Nicholas's cottage was a geometrical picture of figures around a swimming pool. Bright colors, clean lines. To Lily-Ann's eye, it looked like Mondrian and Southern California at the same time.

'That's new,' she said.

'Sophie was flipping through Ocean's old portfolio,' Nicholas told her. 'She bought it for my birthday.'

Lily-Ann looked closer. 'That's Mrs B. In the caftan.'

'And Ocean in the water.'

'What's the other blob?'

'Ocean's wife, when she was pregnant with Riley. I guess that's why it was in storage.'

She squinted. 'I prefer photography.'

'Maybe don't mention that to Ocean.'

'Why not?'

'It might hurt her feelings,' he said.

'Oh, of course.'

She appreciated when people at the Cottages made social cues explicit. Those were the only riddles she didn't enjoy unraveling. She knew that her neighbors explained things to her out of kindness, because Ocean had told her, so now she found it comforting. They helped her, and she helped them. For example right now, by visiting Nicholas.

Hmm. She wondered if Sophie had asked him to invite her, or if he'd realized on his own that he needed her help. Because currently his cottage was a quite acceptable bachelor pad, but Sophie deserved better. Lily-Ann didn't truly care who'd decided to ask for her help, but she still said, 'Does Sophie know I'm here?'

'Yeah.'

'Did she make you invite me?'

'Not exactly.'

'Are you lying?'

'Only a little,' he admitted. 'I don't like anyone going through my things.'

'But for Sophie, you're willing to put up with it?'

'Exactly. And she knew you'd enjoy it.'

'She's sweet.'

'She said she's going to miss you, even though she's only moving across the courtyard.'

'That's silly.' Lily-Ann considered for a moment. 'I'll miss her, too. Okay! Let's start in the bathroom.'

Nicholas looked startled. 'The bathroom?'

'Yes.' Lily-Ann paused, wondering how to break this to him gently. 'How do I break this to you gently?'

'It's okay, just tell me.'

'Your bathroom is horrible, Nicholas. Poor lighting, inadequate ventilation, and insufficient surfaces.'

'There are three lights, a cabinet, and a fan!'

'Mm.' She crossed the living room toward the bathroom, her gaze flicking to the side. 'Oh, and dump your couch. Keep hers.'

'Mine is bigger.'

'Have you ever seen Sophie on her couch?'

'She curls up like a cat.'

'Exactly.'

His expression softened. 'Good point. Thanks.'

'Now, the bathroom.'

She opened the door to a perfectly adequate bathroom. For a man living alone. But she felt protective toward Sophie, and wouldn't accept anything less than the best. So first she needed an opaque shower curtain. No matter how much you loved your boyfriend, you didn't want him watching you shaving your bikini line. Then she needed plenty of *good* lighting and an abundance of surfaces. Lily-Ann worked for an hour before heading to her house for the Kiehl's grapefruit hand soap and the cream body cleanser she'd decided to leave as a housewarming gift.

When she returned, she ignored Nicholas, who was sitting at his desk with his laptop. She walked past him and peered into his bedroom. 'Oh, no.'

He raised his head. 'There's nothing wrong with my bedroom.'

'Your bed's in the wrong place.' She crossed to the bureau. 'And I bet your clothes are—'

'No messing inside the drawers!'

'I'm not messing, I'm tidying.'

'You know what I mean, Lily-Ann.'

'Fine,' she grumbled. 'But the bed would be better against the other wall.'

'You think?' he asked, from the doorway.

'I do.'

While they improved the placement of the furniture, she said, 'What about the caterers?'

'I *know* Sophie doesn't need caterers.'

'I mean at the DeYoungs' house.'

'Oh,' he said. 'They were gone by the time Frank fell. Most of them. A few were waiting in the kitchen for the last of the guests to leave.'

'They could've done something before they left.'

Nicholas straightened from moving the standing lamp. 'What, drizzled vinaigrette on the stairs?'

'Why are you so dismissive of our investigation?' she asked.

'Because we're not investigators?'

'If we investigate, we are.'

'Well, not *trained* investigators.'

'I'm not sure anyone is, despite what you see on TV. So, what about the wine bottle?'

He frowned at the room. 'Um . . .'

'The one that shattered before DeYoung fell, Nicholas. You didn't see anyone else walking around with one?'

'Only me. Maybe a caterer, but I don't remember. And I didn't leave it precariously balanced anywhere. I left it right side up on the buffet table.'

'I'll get Hamilton to ask his cop about the variety. You said you were pouring a Malbec?'

'Uh, maybe? It started with an M.'

'Merlot? Montepulciano? Mourvèdre?'

'Yeah, that's it. Mourvèdre.'

'Nice, ancient grape. We'll have to ask which bottle broke.' Lily-Ann began organizing the bookcase. 'And you noticed nothing else about the guests who remained? Sophie told me that her friend Angela says Jane Sheffield's been widowed twice. She likes to marry older men.'

'How was I supposed to notice that?' She frowned at him.

'That's not dismissive, Lily-Ann, that's my inability to look into a person's eyes and know that two of her husbands died. I don't see how that's motive, though, considering she wasn't married to Frank.'

'True.'

'She seemed normal, for whatever that's worth. Sunny Wheeler is weird, though. He staged a funeral for his seventy-fifth birthday. He's narcissistic and obsessed with cryogenics.'

'Life extension,' Lily-Ann mused. 'Shift the bed a foot to the left. And the Kagans?'

'Kagants. Helene and George. They're not "super-rich weird," just "normal weird." She's got a great vibe, she's immediately likable, and he's like the guy at the cocktail party who you hope monopolizes the conversation. Your family is wealthy, right?'

'Does that make me super-rich weird?'

'Ha! No, you're normal weird like the rest of us.'

For some reason, that pleased her so much that she felt herself smile at the bookshelf.

'What I meant was, maybe your family knows people who know these people?'

'Hmm. Improbable, but possible. I'll inquire.'

'See? I'm helping.' Nicholas shifted the foot of the bed closer to the window. 'Now, who else? There's Pax the massage therapist. He's suspicious as hell.'

'Why is that?'

'Too handsome. And who invites their massage therapist to a party?'

'You think he's sleeping with one of them? Oh, he could be a gigolo! Is that a term we still use?'

'Mrs B probably does.' He adjusted the bed, making everything parallel. 'How's that?'

She surveyed the bedroom. 'Another inch. Right there! Perfect.'

'You know it wasn't a murder, right?' Nicholas rubbed the back of his neck. 'A half-drunk old man fell down the stairs.'

'His wife says CJ pushed him.'

'Yeah, but Ocean can't be that unlucky.'

Lily-Ann considered. 'Should I ask Ocean if she'd rather we didn't investigate?'

'Nah, she'd think we suspect CJ, which isn't great for a new relationship. And sure Karina blames CJ, but she was drinking, too. I heard she doesn't like CJ.'

'There's a large gap between disliking someone and accusing them of murder.'

'True, but just . . . don't get too excited, okay?'

'Why not?'

Nicholas took a breath. 'I'm afraid you'll be disappointed when it turns out there's no mystery. You *and* Mrs B.'

'Ah. That's true. I *do* hope this was murder and not simply another tedious accidental death.'

'Lily-Ann,' he chided.

'Don't worry, I won't share that with Ocean.' She smiled. 'Just Mrs B.'

23

CJ

CJ closed her bedroom door gently behind herself. She exhaled to keep from crying, then crossed to the birdcage. That always cheered her up. Her parakeets whistled and trilled greetings, then Mouse fluttered closer while Mona pecked at her perch.

'At least I have you two,' she said, and opened the cage door.

She cooed at them, but they stayed put, safe behind bars.

She couldn't blame them: she should've learned that lesson and kept to herself. Instead, she'd tried speaking with Karina. That's what Frank would've wanted, after all. And she'd hoped, a little stupidly, that things could change between her and Karina. They'd both loved him. He'd loved both of them. Surely, for his sake, in his memory, they could get along through the funeral at the very least.

Apparently not.

She'd approached Karina at the bocce court after dinner; she'd been playing obsessively since Frank died, as a way to cope with the grief. She'd asked if they could talk, but Karina hadn't even looked at her. Hadn't acknowledged her in any way. She just tensed, her knuckles whitening around the ball in her hand.

So CJ had retreated to her room, aflame with shame and sorrow. Frank deserved so much better. Hell, she deserved better, too. Maybe she should accept one of Ocean's invitations. At least for a walk on the beach, to calm herself a little, if not—

Karina burst into the room and the birds flapped in a panic. 'Get out! I want you gone!'

'Karina, I—'

She hurled the photo in her hand. The frame spun across the room and shattered against the wall. Broken glass tinkled around the picture of CJ and Frank. The one he kept on his bedside table. From her second year with him – before Karina – when he'd taken her on his trip to Costa Rica.

'Get the fuck out of my house,' Karina said.

CJ crouched, shook shards from the photo, then almost smiled at the expressions on her and Frank's faces, in the treetops looking over the zip line that disappeared into the rainforest below.

'The cops don't have a clue,' Karina spat at her, 'but *we* know. You and I know the truth and if you're not gone in twenty-four hours I will – I swear to God, I will set you on fucking fire.'

'Karina, you were drinking! I reached for him, I tried to catch him.'

'I hope you rot, I hope you suffer. You never cared about Frank.'

That's when the rage began pounding behind CJ's eyes. 'I put him first. *I* put him first.'

'Just get out.'

'I always put him first, Karina.'

'Yeah? Well, he put *me* first.'

'Of course he did! You're his goddamn wife! And do you know what he'd want now? Do you have any idea? Because I do. I know exactly what he'd want. He'd want me to stay and—'

'I don't care!'

'And take care of *you*. That's what he'd want. You're petty and selfish but he—' CJ took a breath. 'He loved you, and you need my help. You have no clue how anything works around here. I'll stay one more month, until after the – the funeral. Until you're back on your feet. Because that's what he'd want.'

'Twenty-four hours,' Karina said. 'Starting now.'

After she slammed the door, CJ slumped to the floor beside the broken picture. For the first time since Frank's death, she wanted to sob. Not that she hadn't mourned him. Of course she'd mourned him. Still, she knew he'd insist that she celebrate the good times instead of wallowing in grief. All those years of laughter, of guidance, of stubbornness and kindness.

Yet look at her now, left with nothing but tears.

24

SOPHIE

I finished packing a box of knick-knacks while Anthony delicately wrapped my wineglasses in newspaper. Which I'd arranged on purpose, of course, because watching this big, tattooed man handle fragile things amused me. Maybe that was a little on the nose, considering how that big, tattooed man had taken care of *me* when I'd been fragile.

I never thought I'd arrive at a place where I'd be comfortable with an ex-con living in my little community, but here we were. In my mind, Marigold Cottages was an essentially female space. I mean, Nicholas had a mouthwatering streak of metrosexual in him – the jewelry he wore, the art he loved, how much he enjoyed theatre – but there was nothing female about Anthony.

Except maybe how unashamed he was to care for the other boys. He openly engaged with Miles, equally happy listening to him natter about insects or superheroes. And everyone in the Cottages chatted with Hamilton, but Anthony stopped by most often, usually for a drink in the late afternoon before heading to work. And by 'a drink,' I meant a shot of carrot-horseradish juice or some other Hamiltonian horror.

Also, I didn't want to dehumanize Anthony, but he made me feel secure, like having a guard dog on premises. These days, when I saw strangers lingering at the bus stop outside the Cottages, I figured they were waiting for the bus, *not* waiting to attack me. Talk about personal growth.

I was unpeeling the theatre quotes from my wall, when my

phone rang. Angela's name appeared, along with the surname Givemore Girls, because I hadn't known her well when I'd added her contact info.

'Hey,' I said. 'Thanks for calling back.'

'*C'est bon.* In your message you said you're looking for the tea about the other guests at Frank DeYoung's party?'

'You know I write plays, yeah? I base them on true crime, so I'm digging around for inspiration.'

'Ooh! I love true crime. I'm obsessed with this makeup artist influencer who talks about murder while she does her face.'

'Is her makeup any good?' I asked. 'Send me the link.'

'*Certainement.* But wasn't Frank's death an accident?'

'Sure, but it's still a great background for a play. A dead music producer in a mansion. I'm just looking for inspiration. You know, "based loosely on." So anything you can tell me about the other guests?'

'Especially CJ, right? She's the prime suspect?'

'Absolutely,' I said, feeling disloyal to Ocean.

'She's only interesting because Karina hates her. Jane – you know, my mentor?'

'Yeah, I know who she is.'

'Well, she says Karina is crazy jealous and she's got a serious temper.'

'Really?'

'Apparently she throws things. Let's see, there's George and Helene Kagant. Beard and Bird.'

'Beard and Bird?'

''Cause he's got that Old Testament look and she's like a chickadee. Guess how they made their money?'

'Hedge fund?' I asked.

'Windshield wipers. They invented a new hinge or

something. Frank invested in them early, paid for prototyping and attorneys and all. They sold to a big company and made an absolute mint.'

'How do they know about windshield wipers?'

'George worked as an engineer. For medical instruments, but I suppose the expertise transfers.'

'Huh,' I said. 'So they owe the DeYoungs for investing in them?'

'Big-time. Though Jane says the DeYoungs probably made more money off the patents than George and Helene did.'

'Ooh, I like that as motive. And what about Jane?'

Angela blew a puff of air like a Frenchwoman. 'She came by her money the old-fashioned way. She married it.'

'Her husband died?'

'Both of them.'

'That's pretty true crime-y.'

'Ha! She'd make a great black widow, except at least one died of cancer, which you can't really pin on her. And Jane cares too much about Brand Jane to kill anyone. I mean, no shade, she's done a lot for World of Goods. But that's part of her self-image: she is a good person doing good things.'

I watched Anthony crumple a page from last week's *SB Independent* and wrap it around one of my four unmatched champagne flutes. I felt a pang when Angela mentioned World of Goods. I loved the theatre, I planned to devote my life to the theatre, but World of Goods saved lives by the thousands. The tens of thousands. They shipped vaccines and insulin to war-torn regions; they provided water purification, surgical supplies, and antibiotics.

So I said, 'I wonder if I could volunteer there. At World of Goods. Like, once I learn more about development?'

'You mean volunteer for *free*?' Angela asked.

I couldn't help myself, I laughed. 'Yeah.'

'Huh.' She took a sharp breath. 'Oh! Did I tell you? Jane didn't win the Millerbrandt she wanted!'

'That's the award?'

'Yeah, I guess she's not the best human on earth after all. She's so pissed. She actually thinks Frank didn't support her loudly enough. Tragically, he's too dead to push down a flight of stairs.' She paused. 'Too soon?'

'God, Angela, *yes*,' I told her. 'Wait, was he on the award committee?'

'Nah, but he was a big swinging donor, he could've tipped the scales.'

'Why didn't he?'

'He probably – and I'll deny saying this to my dying day – thought someone else deserved it more.'

I considered that. 'Do you think Karina didn't want him to support Jane?'

'Why would she do that? Oh! Because Jane's skinnier and prettier and better in every way? Nah. Karina already bagged the big money. She treated Jane with a sort of gentle pity.'

'Huh. What's Karina like? Other than resenting CJ. Were they having an affair?'

'Ooh! Karina and CJ! No, no, nobody was having an affair. Frank was a hundred years old and Karina is toxic levels of het.'

'Boring. What do you know about Sunny Wheeler?'

'He's worthless,' she told me. 'He only donates to life-extension scams. And he's handsy, too.'

I growled into the phone. 'How are men still getting away with that?'

'Because we haven't figured out how to procreate without

them,' she told me. 'Also, sometimes they're nice and wealthy.'

'Like Frank DeYoung.'

'Yeah, he was one of the good ones,' she admitted. 'Even minus the millions.'

25

OCEAN

Ocean yawned in the driver's seat as she followed the morning traffic onto State Street. She'd stayed up too late the night before, doomscrolling art videos and stand-up comics and terrifying advice about dating. Even the vocabulary frightened her: 'anxious attachment' and 'breadcrumbing' and 'rizz' and 'situationship.'

'Sleepy?' Mrs B asked.

'Mm. I should join the water aerobics class for a pick-me-up.'

'You absolutely should,' Mrs B said, as warm September air flowed into the car windows despite the early hour. 'But not today. Turn here.'

'It's five blocks too early.'

'Here, here!'

Ocean kept straight through the intersection. 'Why?'

'Now you have to turn around! We're not going to the Y, Ocean. We're meeting CJ for coffee at Common Grounds so we can figure out who murdered Frank DeYoung.'

Ocean glared at Mrs B. 'We're meeting CJ? And you didn't mention this because?'

'You would've complained.'

'I'm still going to complain.'

'Yes, but now I only have to listen to it once. CJ isn't coming to the Y right now. She's so upset, poor thing.'

'I'm aware.'

'Well, awareness isn't enough! She needs a friendly face, so I said we should meet for coffee. Since you were already driving me, I thought I'd bring along my friend with a gift for investigation.'

'So Lily-Ann's going to meet us?'

'Ha! No, I meant you.'

Ocean tightened her grip on the steering wheel. 'Is CJ expecting me?'

'Probably?'

'Let me rephrase that, you horrible old woman. Did you tell her I'm coming?'

'Not in so many words, no. But she *knows* me.'

Ocean didn't bother responding, she just took a left at the drugstore, which also led to the coffee shop.

'Oh, this way works, too,' Mrs B said. 'We have to support her, Ocean. She's innocent, but we still need a strategy for proving that.'

Ocean let out a breath. 'So what's the strategy?'

'How on earth would I know? We'll start with a simple interrogation.'

At a break in the traffic, Ocean turned onto De La Vina Street. She drove in silence, pretty certain that 'interrogation' wasn't part of the new dating lingo. And if she'd known she was seeing CJ, she would've at least put on some lip gloss. Maybe another tank top. The only good thing about this surprise coffee date was that Mrs B was scheming again. The old woman still had a lot of life left in her.

Mrs B's bracelets jangled as she waved toward the coffee shop. 'This used to be a Taco Bell. I once backed my car over that ledge. So you shouldn't worry so much about my driving.'

'Because you were always terrible at it?'

'Exactly. I haven't gotten any worse.'

'I'm not sure that's as comforting as you think.' Ocean parked near the entrance, then hustled around the car in case Mrs B needed help. 'Does CJ know you want to ask about Frank's death?'

Mrs B waved her away. 'The police told her not to leave town, Ocean, she's frightened.'

'I can't believe she agreed to meet you before me.'

'There's a good reason for that,' Mrs B told her.

'Which is?'

'*You* didn't bribe her,' Mrs B said, then strode across the lot and pushed inside.

The door jingled overhead as Ocean followed her in, trying not to think about that 'bribe.' Common Grounds was a fairly generic local café, with a line of flavored coffees in heated urns and nothing more sophisticated on the menu than a chai latte.

'Oh, look!' Mrs B waved enthusiastically. 'She's already here. CJ!'

CJ rose from a table against the tinted window, wearing a gray top and a black skirt. Black beads hung around her neck instead of the usual crystal she wore. For mourning. Her eyes were swollen from crying, though her gorgeous auburn hair still struck Ocean as lush and abandoned.

When Mrs B hugged her, CJ's wry smile looked warm and steady.

Ocean took her in a firm embrace. 'I'm so glad Mrs B bullied you into this. I missed you.'

'Me, too. I'm sorry. I needed to hide my head in the sand for a bit.'

'There's nothing to apologize for. How are you holding up?'

CJ tapped a few loose pieces of paper on her table. 'Better now.'

'Oh, uh, what are—'

'First, you two order, then we'll talk!' Mrs B interrupted, and handed over her credit card. 'This is my treat. Get me a black tea with lemon and sugar, and don't forget the lemon. Or the sugar. And something sweet. Whatever looks good. Shoo, shoo!'

'I'm sorry if you weren't expecting me,' Ocean said, as she and CJ headed for the counter.

'Stop,' CJ said. 'I'm glad to see a friendly face.'

'Oh, right. I suppose his wife doesn't want to keep you on . . .'

'I don't know what I'll do next. Frank hired me right out of college. Honestly, I don't know how to do anything else.'

'What exactly did you do for him?'

'Everything. Managing the staff, dealing with the house. Fixing his phone for the hundredth time. Shopping for clothes, organizing his meds, handling financial advisors and lawyers.'

'So you have experience managing a multimillion-dollar property. That sounds pretty transferrable to me.'

CJ's eyes crinkled with a smile. 'I don't know if I could do this for anyone else.'

'You were close.'

'Like you and Mrs B.'

'So he made you crazy.'

'Ha! That, too.'

'If you did all that for him, what did his wife do? What's her name, Karina?'

'Yeah. She bought things for the house and . . . I guess she gave him something to cherish.'

'He loved her?'

'Yeah. Poor Frank. He so wished that Karina and I got along better. She's always been insecure about me. I was there first, I'm younger. I guess she saw me as a rival? She always felt the need to make clear that I was staff, not family. Except Frank didn't really agree.'

'They fought about that?'

'Frank wasn't big on fighting. He was more of an enabler.'

When they returned to the table with the food and drinks, Mrs B said, 'So enough with your romantic getaway!'

'Is that what that was?' Ocean said.

'Of course! Like a walk on the beach, with less walking. And less beach. So did CJ tell you that she lost her job *and* her housing?'

'Oh, shit,' Ocean said. 'No.'

'Karina kicked me out last night,' CJ said.

'Goddamn.'

'Yeah. I mean, the room was part of my salary. Which mattered less fifteen years ago, when you could still rent in this town. But nowadays? Trying to find a twenty-five-hundred-a-month studio without a job? Impossible.' CJ tapped the paper on the table. 'So even though I know it's a little . . . whatever I'm so grateful for this.'

Ocean looked closer and saw the word *lease*. 'You already found a place?'

'Well, more like the place found me.' She smiled at Mrs B. 'I can't thank you enough.'

'Don't be silly,' Mrs B said, with a smug slurp of tea. 'We're lucky to have you.'

Ocean felt her smile freeze. 'Oh! You're renting Sophie's place to CJ?'

'I *know* I mentioned that to you.'

'Right. Yes, of course,' she said, instead of panicking.

She wasn't ready for this! She wasn't ready for CJ to move across the courtyard. Were they dating? Hooking up? Seeing each other? Oh, god, was this a situationship? She didn't know!

'Is that okay?' CJ asked.

'It's better than okay. It's great. You need a place and we have a place. It's how places work.'

'Am I imagining this?' CJ asked Mrs B.

'No, no, she's absolutely panicking. Look at her poor face! Don't worry, she'll get used to the idea.'

'It's only temporary,' CJ assured Ocean.

'I'm not panicking. I'm just surprised. It's honestly fine. It's great.'

'And now that *that's* settled,' Mrs B sang out, before turning her concerned gaze to CJ. 'Tell us everything you remember about that night. To help the investigation.'

'If you want to,' Ocean added, unclenching her jaw. 'I'm not sure what she told you, but we're not—'

CJ interrupted with a wave of her coffee cup. 'It's fine. I don't mind. Mrs B explained all about the Marigold Cottages Innocence Project.'

'Oh, *did* she?'

'Mm,' Mrs B said. 'And CJ is sure it was an accident.'

'Of course it was an accident! Everyone loved Frank. He was a remarkable man. He was just so . . . kind.' CJ looked down at the foam on her coffee. 'I guess that doesn't sound like much. It's not genius or greatness. Frank had his moments of those, too, but nothing mattered more than his kindness.'

'He sounds lovely,' Mrs B said. 'Now, then, I believe Ocean has questions?'

'You're going to make *me* do this?'

Mrs B made an innocent, fluttery gesture and Ocean sipped her coffee to control her temper. Most of her questions were for Mrs B, and best accompanied by shouting. This wasn't a coffee; it was an ambush. Although of *course* Mrs B had rented Sophie's studio to CJ. She loved nothing more than helping someone in need – and having an excuse to poke around in their business. And it's not like Ocean didn't want CJ to move in. The cottage was empty and she'd been kicked out of the Hope Ranch mansion. Still, she could've used a goddamn heads-up.

'Let's start with his wife,' she said, setting her coffee aside. 'Do you think Karina honestly believes she saw you push him?'

'Definitely.' CJ brushed a strand of her burnished hair off her face. 'She wouldn't lie about that. She doesn't like me, but she wouldn't frame me for murder.'

'Even if she did it herself?'

'She would never kill Frank. She was doing everything she could to extend his life. She'd even started him on a vegan diet. Well, she tried to. For once he dug in his heels.'

'Okay, but people do terrible things for money. Are you in the will? Maybe she wants you out of the way, so she can inherit everything?'

'I am in the will—'

'Aha!' Mrs B said.

'—but I'm not getting enough for her to care about. A

hundred and twenty-five thousand dollars, which is nothing to Karina.'

'That's a pretty specific amount,' Ocean said.

CJ wrinkled her nose. 'Yeah, Frank wanted to leave me a quarter million, Karina wanted to leave me nothing. They compromised.'

'She *told* you that?'

'I didn't mind. He didn't need to leave me anything, you know? He didn't owe me. I owed him. He took care of me for a lot of years, then I took care of him.'

Mrs B asked, 'Are you sure about the size of your bequest?'

'I dealt with the estate lawyers, I've seen the will. It's not a secret. Frank wasn't secretive about that kind of thing.'

'Who else got money?' Ocean asked.

'The rest of the staff. A few distant family members, but the overwhelming balance went to Karina.'

'What about his philanthropic giving?'

CJ's mouth turned down. 'That wasn't his finest moment. He didn't leave anything to nonprofits. He just included language asking Karina to treat them generously.'

'Why not give them the money himself?'

'Because he didn't want to be controlling from beyond the grave. Even though I encouraged him to. What could be more fun than crazy demands in your will? I guess he dug his heels in with *me*, that time.' She smiled at the memory. 'He didn't make any demands in the will, just suggestions. The money is Karina's to spend however she wants.'

Ocean didn't understand estates and trusts, so she texted Lily-Ann and Hamilton to look into them while Mrs B asked, 'Was it normal for Frank to go upstairs before the party was over?'

'Inevitable. He'd say goodbye, then leave Karina to see the guests out.'

Mrs B set her tea cup on the saucer. 'And did anything unusual happen during the party?'

'Not that I noticed. Jane bragged about meeting the Dalai Lama, Karina bragged about her mad bocce skills. Helene ate twice her weight in finger foods, and George talked about a novel I've never heard of.'

'So was it just you and Frank upstairs when he fell?' Ocean asked.

'Karina, too.' CJ's eyes glimmered with tears. 'I was sticking close because he's been so weak lately. She rushed to join us. She didn't like when people saw me taking care of him.'

'Then there was a crash?'

'A wine bottle rolled off the bar. I mean, a liquor bottle. And everyone looked, including Frank.' CJ fell silent, her gaze growing distant. 'That's why he slipped. I reached for him and he fell. I know Karina is grieving, and this isn't about me, but she didn't need to kick me out. I guess I hoped we could put aside our differences, but she blames me for his death.'

She started to cry, then shook her head as if to deny she was crying. Ocean took her hand and Mrs B said, 'Well, we're happy to welcome you to the Marigold Cottages. Do you have a place to stay tonight?'

'A hotel room. There's no rush, I'm okay for a few days.'

As Mrs B demanded that CJ move in the next day, Ocean texted the group chat:

Ocean
Mrs B just invited the prime suspect to live with us

Lily-Ann

I should have anticipated that.

Hamilton

You mean CJ? Your paramour?

Ocean

She's not my paramour

Hamilton

Sorry. Your lady friend?

Ocean looked at her screen blankly for a few seconds.

Ocean

Let's not label the situation

Hamilton

Oh, it's a situationship. Got it!

Ocean closed her phone. 'More coffee, anyone?'

26

LILY-ANN

After the hired cleaning service finished with Sophie's cottage, Lily-Ann let herself in. She liked empty houses. She found them restful, but that wasn't the reason she'd come. She couldn't stand the idea of a new person moving into a dirty cottage, and she didn't trust a service to do a good enough job. So she checked the doorjambs and the ceiling fan and the crack between the stove and the counter.

Everything looked better than she'd expected, so she focused on bleaching the tile grout.

She wasn't sure what to think about CJ moving into the Cottages. She knew that Mrs B enjoyed mysteries and romantic drama, but Lily-Ann imagined how awkward this could be for Ocean. Even if CJ hadn't been suspected of killing a harmless old man. So while she was personally looking forward to questioning CJ, she wasn't sure that inviting her to live here was wholly healthy.

When she finished with the grout, she left her cleaning supplies in the cabinet as a housewarming gift, then headed across the courtyard to Nicholas's cottage. She wanted to talk to Sophie. She enjoyed talking to her. Sophie always chatted happily away, and if Lily-Ann said something wrong, Sophie simply laughed at her and kept chatting.

However, Nicholas answered the door, so she said, 'What do you think about CJ moving in?'

'I think it's extremely Mrs B.'

'By which you mean what?'

'That despite being intrusive, eccentric, and inappropriate, it'll probably get transformed by some Golda witchery into a lovely situation . . . ship. Also, I feel dumb for not expecting it.'

'Agreed. Is Sophie here?'

'She already left for work.'

'Can I arrange your dresser drawers?'

'What? No.'

'It helps me think,' she said.

'They're already arranged.'

'Not *really*, though.'

'Lily-Ann, you can't arrange my drawers.'

'Okay.'

He opened the door wider. 'Do you want to come in?'

'No. I wanted to talk to Sophie. I realized that I haven't asked how her job is going, or if she's worried about you two moving in together.'

'She'd like that,' he said.

'That's what I thought.' Lily-Ann considered. 'Life would be much easier if people just *said* things instead of waiting until they were asked.'

'Less of a puzzle, though,' he said.

'Oh. That's true.'

'You sure you don't want to come inside?'

She didn't have any reason not to enter, and she thought that standing in the doorway was possibly impolite so she went in and said, 'If CJ is guilty, what was her motive?'

'Money?'

'Ocean said it was only one hundred twenty-five thousand.'

'That's a lot of money to most folks, Lily-Ann. People have killed for less. What if she needs the money urgently? Like, it's not the amount, it's the deadline?'

'Oh, that's a good thought.' She wandered farther into his cottage. 'Or what if CJ and Karina are in on this together?'

'I'm not sure we should focus on the woman Ocean's dating.'

'Why not? Though, if they are working together, why would Karina point the finger at CJ?'

'She's betraying her partner in crime?'

'I suppose any of them could be working together.' Lily-Ann ambled past him. 'Or all of them.'

'Hey. Hey!' Nicholas said. 'Stay out of the bedroom.'

She paused at the open door and recoiled at the mess. Makeup was strewn across the dresser, necklaces dangled from the standing mirror, and clothes were tossed across the stuffed chair. 'She's only been here for two days! How did she do this in two days?'

Nicholas ran a hand through his hair. 'Honestly, I've been wondering that, too.'

'Maybe *Sophie* pushed the old man down the stairs.'

Nicholas gave a surprised laugh. 'Lily-Ann, did you just make a joke?'

'I did,' she said, then a thought struck her. 'Hold on.'

He waited, but not for very long. 'Yes?'

'How's *your* work going? Are you worried about Sophie moving in with you?'

'Work is annoying, and I've never been happier.'

She considered that. 'I like having Anthony around. I don't know why.'

'Possibly because you love each other?'

'Also, he's tidy,' she said.

On the way back to her cottage, she thought more about what he'd said. '*Because you love each other*.' Did they? She liked how Anthony treated her. She liked how he talked to her and how he touched her. She liked how she felt with him: steady, strong, stable. And she liked how *she* treated *him*. She liked taking care of him, sharing her thoughts and her world.

She and Anthony made each other happy. She'd never felt that before. Everything just fell into place with them. Talk about tidy.

Maybe she shouldn't worry so much about CJ moving in. Maybe the Marigold Cottages would have another romance instead of murder.

27

VERNON

The medical examiner's report about Frank DeYoung's death contained no surprises. Blunt force trauma, injuries consistent with falling down the stairs.

'So what's all this?' Vernon asked the ME, tapping the addendum.

She adjusted her reading glasses. 'Medical conditions, previous procedures, medications. DeYoung was well looked after.'

'He had six doctors?'

'At his age and income bracket, that isn't so uncommon.'

'Huh. How long did he have to live?'

'Life expectancy? No idea. I'm not an actuary, Enible. Five years, maybe.'

'So nothing here is acute?'

'Only the blunt force trauma. His blood was at point-oh-four, just a little tipsy. But interacting with tamsulosin, that's his prostate medication, alcohol can lead to dizziness and fainting.'

'Huh.' Vernon flipped to a photograph of the dead man's naked back, a stretch of papery skin scattered with moles and white hairs. 'Now talk me through this.'

'Bruises on his lower back,' she said, pointing to smudges on the corpse's fish-belly white skin.

'Those are bruises?' he asked, though of course he'd already read the full report. He'd learned to talk to specialists in person despite what he thought he understood – sometimes they'd drop an opinion that they knew was factual but were unwilling to commit to paper.

'Yeah.' She spread her fingers and pressed them into the desktop. 'The pattern is not inconsistent with a handprint. Thumb there, the dark mark, and forefinger there.'

'Pinkie there.' He pointed.

'No, that's unrelated discoloration.'

He grunted. 'What else can you tell me about the hand?'

'I don't even know it *is* a handprint, Enible. The only reason it's there at all is the decedent's propensity to bruise. Could be from the chair he sat on, or he fell against a towel rack the day before.'

'How long premortem did it happen?'

'I can't tell that, either.'

'If it is a hand, what's the gender of the pusher?'

'Sex,' she said. 'There's no way to tell. A small hand with spread fingers looks like a large hand.'

'Can you match them against the people of interest?' Vernon asked.

'No. Except *if* it's a hand, it's a right hand. So nobody without a right hand.'

'That narrows it down,' he said. 'What makes someone bruise that easily?'

'A dozen things. Blood thinners, Cushing's disease, vitamin deficiencies. And age. Mostly age.'

On his way out, Vernon tugged his shirtsleeves down to hide the bruise on his forearm from where he'd knocked into his car door. Even the ME was a goddamn kid these days. He reread the reports at his desk. There was nothing there except for the eyewitness who insisted it was homicide. And that eyewitness had just inherited a massive fortune from her dead husband, so he wasn't about to ignore her.

He grabbed lunch at Hamburger Habit before taking La Cumbre Road to Hope Ranch. When he parked at the DeYoung mansion, he wiped his face with a paper napkin and realized that his hands still smelled of ketchup. Not the best impression, so he dug around for the lavender hand sanitizer that his wife made him keep in the glove compartment.

No one answered the front door. He rang again and one of the gardeners pointed around the side of the house. He called, 'Gracias,' then followed a path to where he found Karina DeYoung in a one-piece bathing suit lounging by the pool, which was not what he'd expected from the grieving widow. She was sitting on a chaise in the shade of a big umbrella, flipping through a leather-bound book. She'd struck him as mousy on first sight, but her swimsuit revealed a tidy body. Well, except for the sun damage that had left moles and age spots on her skin.

'Ms DeYoung,' he said.

'Missus,' she corrected him, before raising her gaze. 'Oh, Officer . . . um, I've forgotten your name.'

'Detective Enible. I have a few questions, if you don't mind.'

She closed the book with manicured fingers. 'I hate to imagine what you think, finding me at the pool. But this was our spot, listening to the surf. Frank read the *LA Times* here every morning. He refused to subscribe online, he liked the feel of paper in his hands.'

As he sat, he realized her book was a photo album. So he asked her about it, and she showed him pictures of her life with Frank. Then she said, 'Everyone thinks – you think – that I married him for his money. And y'know what? It didn't hurt. He used to laugh when I'd say that. It shocked everyone, and he liked that. But he's the first man who really *courted* me. You wouldn't understand. He was a good man. That's rare.'

'You think CJ Moore pushed him down the stairs.'

She closed the photo album with a gunshot snap. 'I don't think it, Detective, I know it. I saw her.'

'Why did she do it?' he asked.

'I don't know. She thought they were closer than they were, which was sad and deluded. He must've done something to piss her off. Like try to establish healthy boundaries.'

'She lives here?' he asked.

'She did. Rent free. For years. Not anymore.' Karina cleared her throat. 'Why haven't you arrested her?'

'She says she reached for your husband to catch him when he stumbled.'

'There's a difference between catching and pushing.'

'Nobody else reported that, ma'am.'

'I know what I saw, just like I know how you see me. As a trophy wife, and not even a good one.'

'I don't know enough trophy wives to judge.'

She gave a quick laugh. 'A cop with a sense of humor?'

'I'm a special case,' he told her. 'Did you see anyone with that Amaretto bottle that broke?'

'No, though CJ usually mixed them for him.'

He asked about the other guests, then said, 'What do you know about Sophie Gilman and Nicholas Perez?'

'Who? Oh, right, no, I'd never met them before. I certainly wasn't expecting them. I suppose they were CJ's guests. Oh!' She sat up straighter, and the sunlight painted a stripe across her shoulder. 'You think they helped her.'

'No, ma'am,' he told her. 'I'm not suggesting anything of the kind.'

Even as he said the words, he wondered if they *had* conspired with CJ Moore. He didn't trust anyone at Marigold Cottages. Well, he'd trust them to babysit a child or return a wallet, just not to follow the law. They'd played games with the murders on the property earlier in the year, and now two of them appeared at another crime scene? That raised questions.

So as Karina kept insisting that she'd seen CJ push her husband down the stairs, he wondered what might connect Nicholas and Sophie to this death. Some not-entirely-legal sense of justice or morality, probably. Protecting the charity money? That sounded like them.

'I'm not wrong, Detective,' Karina was telling him. 'Frank loved me. He loved me and I loved him, and we didn't have much time left. We knew that.' Her smile looked sadder than her tears had. 'He was slowing down, but he was still *him*. And CJ stole those final years from us. She stole our trips to Monaco and Aspen. She stole a thousand mornings sitting here, around the pool, listening to the surf.'

He gave her a moment, then said, 'Do you have any family who can stay with you for the next few weeks?'

'No.'

'How about friends?'

'Well, Helene and George will stop by. They stayed with Frank for a few years so they're completely at home here.'

'They stayed for years?' he asked.

'It's a big house, and they'd put all their money into their new business.'

'Well, thank you, ma'am.' He stood from his chair. 'And again, my condolences.'

She squinted up at him. 'I *saw* her, Detective. How much more evidence do you need?'

Vernon was beginning to wonder that himself. Was one tipsy eyewitness – who resented the accused – enough to build a case on? No. Not even with all her money. However, was all that money enough reason to keep digging? Yes. And CJ was at the top of his list.

28

OCEAN

Ocean worried that Sophie's old cottage wasn't ready for CJ's too-abrupt arrival. Well, no. The truth was, even though she wasn't sure how she felt about this whole girlfriend-across-the-courtyard thing, she wanted to make a good impression. So she let herself in and was immediately struck by the cleanliness.

Ah. Of course, Lily-Ann had already taken care of things.

So Ocean switched to worrying about Mrs B's casual approach to landlady-ing. She'd long been concerned that Mrs B would run afoul of tenant laws, because she never even pretended to care about them. She charged whatever she wanted, and had absolutely no boundaries. And inviting CJ seemed like a bad idea, her own relationship aside, considering the Marigold Cottages' history with homicides. Why ask a murder suspect, even one whose laugh brightened Ocean's world like cadmium yellow, to live there?

The last thing they needed, considering the secrets from six months earlier, was another reason for the police to be snooping around.

Ocean stood in Sophie's empty living room, wondering if

accenting the cottage with a few vases of fresh-cut flowers would be weird and stalkerish. Probably. She exhaled, trying to let the blank serenity calm her. She liked to think of her own cottage as eclectic, but she cared enough about aesthetics to admit that it was mostly chaotic. Maybe she needed Lily-Ann to organize her life. Or adopt her kids. Ha. Yeah, that would—

A knock sounded at the open door and when she turned, CJ said, 'Well, if I knew *you* were included in rent, I would've moved in a long time ago.'

Ocean blushed. Actually blushed. 'Oh! I was, um, just doing a final walk-through.'

'How does it look?'

'Good! Good. I didn't expect you until later. I was going to bring housewarming flowers but I didn't. Oh, god, I sound like Lily-Ann.'

CJ gazed at her face. 'Well, everything looks perfect to me.'

'You stop.'

'You know what I realized about you?'

'I've got great arms?'

'You're more comfortable being needed than wanted.'

'Isn't everyone?'

'No, Ocean. Everyone isn't.' She peered around the living room. 'This is wonderful. I can't thank you enough.'

'That's all on Mrs B.'

CJ gave her a lopsided smile, her wing-tipped eyes twinkling. 'I mean that you're not freaking out too much.'

'I'm not freaking out at all!'

'Well . . .' CJ stepped into her arms. 'Just the right amount.'

Ocean smelled the apple scent of CJ's shampoo. 'You have glorious hair.'

'One of the few good things I inherited from my mother.'

'Do they, uh, do your parents know what's going on with you?'

CJ left her arms. 'They wouldn't care.'

'I'm sorry, I shouldn't have—'

She stepped out the front door. 'Stop apologizing and tell me which way to find Anthony.'

'Oh!' Ocean said, following her. 'I think he's . . .'

'Not here at the moment,' Lily-Ann called from her porch, making Ocean wonder if she'd been listening through the window.

CJ gave a little wave. 'Oh! You must be Lily-Ann. I'm CJ. Mrs B said Anthony might help me move in? There isn't much but I'm renting the van by the hour.'

'I'll help,' Ocean said.

'We need a man,' Lily-Ann said, then saw Ocean's expression. 'What? That's what they're *for*.'

'Well, I brought one,' CJ said. 'But I want two. I'd rather not wrestle half that couch again. Pax is here.'

Ocean tilted her head. 'Pax the masseuse?'

'He's the closest thing I have to a coworker.' CJ's cheeks pinked as she gestured toward the street. 'He offered to help.'

'You have a crush on him!' Ocean said, enjoying CJ's uncharacteristic embarrassment.

'I do not! Well, maybe I did, but only for a second. Wait till you see him.'

'I am immune to the charms of men,' Ocean loftily informed her, then gave a soft whistle when a compact, beautifully built man ambled onto the property. 'Okay, yeah.'

His light eyes contrasted prettily with his unshaven face. He was wearing a tight T-shirt with the words KNEAD YOU across the chest. He looked like Michelangelo's *David*, dressed in SoCal casual, with amazing sandy-brown hair. His jawline alone could launch a thousand ships.

'All that and he's into astrology, too,' CJ whispered.

'You're such a *girl*,' Ocean murmured.

Pax gave a yawning smile as he reached them. 'Morning.'

'I knew this was too early for you,' CJ said. 'Pax, this is my Ocean, and that's Lily-Ann.'

Ocean said hello, trying not to parse how she'd been introduced.

'You also worked for Frank DeYoung?' Lily-Ann asked.

'Well, not on the payroll.' Pax stifled another yawn. 'But he always felt so much better after a massage that his wife had me coming by four days a week.'

'Plus, once for her,' CJ added. 'Because she felt left out.'

'Maybe I'm just that good.'

'Uh-huh. Anyway, when Pax heard I got kicked out, he offered to give me a hand moving. He's sweet that way. I just thought Anthony would make it easier.'

'We'll manage,' Ocean said, then heard a tapping from across the courtyard.

When she peered closer, she saw Hamilton at his window. He caught her eye and gestured frantically toward Mrs B's cottage, mouthing unintelligible words.

'Er, though apparently I'm needed . . .'

'We'll get started without you,' CJ said, and invited Pax inside to show him the cottage.

Ocean stood there for a moment, unsure. She was so unsure that she didn't even know what she was unsure about. Then Hamilton tapped more urgently, so she bustled across the courtyard toward Mrs B's front door. When she turned the corner, she found Detective Enible on the stoop.

'Ocean Mistral,' he greeted her.

Ocean felt her heart thump. 'What are you doing here?'

'Found myself in the neighborhood, thought I'd say hello.'

'Yeah? I'll let Mrs B know.'

'I haven't even knocked yet.'

'Don't bother.' Ocean worried that she sounded too defensive so she added, 'She's busy right now.'

'How about Sophie Gilman?' The detective jerked his head toward Sophie's former cottage. 'Looks to me like she's left town.'

Ocean remembered, belatedly, that she wasn't supposed to talk to cops. Anthony had made that clear: don't explain, don't justify, don't argue. Don't even respond to the most innocuous questions.

After a silence, Enible said, 'Damn, Anthony trained you well. Never mind. I'll find Sophie at her job.'

What a prick.

'She's usually home by six,' Ocean told him, because she knew Sophie would hate the cops stopping by her office.

'Where's home?' he asked.

'She moved in with Nicholas.'

Enible hitched up his pants in satisfaction. 'Is that right? I knew the two of them were dating. Or what does my daughter call it? Talking? Hooking up?'

'I wish I knew.'

'Aren't you going to ask me how I know they're dating, Ms Mistral?'

'I know how you know.'

'That's right, they were together at the Hope Ranch party where Frank DeYoung died.'

'When he fell down the stairs,' Ocean said.

'His widow thinks Sophie and Nicholas's friend pushed her.'

Ocean managed not to glance toward CJ's new cottage. 'People believe all kinds of things.'

'Never have truer words been spoken.' Enible scratched his nose. 'Still, I'm obliged to inquire. The widow wonders why, if the friend planned to kill Frank DeYoung at the party, did she invite two of her friends along? What were they doing there?'

'It's almost as if the friend didn't plan to kill anyone,' Ocean said.

'As a thought experiment, though, if you'll indulge the—'

'CJ's not *their* friend!' Mrs B said, opening the screen door behind him. 'She's mine.'

The detective smiled in what looked like genuine pleasure. 'Mrs Bakofsky, how good to—'

'You don't have to talk to him,' Ocean cut in. 'He arrested you for no reason.'

'Everyone makes mistakes, dear.' Mrs B stepped out of her cottage, her pink silk caftan fluttering. 'I met CJ at the YMCA. She helps with my bra straps. I'm not as flexible as I used to be, and clasps are fiddly. We've known each other for, oh, a year or two now? Time flies at my age. Which is ironic because I only shuffle. What was I saying?'

'You've known CJ Moore for two years.'

'Approximately! Write that down! Approximately. I'm only guessing.' She sniffed at him. 'We talked once or twice a week. She drove me home a handful of times and I gave her coffee and advice. I'm a bit of a yenta.'

'I don't know what that is,' the detective said.

'A busybody,' Ocean murmured.

'Also a matchmaker!' Mrs B peered at Enible. 'Speaking of which, are *you* married? You look married, but you don't act married.'

'Uh,' the detective said.

'Oh! There's your ring. Your wife's not dead, is she? No? You're too young to be a widow. Or do I mean a widower? Do we still say widower? Language keeps changing, doesn't it? That's one thing I love about it. I've been speaking English my whole life and there's still so much to learn. I suppose that's true of culture. What's that phrase you use, Ocean? "Culture is upwind of language"? That's not it! It's close, though . . .'

As she continued to babble, Ocean felt a sort of glee bubbling in her chest. Of course, Mrs B couldn't *not* speak to the cops. She couldn't not speak to anyone. But damn could she bury the detective in an absolute avalanche of charming bullshit.

Enible caught on a minute later, when Mrs B paused for a breath. 'Well, that clears it right up,' he said. 'Now if you'll excuse me, I'll go knock on Nicholas's door.'

He'd barely vanished around the corner before Pax appeared from the courtyard, looking gorgeously mussed from moving furniture. Ocean cringed at the close call: if the detective had met another one of the DeYoungs' party guests at Marigold Cottages, he'd suspect them *all* of pushing the old man down the stairs.

She needed to keep Pax away from the cop, so she grabbed his arm and dragged him inside Mrs B's cottage, saying, 'Let me get you the mailbox key.'

'Oh, sure.'

When she was sure the detective was gone, she released him. 'Sorry about that.'

Pax gave an inquisitive smile. 'You didn't want the cop to see me?'

'CJ's got enough problems, she doesn't need the police

investigation to zoom in on her new home.'

'Yeah, she can't catch a break. First losing Frank, then losing her room. We aren't close, but it looked like she needed a friend.' He shrugged one muscular shoulder. 'It's like Krishnamurti said, "The worst of times is always better with a friend."'

Ocean was ninety percent sure that was a Winnie-the-Pooh quote, but she said, 'Very wise.'

'So is the cop here to arrest her?'

'Not if we can help it,' Ocean said, then texted the Murder Collective.

29

NICHOLAS

Financial projections blurred in Nicholas's vision. He rubbed his eyes and stretched in his office chair, trying not to fixate on the State Street revamp. Turning eleven blocks into a pedestrian arcade, giving Santa Barbara more of a 'European' appeal to tourists, made some sense. But so had Paseo Nuevo, decades ago. Now, without any anchor stores, it was becoming a dead mall. Another problem to deal with.

What annoyed him most about the State Street project was that he didn't have a strong preference either way. He wasn't sure what to push for, what to support, so he just glowered at the screen until his phone dinged.

Ocean
We need to meet

Hamilton

Yes! I have news.

Well, we have news.

Miles helped, he joined a party raiding into the voidlands.

Ocean

That detective is sniffing around the Cottages. Edible.

Oh ffs, you know who I mean

Lily-Ann

Why?

Hamilton

Because the cop I know will give us information if we help him beat the vault.

Sophie

Autocorrect is a bitch

Lily-Ann

Not you, Hamilton.

Anthony

W repa

Nicholas smiled at Anthony's inability to text and added, I agree with Anthony, just to join in.

Lily-Ann

Why is Enible sniffing around?

Ocean

Karina the widow thinks CJ pushed Frank.

The cop wonders if she invited S&N to the party to help with murder

Hamilton

What is S&N?

Oh! Forget it. I see now.

Nicholas stopped smiling and said, 'Fuck.'

Nicholas

He thinks we're involved?

Sophie

That's not good

Anthony

Sorrry I hit send brfr

Lily-Ann

Don't worry.

Enible can't finesse the evidence to implicate you.

Sophie

What should we do then?

Lily-Ann

What we discussed. Hamilton's talking to his cop friend.

Did you talk to your networking friend Angela?

Sophie

A little. There's more to ask.

Lily-Ann

Ocean, you asked around about the other guests?

Ocean

Not yet I'm busy!

Can we talk about the fact that CJ lives here now?

Sophie
Yeah that kind of implicates us

Ocean
I am freaking out.
Not freaking out but . . . Not because of that, Sophie.

Hamilton
You think she's guilty??

Ocean
No! I think she's the first woman I've been this interested in since Zoe. My ex

Nicholas
And now she lives directly across from you.
That's great and also I will bring you a bottle of whiskey

Ocean
That's not why I texted
Edible isn't going to stop poking around.

Lily-Ann
That's fine. We have nothing to hide.

Nicholas winced, afraid one of the others would mention that they absolutely needed to hide the truth about James Dedrick and Gregory Ybarra, who'd been murdered at the Marigold Cottages last spring. If any of the tenants got arrested again, there was nothing stopping the cops from searching their phones.

Lily-Ann
Especially not while writing in a digital medium that the cops can search, ha ha.

Nicholas

Ha ha

Sophie

Ha ha

Anthony

aa

Hamilton

The autopsy found blunt force trauma to the head but also slight bruising on his back.
Possibly from being pushed but more likely from any of the other 231 things that can bruise an eighty year old man who bruises easily.

Anthony

DO NOT TLAK TO COPS

Lily-Ann

Thank you, Anthony.

Nicholas

Maybe we should also stop interfering in a murder investigation

Ocean

Yes That

Lily-Ann

Mrs B is here, and she says 'We're not interfering. We're helping an innocent person who is wrongfully suspected.'
And also says you two are ungrateful children.

Nicholas took a moment to enjoy being lumped in with Ocean as one of Mrs B's children. Both of his biological parents were dead. The widow of his biological father was as close as he had to a parent now, and he liked knowing Mrs B felt the same.

Lily-Ann
It's probably not even a murder.

Sophie
You HOPE it's murder.

Lily-Ann
That's beside the point. We should meet CJ as a group.

Nicholas
What a lucky woman

Hamilton
At my house! I'll make moussaka.
And chocolate mousse.
A double moose meal.

Anthony
CAP SLOCK

The conversation drifted, and Nicholas fiddled with his mouse. He didn't care much about Frank DeYoung's death, but he was terrified about the detective poking around in their lives. What if someone – well, Mrs B – let something slip about the previous murders? And considering that Detective Enible already suspected him and Sophie, he might simply adjust the evidence to fit like he had with Anthony's arrest. Which meant they needed to unequivocally prove CJ innocent.

Whether she'd killed the guy or not.

30

SOPHIE

I promised the Collective that I'd squeeze more information from my networking friend Angela, so I arranged to meet her for lunch at Leadbetter Beach. To my surprise, Nicholas asked to join us; he wasn't Angela's biggest fan.

He picked me up at my office and we chatted happily as he drove to the beach. Well, I chatted happily. I'm more of a talker than Nicholas, but he usually contributed better than this. So as he flicked the turn indicator I said, 'You're worried about Detective Enible, aren't you?'

'I'm *afraid* of Detective Enible.'

'So you came along to help me pick Angela's brain?'

Nicholas pulled into the public lot at the beach. 'That, plus I can't think about State Street for another minute.'

'Also for the fish and chips,' I said, 'because that's what we're splitting.'

We didn't often see each other midday, even though we both worked downtown. I liked how he looked in his Santa Barbara business clothes, a forest-green button-down tucked into black trousers that were just the right amount of not skinny. He asked the restaurant server for a beach table and we waited for Angela to join us. I kicked off my chunky loafers to run my feet through the warm sand. The ocean sparkled with midday sun and we watched kite surfers skid across the surface while seagulls squawked on the fence to the parking lot.

'Should I take off my boots?' Nicholas asked.

He was wearing black Red Wings, which I really dug for

some reason. 'Nah, you'll only regret it when you have to put them back on.'

'How come you won't?'

'I'm just that carefree,' I said.

He started to make a teasing reply when he spotted Angela slinking through the tables with her bouncy blonde curls, form-fitting white suit, and black stiletto sandals. Which was ridiculous. Nobody wore stilettos to work in Santa Barbara.

Nicholas stood to greet her, because he was a gentleman. Specifically, he was *my* gentleman, so I didn't love how Angela eyed him. I knew she was hanging out with a guy from Montecito, where Prince Harry and his family lived, so I greeted her with, 'Hey. How's Jasper?'

She gave me a kiss hello, then said, '*Zut alors*! I need a man who doesn't think school nurses are giving kids sex change operations.'

'How would that even work?' I asked, wondering if anyone in France ever said *zut alors*.

'I was afraid to ask,' Angela said, folding herself elegantly into a plastic chair. 'He probably thinks they're in league with' – she lowered her voice to a foreboding whisper – 'librarians.'

I laughed. 'At least tell me he disqualified himself *before* you slept together.'

Angela shot me a guilty look.

'Oh, Angela.'

'I know! I should be using my hotness for good.'

'I hope at least he donated to Bright California,' Nicholas said.

She winked at him. 'That's how he got a second date.'

The server came and Angela ordered fish tacos and a margarita while Nicholas and I stuck to fish and chips and iced tea. I was okay with wine, but what kind of monster can stop after a single margarita?

'So is World of Goods suffering since Frank's death?' I asked, scrunching my toes in the sand. 'Because of losing such a big donor?'

'The opposite,' Angela told me.

'What, they're doing better than ever?'

'Yup. Jane's been meeting her heavy hitters, talking about Frank. Mentioning how life is uncertain, don't they want to leave a legacy? She's raking in the cash.'

'Damn, she's good,' I said.

'Yeah, and driven by incandescent fury at losing the Millerbrandt Award.'

'What's that?' Nicholas asked.

'Like the highest-status nonprofit fundraising award in the country,' Angela told him, as the waitress started setting our food on the table. 'Jane hit the short list but didn't quite win.'

'The short list is nice though.'

'Not for Jane. She's one of those people who believe that "second place" just means "top loser."'

I reached for a French fry. 'Ha! Well, Karina must be writing a huge check in his memory. The Frank DeYoung Clean Water Initiative or something.'

'That's exactly what Jane was pushing for,' Angela told me. 'But she's not.'

'She's not what?' Nicholas asked.

'Karina isn't writing a huge check. Or a small check. Or any check. Karina is suspending all giving as of now. Jane just told me. World of Goods is getting nothing from the DeYoungs.'

'So much for Frank's legacy,' I said.

Angela shrugged. 'Karina wants to remodel the house.

And to buy an Italian yacht to live on half the year. She's always dreamed of owning one but Frank thought it was too ostentatious.'

Nicholas jingled the ice in his tea. 'On the bright side, she can name it *The Legacy*.'

'Not helping,' I told him, then frowned at a sudden thought. 'Wait. Is that, like . . . motive?'

'What?' Angela asked.

Nicholas gazed at me. 'You mean Karina wants an Italian yacht, but can't get one while he's alive. But now that he's gone . . .'

'Yeah, but she only had to wait a while. She would've inherited soon enough.'

'Who wants to wait years and years for their yacht? Not me.'

'What do you mean, motive?' Angela asked.

The tourist family at the next table stood to leave and two seagulls swept in, shrieking over abandoned French fries.

'Just ghoulish curiosity,' Nicholas lied.

I nodded along. 'My play needs drama, so we're looking for angles. Plus, our landlady is friends with CJ. And our friend is friends with her, too. Uh, what does Jane think of her?'

'Not much,' Angela said. 'Jane doesn't talk about the help.'

'Ouch,' Nicholas said.

Angela brushed her hair behind her ear. 'Yeah. I love her, but she is what she is, you know?'

'What do you think happened with Frank?' I asked.

'He tripped.'

'You don't think CJ pushed him?'

'Ha! No way. She's like toxic levels of sweet. So selfless and helpful.' She made a face. 'On the other hand, maybe that's the type who snaps.'

I grabbed another French fry. Yeah, anything was possible, but only one thing was likely. An elderly man stumbled. And Karina, from resentment or grief or wine, or a combination of all three, imagined that she saw CJ shove him.

Angela drained her margarita. 'Welp, that should get me through the afternoon of talking to donors.'

'*Bonne chasse*,' I said.

31

CJ

CJ felt guilty for enjoying herself so soon after Frank's death. She didn't deserve it. That's why she'd almost told Ocean not to help her settle in. However, she could imagine Frank's teasing dismay if she clung to her unhappiness. She could imagine his insistence that she resume life without him. She could even more vividly imagine him laughing at her dippiness about Ocean.

He'd always been baffled but supportive that she'd dated both men and women. He'd said awkward things, but never maliciously – and he'd loved when she'd mocked him for being an elderly fuddy-duddy. He would've liked Ocean. Well, he would've thought Ocean was 'the man' that a woman like CJ needed, because Ocean was strong and direct and no-bullshit.

There was nothing masculine about her, though. She was fiercely female. And intense enough that her undiluted focus made CJ a little weak in the knees.

CJ was a full head taller than Ocean, yet constantly struggled against the urge to fall into her arms. At least for now. Ocean already took care of her kids, Mrs B, and her neighbors – CJ didn't want to become another item on that list. She wanted to take care of Ocean. Now that Frank was gone, she had room in her life for someone else. Someone who didn't need their medications sorted. And while CJ wasn't surprised at how much she missed Frank, she was a little taken aback that she also missed *caring* for someone. How central that was to her nature.

She wanted to be the person Ocean needed, not just the other way around.

So while they'd spent the last two hours together, drinking mojitos and setting up her new cottage, she hadn't let Ocean fetch her birds. Instead, she'd taken up Pax on his offer to bring the parakeets from Hope Ranch.

'You really had a crush on him?' Ocean asked, tightening the kitchen sink faucet to stop a slow leak.

'For twenty minutes, yeah.' She closed the silverware drawer. 'I mean, he's gorgeous.'

'As an artist, I cannot disagree.'

'And he's got gentle energy, you know? Plus, he doesn't make fun of my crystals.'

'I'm glad you're wearing them again.' Ocean stepped closer and touched the crystals hanging on CJ's necklace. 'They're very you.'

CJ felt her breath catch – and her phone dinged on the counter. She ignored it, too busy basking in Ocean's attention, but Ocean looked and said, 'That's Pax, he just parked with the birds.'

'Okay.'

'How long have you had them?' Ocean asked.

'The birds? Uh, I got Mouse like ten years ago. He needed a friend so I got Mona a couple months later.'

'Frank didn't mind them in the house?'

'He liked them. Everyone likes them. Even Karina. Pax brings them persimmons from his tree.'

'Them or you?'

CJ felt herself grin. 'Are you jealous? Sadly, them.'

'Were you the one who found Pax for Frank?'

'No. One of his old guy friends recommended him.'

'When was that?'

'Are you interrogating me?'

'Just trying to prove your innocence.'

'Hmm. I guess Pax started coming around maybe six months ago? His business card says, 'Many Hands Make Light Work.' I think that's, like, his personal motto. Always happy to pitch in.'

'Did you ever get a massage?'

'Nah. It would've been weird.' She shot Ocean a flirtatious look. 'I could use one, though. My shoulders are killing me.'

'I'm good at back rubs. Sculptor's arms.'

'I'll be the judge of that . . .'

'We're here!' Pax called from the front door.

'Rain check,' CJ said, then downed the end of her mojito before heading to the living room.

Pax carried the birdcage inside, wearing a long-sleeved tee with a graphic of a colorful Darth Vader holding a gift basket above the logo DARTH NEIGHBOR.

'Two parakeets,' he announced, 'straight from Costa Rica.'

'They're from Australia,' CJ told him.

'Oh. I don't know why I thought that.'

'Probably all the Costa Rica maps in my room.'

'What's up with those?' Ocean asked, because she'd hung two of the framed ones.

'I spent a few months there on holiday. I loved it.'

'When was that?'

'Frank took me. He expensed me as a secretary but it was mostly an excuse to share a luxury vacation with me.'

'What a boss,' Pax said, setting the cage in the corner.

'Yeah. He took me on most of his trips before he married Karina. He liked the company, and—'

Out of nowhere CJ began to weep. She couldn't speak, and she couldn't stop, so she rushed to the bathroom. She looked at herself in the mirror for a long, ugly moment. Then splashed water on her face. Then she kept crying, so she splashed more water on her face.

When she'd finally pulled herself together, Pax was gone and Ocean was waiting at the kitchen table. CJ wanted Ocean to hold her and rock her, and promise her that everything would be all right. But she didn't want to add to her burden. She didn't want this new fragile relationship to be based upon needing comfort while she mourned Frank.

She sniffled. 'I just think I need some time alone.'

Ocean stood from the table with a soft smile. 'Let me know when you want that back rub.'

32

LILY-ANN

Anthony's muscles tensed beneath his skin as he did one of his kettlebell routines, moving with a grace that still surprised Lily-Ann. His shoulders bunched, then stretched, and his thighs thickened as his big hands tightened on the handles. She sat at the small kitchen table in his studio, working on a spreadsheet for the Murder Collective, but she was having trouble concentrating.

Then Ocean rapped on the door and stepped inside. She took two steps toward Lily-Ann before she stopped, watching Anthony with a clinical eye.

Then she said, 'I need you to model for me.' Anthony grunted.

'Twenty-five dollars an hour.'

'In the nude?' Lily asked.

'Undraped.' Ocean tore her gaze away and sat across from Lily-Ann. 'Uh, and I wanted to talk to you before dinner.'

'Are you bringing cheese and crackers?'

'I'm bringing Cheez-Its, like I told you.'

'Oh.'

'Mrs B wants the kids to come, and I had to lure them with Cheez-Its.'

'How do they feel about kettle corn? I have an extra bag.'

'They'd love that.'

Lily-Ann liked Ocean's children more than she usually liked kids. Miles was attached to Anthony, which pleased her, and Riley came to her for advice. Only about math careers and beauty regimes, of course – the emotional stuff she left for Sophie – yet she still treasured the interactions.

'Is that all you wanted to talk about?' she asked.

'No, I also wanted to tell you not to grill CJ about Frank DeYoung's death.'

'I won't.'

'By "grill," I mean ask anything.'

'Oh.' Lily-Ann frowned. 'Why?'

'We're just introducing ourselves to the new neighbor, who I happen to be dating. Mrs B wants to welcome CJ and have her greet everyone at Hamilton's. This is not a meeting of the Murder Collective.'

'All right. I understand.' Lily-Ann tried to conceal her disappointment, then closed her laptop and asked, 'May I grill you instead?'

'About CJ?' Ocean frowned. 'I guess.'

'About her and Frank DeYoung.'

'Not about your love life,' Anthony added.

'Oh!' Ocean leaned back in the chair. 'Sure.'

So Lily-Ann asked, 'What if someone *did* interfere with the flooring? Was there a rug at the top of the stairs? Something that intentionally tripped him? What about his shoes? We need the caterer's contact information. And the cleaner's.'

'If they'd noticed anything, they would've told the cops.'

'Not if they're undocumented.'

Ocean tilted her head. 'True.'

'Sabotaging his medication would work, too.'

'Mm. CJ helped him with that. And the autopsy found nothing.'

'Hamilton says the broken wine bottle was actually a broken Amaretto bottle,' Lily-Ann reported.

'Okay.'

'They're more fragile.'

'Like CJ,' Ocean said.

'Is she?' Lily-Ann clicked a manicured nail on her laptop. 'Then I'm not sure I see any productive way forward on this case.'

'Because there wasn't a murder, Lily-Ann. We're doing this to keep Mrs B happy, that's all. And to support CJ, who doesn't have anywhere else to go. If you heard her talk about Frank DeYoung, you'd know she adored him. The most suspicious thing about her is that she doesn't seem to have much of a life outside of work.'

'Lucky woman,' Lily-Ann said.

Ocean laughed, though Lily-Ann hadn't been joking. 'I guess she's been focused on Frank. Did Riley tell you she thinks Pax has a crush on CJ?'

'Does he?'

'I don't think so. CJ doesn't think so. But Riley saw him bringing extra bird stuff over for the parakeets.'

'Nice guy,' Anthony said, without pausing his push-ups.

'Suspicious,' Lily-Ann said. 'Riley's right.'

'Why's that?' Ocean asked.

'You can't trust a man who's that handsome. How's your relationship with CJ?'

Ocean looked flustered. 'I don't know. Good. Except for Frank's death. Also, Riley thinks she's too young for me.'

'You're not even ten years older, that's nothing. Do you love her?'

'What? No, Lily-Ann. Not yet. It's too early to tell.'

'But you're falling for her?'

'She's in the middle of a pretty major disruption in her life.'

'So you *are* falling for her?'

'Okay, when I said you could grill me, I didn't expect it to go this far.'

Lily-Ann tried to think of a new subject, but nothing sprang to mind so she said, 'I'm trying to think of a new subject but nothing springs to mind.'

'Sometimes, Lily-Ann,' Ocean said, as she stood to leave, 'I fall in love with you all over again. Anyway, Anthony, let me know about the modeling.'

He grunted between his sit-ups.

Lily-Ann wasted a few minutes wondering what she'd done that was lovable. Then she returned to work until Anthony finished his workout. He stood and wiped sweat from his face with a hand towel.

'You didn't tell her that you agree CJ is too young,' he said.

'No,' she said. 'It didn't seem helpful.'

He crossed the studio in two steps. 'Look at you.'

'I don't know, maybe I should've—'

Anthony put his rough, hot hands on her face and kissed her so thoroughly that she forgot what she should've done.

33

VERNON

Vernon leaned back at his desk and gazed in almost-religious gratitude at the station ceiling. Information kept falling into his lap from the clear blue sky.

First, the primary suspect – well, the *only* suspect, CJ

Moore – had moved into the Marigold Cottages. After inviting two tenants to the death scene, she'd joined that tight-knit community of eccentrics that was mixed up in previous murders. That gave him a nice juicy lead to follow up on.

Second, he'd gotten an email from an LA law firm. Sworn testimony. Another eyewitness. Jonathan 'Sunny' Wheeler, who'd sent an affidavit instead of submitting to an in-person interview. Of course, Vernon would insist upon one, but Wheeler was so rich he'd end up talking to the lawyers. Still, that was fine. You took what the gods gave you.

As he typed up the details, his computer dinged with yet another notification – this one from the officer who did forensic accounting. He scanned the message, then read more closely. Good things came in threes: Frank DeYoung had withdrawn a thousand dollars from an ATM, three or four times a week for the past four months.

'Damn,' Vernon murmured. 'Fifty-five thousand dollars in total.'

What did a guy with that kind of money want with all that cash?

Something untraceable, that's what.

Vernon phoned the LA law firm about conducting the interview with Sunny Wheeler, then left the station to visit the Marigold Cottages. He liked them, sure, they amused him. They also brought an outsider's perspective to . . . well, everything. That made their weird insights valuable.

And in this case, one of them in particular might know about untraceable cash.

Vernon parked a block away. He felt like he should suspect the tenants of accomplice liability – aiding and abetting – but he didn't, not really. Say what you would about the eccentrics of Marigold Cottages, they'd never mess with an elderly man who funded a bunch of charities. Of course, none of them would speak to Vernon. Or wouldn't *communicate* with him. Golda Bakofsky had a gift for speaking forever without saying anything.

But one of them, at least, would listen. And there was only one person on the property who you might hire for fifty thousand dollars in cash. Fifty thousand dollars for a job you wanted to stay hidden.

He paused at the Little Free Library out front, looking at the books. All fiction. He didn't see the point. He headed up the three stairs, turned past Ocean Mistral's place toward Anthony's studio apartment. He knocked, then went inside without waiting for an answer.

The apartment looked like he remembered, small and tidy. A workout section, a bed, and a small table with two chairs and a bowl of fruit. The only differences were the faint scent of perfume and the childish pictures on the fridge, mostly of whales and walruses.

Anthony appeared from the bathroom, naked but for his boxer briefs, scrubbing his bald head with a fluffy lavender towel. His shape reminded Vernon of an old-timey strongman, both muscle and meat, not like the bodybuilders you saw now with zero percent body fat.

'I've got to start going to the gym,' Vernon said.

'Detective Enible,' Anthony said.

'Let me guess. The towel was a gift from Lily-Ann Novak.'

'There are different kinds of cotton,' Anthony told him.

'That's old news. I'm married.' He took a seat at the little table. 'You mind if I sit?'

Instead of answering, Anthony draped the towel around his neck.

'You're guilty of *something*,' Vernon told him. 'We both know that. Two bodies dropped on this property within months of your moving in, that's not a coincidence.'

Anthony went to the closet and took a polo from a hanger and pulled it over his head.

'How're you doing for money?'

'Fine,' Anthony said.

'You making minimum wage?'

He stepped into a pair of pants. 'Seventeen fifty.'

'You get a raise?'

Anthony sat across from him, looking politely attentive. 'That's the starting pay.'

The guy could give lessons in stonewalling without pissing off a cop.

'So you're washing dishes for high school wages while Lily-Ann Novak's got seven zeros in her portfolio.' Vernon took an avocado from the fruit bowl. 'You and I both know that does things to a man's self-esteem. So what do you do? A man with your background? You leverage what you know. Maybe working under the table. Cash only.'

'You don't care if I'm working for cash,' Anthony said.

'No. Have you heard about Frank DeYoung? Of course you have, there are no secrets in the Marigold Cottages.'

'There's Hamilton's buttermilk recipe.'

Vernon let out a huff of laughter despite himself. He was comfortable with Anthony. He respected him in a way. They played by the same rules. 'All right. Over the last few months, Frank DeYoung withdrew a small fortune in cash.

Fifty thousand dollars. There's no trace of that money, unless you've got something to tell me.'

'I don't,' Anthony said.

'Damn. I didn't think so.' He felt the weight of the avocado in his palm. 'Do you know CJ Moore? The DeYoungs' housekeeper?'

'I've heard the name.'

'Your new neighbor. She knows Mrs B from the Y, so say she mentions that her boss needs some under-the-table help. Mrs B happens to know a guy who is not too encumbered by the law.'

Anthony just looked at him. 'That's you.'

'I figured.'

'Yeah, but you're not dumb enough to take the risk. That would make my life too easy. Okay, I'll come clean. Marigold Cottages is involved *somehow*. I know that. Two of you were there when the old guy died, and my only suspect now lives across the courtyard. So I have to investigate, right?'

'I can see that.'

'However, I'd rather not waste my time. So how about this? If there's anything I should know, you'll tell *me*. And in exchange, I'll keep other cops from stomping around your private paradise.'

'I'll pass that along,' Anthony said.

'Oh, and one more thing.' Vernon showed him the avocado. 'You mind if I take this with me? It's taco night and my wife makes the worst guacamole.'

'It's all yours.'

'The secret is adding too much salt and eating it right away.'

Anthony nodded stonily. 'Salty and fresh, huh?'

'Ha. Yeah, just like the Marigold Cottages.'

34

LILY-ANN

Lily-Ann was the first to show up at Hamilton's cottage that evening, as usual. She wanted to ensure everything looked okay while meeting the suspect. Though she should probably think of her as 'CJ.' She wasn't sure how to deal with Ocean dating the suspect, so she decided to ignore it.

Anthony stepped inside wearing the Loro Piana polo she'd given him, and Hamilton cornered him with questions about installing a cat door. Ocean arrived next, with her kids and Mrs B. After saying a vague hello, Riley slumped onto the couch with her phone, while Miles went into Hamilton's office to enjoy his three-monitor computer setup.

Nicholas came in with a plate of Sophie's shortbread cookies and a box of buñuelos from a bakery on the Lower Eastside. Sophie followed, chatting with CJ, who was wearing a prettily cut but all-too-gray top and black pants. She looked drab, at least from the neck down: her elaborate makeup was on point, as ever. Lily-Ann wanted to suggest that she wear bolder colors. Maybe once they knew each other better. Or when CJ wasn't mourning her dead boss.

'There you are!' Mrs B glided across the room toward CJ, arms wide, the sleeves of her royal blue caftan billowing. 'Give me a hug! You met everyone, I think, except this is Hamilton, he wants to get a cat, and Ocean's children, Riley and – where's Miles? Oh, he's in the other room, on the computer.'

'I met him, already. He told me about Montevideo.'

'He does love his computer games!'

CJ nodded, her eyes sparkling. 'Thank you again. I was two weeks away from living in my car.'

'Don't be silly!' Mrs B waved a bangled wrist, then addressed everyone. 'CJ's been such a big help at the Y. You can tell so much about a person, can't you, from what they do for no reason? Or for no *reward*, I should say. I suppose there's always a reason, isn't there? What smells so delicious?'

'Eggplant rollatini,' Hamilton told her. 'Which are like marinara rollups. Every food should have a rollup variety. Chili con carne, pizza. Everything.'

'Chili dogs and calzones?' CJ suggested.

'Whoa!' Hamilton rocked back on his heels. 'I see why Ocean's falling for you.'

Lily-Ann caught Ocean throwing a sharp glance at him, but she didn't respond. She appeared to be avoiding CJ, or perhaps simply giving her space.

'Er, there are drinks in the kitchen,' Hamilton continued. 'Kombucha and lemon water and beer, except I forgot the beer.'

'Why do people persist in thinking they can improve upon wine?' Lily-Ann asked, pouring herself a glass of the local Syrah she'd brought along.

'Kombucha is like wine,' Hamilton told her. 'Except without grapes. And with a symbiotic bacterial growth and yeast culture in a mat of biofilm.'

'Yum,' Ocean said.

'Who wants a glass?' Hamilton asked, a little forlorn. 'Anyone? No?'

'Yes,' Anthony said.

Hamilton brightened and poured a glass of murky liquid, then everyone started chatting and eating and Lily-Ann watched for a moment before joining CJ and Sophie at the table near the window. She listened to them talk about the New Vic, then about how CJ sometimes went to trivia nights.

'You'd like that,' Sophie told Lily-Ann.

Lily-Ann preferred puzzles to facts, so she said, 'Hamilton would.'

'I'll invite him next time,' CJ said.

Sophie made an apologetic face. 'That won't work.'

'Hamilton doesn't leave the house,' Lily-Ann explained.

CJ stopped mid-sip. 'Not ever?'

'Only in case of a medical emergency.'

'Oh, well . . .' She gave a little smile. 'Let's hope he stays healthy.'

Lily-Ann liked that response. She tapped her fingernail on the table, trying to think of something to say that didn't involve Frank DeYoung's death. 'Have you had your colors done?'

'I'm sorry?' CJ asked.

'Your colors.'

'Oh, Lily-Ann,' Sophie chided. 'Not yet.'

There was an awkward pause before Ocean appeared with Miles in tow. 'Hey, CJ, look who's eager to say hello.'

'Hello!' Miles told CJ. 'Also, I didn't *not* want to say hello.'

'I dragged him out of a dungeon,' Ocean said.

'It was a feast in the great hall of a castle, Oma.'

'Speaking of feasts,' Sophie stood. 'I'm getting more food. Take my seat, Ocean.'

'Are you playing *Baldur's Gate*?' CJ asked Miles.

'Ooh! Are you a gamer? We should start our own guild! There's me and Hamilton, except he's already got a guild, and Anthony, except he doesn't play. He just watches, because he doesn't like playing, and actually it's *Realm of Rangers*.'

'I haven't tried that one.'

'You should come to game night.'

That sounded like a nightmare to Lily-Ann, but CJ smiled at the offer. Well, maybe not at the offer, but at the sweetness with which it was made. CJ asked Miles what he played and he started babbling about healers and artifacts.

Lily-Ann looked to Ocean for approval about how she'd managed not to ask about Frank DeYoung's death.

Ocean sketched a little bow of gratitude and refilled her wineglass.

Sophie joined Riley on the couch, and Lily-Ann tuned in to Mrs B's story about her frenemy at the YMCA, who criticized her for monopolizing the hair dryer to dry her entire body. 'It's too damp in the locker room to rely on a towel.'

'CJ's lucky you don't ask her to towel you dry,' Ocean said.

'Don't be ridiculous!' Mrs B said, and eyed CJ speculatively.

Then Ocean passed around her phone to show off a photograph Riley won an award for at school, which made Riley squirm and Lily-Ann wonder if she preferred photography after all.

Finally, when CJ was halfway through her second glass of wine, Lily-Ann couldn't take it anymore. She needed to know more about the other guests at the murder scene. 'So CJ, how well do you know George and Helene Kagant?'

'Fairly well. They're lovely.'

'They're the windshield wiper tycoons?' Nicholas asked.

Sophie nodded. 'The ones Angela calls Beard and Bird.'

'Ha!' CJ took another sip of wine. 'That's perfect. They're great – and trustworthy enough that Frank loaned them money. Helene is the nicest person in the world, and George is dippy for her. Actually, he dated Karina back in the day.'

'Whoa,' Sophie said.

'Long before he met Helene. He was an engineer, she worked at the same place.'

'How did Frank and Karina meet?' Lily-Ann asked.

'I think through George, actually. He invited her to a party at the house, she wowed everyone with her bocce skills.'

Sophie gestured with her fork. 'Was she on the prowl?'

'For a rich husband, you mean?'

'Yeah. Like, if that's what you're looking for in a marriage, then you have to wait and wait and wait to buy your yacht, to start remodeling the—'

'We're not talking about that,' Ocean said, trying to keep the conversation away from murder.

'It's okay, Ocean,' CJ reassured her. 'I don't mind.'

'I'm pleased to hear that,' Lily-Ann said. 'You were telling us about George?'

'Right. Um, he's clever, funny, a sort of off-kilter intellectual. He needs a Helene, though. A woman who's smarter than he is but lets him talk. Of course, the difference with George and, say, Sunny, is that George actually knows things.'

'Sunny was Frank's best friend?' Ocean asked.

'Well, his oldest friend.'

'You don't like him?' Ocean asked CJ.

She made a face. 'Sunny is a lot. But he's so awful that it comes around to being almost endearing? I don't know if Frank actually liked him or just loved him. They were more like brothers.'

'Where is his money from?' Lily-Ann asked, angling toward a motive.

'Investments. The story is he hustled his way into a little money young, then spent the last fifty years growing it.'

Nicholas refilled CJ's wineglass. 'He told me about his fake funeral.'

'Yeah. Imagine him bursting out of his casket like a stripper from a cake.'

Sophie made a face. 'He's this old lizard-y bald guy with sunglasses and gold chains.'

'I want a garden party for my funeral,' Mrs B announced. 'Here, in the courtyard, with a soft-serve truck and free tacos. Tons of marigolds obviously. Oh! And churros. Also, egg creams. Does anyone make egg creams anymore?'

'You mean like a Kinder Egg?' Miles asked.

'*You're* my Kinder Egg!' she said, kissing the top of his head.

And Sophie said, 'Sounds like it's time for dessert.'

Lily-Ann wanted to keep questioning CJ, but she didn't want to get the stink eye from Ocean, so she waited until she'd finished the shortbread before asking, 'Did you introduce Pax to Frank?'

'Pax is the massage therapist,' Nicholas explained to Mrs B.

CJ shook her head. 'No, Frank heard about him from what he called the "raisin vine." Which is like the "grapevine," only more wrinkled.'

Mrs B hooted. 'I like him!'

'Pax almost exclusively works with the elderly. He specializes. Well, it *should* be special considering he charges three hundred for ninety minutes.'

'Three hundred dollars for an hour and a half?' Riley said, reaching for a second piece of shortbread. 'Well, now I have a career goal.'

'If he goes once a week, what is that annually?' Nicholas asked. 'Fifteen grand per client?'

'He came four or five times a week,' CJ told him. 'Usually

four for Frank, once for Karina, and of course he has other clients.'

Nicholas whistled. 'Sixty grand a year, at one house. Not bad for nine hours a week.'

'He massaged Karina, too?' Ocean asked, not quite looking at CJ.

'Yeah, she was jealous about the time Frank and Pax spent together. She wanted to get involved.'

'Could they be having an affair?' Riley asked.

'What do you know about affairs?' Miles asked.

'More than you, dingus.'

'Children, please,' Ocean chided.

'*Were* they having an affair?' Hamilton asked.

'Pax and Karina?' Sophie asked.

'Or Pax and Frank,' Lily-Ann said.

CJ almost spilled her wine. 'Oh, god, no! God bless him, Frank was not gay. When I told him I was bi, he thought that meant he needed to refer to me as "they."'

'Ha!' Ocean licked cinnamon off her fingers from the buñuelos Nicholas had brought. 'So maybe Pax and Karina?'

'My friend Angela would be so pissed,' Sophie said. 'She's got her eye on Pax.'

CJ wrinkled her nose dubiously. 'Maybe. I mean, I'd love to resent Karina for cheating on Frank, but sometimes a massage is just a massage.'

'Pax Heron!' Hamilton said, poking his head in from his office. 'He doesn't have a website, at least not under that name.'

'Not having a website is a flex,' Lily-Ann told him. 'It means he's exclusive.'

CJ brushed a lock of her hair behind her ear. 'He takes

clients from word of mouth. He's got a waiting list. If you know, you know.'

'Dream job,' Riley said.

'You can practice on me, Riley,' Mrs B told her. 'See how much you like raisins.'

Riley tsked. 'Don't talk about yourself like that, Mrs B. You're more of a—'

'A prune? Terrible child! Just like your mother!'

'I was going to say "a fine wine."'

'Oh!'

Riley nodded solemnly. 'Because you're always complaining.'

'Zing!' Miles said.

Mrs B's laughter rang out so sweetly that everyone else laughed along. After that, the conversation shifted to the downtown revitalization project and – as always – housing prices. Which bored Lily-Ann, so she headed into the kitchen to start rinsing dishes. Hamilton joined her, and twenty minutes later she heard Sophie say, 'Welp, you've survived your first Marigold Cottages dinner.'

'I can't remember enjoying a dinner more,' CJ said.

'If you need anything and Ocean's gone, feel free to knock on anyone's door,' Nicholas told her. 'Lily-Ann usually works from home, and Hamilton is always here. I like to tease, but he's a solid guy.'

The last few words carried so clearly into the kitchen that Lily-Ann suspected Nicholas had intended for Hamilton to overhear. And sure enough, Hamilton paused at the dishwasher before he placed the dirty knives in the rack. He didn't say anything but she could tell he was smiling.

35

OCEAN

Early the next morning, Ocean stood in her kitchen, gazing out the window toward CJ's cottage. Weighing the wisdom of knocking on her door with a couple of lattes or a bouquet of flowers. She understood CJ wanting alone time after the sudden, shocking death of her friend and mentor. She genuinely got that. Before the kids, she'd tended to retreat into the bleak comfort of her own mind at such times.

Yet, as she got older, Ocean valued Mrs B's approach more and more. People needed people. On the other hand, their relationship was so new – barely even budding – that she didn't want to step on any of CJ's boundaries.

So instead of making lattes or cutting flowers, she stared through the window.

'Oma,' Riley said, behind her. 'You're worse than a middle schooler. Do you want me to pass her a note saying "Do you like me? Check yes or no."'

She turned and saw Riley dressed for school in baggy jeans and a halter top she'd upcycled from a black silk blouse Ocean's ex had left behind. She had a better sense of style than either of her mothers, which pleased Ocean. She'd always nurtured her daughter's creativity . . . and of course Riley had inherited her sarcasm.

'Listen, I'm not good at this, okay?'

'You really aren't.' Riley hugged her. 'But you deserve to be happy.'

'Yeah?'

'Yeah. So go talk to her.'

'Okay, thanks.'

'Fix your hair first,' Riley said, as she left the house for school. 'You look like Rocket Raccoon.'

So Ocean went to the bathroom and wrestled with her hair until it looked exactly the same as when she started. She applied lip gloss, then crossed the courtyard. There was no answer when she knocked on CJ's door so she figured she was still asleep. She'd had a lot to drink last night and nowhere to be this morning, so she didn't blame her for sleeping in. She'd catch up with her later.

Thinking about last night reminded Ocean that the Marigold Collective needed to prove CJ's innocence. That was the one way she could help with her grief, to get Karina off her back. So she decided to head downtown to dig for DeYoung-related gossip. She knew a lot of struggling artists, but only a few who might be familiar with philanthropists.

She started at The Spot, located a block from the art museum. The owners, Thomas and Petra, claimed that the gallery name was in honor of Pointillism, because they'd met in front of a Seurat painting in Paris, but Ocean knew the truth: they loved dalmatians.

Inside the gallery, classical music drifted from the speakers and a few visitors inspected the heavily framed California landscapes on the walls. Petra approached with a click of heels and a professional smile. She was the kind of woman Mrs B called 'waspy,' while Thomas was a charmingly ramshackle Brit.

'Welcome to the gallery,' Petra said. 'Feel free to—'

Thomas interrupted. 'Ocean! It's been a long time.'

'Oh!' Petra said. 'Sorry, I'm on autopilot.'

'It's great to see you.' Ocean drifted around the gallery until the guests left, then asked, 'Did you hear about Frank DeYoung?'

'Such a tragedy.' Thomas clicked his tongue. 'He was a good friend of our friends George and Helene.'

'I think I've heard of them,' Ocean said. 'The Beard and the Bird?'

Petra gave a honking laugh. 'Oh, god, that's perfect.'

'Actually,' Thomas said, 'they were there the night he fell.'

The three of them agreed that while Frank's death was tragic, he'd lived a full life and had helped World of Goods become a major nonprofit.

'He was involved in the arts, too,' Thomas said. 'Donated to the symphony mostly. And didn't he support medical research?'

Petra sniffed. 'No, he just supported that friend of his.'

'Sunny Wheeler?' Thomas asked.

'That's the one. Frank took far too good care of Sunny when he got into legal trouble with his life-extension company. Frank covered for him.'

Thomas shook his head. 'I thought he got in trouble for sleeping around?'

'No, it was a medical thing. He wasn't practicing medicine without a license, but along the same lines. Frank dropped a truckload of cash on the AMA or somebody, and it went away.'

'Don't listen to Petra,' Thomas told Ocean. 'That's all unfounded gossip.'

Petra winked. 'The best kind of gossip.'

Ocean grinned and said, 'Speaking of which, I heard Karina is cutting off their donations. Like, completely? She feels like she missed the "spending money" phase of the marriage.'

'In her defense,' Thomas said, 'that sounds like a super fun phase.'

The bell over the door jingled and Petra greeted the group of tourists entering. Ocean said goodbye and headed outside. She transcribed the conversation to the group chat before she forgot anything.

She couldn't imagine that Sunny's history of legal troubles mattered in the slightest, but it was new information, at least. And one step closer to clearing CJ.

36

SOPHIE

My father phoned while I was eating a salad at my desk at work. I considered answering, but didn't. I'd been at my new job for two months, learning the ropes, and now I wanted to make my own mark. After the party in Hope Ranch, I'd started thinking about the Big Names. What the Givemore Girls called 'high-capacity individual donors,' the ones who dropped a hundred grand without blinking an eye.

There were a few famous Santa Barbara philanthropists, but I needed to focus more on the level of Frank DeYoung, the ones who flew under the radar. So I'd spent the last few days researching. I took special note of a real-estate mogul called Steven 'Swede' Braby and a self-described 'Wall Street asshole' named Douglas Sudmayer. I got excited at the prospects of the improbably named E. E. Elliot and a Montecito old-timer called Horace Ashley, before I discovered they'd both died in the past year. A natural hazard of trying to raise funds from the elderly.

After I finished my salad, I checked my voicemail for the transcription of my Dad's call.

'Hey, sweetie! Hope you're loving your new job. It sounds like a big responsibility, but nothing you can't handle. Good luck researching those funders. You were always great at research. Remember that history project about Carthage? I love that one and the . . .' A pause. 'Mom's telling me not to brag about your middle-school work, but you looked so cute in your colander helmet.'

I skimmed to the end: '. . . looked up that Word of Goods place you mentioned. Remarkable. Helping with natural disasters. Refugee camps. Shipping mosquito nets to developing countries. Such important work. And now you're in the same industry. Or near enough.'

'Near enough,' I said.

I mean, he wasn't wrong. World of Goods was amazing. They saved lives every day, while I focused on staging one more production of Shakespeare. Still, I thought about what Frank DeYoung told me and refused to spiral. I *was* a playwright. And music, theatre, dance, visual art, literature: they made us human. So maybe I wasn't saving lives but the work was still important.

And I was trying to help Mrs B prove CJ's innocence. Well, not just Mrs B, Ocean had a hefty stake in the outcome, too. So I texted the Marigold Cottages Murder Collective chat to tell them what I'd learned that morning.

Sophie

Everyone at The New Vic loves Helene and George

Hamilton

They're the Kagants, for those just tuning in. Beard and Bird.

Lily-Ann

Wait! Everyone wait.

Anthony is trying to text.

(Give him a minute.)

Or four.

Anthony

The windwield wiper typos

Typons

Typhoons

Lily-Ann

The windshield wiper tycoons.

Sophie

The only suspicious thing about them is that they've known both Jane and Karina for decades

Hamilton

We should reconsider the tripwire.

Nicholas

Why not quicksand, Wile E?

Sophie

He doesn't mean a tripwire-tripwire, Nicholas.

Any kind of trap or mechanism.

Anthony

Tycoons

Lily-Ann
Ask George and Helene about Karina's background.

Sophie
Will do. Apparently they're completely chill
And happy to gossip

Anthony
mec anims

I smiled at Anthony's attempt to text, then grabbed my bag and went outside into the balmy California afternoon.

Ocean
Are there phones for people with sausage fingers?

Hamilton
Sausage fingers are the wurst.

'Ha!' I said aloud, reading my phone as I walked toward home. Wurst. Only Hamilton and I would enjoy that. And probably Mrs B, but she liked to pretend she didn't text.

Lily-Ann
Anthony would like me to convey that he is giving you the sausage-finger at this very moment.

Nicholas
When do we tell Mrs B that this ridiculous 'investigation' is finished?

Oh, Nicholas. You're so transparent. He liked to pretend that he was disgusted by the whole concept of investigating crimes, but we all knew he just worried about Mrs B.

Lily-Ann
The detective spoke to Anthony yesterday. He asked if Frank DeYoung was paying Anthony for something.

'What the hell?' I muttered, stopping on the sidewalk.

Sophie
Something?

Nicholas
Something?

Ocean
What exactly?

Lily-Ann
One moment. This is news to me. Anthony is explaining.

Nobody texted anything – not even Hamilton – until I'd walked another four blocks. And then this very enlightening message appeared:

Anthony
Not suss pisces

Lily-Ann
I'm taking his phone away. He says Enible wasn't suspicious. He wants our help.

Sophie
Why should we help him?

Lily-Ann
According to Enible, Frank DeYoung withdrew 50k in cash over the past months to pay someone without leaving a paper trail.

Nicholas

How does he know it was to pay a person? Not for something else?

Lily-Ann

Anthony thinks he's guessing. Enible suspected the only thing we could offer a wealthy man under the table is muscle-headed thuggery, ie Anthony.

Ocean

Lily-Ann!

Lily-Ann

Sweet, soulful thuggery.

Ocean

Better

Nicholas

Sounds like Sophie's kind of romance novel The Thug and the Thespian

I typed furiously, as I waited at the crosswalk a few blocks from the Cottages.

Sophie

The Princess and the Peabrain

You're in that one.

Hamilton

The bestselling romance of all time is Fifty Shades of Grey.

Ocean

We're discussing fifty thousands of dollars, Hamilton.

What does Enible expect us to do with that information?

We can't track it. We can't do anything

Lily-Ann

He wants us to keep our ears pricked. And snoop around CJ.

Sophie

Speaking of snooping around CJ, what do we all think of Pax?

Ocean

Sensitive new age guy. Out there sharing his light with the world.

Sophie

Ugh.

Having expressed that so eloquently, I crossed Garden Street, heading for the front entrance of the Marigold Cottages.

Lily-Ann

We need to add Frank DeYoung's missing 50k in cash to our spreadsheet.

Ocean

Also that Karina and George have known each other longer than anyone else. And Sunny's money/law problems.
All gossip from this morning, but seemingly accurate.

Lily-Ann

Sophie, can you determine if Jane cared enough about losing the Millerbrandt Award to lash out?

Hamilton

Who is Millerbrandt?

Lily-Ann

A career-making non-profit award that Jane might have blamed Frank for not winning.

Hamilton

Cops. Here. Now.

That was when I noticed the police cars. I'd walked past them without seeing them, too busy with my phone. I climbed the steps and spotted two officers in uniforms approaching my old cottage with Detective Enible. My stomach soured. I'd seen too many videos of cops bullying people. Not in Santa Barbara! I've only ever had friendly interactions with the SBPD. Still, those videos replayed in my mind.

'D-detective!' I called.

He turned. 'Sophie Gilman.'

'I – hello. Um, that's my – can I help you?'

'You don't currently live here, do you?'

I flushed. 'No. But, um . . .'

'CJ Moore lives here now.'

'I – I don't . . . uh.'

'If you could move back a smidge?'

I took a step back.

'There you go,' Enible said. 'Much better.'

I wanted to say something, maybe to object, but I didn't know how. And while I stood there dithering, I heard the happiest words in the English language.

37

OCEAN

'What the hell is going on here?' Ocean yelled, marching around the corner in her paint-splattered overalls.

Detective Enible's placid gaze shifted toward her. 'Oh, just serving a legally issued arrest warrant.'

'Another one?' Ocean's skin prickled with fear. 'What do you think, third time's a charm?'

One of the cops took a threatening step toward her, but Enible raised his hand to stop him and said, 'If at first you don't succeed, Ms Mistral.'

'Really? A motivational quote?'

'Some days they're all that keep me going.'

'I'm sorry to hear that.'

'That I rely on motivational quotes or that I keep going?'

'Yes.' Ocean almost pinched the bridge of her nose before she remembered her hands were smeared with paint. 'So who're you arresting this time?'

By way of answer, Enible knocked on CJ's front door.

Ocean's first impulse was to jump on his neck and drag him down to her level. However, she was a respectable mother of two, so she merely yelled, 'No! CJ! CJ, it's the cops! Don't talk to this prick without a lawyer! Don't say a word!'

When CJ opened the door, her eyes were shaky and her pale face looked even younger. She wore oversized gray joggers and hadn't even applied her trademark eyeliner or bright red lipstick.

'You're under arrest for the murder of Frank DeYoung,' Enible told her.

'N-no,' CJ stammered, before covering her mouth with her hand.

'You have any goddamn evidence this time? Sophie! Keep recording this.' Ocean raised her voice to a bellow. 'You too, Hamilton!'

CJ swayed as Enible read her rights, then one of the

uniformed police officers spun her around and cuffed her. She started crying, but didn't say a word.

'You get off on this?' Ocean snarled at the uniformed cop as Enible held her back. 'Proud of yourself?'

'Ocean, stop,' CJ whispered, as she passed her.

'Say nothing!' she snapped. 'Don't defend yourself, don't explain, don't say a word! I'll get you a lawyer, do not speak.'

Enible cleared his throat almost apologetically. 'I didn't realize CJ Moore's connection to the Marigold Cottages was romantic.'

'Shut up, Enible!'

He nodded sadly, then, and followed the cops out to the squad cars. Ocean glared at the police leading a silently crying CJ away. She wanted to scream. She wanted to break something.

'Oh, no,' Sophie said, her voice shaky. 'Oh, that poor thing.'

Ocean hugged her. She needed it more than Sophie. She felt a hitch in her breath and forced herself to exhale slowly, calmly, until the red tint in her vision faded away.

'I guess they got more evidence?' Sophie tentatively suggested. 'Should we ask Hamilton if his cop friend knows anything?'

'Yeah.' Ocean breathed again. 'And I need to see about that lawyer.'

Sophie chewed her lower lip. 'You know how I know CJ's innocent?'

'How?'

'Because she's so into you. And, I mean, surely you don't fall in love if you're waiting for the axe to fall?'

'I don't know, Sophie. Do we ever choose the right time to fall in love?'

'Oh! Um . . . so, who's going to tell Mrs B?'

Ocean groaned because she knew she was. Of course. And the last time one of Mrs B's tenants had been arrested, she'd turned herself in for the crime. Of course, she'd been guilty, but that was hardly the point. She wiped her hands on her overalls and headed for Mrs B's cottage.

38

LILY-ANN

For the first time ever, Lily-Ann didn't prepare a meal for a meeting of the Marigold Cottages Murder Collective. She needed to email a project to her boss before the deadline, and didn't have time to throw anything together. So she didn't bother objecting when Nicholas ordered pizzas from Capriccio.

She didn't arrive first, either. When she walked into Hamilton's cottage, she found Sophie already there, listening to Hamilton talk about cats.

'I'm partial to ragdolls and British shorthairs,' he was saying, 'especially the blues, who are supposed to have what's called "pineapple eyes," though I'm not sure what that implies.'

'Maybe just the color?' Sophie suggested.

'Oh! Is pineapple a color?'

'Orange is,' Lily-Ann said, closing the front door behind herself. 'And lemon.'

Hamilton's brow knotted. 'Surely, not all fruits are colors.'

'Lime,' she said. 'Avocado.'

'Stop teasing him,' Sophie told her, with a quick smile.

Lily-Ann hadn't been teasing. 'You should adopt one from the shelter, anyway.'

'Then I'd have to go to the shelter,' Hamilton said.

'I'll go for you,' she told him.

'You'd do that?'

'Of course.'

Hamilton snapped his fingers. 'Grape!'

'What?' Sophie asked.

'Another fruit color.' He started for the kitchen. 'Let me grab some drinks. Then we can talk about the police reports.'

'Did your cop friend give you the files for Frank DeYoung?' Lily-Ann called after him.

'Definitely not,' Hamilton said from the kitchen. 'No. Nope. That would put his job in jeopardy. He didn't give me anything, I merely happened to notice a file he accidentally attached to an email. By accident.'

Lily-Ann sat on the couch. 'So you know why they arrested CJ?'

'Milco, tamarind soda, or water?' he called.

'Water,' she said. 'With ice and a slice of lemon.'

'What's milco?' Sophie asked.

Lily-Ann felt her lips thin. 'Half milk and half Coke.'

'I'll have Coke, hold the milk!' Sophie called, then glanced at Lily-Ann. 'How does he come up with these things?'

'He likes beverages.'

'Then why does he do such terrible things to them?'

Hamilton brought the drinks, his Birks scuffing the floor. 'They arrested CJ because another witness came forward. Should I wait for everyone else?'

'Anthony's working.' Lily-Ann took a glass from Hamilton,

enjoying the coolness on her fingers. 'But Ocean and Mrs B should be here any minute, so let's—'

'It's just me,' Ocean said, as she opened the screen door. 'Mrs B's staying home, drowning her sorrows in sherry and sudoku.'

Sophie made a sympathetic noise. 'How are you holding up?'

'I'm okay,' Ocean said.

Lily-Ann suspected that the quaver in her voice gave lie to her words. She wanted to ask, but she resisted the urge.

'Mrs B said that while CJ might not always stay in her lane at the YMCA pool, she's not a killer.' Ocean scratched her wrist, sending paint flecks to the floor. 'I think she's been dreaming of proving her innocent and feeling better about what we did last time.'

Lily-Ann was absolutely content with what they'd done last time. Everything had worked out fine, as far as she was concerned. So she didn't reply, she simply went to the kitchen for Hamilton's dustpan, then swept the paint flecks from the floor.

'At least the cops won't think *Mrs B* is a suspect,' Ocean said, her voice still tight. 'She can't, like, claim she was hiding in a closet in the DeYoungs' mansion.'

'Also, there's a new witness who says CJ pushed Frank,' Hamilton said.

Sophie peered at her drink as if to check for milk. 'Well, shit.'

'What new witness?' Ocean asked, from between her teeth.

'Sunny Wheeler came forward. He presented written testimony through his lawyers, which frankly is how *I'll* testify, if I ever have to testify for anything, via a written statement that my lawyers drafted, so I can ensure accuracy as well as—'

'Hamilton,' Lily-Ann cut in.

'Er, right. So the news is Sunny *also* saw CJ push Frank down the stairs.'

'Oh, come on!' Ocean said. 'That can't be true.'

A corroborating witness. Well, that was unexpected. On the other hand, while Lily-Ann didn't trust Mrs B's judgments, she trusted her sentiments. Also, Mrs B had stood by Anthony despite his history, despite his appearance; plus, Lily-Ann owed her for creating the oasis in which she lived – so she'd keep digging.

'Why didn't he say anything at the time?' she asked.

Hamilton fiddled with a button on his short-sleeved shirt. 'Reading between the lines of the statement? Because he's old, in shock, and lost a good friend.'

'And that's enough to arrest CJ?' Sophie asked.

'Two extremely wealthy, entirely respectable eyewitnesses, plus the bruising?' Hamilton said. 'More than enough.'

Ocean rubbed her face. 'I sure can pick 'em.'

'What about motive?' Lily-Ann asked.

'I don't think they've gotten that far,' Hamilton told her.

'Could Karina have paid Sunny to back her up?' Ocean asked. 'If he has legal problems like my artist friends mentioned, he probably also has money problems.'

'The fifty grand in cash?' Lily-Ann asked. 'Did that go to Sunny?'

'No clue,' Hamilton said.

Ocean took a deliberate breath, so slowly that even Lily-Ann realized she was wrestling with her temper. 'But why? Why would CJ hurt Frank? She loved him.'

'I don't know,' Lily-Ann said, returning the dustpan to the closet. 'Maybe she doesn't know either. It doesn't matter. Two people saw her.'

Sophie made an unhappy noise. 'I guess sometimes the most obvious thing is what happened.'

'The most obvious thing is that he fell,' Lily-Ann said, trying to identify the uncomfortable feeling nagging at her.

'Exactly!' Ocean said. 'So what we need to investigate is why these pricks are trying to frame her.'

As the others responded, Lily-Ann gazed toward Ocean without seeing her. CJ could've killed Frank in any number of ways, at any point in the past or coming year. Even if she was guilty, that didn't mean she was stupid. Why commit homicide in public, in front of his friends? Well, maybe that was exactly why: so she'd be shielded by the unlikelihood of her actions. Except what about the Amaretto bottle smashing at exactly the right time? Had that been planned?

'Welp,' Ocean said, setting her glass aside and standing. 'I better go tell Mrs B about this new statement.'

Hamilton looked alarmed. 'You're leaving? What about the pizza?'

'I'll have Nicholas deliver them,' Sophie said, following Ocean to the door.

Lily-Ann watched them go without saying goodbye and ignored Hamilton as he complained about a lonely slice. She gazed at the hedge through the window until she identified that uncomfortable feeling: it was how she felt when she'd almost finished a jigsaw before discovering that it was incomplete.

A piece of the puzzle was missing.

39

SOPHIE

I called Nicholas and told him to drop the pizzas off at various cottages – the veggie for Ocean and her kids, the cheese for Hamilton, the spinaci for us, and nothing for Lily-Ann because she'd rather eat her own cooking.

'What about Hamilton?' he asked on the phone.

'He gets the cheese,' I repeated.

'No, I mean – he was planning on hosting everyone.'

'Right, but we're not there anymore.'

'It's just, Hamilton loves having people over.'

'Are you worried about hurting his feelings?'

'Of course not,' Nicholas grumbled. 'A little.'

So I silently vowed to never let this man go and said, 'Bring ours to his cottage, we'll eat with him.'

I went home to grab a few bottles of beer, and changed into sweatpants to further enhance the pizza-eating experience. When I got back, Nicholas and Hamilton were sitting across from each other, two pizza boxes on the coffee table.

I cracked the beers and offered the first to Hamilton.

'It's not flavored,' he said.

'It's beer-flavored,' Nicholas told him.

He took a sip, and a knock sounded on the screen door. The three of us turned to the door and waited. We expected a Marigold tenant to simply walk in, so we didn't respond until a man said, 'Hello? It's Pax? CJ's friend?'

'Oh,' I said. 'Hi!'

'Come in, come in,' Hamilton intoned, in his innkeeper's voice.

'Thanks.' Pax stepped inside, wearing a shirt with pictures of dogs across his muscular chest. 'I'm sorry to bother you.'

'Would you like a glass of small-batch artisanal kombucha? Oh, and feel free to keep your shoes on.'

Pax eyed the complete absence of shoes on the entryway floor, then said, 'Uh, thanks.'

'We've got plenty of pizza, too,' Nicholas told him.

'I really just wanted to talk to you about CJ?'

'Sure.' Hamilton gestured to the couch. 'Make yourself at home.'

As Pax took a seat I realized that the text under the bland-looking dog on his shirt said NAMASIT and the text under the rainbow-colored dog said NAMASTE. Cute.

'So I don't know if you heard the cops arrested her?' he asked.

'We know,' I told him.

'Right. Well, she asked me to take care of Mouse and Mona – her parakeets.'

'She has birds?' I asked.

'I want a cat,' Hamilton said.

'Why didn't she ask Ocean?'

Pax shrugged one of his muscle-y shoulders. 'She, uh, she's afraid of imposing on her. A few dates, and she's already living across the courtyard. She doesn't want to make Ocean take care of her. She, uh . . . I just wanted to talk to someone about this. The cops can't genuinely think she killed Frank, right?'

'They've got eyewitnesses,' Hamilton said.

'Karina? Surely, that's not enough to convict her?'

I swallowed a bite of pizza. 'What did she tell you about the accident?'

'Frank tripped, she reached for him. Karina never liked her, she imagined the shove.'

'Two people saw her push him,' Hamilton said.

'What? No. I was there. No one else said a word.'

'Sunny Wheeler just came forward.'

'This doesn't make any sense.' Pax shifted on the couch. 'You've met CJ. She's better than that, she's more *evolved* than that.'

'Why would they lie?' I asked him.

'Well, Karina saw what she wanted to see. But Sunny? Yeah. I don't know.'

'Why didn't he speak up immediately?' Nicholas asked. 'Did Karina bribe him?'

Pax shook his head regretfully. 'That part is very Sunny. Taking his time to think through what speaking up meant for him.'

'Didn't he send in a written statement?' I asked Hamilton.

Hamilton nodded. 'I'm sure once the cops interview him, they'll learn more.'

'They'll learn he was too drunk to know what he was seeing,' Pax insisted, then he gave an apologetic smile and stood. 'Sorry for crashing your pizza party. I just – the whole thing is so mind-boggling. And now there's a second witness.'

'Maybe Sunny's covering his tracks,' I suggested.

Nicholas nodded. 'Yeah, apparently Frank helped Sunny with a legal problem, so they could be, like, entwined somehow.'

'I love a tragic backstory,' I said.

'That's so playwright of you.'

I chased my last bite of pizza with a sip of Nicholas's beer.

'We need to talk to Sunny. And I still think we're overlooking clues in the staging. Like in the background. Obvious things we're overlooking.'

'Not your killer ice cubes again,' Nicholas said.

'You could murder someone with an icicle and there'd be no weapon once it melted,' I informed him.

'Is that from an Agatha Christie novel?' he asked.

'*Die Hard* 2,' Hamilton murmured.

'I'm just saying those ice cubes on the stairs were suspicious,' I told them. 'Anyway, there's only one thing that will make them dismiss CJ as suspect.'

'What's that?' Pax asked.

'Finding a better suspect.'

Even as the words left my mouth, I felt Nicholas tense. Like I was about to admit to Pax that we'd 'found' better suspects for the murders of James Dedrick and Gregory Ybarra and framed Lily-Ann's ex-husband, Piotr.

So I added, 'That is, the person who actually *did* kill him.'

'Or we can prove it was an accident,' Hamilton said.

'Is that possible?' I asked. 'To prove that nobody did it?'

'Probably not,' Pax said, scratching his flat stomach through his namaste shirt. 'I can't see the police backpedaling from "we found the killer" to "oops, he just tripped." They'll keep going until someone's in jail for life.'

40

OCEAN

The scent of potting soil wafted around Ocean as she crouched in the courtyard. A leaf blower roared across the street, and Miles peered at her from beside the planter, all big eyes and silent pleading.

She pretended she didn't see him, and focused on planting the new trays of marigolds.

'O-ma!' he said.

'I'm sorry,' she told him, 'there's nothing else we can do.'

His eyes got even bigger. 'Puh-leeease!'

'Honeyboy,' she told him, unable to keep the fondness from her voice. 'I called a bunch of lawyers and she doesn't want visitors. I'm not sure what else we can do.'

'I don't mean about CJ!' he said, suddenly indignant. 'I'm not even talking about her.'

'Oh,' she said. 'Oh, right.'

'You barely know her. You went on like three dates!'

Ocean wiped dirt off her cheek with an even dirtier finger. It had been more like five dates, but he wasn't wrong. Maybe she was trapped in the lesbian urge to merge, but she couldn't stop thinking about getting CJ out of jail. So much so that she assumed everyone else was worried about the same thing.

'I'm sorry,' she told Miles. 'I'm still a little shaken up. You're talking about Anthony.'

'Of course I'm talking about Anthony! I don't get it. They keep asking for volunteers.'

'You do get it.' She clunked her trowel for emphasis.

'Anthony can't chaperone an elementary-school field trip because he's a felon.'

Miles plucked a dead leaf from a stem. 'He *was* a felon.'

'Once a felon always a felon.'

'People change! Can you think of anyone else in the whole entire world who'd keep us safer than Anthony?'

'Not even close,' Ocean admitted. 'But that's still not enough to convince your principal.'

'You'll talk to her, though?'

'I'm not sure she's even allowed to change her mind.'

'Pleeeeeease?'

'Fine,' she said. 'I don't think I'll get anywhere, but I'm proud of you for sticking up for him.'

'I learned from the best!' he sang out, before scampering inside. 'Thank you!'

Squatting beside the trays of yellow and gold marigolds, Ocean raised her face to the sun. She listened as a mockingbird's song replaced the leaf-blower noise. He'd learned from the best? Who? Mrs B? Ocean wasn't sure she was good at anything at the moment.

She continued planting and was watering the freshly filled terracotta pots when Pax crossed toward her from CJ's cottage. 'Hey, do you need a hand?'

'Oh, Pax. Um . . .'

'I'm sorry! Maybe the others didn't tell you that I'm stopping by once a day to—'

'Take care of CJ's birds, right.'

'I hope that's okay with you?'

Ocean huffed a laugh. 'It's fine. Though she's silly for not asking me. I'm right here.'

'I guess she doesn't want to make a bad impression on you.'

'While she's in jail.'

Pax winced. 'I can't believe – I mean – this is all going terribly.'

'Yeah.' Ocean peeled off her gardening gloves. 'She asked you to stop by indefinitely?'

'No, no. I'm supposed to take them home, but I don't want to manifest that CJ is gone for good. Like if I keep coming by, that means she'll be back soon.'

'I can have the kids handle that if you want.' Honestly, having Pax hovering around wasn't exactly helping her mood.

'Thanks. I'll let you know.' When he rubbed the back of his head, his bicep bulged. 'I guess I'm being naïve. I mean, the evidence is watertight, but her aura feels innocent, you know?'

Ocean grabbed the empty flat of flowers. 'I do know.'

'She's not a killer.'

'Yeah.' She considered the freshly planted flowers. 'I guess we have to hope the real killer pushes someone else down a stairway.'

'Don't even say that,' Pax told her, his chiseled face perfectly humorless. 'That's a terrible thing to hope for.'

'Then what should we hope for?' she asked, looking for a real answer.

'We should . . .' He gazed thoughtfully toward the street. 'I guess we should hope that our dreams align with the universe.'

But Ocean had never been into that kind of mumbo jumbo, despite being raised by her parents and her relationship with Mrs B. She believed in protecting the ones you love. And while she didn't know exactly how she felt about CJ yet, she'd do whatever she could to protect her.

41

CJ

The prison guard left her in a tile room, with tile walls and tile floors. When he closed the door, CJ almost gagged at the stench. Stale sweat and fresh body odor. Then the crackle of a microphone dragged her attention to a woman sitting behind a rectangular window in the wall.

The woman looked fifteen years younger than CJ, with heavy lipstick and thick eyebrows. Through the window, she handed her scrubs that said PROPERTY OF SANTA BARBARA COUNTY JAIL, along with a bin with her linens and a printed guide of jail rules.

Nothing happened for an hour after she had changed. She sat against the wall, then realized the squiggles on the tile floor weren't designs, they were curls of hair. She stood and read the guide until a guard came and took her along a corridor to what he called a 'tank,' which was a room with eight double-bunks. A few of the women inside the tank studied her. Some of them talked to her. One kept hitting herself in the head with the heel of her hand.

CJ couldn't stop crying. She couldn't do this, she couldn't stand it. She couldn't bear it. She needed help, but when the intake officer had asked for her next of kin, the only person she could think of was Frank.

42

VERNON

For his last birthday, Vernon's wife gave him a plant for his desk. She'd said he needed a 'work friend,' which their daughter had thought was the height of humor. Apparently this particular kind of plant 'fainted' when the soil got dry, then perked up immediately when you watered it.

Vernon liked that. Nice and straightforward. Unlike the case against CJ Moore, which depended far too much on eyewitnesses. Wealthy and connected eyewitnesses, but still.

He was watering the plant when his desk phone rang. 'This is Enible.'

'Detective, hello. This is, uh, Karina DeYoung?'

'Mrs DeYoung,' he said, to assure her that he remembered her. 'Good afternoon.'

'I, uh – I wanted to thank you for handling this with sush . . .' She cleared her throat. 'Such professionalism.'

'Just doing my job, ma'am.'

'Mm. Well, the reashon I called is, I found something I think you'll want to see.'

'What's that?'

'A bag full of money. Cash. Addressed to CJ, which—'

'Did you touch it?'

'Of coursh I touched it.'

Fair enough. She was clearly half-drunk; he couldn't expect her to keep her curiosity to herself.

'How elsh would I know what was inside?' she continued.

'That's fine,' he said, not wanting to upset her. 'Don't let anyone else near it. I'll be there in ten minutes.'

When he left the station, he walked into a wall of heat. Santa Barbara summers were cool but Septembers could be brutal. He cranked the AC in his car and regretted his choice of blazers. He'd grabbed one of his thicker ones this morning without thinking. Eight minutes later, the wheels of his Chevy pattered over the cobbled drive of the DeYoung property. He parked and stepped back into the heat. Damn. He looked longingly toward the back of the house, dreaming of a world in which he could take a dip in the pool.

When he knocked on the front door, Karina DeYoung greeted him in leggings and an oversized T-shirt, her face haggard and her hair clumped. Sloppier than he'd expected, but grief was never a straight line. She gazed at him without recognition for a few seconds, then ushered him into the cool foyer. There was no AC, which surprised him, but the room was so grand that the heat didn't dare enter.

'I know offishers searched CJ's room,' Karina DeYoung said, her voice slurred with booze. 'They didn't find anything there, or I guess in her new apartment?'

'Yes, ma'am,' he said, not committing either way.

'Well, she used our storage freezer. I forgot, until I . . . remembered. The big one downstairsh. So I went with a trash bag to clean it out.'

'You found the cash in the freezer?'

Karina blinked at him, a little too slowly, and he wondered if she'd popped a few pills along with her calming glass of wine. 'I mostly found bags of smoothie fruit.'

'What's that?'

'Fruit for smoothies.' She swayed, then caught herself. 'But then, um . . .'

'You found the money?'

'In the freezer? No. I realized I hadn't gone through his paperwork. In what he called his office. That's where I found the envelope. The bag. A bag, not an envelope.'

'Show me?' he said, when she didn't move.

'Oh! Yes.'

She stepped with great care as she led him past the stairway to an even cooler corridor with a tile floor and oak paneling. She winced when she noticed him looking, and started talking about remodeling.

'I like it the way it is now,' Vernon said.

She gave him a mildly poisonous look, then led him to a recessed nook with a window facing the garden. A roll-top desk with dozens of pigeonholes stood against the wall, beneath a watercolor painting of what looked like the palm trees along Cabrillo Boulevard. There was a beige recliner – the kind that helped old people stand – with two remotes propped on the arm, and a narrow wooden chair. Framed photographs lined the top of the desk, a big formal one with Karina and Frank and smaller casual ones with CJ and Frank. A handful of autographed photos of now-obscure musicians lined the opposite wall of the nook. The desktop was tidy, with two notebooks, a flip calendar, two 'healthy eating' cookbooks, a stack of World of Goods literature, and a well-thumbed directory of what looked like freelancers in the music industry.

'This is his office?' Vernon asked, because he'd expected a room with a door.

'He used to work in his studio, across the garden. But he's been having trouble with his balance, so we moved him here.'

'Ah.'

'There.' Karina pointed to a Trader Joe's bag on the table beside the recliner. 'That's it. That's the evidensh.'

Okay, then. Vernon took a few pictures, squeezed his hands into gloves, and opened the bag. Money. A lot of money in twenty-dollar bills. He grunted as he crouched to look closer, then he lifted the handles to feel the weight. Five, six pounds.

Fifty-five thousand dollars in cash, if he didn't miss his guess.

Inside, he found a torn slip of paper with *For CJ* written on it.

'That's his handwriting,' Karina said. 'Frank's.'

'Where did you find it?'

'Behind the big chair.'

He took a picture of the gap between the recliner and the wall. 'Any idea what it was for?'

'No,' she said. 'No. No, I don't have any idea.'

Could be any number of things, including some that verged on the innocent. Though an old man setting aside untraceable cash for the young female employee didn't sound entirely innocent. At least Vernon now knew where the ATM money ended up. Though not why. Hmm. He didn't see how this helped his case. At least not beyond presenting hard evidence that Frank DeYoung and CJ Moore were entangled more tightly than most employers and employees.

He rifled through the bag as he considered the legal ramifications. Just cash. A bag of petty cash, for these people, tucked away in a quiet hallway. He could pay for two years of college for his daughter with that money – well, after the police scholarships.

'Thank you for calling me,' he said.

'They weren't sleeping together,' Karina told him.

'No?'

'No, Officer. Though she was controlling.'

'In what way?'

She flicked a World of Goods flyer with her manicured fingernail. 'Fifteen years ago, he wasn't tossing his money at hopeless causes. That's CJ's influence.'

'What's your guess, then? What was he paying her for?'

'My guess is she manipulated him into wanting to take care of her. She wrapped him around her little finger until he thought of her as a daughter. She convinced him it was normal for him to pay her way.'

'Then why'd she shove him down the stairs?'

She recoiled at the brutal language, as he'd intended. 'How should I know? Maybe that money was a parting gift? Maybe he was cutting her off and she – maybe he threatened to remove her from the will? I don't know. That's your job! My job is just – just . . .'

'To take care of yourself during this difficult time,' he said.

Her face crumpled, like she was about to cry. 'Yes. Thank you. Yes.'

Vernon was about to leave, when a thought occurred to him. 'The laptop. Who used it?'

'Frank and CJ. Mostly CJ. He liked her to show him what 'the young people' were doing online.' She rolled her eyes. 'The young people. As if she's a child!'

'Mm. I believe nobody logged this device?'

'They used to giggle over videos of hikers slipping in the mud, or a bride tripping into her wedding cake. I'd hear them from upstairs, wheezing with laughter.'

'With your permission, I'll seize the laptop in an evidence hold.'

'Be my guest,' she told him.

He wrote her a receipt she didn't want, then started inventorying the desk, just in case. She walked away without a word, and he looked toward the hallway where she'd disappeared.

Grief did funny things to people, but so did guilt.

43

OCEAN

Ocean stepped from her cottage and locked the door behind her. She paused a moment, feeling the sun-drenched air on her face, then crossed the courtyard toward her car. She needed to pick up Riley at school, to drive her to a friend's house on the Mesa. Normally, she would've made her take the bus, but she wanted to spend time with her. Even if Riley was in a mood, Ocean still found her comforting.

She unlocked her car and paused again. Something felt wrong.

Well, of *course* something felt wrong: the woman she'd been dating was in jail, accused of murder. She'd really liked her, too. She still did, but what if that was just more proof that she couldn't trust her own taste? First Zoe, now CJ.

She gazed blandly at the Marigold Cottages parking spaces, then shook herself. Enough mooning. Whatever her romantic failings, she needed to help CJ. And to talk to Riley about cheering up Mrs B, who was as rattled by the arrest as Ocean was.

Even worse, Mrs B kept trying to pretend she was fine. She

was not good at pretense. She still smiled and hugged, asked intrusive questions and offered unsolicited advice, but Ocean saw the cracks in her cheeriness. And she felt helpless to do anything about it. She struggled to see CJ as a murderer; she'd tossed and turned for three nights in a row, wrestling with that, but she had to face the fact that two people had seen her push Frank DeYoung down the stairs.

She started her car, and a rattle sounded from the left rear wheel. One more thing not to think about too closely. She couldn't afford a serious repair, so she pretended she didn't hear anything. Which almost worked, except a formless worry kept tugging at her as she drove to Riley's school.

A *new* formless worry, like she'd missed something important. Something outside the Cottages?

Huh. She thought back, but nothing occurred to her.

She pulled to the curb at the high school and Riley slammed inside and said, 'Why would he say that?'

'What?' Ocean asked.

'Yeah, no.'

'*What*?'

Riley turned to her and hissed, 'Not talking to you!'

'Oh.' Ocean started driving, then four blocks later said: '"Thanks for the ride, Oma. How was your day? Let me tell you about chemistry class."'

'Bio,' Riley corrected.

Ocean eyed her. 'Are you talking to me now?'

'Duh. And I'm taking bio, not chemistry. I'm not taking the AP test, though, so don't ask.'

'I didn't know there was an AP test.'

'Of course there's an AP test.'

'Are you taking it?'

To her relief, Riley snickered. 'You're such a dad.'

Ocean mock-gasped as she began to drive up Carrillo Hill to the Mesa. 'That's the meanest thing you've ever said to me.'

'I need to up my game.'

'Ha. So Mrs B is pretty upset about CJ.'

'As if you aren't.'

'I'm okay,' Ocean said. 'I mean . . . I'm okay.'

Riley turned in her seat to look at her. 'Can we talk about how weird it is that everyone at the Cottages keeps getting arrested?'

'Is that weird, or is that just Mrs B?'

'Point.'

'I'm thinking of taking her for a spa day to cheer her up,' Ocean said. 'And she'd love if you came along. What do you think about girls' day out in Ojai?'

'You can afford a spa day?'

'Well, uh . . .' Ocean felt her face warm. She hated that her children had to worry about her finances. 'I'll have Mrs B pay.'

'You're as bad a daughter as I am!'

Ocean smiled. 'And that is the *nicest* thing you've ever said to me, my sweetest child.'

'Second sweetest. Sure, I'll come – if I can get another piercing.'

'Anywhere on the ear,' Ocean bargained. 'And you're paying for it.'

'Deal,' Riley said, then tapped at her phone for a minute. 'Why's Mrs B so upset?'

'I guess she's closer to CJ than I thought,' Ocean told her, instead of the truth: that Mrs B felt guilty about the murders earlier in the year and wanted to redeem herself. To redeem them all.

'Yeah, or she's desperate for you to find someone.'

'Oh, god. I hadn't thought of that. You think so?'

Riley snorted as they crested the top of the hill, but didn't answer. The sparkling sea unfurled in front of them. It always looked impossibly high and full from this angle, and Ocean vowed that one day she'd capture that sense of swollen over-ripeness in paint.

'Is she going to be okay when it turns out CJ actually killed the old guy?' Riley asked.

Ocean glanced at her. 'You think she's guilty?'

'Of course she is.'

'Well, whichever one of us is right, I bet it's more complex than we think.'

'Why?'

'Because everything always is.'

'Huh. That really sucks.'

Ocean laughed. 'Totally.'

'You can be wise sometimes, you know that?'

'Aw. Thank you.'

'But she's still guilty. Cool eye makeup though.'

'Yeah.' Ocean pulled to the curb outside Riley's friend's house. 'Well, I suspect that what matters most to Mrs B is motivation. She doesn't really care about the law.'

'Like that poster at Grandma and Grandpa's house. "Justice without mercy is cruelty."'

'Oh, god, I forgot that,' Ocean said. 'She's exactly like them.'

'Except she's nicer.' Riley left the car, then said, 'Thanks for the ride, Oma.'

'Don't mention it,' Ocean said.

'How was your day?' Riley asked, then closed the car door.

'I'm laughing!' Ocean shouted after her.

Riley waved goodbye and Ocean smiled as she pulled away. She'd miss it when Riley didn't need her for rides anymore. Which reminded her that she should talk to Mrs B about borrowing her car. Then she wouldn't have to worry about the rattle, which still—

Ocean jerked to a stop at the intersection. Oh, shit. Shit!

That's what she'd missed outside the cottage: Mrs B's car.

There'd been an empty space where the car should've been. Mrs B had already been to the YMCA that morning. She didn't have any appointments. Yet her car was gone.

She was probably fine. Of course she was fine. But what if she wasn't?

44

NICHOLAS

Nobody planned the city planning meetings. Nicholas had once written a satirical interoffice memo about it, but everyone thought he was being serious. So much for his passive-aggressive business communication skills.

The two-hour meeting oozed across the morning, suffocating every other item on Nicholas's calendar. When one o'clock finally rolled around, he handled a few urgent tasks while eating a farmers market pluot at his desk. A single pluot. The only downside of falling for Sophie was he'd gained ten pounds. He preferred spending time with her to going to the gym. Even worse, she found their relationship invigorating, and was jogging more than ever, like a traitor.

When he finished the pluot, he left his office for a late 'official' lunch hour with two fresh copies of Sophie's play. He'd clipped her new card to the top of each and scrawled brief cheery notes, one for Helene Kagant and one for George. He'd chatted with them a few times since the party and asked for their feedback on the script.

Sophie was going to kill him.

Unlike the DeYoungs' place, the Kagants' property made him jealous. They lived in that sweet neighborhood of funky houses and apartments a block from West Beach. Despite the obvious wealth, the vibe was unpretentious and casual. He'd planned to drop the scripts at the front door without bothering George and Helene – he didn't want to pester them – except as he walked up the path, Helene called to him.

'Nicholas, is that you? Did you bring Sophie's play?'

He shaded his eyes with the scripts and caught sight of her at a round table on the front patio of her white Spanish-style house. 'It is and I did.'

'Good, because I'm stuck on this crossword! Come, sit with me.'

Helene was wearing a gray dress with asymmetrical detailing that reminded him of origami. An open magazine sat on the table beside a glass of iced tea and a mostly demolished bowl of tortilla chips. A white kitten slept in her lap, and at least four adult cats eyed Nicholas from the screened front door.

'How many cats do you have?' he asked, taking the seat across from her.

'Right now? Nine, but most of them are fosters. I can't stand them being locked in those tiny cages.'

Which reminded Nicholas of CJ – and then of Ocean. She couldn't catch a break. A few months earlier, when he'd taken Mrs B out for coconut cake to celebrate her wedding anniversary to his father, she'd told him that she worried Ocean had given up looking for someone special. She had so much to offer, she was so wonderful, yet she'd been burned so badly that she was afraid to touch the stove again. While he'd wrestled with that metaphor, she'd demanded that he scour other city employees for single gay women. Because sure, that wasn't creepy. He'd agreed about Ocean, though: She deserved better. She deserved the best.

'Yeah,' he told Helene. 'Cages.'

'I'm on the board of a cat shelter. I try to give the older cats a staycation now and then. And occasionally a younger one.' She stroked the kitten in her lap. 'If you happen to fall in love with Mr Betty, he's available.'

'I might know someone who's looking. Can I take a picture?'

'Of course!'

Nicholas snapped a couple photos of the sleepy kitty before setting the copies of Sophie's play on the table. 'Thanks so much for having a look.'

'I'm happy to.' Helene's eyes sparkled. 'And George absolutely adores this kind of thing.'

'Oh, good. He struck me as pretty literary.'

'I'll tell him you said that! He'll love it.' Her expression changed. 'Though that was a rough way to meet, considering what happened.'

'Yeah.' Nicholas was surprised that she'd brought up the party, and wondered what Lily-Ann would want him to ask. 'Did you, uh, hear the police arrested CJ?'

Helene made a dismissive face. 'They finally decided to trust Karina?'

'Only because now Sunny Wheeler also says he saw her push Frank.'

'Oh.' She frowned. 'Odd that he didn't mention that at the time. Sunny is not exactly shy. The only reason he'd ever bite his tongue was if he thought tongue-biting was the key to living longer.'

Nicholas sputtered a laugh. 'Why would he claim he saw CJ push Frank if he didn't?'

'Maybe he did. On the other hand, he's not the least gullible person I've ever met.'

'Er, so was CJ having, like, an emotional affair with Frank?'

Helene scoffed. '"Emotional affair." They were like father and daughter.'

'And how about Karina?'

'Frank loved her. He really did. He worried about her. I'm not sure Karina was . . . the right person for him? He could've been happier. But he loved her, and she loved him, in her way. She's really shaken up.'

'You and George knew Karina before any of you met Frank DeYoung, right?'

'Forever ago, yeah.' Her eyes twinkled. 'You'll never guess how. We were part of the same bocce league. George and I were so bad, but they needed to make up the numbers.'

'What did she do back then?' Nicholas asked. 'I think someone told me she was an engineer?'

Helene ate the last tortilla chip. 'No, she worked with engineers in the design department. Something like that.'

'Oh. Uh . . .' Nicholas wasn't sure if he was learning anything, but this seemed like a great opportunity, so he said,

'Uh, I don't want to offend you – I *am* sneaking around asking you to read Sophie's stuff, after all.'

'But you want to know about Frank's investment in our business?'

'Yeah,' he admitted.

'He loaned us a half-million dollars and let us live with him for two years for free, after we invested every cent of our own in the business. Without Frank, we never would've gotten off the ground. Of course, he didn't do too badly for himself investment-wise. Though we—'

She stopped as Nicholas's phone rang with a call from Ocean. That surprised him: they texted, they didn't call.

'Sorry,' he said, standing from the table. 'I should take this, and get out of your hair. Thanks so much for everything.'

'You're very welcome,' Helene told him. 'We'll let you know about the play.'

Nicholas answered the phone as he walked back to his car. 'Hey, Ocean.'

'Is Mrs B with you?' she asked.

'No, she's – you don't know where she is?'

'Her car's gone. I'm hoping someone drove her somewhere.'

'Text the group chat.'

'I did, Nicholas. You didn't respond.'

'Oh, sorry.'

'I'm sure she's fine,' Ocean said. 'It's not like she forgot how to drive a car.'

'When did you notice she was gone? You want me to check the YMCA for her car?'

'Would you?' she asked.

'I'm on the way.'

Mrs B had been taking care of herself for longer than any

of them had been alive, so Nicholas wasn't *that* worried. Still, he trusted Ocean's opinion about this kind of thing. She joked about her 'mom senses,' but she'd learned good judgment the hard way: by raising kids. And he had to admit that while Mrs B was as bright and lively as ever, she'd become more easily distracted lately and maybe a little dippier.

By the time he pulled into the YMCA parking lot, the Marigold Cottages Murder Collective chat had eighty-four notifications. He drove along the first aisle, scanning for Mrs B's car, then paused and scrolled through the texts. No one had any idea where she was: Sophie hadn't seen her; Hamilton accidentally pasted in a recipe for a pineapple upside-down cake; Ocean announced that she wasn't at the grocery store nor the library; Hamilton apologized for accidentally pasting in the recipe; and so on.

Nicholas crawled through the parking lot with no luck.

She'd been gone for three hours.

45

LILY-ANN

Lily-Ann frowned at the picture frame on her living room floor. She knew the top was perfectly aligned with the door, because she'd already checked twice. Despite that, she checked for a third time. And sure enough, the picture was still in the right place. Unlike herself. She felt uncomfortably out of place. She sat and frowned at her phone, at the 'Mrs B is missing' updates buzzing every few seconds.

'You want to check See's Candies?' Anthony stepped in from the kitchen in his flour-dusted apron. 'You know how she feels about peanut crunches.'

'I'm not upset about Mrs B,' Lily-Ann said.

'No?'

She looked up at him. 'No.'

'She's missing.'

'She's fine. I'm just . . . agitated.'

'Why?'

She didn't want to tell him, because despite years of therapy she didn't entirely embrace the theory that talking about your problems helped with them. It was like thinking that talking about dinner sated your appetite. Plus, she wasn't comfortable needing that sort of back-and-forth. Though, what else had she paid all those therapists for? And say what you will about Lily-Ann Novak, she tried.

'What exactly do we know about Frank DeYoung's death? The cause, if we trust the police. The time and location. Two eyewitnesses claim CJ pushed him, but eyewitnesses are notoriously unreliable.'

'Okay,' he said.

'What I'm trying to say is proof is difficult. Proof is specific and fragile. However, suspicion lingers. *Consequences* linger. And the opposite of innocence isn't always guilt.'

'I don't understand.'

She took a breath. Yeah, she needed to try a little harder than that. 'I'm talking about the last time, about—'

To her relief, her phone buzzed again. She happily fell silent and checked the screen. Hamilton was notifying the group chat that there hadn't been any emergency medical admittances that day. So Mrs B wasn't lying injured in a hospital bed. Everyone else on the group chat expressed relief, but Lily-Ann wasn't surprised. She suspected she knew exactly where Mrs B had gone, and why. And if she was correct, she expected that she'd return shortly.

'Lil,' Anthony said, crouching in front of her, his heavily muscled forearms resting on her knees.

'You're all floury,' she said, watching the dust swirl from his apron. 'I'll need to vacuum.'

'I know,' he said.

She put her palm on his arms, to feel his strength. 'Waverly called.'

'Your sister-in-law.'

'Ex-sister-in-law.'

'Again?'

'Twice this morning.'

'Did she say anything new?' he asked.

Lily-Ann frowned at the picture frame. 'No, it was the same as always: Piotr is in prison because of me. Their family is broken because of me. Which is not entirely unfair.'

'He tried to kill you,' Anthony said.

'I know.'

'He got off easy.'

'*I know.*'

He eyed her flatly and waited for her to continue.

'Waverly and her mother believe Piotr tried to kill his controlling, estranged ice queen of a wife. That they believe. But they also believe he's incapable of killing anyone else, and that I'm fully capable of framing him.'

'He got off easy,' Anthony repeated, in his rumbling voice.

'I don't feel bad about Piotr. I don't. But his mother and sister treated me okay and I . . . I put Piotr in jail for the rest of his mom's life. And they suspect me.'

Anthony's face blanked at the pain in her voice. His hands flexed by his side. One thing she'd learned about him was he didn't hold on to tension when he felt the urge to lash out; he became looser, more relaxed.

'Don't you dare get involved,' she told him.

He ducked his head in acceptance, and she watched the muscles in his neck and shoulders moving under his inked skin.

'I hate that they hurt you,' he said.

'I like that you hate that.'

'Trust yourself.' He put his palm against her cheek. 'Trust yourself half as much as I trust you.'

He meant about the decisions she'd made to protect her friends. And about her ability to remain undetected no matter what Piotr's family suspected. She started to tell him that she'd try when her phone buzzed again.

Ocean
She's back
The old bat

Hamilton
Where was she?

Sophie
Is she ok?

Nicholas
She's fine

Sophie
How would you know? Nicholas is sitting two inches from me pretending he knows things

Ocean

He's right

Nicholas

Ocean wouldn't call her an old bat if she wasn't fine

Ocean

She's worse than fine. She's pleased with herself like the cat who ate the canary

Hamilton

Is the canary in that adage the same one who is in the coal mine?

Nicholas

You think there's a cat in the coal mine?

Hamilton

If so, 'the cat who ate the canary in the coal mine' would refer to feeling smug about impending disaster.

Sophie

There's probably a German word for that.

Anthony

Gld shook

Nicholas

Mein Gott, Anthony, I didn't know you spoke German.

Lily-Ann looked up to see Anthony wincing at his phone. '"Glad she's okay,"' he translated.

'Maybe stick to emojis?' she suggested.

'I don't understand them. Riley told me the smiley is sarcastic.'

She texted as she spoke. 'No one ever misinterprets a thumbs-up.'

Lily-Ann

Anthony and I are glad she's okay

Hamilton

So where did she disappear to?

Ocean

She won't tell me.

Ocean

Says she'll show us tonight at Hamilton's house?

Hamilton

Sounds great. With rings on your fingers and bells on your toes.

Lily-Ann

Anthony is baking baguettes as we speak.

Hamilton

Ooh! I'll make Italian sodas. Anyone like any flavor more than Spicy Lavender?

Nicholas

Yes.

Hamilton

How about Salted Egg Yolk?

Nicholas

I cannot tell if you're joking.

Hamilton

Custard-y!

Anthony looked at Lily-Ann. 'You still think you know where Mrs B went?'

'Absolutely,' she said.

And while she knew that this didn't reflect well upon her, she was relieved. She *wanted* to think about Frank DeYoung's murder, about CJ's guilt, about this new cast of suspects. About why anyone would kill a good man with only a few years left. Because that was so much better than thinking about having framed her ex-husband.

She didn't say that, though. She just watched Anthony as he labored over his phone for two minutes, then sent her a thumbs-up.

46

SOPHIE

When Nicholas and I arrived at Hamilton's, we found Lily-Ann frowning at the buffet table. I understood the feeling. Hell, Ocean was brokenhearted and Mrs B had run away from home. We needed to help CJ. Urgently. We needed to prove her innocence and free her from jail. Which meant we needed to find the real killer.

Still, I hadn't quite stopped smiling at Nicholas's faux complaints about his new bathroom setup. 'Everything is too damn convenient! It smells like a rose garden in here!'

I'd put my hair in a high pony, because Lily-Ann felt unnerved if I wore it any other way outside of work. We had a special relationship. An unspoken one. So unspoken that I was only halfway sure *she* knew it existed. I saw her as sort of a big sister. I was an only child and I wondered what it said about me that I'd chosen her as an older sibling. Probably that I valued sensible reliability with little emotion.

I went straight to where she was adjusting the stack of napkins and reported in about my research into the non-CJ murder suspects. 'I've been looking for donors for work,' I told her. 'So I asked around about Sunny Wheeler. It's such a small town, all the rich people know each other. He's well-liked but not entirely trusted.'

'Not trusted how?' Lily-Ann asked.

'Basically, Sunny Wheeler is a little too into Sunny Wheeler. Plus, he lost money in a big investment? Sounded like normal rich-guy stuff.'

'Mm,' she said. 'Did you ask about Karina?'

I made a face. 'She wasn't involved in giving. Everyone knew Frank better, and liked him more. They made him sound old-fashioned, but in a good way? Though I guess he'd been declining pretty steeply the past year or two.'

'I did some investigating myself this afternoon,' Nicholas said, moving to stand beside me.

'What?' I squinted at him. 'When? Where?'

'I, um, ran into Helene Kagant. Downtown, on my lunch hour. She was having iced tea and doing a crossword.'

'Details we didn't need.' I eyed him suspiciously, because he sounded evasive. 'What'd you find out?'

'Not much. Turns out Karina isn't an engineer, she just worked with them. Uh, she's apparently a killer on the bocce court.'

'So to speak.'

He bumped me with his hip. 'Is bocce the same as lawn bowling?'

'No idea.'

'I don't see the pertinence,' Lily-Ann said.

'Where exactly did you run into her?' I asked.

'Just, y'know, downtown.' Nicholas gestured meaninglessly. 'Oh, and Helene's a serious cat lady. She fosters for the local shelter. I took a picture of a kitten for Hamilton.'

'So you went to her house!'

He looked shifty. 'What? No.'

'She happened to be carrying a kitten around?'

'I mean, I didn't go inside her house. And she lives downtown, so—'

I narrowed my eyes. 'Nicholas Perez! Did you bully her into reading my play?'

'Aw. You've never both-named me before.'

'You've never deserved it before. Would you stop undermining me?'

'I'm not undermining you. You're undermining you! You're amazing, your play is amazing. You just need to get more eyes on it.'

'Which I'll take care of when *I* want to.'

'Okay, okay! I'll stop.'

'Thank you.'

'After I follow up on the copies I already handed out.'

I felt my lips thin. 'How many is that?'

'Oh, is that Mrs B?' he said, turning away.

I reached to pull him back but it *was* Mrs B. She drifted in from the courtyard with a flutter of her silk muumuu and a bouquet of marigolds with overlarge round yellow blooms.

Hamilton and I called her name and Nicholas smiled like a schoolboy. Ocean gave her a relieved, wary, exhausted, adoring look that was extremely daughterly.

'You're all here!' Mrs B said. 'Well, almost all. Not CJ. You didn't invite the children, Ocean?'

Ocean set a pitcher of iced tea on the table, which she'd made after we'd all refused to run to the market for Hamilton's egg yolk-flavored Italian syrup. 'Not until I know where you disappeared to.'

'What does that have to do with anything?'

'For all I know, you were off getting boudoir photographs.'

'Ooh, I should look into that! Not photographs, paintings. If only there were an artist I could hire.' She gave the flowers to Lily-Ann and turned to Hamilton. 'How about a glass of your kombucha?'

'She'll have Ensure,' Ocean said.

Mrs B made a face. 'Fine, but only if you have butter pecan.'

'Of course he has butter pecan,' Nicholas said.

'My favorite kind of pecan!' Hamilton flip-flopped into the kitchen.

Lily-Ann arranged the flowers in the vase, and I opened my mouth to ask Mrs B where she'd gone, but Ocean got there first. 'Are you going to tell us where you disappeared to?'

'After dinner,' Mrs B said.

Ocean said, 'Golda, I am already on edge.'

'Please?' Mrs B asked, then at Ocean's expression of begrudging agreement she said, 'Thank you. Now, where shall I sit?'

Nicholas pulled out a chair, and she gave him a buss on the cheek. 'Such a gentleman. You're a lucky woman, Sophie.'

'Lucky-ish,' I grumbled, still annoyed at his interference.

'I'm in trouble,' he told Mrs B.

'Oh-ho!' Her brown eyes brightened with interest. 'What have you done now?'

'Believed in her,' he said.

'Everyone sit,' Lily-Ann said. 'Who wants wine?'

I said I did, and nobody shot me a dirty look, which I appreciated. I knew I had to be careful with alcohol, but one glass at Hamilton's house before strolling home across the courtyard with Nicholas? Even I couldn't get in trouble with that. Lily-Ann had made enchiladas and Hamilton produced a nice, normal green salad. In an obvious attempt to keep the conversation light – not about CJ or Mrs B's disappearance – Ocean told us that Miles was trying to get Anthony approved as a chaperone for his weeklong school trip to the Channel Islands. 'He's considering picketing the principal's office with a sign about felons' rights. He still spells "school" wrong half the time, but "felon" is no problem.'

'He's great in *Realm of Rangers*,' Hamilton said, helping himself to another serving of enchiladas. 'And my friend, the cop who plays Cyntria? He's so grateful for Miles's healing that he's still sending me an update every day.'

'Goodness!' Mrs B said. 'About CJ's case? Have you learned anything important?'

'Not really, though I haven't checked his message today. I made the salad instead.'

'It's so good,' I told him.

'The snap peas are fresh from the farmers market.'

'Do they deliver?'

'I asked Anthony to pick them up.'

'You're baking baguettes, drinking kombucha and shopping at the farmers market?' Nicholas asked Anthony. 'What have you become?'

Anthony's eyes crinkled. 'I'm doing yoga, too.'

'God help me,' Lily-Ann said. 'He does the happy baby pose on my living room floor.'

Chuckles rippled around the table even before Mrs B asked what on earth the happy baby looked like.

'When Anthony does it?' Nicholas said. 'A joint venture of Pampers and Harley-Davidson.'

We laughed more, finished dinner, then passed around a box of See's chocolates Ocean had picked up while looking for Mrs B.

'Peanut crunch!' Mrs B said, dipping into the box. 'And here's something even sweeter. CJ's coming home.'

An uneasy silence spread around the table even faster than the chocolates had. Ocean lowered her gaze, though she gave a faint smile when Anthony, who was passing behind her, briefly squeezed her shoulder.

'That feels unlikely,' Nicholas said.

I looked away from my dark chocolate truffle. 'They did arrest her for murder, after all. How is she coming home?'

'Well, I suppose,' Mrs B said with another airy jangle of her bracelets, 'that someone bailed her out.'

'Oh, shit,' Ocean said. 'What did you do?'

'Nothing!'

'What did you do!'

'Well, I . . . I went to talk to her and everything fell into place.'

'Golda. Spill.'

Mrs B huffed. 'Stop looking at me like that! This is good

news. Wonderful news. It's exactly what you wanted! CJ will be home tomorrow.'

'How?'

'Well, you know, everyone really is trying their best. Nobody *means* harm, it's just that sometimes we get muddled, so I went and tried to un-muddle things, that's all.'

'Sure,' Ocean said. 'Now explain using words.'

'My assumption,' Lily-Ann told Ocean, 'is that Mrs B used the Cottages as collateral to bail out CJ.'

47

LILY-ANN

Lily-Ann watched the reactions to her statement on the faces around the table. The surprise struck her as odd. Of *course* Mrs B had risked the Marigold Cottages for CJ. Nothing could be more in character. They were only YMCA locker room buddies? Well, naturally you'd risk your home for a kind stranger. Your unofficially adopted daughter had gone on a few dates with her? Nothing could possibly matter more than that!

'Well, fuck,' Ocean said, pinching the bridge of her nose.

'Now you're being silly,' Mrs B told her. 'It was the right thing to do, because she's innocent. And you can take her out to dinner to celebrate!'

'Fuck.' Ocean considered for a moment, then added: 'Fuck.'

'You bailed her out using . . . what exactly?' Sophie asked Mrs B.

'Bail isn't bail,' Hamilton said, but everyone ignored him.

'She used the Cottages,' Lily-Ann told Sophie. 'Unless there's a substantial amount of wealth of which I'm unaware.'

'Er,' Mrs B said. 'Well, I didn't really *use* the Cottages.'

'What does that mean?' Sophie asked.

'As long as CJ shows up for her legal proceedings,' Lily-Ann said, trying to share information and hold off Ocean's explosion, 'nothing happens. However, if she flees, Mrs B loses the property.'

'Loses like . . . loses?' Sophie asked.

'Yes.'

Ocean grunted. 'And my kids lose the only home they've ever known.'

'She won't run,' Mrs B said. 'She'd never do that to us – or herself! She'll stay while we prove her innocence.'

'Bail doesn't exist in California anymore,' Hamilton said. 'Mrs B probably posted a property bond to afford the services of a pretrial consultant to secure CJ's release. Which is extremely bail-like without actually being bail.'

'She won't run,' Mrs B repeated.

'It's your property,' Ocean said, her voice clipped. 'You have every right to do what you want with it.'

'You're upset,' Mrs B said.

'Of course I'm upset! Miles and Riley live here. You should've told me.'

'But you're falling for CJ! I've seen you looking at her.'

'Sure, and my taste is so impeccable that my wife never left me and the kids.' Ocean rose angrily from her chair. 'You turned a few dates into a massive uncertainty in their lives.'

'I, I didn't think—'

'That's exactly the problem,' Ocean snapped, before she walked out.

The screen door slammed shut and Mrs B said, 'That was poorly done of me. I . . . I didn't think it through.'

'She's just surprised,' Sophie told her. 'She'll come around.'

'And we won't let CJ run away.' Hamilton frowned at his phone, his bushy eyebrows beetling. 'Despite whatever new evidence suddenly comes to light.'

'She's not going to *try* to run away!' Mrs B insisted. 'Stop saying that!'

Sophie clearly couldn't stand to see Mrs B so unhappy. 'That's right. Even if she's guilty—'

'Which she isn't,' Mrs B said.

'—she's not about to run. She worked the same job for her entire adult life. She isn't a flight risk and she lives right across the courtyard. She's surrounded by, um . . .'

'Busybodies?' Nicholas suggested.

'By *interested parties*,' Lily-Ann offered, 'who won't let her run. We'll watch her.'

'Well!' Hamilton said. 'Someone should go after Ocean. And someone else should make sure CJ has a ride home from the jail tomorrow. And a third person should, um, get to bed early because he has a big meeting at five in the morning. That one is me. I'm the third person.'

'Are you kicking us out?' Sophie asked.

Lily-Ann caught the disbelief in her voice. Hamilton always tried to keep a dinner going as long as possible, he never cut one short.

'No, no,' Hamilton said. 'Not "kicking" exactly.'

'I'll talk to Ocean,' Mrs B said.

'That's a terrible idea,' Nicholas told her. 'If you two talk right now, there'll be another murder.'

'I'll talk to her,' Sophie told Mrs B.

Mrs B laid her palm on Sophie's cheek. 'You're so darling.'

When Lily-Ann stood to leave, Hamilton said, 'Actually, Lily-Ann, could you stick around to help me clean?'

She said yes, and Sophie and Nicholas exchanged a look, and Mrs B fluttered around the buffet table until Lily-Ann said, 'Nicholas will escort you home.'

He took the hint. 'Right. Let's go.'

'Oh, Nicholas.' Mrs B took his arm. 'Tell me this will all work out.'

As Sophie followed them to the door, Lily-Ann reflected that Mrs B hadn't simply put everyone's homes at risk, but Nicholas's inheritance. Yet there was Nicholas, smiling down at her, trying to comfort her. And there was Sophie, watching with her face wreathed in love.

Now what did Hamilton want to discuss in private?

48

OCEAN

That night, Ocean dreamed of newspaper 'For Rent' ads, the most terrifying Santa Barbara nightmare. She woke late and grumpy so she drove Riley to school in silence. She was starving as she headed home, probably because she wanted to eat her feelings about Mrs B using the Cottages as collateral. For what? To help her bra-strap adjuster at the YMCA? To redeem herself for lying to the cops during the previous murders? Or to help Ocean get a date?

Because c'mon. She liked CJ, she liked her brightness and

enthusiasm and the noises she made when Ocean kissed her. But you don't risk your home for someone after five dates! Hell, what did that say about *Ocean*, that she couldn't find a woman if Mrs B didn't bail one out of prison for her?

So instead of planning a lesson for her students, she planned fat slices of toast slathered in butter.

She was halfway across the courtyard to her cottage when Sophie called out, 'You're heading the wrong direction!'

'You're telling me,' she muttered.

'What?'

'What?'

'Didn't you get Lily-Ann's text? She's taking us to breakfast at Régina's.'

The perfect timing cheered Ocean. 'Oh! Thank god! But why?'

'Secret Lily-Ann reasons.'

'Just us?'

'No boys allowed! She told Anthony he wasn't invited.'

'I'm sure she communicated that very politely.'

'Oh, absolutely. She said, "You're not invited."' Sophie gestured toward the street. 'Will you drive? We're meeting her there.'

'Sounds good,' Ocean said.

She tried to stick to a strict work schedule, because she was terrified that if she slacked for two days in a row, she'd forget how to work. But she needed a break – and Régina's was forty bucks per person even before mimosas. She couldn't afford that, so screw her schedule. She drove Sophie southward, then took the exit toward the bird refuge. The restaurant looked shabby and cozy before you took in the quality of the mismatched silverware and the casually arranged pillows on the overstuffed furniture.

Sunlight flooded in from the front door, through arches that separated the bar area from the dining rooms. The air smelled of orange peel and cardamom – or something fresh and herbal. Only a handful of tables were occupied on a weekday morning, so the murmur of conversation was barely audible beneath the classical music playing over the speakers.

Lily-Ann had chosen a table on a raised floor, beside a window with a view of the patio, where furled umbrellas rose above the tables. She wore an elegant white blazer over an olive-green tank dress, while Sophie made thrifting look chic. Meanwhile, Ocean was in brown carpenter pants and the chambray blue button-down she liked to teach in.

After the waitress returned with drinks, Sophie raised her orange juice and said, 'To Lily-Ann's sudden urge for coconut parfait.'

Ocean toasted her. 'And her generosity.'

'So are you and Mrs B okay?' Sophie asked Ocean. 'I mean with each other?'

'We're always okay,' Ocean admitted, almost grudgingly. 'She wants to make her famous mamaliga tonight, which is her idea of an apology, and I managed not to tell her that Riley hates the texture of boiled cornmeal.'

'Ha. And what about CJ coming back today?'

'I'm trying not to think about that, thanks.'

Sophie flushed. 'Oh, god, I'm sorry, I didn't mean—'

'I'm kidding! I mean, I don't know. I'm happy she's out, of course. She won't run or anything, I know that, but I'm still pissed at Mrs B for risking the Cottages. And do I want the kids in the middle of another murder investigation?'

'Yeah, that's a good point.'

Ocean let a little of her dismay creep into her voice. 'I just need to take another ten years off from dating.'

'You don't,' Lily-Ann said, in her flat way.

'Why's that?'

'Because you are a remarkable woman,' Lily-Ann said, still in her flat way.

Ocean actually felt herself blush so she said, 'Oh, shut up.'

Lily-Ann looked to Sophie for an explanation of that but Sophie just said, 'I kind of wonder if Mrs B set this up on purpose. I mean bailing out CJ. Like, now we *have* to keep investigating. We need to prove CJ's innocence so the bank doesn't repossess the Marigold Cottages.'

'You think she *planned* it?' Ocean asked.

'Well, I'm trying to think like a writer. In a play, everyone has ulterior motives, often concealed even from themselves.'

Ocean sipped her latte as she considered. 'That's crazy and manipulative. So, yeah, I wouldn't put it past her.'

'And look at us now.' Sophie gestured with her menu. 'It completely worked. Lily-Ann summoned the strike team to prove CJ's innocence.'

'The strike team?'

'The special investigations unit of Marigold Cottages.' Sophie paused as the waitress walked past. 'Except when there's so little evidence, how do we prove she didn't do it?'

Lily-Ann finally spoke. 'There's more evidence than you know.'

49

LILY-ANN

Despite how often she'd gone to Régina's with her murderous ex-husband, the restaurant felt safe to Lily-Ann. That's why she'd invited Ocean and Sophie there to break the bad news, in an attempt to soften the blow. Well, that wasn't the entire truth. She also missed the coconut yogurt parfait. And perhaps she'd stolen this strategy from Hamilton, but she enjoyed turning a casual conversation into a social occasion. Look at her, Lily-Ann Novak, enjoying a fancy breakfast with her girlfriends on a weekday morning.

'What kind of evidence?' Ocean asked.

The waitress arrived before Lily-Ann could respond. Sophie asked for the smashed avocado toast with pickled radish and tomato confit. Ocean ordered the shakshuka, which impressed Lily-Ann. That was real breakfast, and one of the most expensive things on the menu. She appreciated that Ocean didn't hold back out of misguided concern for the cost.

'I'd like the coconut parfait,' Lily-Ann told the waitress. 'Except with passion fruit instead of dried cranberries, and no strawberries, and a drizzle of maple syrup instead of honey.' When the waitress left, she looked at the other two women and said, 'I know you're laughing at me.'

'It's a pleasure to watch someone who knows what she wants,' Ocean told her.

'And who is certain there's passion fruit in the kitchen!' Sophie said, reaching to touch Lily-Ann's forearm as if to reassure her they were teasing.

'I used to come here with Piotr,' she explained. 'I want to create new memories.'

'As long as you keep paying,' Ocean said.

Sophie smiled. 'I like the word "shakshuka." What even is it?'

'Poached eggs in a savory tomato sauce,' Lily-Ann told her.

'With marinated feta,' Ocean said. 'At least if you order it here.'

Lily-Ann decided that was enough chitchat. 'The police found the fifty-five thousand dollars in cash from Frank's ATM withdrawals, in a Trader Joe's reusable bag with a note that said "For CJ."'

Ocean frowned as if she didn't quite understand and Sophie said, 'Oh, shit, is that why Hamilton asked you to stay last night? His cop friend told him?'

'Yes. He didn't know how to break it to Mrs B or Ocean.'

'Me?' Ocean asked.

'He thinks you're in love.'

'Five dates!' she said.

'Nicholas said you glow when you see her,' Lily-Ann said.

Sophie wrinkled her nose. 'He told you that?'

'I asked him.'

'Enough about my radioactivity,' Ocean said. 'Do we know *why* Frank was paying CJ fifty grand?'

'We don't.'

'So, wait . . .' Ocean slouched in her chair. 'He's been withdrawing cash for months but never actually gave it to her? That's weird. Why hoard it?'

'That is a good question,' Lily-Ann said. 'Here's another one: Is the fact that Karina found the money the day after CJ's arrest a little too convenient?'

'You think she set her up?' Sophie asked.

'I think it's a possibility.'

The conversation paused while the waitress served them, then Lily-Ann asked for a side of lime wedges and Ocean took a bite of shakshuka and said, 'Oh, god, this is so good. Um. Okay, say Frank withdrew the cash for an innocuous reason. Like dodging taxes.'

'Innocuous,' Lily-Ann deadpanned.

'That works,' Sophie said. 'Like they were going to pay someone under the table for working on the house, something like that. So first, Karina pretended she saw CJ push her husband, then she found the cash and added a note saying it was for CJ.'

'Huh,' Ocean said. 'Maybe you're onto something.'

'It's a good, simple frame-up. Easier than some others . . .' Silence fell until Sophie cleared her throat. 'If we're right, how do we prove it?'

'We talk to Karina, I guess,' Ocean said. 'And to Sunny Wheeler. Mostly to him. How do we explain his testimony?'

Sophie frowned at her avocado toast. 'He's the key. He *suddenly* remembered he saw CJ push Frank? Talk about convenient.'

'Yeah, that's got to be bullshit. Which means he's hiding something.'

'Perhaps,' Lily-Ann said. 'Eyewitnesses are tricky. For most people, memory is deeply unreliable.'

'Not for you?' Sophie asked, with possibly a teasing tone in her voice.

Lily-Ann squeezed lime onto her parfait. 'No.'

'Are you eating toast with a fork?' Ocean asked Sophie.

'What?' Sophie paused with the fork halfway to her mouth.

'There's too much stuff on top to eat with my hands.'

'Okay.'

'It's messy!'

'Do you eat your burgers that way, too?'

'No, Ocean.' Sophie flipped her the middle finger. 'I use my fingers.'

'Also,' Lily-Ann said, as they laughed, 'CJ searched the web for "painless ways to kill an old man."'

The two of them stopped laughing.

'That is the other piece of evidence the police unearthed,' she explained.

'She googled ways to kill Frank?' Ocean said, her shoulders slumping. 'Well, that's a bit damning.'

Lily-Ann couldn't abide the imprecision. 'She searched online for how to kill a man who was roughly Frank's age with roughly his medical condition. At least, the police believe it was her. The searcher used a laptop in the house, in Frank DeYoung's office, not CJ's personal computer or her phone so—'

'Karina could've planted the search,' Sophie interrupted.

'Searches,' Lily-Ann corrected. 'There were two.'

'Well, shit,' Ocean said.

'They date back four months.' Lily-Ann dabbed at her mouth with her napkin. 'So if Karina framed CJ, she started at least that long ago – before the cash withdrawals – and she planted the evidence deep. However, Frank DeYoung also used that laptop.'

'Why would he search . . .' Ocean trailed off. 'You think he wanted to die by suicide?'

Sophie made a thoughtful noise. 'Everyone says he'd been slowing down.'

'It's possible,' Lily-Ann said, 'but if he were thinking of euthanizing himself, I suspect he would've searched something like "how to kill yourself," not "how to kill an infirm old man."'

Sophie forked another section of her toast. 'Which means we're back to trying to prove that Karina framed CJ.'

'Or to admitting that she's been guilty all along,' Ocean said.

'I don't think she is,' Sophie said.

Lily-Ann decided against asking for more maple syrup, then said, 'The computer searches don't strike me as a big deal.'

'Why not?'

'It's normal curiosity, isn't it?'

'Searching how to kill someone?'

'Yes. I mean it's an interesting question.'

'It might be interesting, Lily-Ann, but it's not normal.'

The certainty in Sophie's voice surprised Lily-Ann. 'Are you sure?'

'Yes.'

'Hmm.' She looked to Ocean. 'You've never searched that about Mrs B?'

Ocean covered her mouth to keep from spitting out her coffee. 'No! No, I've never searched that, Lily-Ann.'

'Why not?'

'Why would I? I've searched for senior housing and memory care. I've searched if those garlic pills she takes are a scam. I have not, however, searched how to kill her, painlessly or otherwise.'

'Huh,' Lily-Ann said, a little taken aback by the lack of curiosity on display.

'Oh, god.' Sophie gaped at her. 'Tell me you haven't searched how to kill Mrs B!'

'Not Mrs B, no. Though I will now.'

'Of course you will.'

'Hamilton and I searched for ways to dispose of a body,' Lily-Ann admitted, 'after two of them appeared on the property. We were curious. It's more difficult than you might imagine.'

'Okay, but CJ isn't you.' Ocean set her fork down. 'What if she actually is guilty? Then she'll run. And Mrs B will lose everything.'

'We'll *all* lose everything,' Sophie said.

'I don't think she's going to run,' Lily-Ann said, trying to allay their fears. 'But I'll admit this puzzle just became much more interesting.'

50

NICHOLAS

To Nicholas's relief, the monthslong logjam finally broke, and the State Street master plan meeting turned suddenly, shockingly, productive.

'So that's the quick pitch?' The councilor lowered her glasses and read from her screen. '"A pedestrian-friendly city core that connects existing paseos into a vibrant State Street neighborhood with mixed-use buildings and unique tourist appeal."'

'And we're extending this to the eleven hundred block?' another member asked.

Nicholas said, 'From five hundred to twelve hundred.'

'We're going to piss off a lot of car people,' one of the holdout councilors warned.

Nicholas's phone buzzed with a text from Sophie, but he didn't have a chance to respond until he returned to his office an hour later. She told him to expect yet another meeting of the Marigold Cottages Murder Collective when he got home – and asked him to check the county records of all the suspects.

He texted back ha ha, absolutely not, don't even joke, then he called her.

'In the future,' he said, while searching the databases, 'if you want me to break the law you need to tell me using your words, not in an archived digital format.'

'Did you know that Lily-Ann and Hamilton searched how to get rid of a dead body?'

'What?'

'Just out of curiosity, after . . . Dedrick and Ybarra.'

'Of course I didn't know, but I've never been less surprised.'

When Sophie put him on speaker, he started reading property tax information, building permits, DBAs, and other legal notices. 'Huh. Sexy Jane Sheffield owns more property around town than I expected.'

'Can we not call her Sexy Jane?'

'Jezebel Jane?' He frowned at his screen. 'Apparently she inherited the properties from one of her late husbands. So maybe that's worth a second look.'

Sophie didn't respond, though he heard her chatting with a coworker in the distance.

'Sorry, I'm back,' she said, a few minutes later.

'I found a business license for Pax Heron,' he told her. 'DBA Pax Bodywork. What a boring name. If he were a chiropractor it could be, like Pax Cracks. Ooh, Pax Cracks Backs. What's wrong with Relax with Pax or—?'

'Is there contact info?' Sophie asked.

Usually she'd play along. 'What's wrong?'

She sighed. 'There's more evidence against CJ. I'll tell you tonight.'

'Oh. Well, CJ doesn't show up anywhere. I guess she's lived the sort of blameless life that doesn't involve local government.'

'Just a second,' Sophie said to someone in her office, before asking Nicholas, 'Can you email Lily-Ann anything important? I've got to run. See you at home.'

'Love you,' he said to himself, since she'd already ended the call.

A few minutes later, he discovered that Helene and George Kagant had bought their current house ten years ago, for a small fortune – and half of what it was currently worth. Apparently there was good money in windshield wipers; Frank DeYoung must've made an extra fortune by funding their work.

'Last one,' he told himself, then searched for Sunny Wheeler.

He didn't find much, considering Wheeler was a thousand years old and had lived in Montecito for fifty of them. The only unusual real estate transaction was Wheeler's purchase of a fifteen-acre property off Route 192. Wheeler had immediately transferred the title to VivX Inc., which was some sort of life-extension company.

Which checked out for Mr Fake Funeral on My Birthday.

Nicholas dug around and discovered that VivX had gone bankrupt years later. Which was weird, considering the amount of money Wheeler had poured into it. He thought about getting back to work, but the last fifteen minutes of the day wasn't enough time to get anything done. So he researched Frank and Karina DeYoung instead. Somewhat to his surprise, neither Karina nor Frank appeared in connection with any property other than their primary residence in Hope

Ranch. Even more surprising: over the past few years, Karina had arranged for demolition permits and design reviews and CEQA documents, but she'd never followed through.

Which meant what?

That she'd paid for major renovation plans, presented them to Frank, and he'd vetoed them? You marry a guy, think you're partners, then when you want to upgrade the house suddenly the money is all his? Was that enough to kill an old man for?

He heard Anthony's voice in his head. '*People have killed for less.*'

51

SOPHIE

After we moved in together, I realized that whenever I tucked my feet under myself on a sofa, Nicholas gave me a smoldering look. Was it just him? Did other men have a thing for women on couches? I had no idea. That felt like the level of question the Murder Collective was qualified to answer, but sadly we were too busy with a murder investigation for me to ask.

Well, mostly we were waiting for CJ to join us, now that she was out of jail.

We had questions for her, by which I mean Lily-Ann had questions for her. Also, Ocean had . . . I didn't know what. Second thoughts? Desperate hopes? Acute regrets? Mostly just insecurity for dating a woman accused of murder. Poor Ocean. She deserved love more than anyone, she was so generous with herself, with her strength and her kindness, yet she was starting to think her love life was cursed.

The rest of us mostly wanted to judge for ourselves if CJ was likely to flee to Mexico, dodging her court appearances, violating the property bond, and making us homeless.

While we waited, Lily-Ann talked us through our current priorities. All of us except Mrs B, who was coming with CJ. Well, and Anthony, who was at work. So Nicholas, Ocean, and I made suggestions while Hamilton took notes on his whiteboard.

THE TINY QUESTIONS

1) Is there a secret from George and Helene's (aka Beard and Bird) shared past with Frank that they need to keep hidden? Sophie wants a dark backstory.

2) How much did Jane Sheffield's personal success depend on Frank's donations to World of Goods? Why didn't he support her more with this Big Award she wanted?

3) Did Jane's husbands die naturally?

'That doesn't even rise to the level of an *unimportant* question,' Lily-Ann said when Hamilton added the last one himself. 'She wasn't married to Frank.'

'On the other hand,' Hamilton told her, 'I am in charge of the whiteboard.'

'The first rule of brainstorming club,' Ocean told Lily-Ann, 'is not to judge the brainstorming.'

'Because suspending judgment is such a productive approach.'

'Exactly,' Ocean said, ignoring her sarcasm. 'Does anyone have anything about Pax the masseuse?'

Nicholas and I collaborated on the next one.

4) Was Pax having an affair with anyone?

5) C'mon, he's hot and this is a bunch of rich people! Surely, they were sleeping around.

'Now CJ,' Lily-Ann said.

'We can't write down our doubts about CJ,' I told her. 'She'll be here any minute.'

'She can answer them when she arrives.'

'Uh, no. Suspecting her of murder is insulting. For her and . . .' I glanced at Ocean. 'And maybe Mrs B.'

'Ah,' Lily-Ann said, and I could tell she wanted to ask why that mattered but she didn't. 'So with CJ, we're wondering about the bag of cash and the homicidal web searching.'

'When you put it that way, it sounds bad,' I said, and decided not to mention my suspicions about ice cubes.

Lily-Ann cleared her throat, then told Hamilton to start listing the more pressing items.

THE BIG QUESTIONS

1) What if several guests worked together to kill Frank?

2) Did Karina want to remodel the mansion so much that she killed her husband? Why else would she want to get her hands on the money immediately?

3) Was the liquor bottle rigged to fall? If not, did the accident lead to a crime of opportunity?

4) Karina happened to discover the bag of cash? Suspicious timing. What was purpose of cash?

5) What led Sunny Wheeler to 'suddenly' remember seeing CJ push Frank? What does he gain from his testimony?

6) Frank bailed Sunny out of a scandal? What exactly happened? Is Sunny hiding something? Did Frank know his secret?

'So Sunny Wheeler is our second priority,' Lily-Ann said, as Hamilton wrote. 'Or he's tied for second with Karina, but the grieving widow is difficult to question.'

'We can corner her at the memorial service,' Hamilton said.

'There's a memorial service?' Lily-Ann asked.

'Of course there's a memorial service,' I told her. 'And we are not cornering her there.'

'Maybe "cornering" was the wrong word,' Hamilton said.

'Questioning?' Lily-Ann suggested.

Nicholas nodded. 'Sure, everyone loves uninvited guests questioning the widow at a funeral.'

'Fine,' Hamilton said. 'I'll cross the memorial service off my list.'

'Why?' Lily-Ann asked.

I didn't want him to encourage her to crash the memorial service, so I said, 'If Sunny and Karina are the second priority, who's the first?'

'CJ,' Lily-Ann told me. 'We need to agree what to ask her before she gets here.'

'Shouldn't we brainstorm that with Mrs B?' I asked. 'It's her property on the line.'

'God, no,' Ocean said. 'She'll ask any old nonsense, like she did at the dermatologist.'

'Would you stop dropping hints about that?' I demanded. 'What did she do?'

'The wound is too raw. Maybe in a few months I can speak of it.'

'C'mon, spill.'

'You know you want to,' Hamilton said.

'Fine.' Ocean took a breath. 'Mrs B's been going to the same dermatologist for ten years, okay? She loves him. She says he's gay and married and lovely. I didn't want her driving herself, so I went in with her for her scan.' Ocean took a slug of beer, then stared at the bottle in horror. 'What the heck, Hamilton, why can't you buy normal beer?'

'It's hickory-flavored,' Hamilton told her.

Ocean plopped the beer bottle on the table. 'Ugh, the aftertaste.'

'Back to the derm,' I said. 'Please.'

'Right, so I'm with her in the office. She asks about the doctor's family and he says, 'Ooh, we're pregnant!' And Mrs B says, "Mazel tov."'

'So far so good,' Nicholas said.

'Right. Now guess what she asked next.'

'Uh, when's the due date?' I asked.

'If they chose a name,' Hamilton suggested.

Ocean spread her arms as if to appeal to the group. 'Both good questions, the kinds of things a human might ask. But no. No, that's not what she said.'

'What'd she say?' I asked.

'She said, and I am not making this up, "Mazel tov! Did you use *your* sperm?"'

Hamilton barked a laugh and Nicholas groaned but Lily-Ann tilted her head. 'In a marriage with two men, surely that's not an *entirely* incomprehensible question.'

'Sperm is *never* a polite subject, Lily-Ann,' Nicholas said.

'I'm not done!' Ocean said. 'So she said, did you use your sperm? Now guess how the doctor answered.'

'Yes?' I said, while Nicholas said, 'No?'

Ocean exhaled deeply. 'After a pause that lasted way too long, he said, and I quote, "Yes, and my wife's egg."'

'No!' I said.

'What?' Lily-Ann asked.

'He's not gay,' Ocean explained.

'He's not gay,' I repeated, to Lily-Ann. 'So what happened was, this straight doctor told an old lady that his wife was pregnant and she said, "With whose sperm?"'

Hamilton drained his beer. 'Wow.'

'Very wow,' Ocean agreed. 'Now guess why she thought he was—'

The door to Hamilton's cottage opened and CJ helped Mrs B inside. Not that she needed help, but I knew her tricks now: she was helping CJ by pretending that she needed help. Vintage Mrs B.

'Welcome back,' I told CJ. 'I'm so glad you're, um . . .'

'Free,' Lily-Ann said.

'Free as a bird!' Mrs B said.

'Free as a canary,' Hamilton said. 'On a hot tin roof!'

Which pretty much ended that conversation.

52

LILY-ANN

'We brainstormed a little before you arrived,' Lily-Ann told CJ.

'I – I can see that.' CJ glanced nervously at Ocean, then at the whiteboard. 'That's a lot of questions.'

'Don't worry, dear,' Mrs B said, as CJ helped her into a chair. 'We're in this together. And we've cracked harder cases in the past.'

'Cases?' Nicholas asked.

'Case,' Sophie corrected. 'We've cracked a harder *case* in the past.'

Mrs B tsked at them but Lily-Ann kept watching CJ, wondering about her. She certainly didn't come across as a flight risk, wearing an oversized stripy sweater and jeans. Her signature eyeliner was missing, but she did have on red lipstick. She didn't look like a killer either, but the jury was still out about that.

Ocean handed CJ a glass of tolerable Malbec and said, 'I'm glad you're back.'

'Thank you,' she replied.

There was a pause, or perhaps Lily-Ann imagined the pause, as the two of them looked at each other. So she said, 'We have a few questions.'

'I noticed.' CJ gave an uncharacteristically timid smile. 'But first I want to thank you. All of you. I already thanked Mrs B for, um . . .'

'It's nothing, darling,' Mrs B said.

That was such an obvious lie that Lily-Ann almost spoke up. Using her property as collateral for this near-stranger was absolutely not nothing. CJ owed her a debt that she'd never repay, and Lily-Ann wanted to ensure that she understood that – that they *both* understood that. However, before she could open her mouth, she was struck by the notion that if Anthony were there he'd give her a look, so she didn't say anything.

'I'm a little horrified that Mrs B bailed me out,' CJ continued, looking to each of them in turn. 'But mostly grateful. This was the worst week of my life and – and Mrs B told me you're trying to prove my innocence, and I can't thank you enough.'

'Now *that* is genuinely nothing,' Mrs B told her. 'Everyone needs a hobby, and I never had a knack for pottery. We positively enjoy investigating.'

Lily-Ann frowned at CJ. 'Even if we find you guilty.'

'Which we won't!' Mrs B blurted. 'Because you're not.'

'Of course not,' Sophie said.

'Still,' Ocean told CJ, 'Lily-Ann's right to warn you. "Investigating" sounds good, but "gossiping, meddling, and prying" not so much.'

Mrs B pointed her glass of rosé at Ocean. 'Stop tormenting her, you ungrateful child.'

'I'm just saying there's no telling what we'll do, because we don't know what we're doing.'

'We might even find evidence against her,' Lily-Ann said, trying to move things along.

'There is no evidence against her,' Mrs B said, 'because she's not guilty.'

'The police found fifty-five thousand dollars in cash in a bag with her name on it.'

Mrs B blinked. 'Pardon? Fifty-five thousand *what*?'

Lily-Ann caught CJ's gaze. 'Were you aware of that?'

'Yes, I – the detective told me.'

Lily-Ann didn't speak, waiting for the silence to become oppressive, to increase the pressure on CJ. She personally never minded an extended silence – in fact, she found them restful – but she knew that was a minority opinion.

However, Sophie spoke first. 'So what *do* you know about the cash?'

'Nothing,' CJ said, looking at her hands. 'Like I told the police, Frank might've wanted to surprise me. He was generous, and he liked to make the occasional grand gesture. He never did anything like that before though, and cash wasn't really his style so . . . I don't know.'

Nicholas asked, 'Did he often keep that kind of cash around the house?'

'No. Never. Not that I saw.'

'And you would've seen?'

'Absolutely.' She tilted her chin up slightly. 'I worked for him but we were partners. Well, he paid me, he was my employer, but my job wasn't to assist him, not really. My job was to act as an extension of him. And to do that, I needed to know what he wanted. Not what he *said* he wanted, what he really wanted.'

'That's a lot of trust,' Sophie said.

CJ gave a quick little smile. 'I was very good at my job.'

'Did your job change as he got older?' Ocean asked, an echoing smile appearing for an instant on her face. 'In my experience, caretakers sometimes think they know better than their elderly charges – and they're absolutely right.'

'Ha!' Mrs B said.

'It changed a little the past few years,' CJ admitted. 'As Frank's world shrank.'

'Karina thinks he was paying you to keep quiet about your affair,' Lily-Ann lied, to see how CJ responded.

'No, she doesn't!' CJ scoffed. 'Not even if she said she does. She knows that's a lie.'

'Hm,' Lily-Ann said, and doodled fifty thousand in her notebook because she wanted CJ to worry about what she was writing.

'You didn't know he was withdrawing money from an ATM?' Ocean asked.

'No, which is odd. That he didn't tell me. Also, he never used cash. And if he did, he wouldn't use an ATM, a concierge would've delivered it.'

'A bank concierge?' Hamilton asked.

'When you have Frank's kind of money, the bank comes to you.'

'So you know nothing about the cash,' Lily-Ann said. 'Not even where Karina found it?'

CJ shook her head. 'The officer didn't mention that.'

'How about the searches on your laptop, for ways to murder an old man? The easiest ways to kill a man in Frank's position?'

'That's not my laptop!' Red spots appeared on CJ's cheeks. 'It's a household laptop.'

Nicholas spoke more gently. 'Did anyone use it besides you and Frank?'

'Not that I ever saw. No. But anybody could have.'

'Was it password protected?' Hamilton asked.

'No. No.'

Lily-Ann tapped her pen against her notebook. '*Did* you

search for ways to kill a man in his condition?'

'To kill Frank?' CJ asked.

'Is that a yes?'

'No! No, that's not a yes.'

'So you think that between four and six months ago, Frank himself searched how to painlessly murder an old man?'

'I don't know. I don't know what Frank searched.'

'Who else has access to the laptop,' Nicholas asked, 'other than you and Frank?'

'Karina. The cleaners, the gardeners. Anyone we ever invited into the house.'

'We?' Lily-Ann asked, then tapped a quick message on her phone.

'They. We. I did a lot of the inviting. Anyone could've used the laptop.'

'Anyone *could* have,' Sophie said, 'but who *would* have?'

'I don't know. Nobody.' CJ started crying silently. 'Ev . . . everyone loved him.'

Apparently that was too much for Ocean. She crossed the room, slipped onto the sofa beside CJ, and put her arm around her.

CJ buried her face in Ocean's shoulder and sniffled. 'Everyone loved Frank.'

'Possibly not everyone,' Lily-Ann said, because the moment called for rationality, not sympathy.

Mrs B tsked. 'Lily-Ann!'

'Unless you think he tripped?'

CJ raised her head. 'Of course I think he tripped!'

'Well, I think you're lying about the online searches.'

'Why?' Mrs B demanded. 'Why would you think that?'

'Anything else is too bizarrely unlikely. Four months ago,

someone *else* used CJ's work computer to search for ways to kill her boss? And did you see how she reacted?'

'Like a *person*! There's no reason to attack her.'

'We're not here to attack CJ, Mrs B,' Nicholas said. 'We're here to help her. However . . .'

'We can't help her if she doesn't tell the truth,' Hamilton continued, looking up from the group text Lily-Ann had sent, telling everyone to press CJ.

'That's true.' Sophie's sweet smile turned sympathetic. 'I'm sorry, CJ, but he's not wrong.'

'Very not wrong,' Nicholas said.

Sophie put her hand on Nicholas's arm. 'We're the only people who won't assume you're guilty. It's us or nobody. And we don't care what's legal, we only care about what's right.'

'Is that . . .' CJ sniffled. 'Is that true?'

'Yeah,' Ocean said. 'All too true.'

'We don't judge,' Lily-Ann told CJ. 'None of us is in a position to judge. For example, I've searched for ways to poison Anthony.'

'You have? Why?'

'Curiosity,' Lily-Ann said.

CJ's teary gaze flicked to Ocean. 'Um . . .'

'No, I haven't searched ways to get rid of Mrs B,' Ocean said, giving her arm a squeeze, 'but only because I already ordered an anvil from Acme.'

The joke eased the tension more than Lily-Ann liked, so she said, 'And I'm not the only one with a problematic search history. Hamilton searched for commercially available drones able to deliver a package of C4 and a detonator.'

'What on earth?' Mrs B sputtered.

'You did not!' Sophie said.

'I'm interested in the future of asymmetrical warfare,' Hamilton lied, surprisingly adept, considering that Lily-Ann had just invented that.

'Then there's Nicholas,' Lily-Ann said. 'However, in the interest of decorum, I won't share the contents of a young man's search history.'

'I like big toes and I cannot lie,' Nicholas said, at which Sophie tucked her feet more tightly beneath her on the couch.

'So you searched for ways to painlessly kill Frank,' Lily-Ann told CJ. 'So what? That's normal curiosity. We're a morbid species.'

CJ fiddled with the cuffs of her overlarge sweater. She looked at Ocean, closed her eyes, then finally said, 'Six or seven months ago, Frank started getting worse again. Tired and unhappy. Just . . . terribly unhappy. There was nothing acute, it was the combination of everything.'

'Getting old isn't easy,' Mrs B said.

'Yeah. His joints ached, he struggled to dress himself. He was getting brain fog. He took no joy in anything. Just discomfort. For a few months, things looked pretty dire.'

'That's so tough,' Nicholas said.

'He was uncomfortable and confused,' CJ continued, 'but not so confused that he didn't know he was confused, which made it so much worse. The good news was, they adjusted his medications, his potassium . . . and he bounced back.' She smiled wistfully. 'Frank was full of surprises.'

'Which leads us to the laptop?' Ocean prompted, her voice gentle.

CJ spoke so softly that Lily-Ann barely heard. 'Frank didn't want to linger. He told me a hundred times that nothing scared him more than spending the end of his life bedridden and confused. And with his money, they'd never let him die. They'd keep him alive even when there was no *him* left.'

'You wanted to help him.'

'I didn't! I didn't *want* to help him, not with that. But I owed him.'

Mrs B reached out from her seat to pat Ocean's knee. 'We all need someone in our life who we can trust to do terrible things.'

'So you searched online for ways to help,' Lily-Ann said. 'Doing your job for him, as always.'

'Exactly, yes,' CJ said, as if surprised that Lily-Ann understood. 'That's it exactly.'

Lily-Ann let her gaze skim the whiteboard as the conversation focused on Frank's health and CJ's emotions. She was starting to suspect that she understood the basics of the murder. However, she still struggled to link the facts she knew, the connections she suspected, and the as-yet-unresolved questions. Primarily Sunny Wheeler, but also the money, the liquor bottle. Still, nothing was tidy about human lives: even if she solved the primary riddles, she'd end up with pieces left over, with edges that didn't quite fit together.

Her attention returned to the group when Ocean asked, 'CJ, do you think you're being framed?'

53

SOPHIE

CJ blinked at Ocean. 'Framed by Karina?'

'Her and Sunny,' Ocean said, 'but mostly her.'

'No,' she said. 'No.'

To my playwright's ear, she sounded too confident. Like she was trying to convince us of Karina's innocence – or trying to convince herself. There were just too many oddities floating around. The secret cash, the fact that only Karina 'saw' the push – until Sunny Wheeler suddenly jumped on the bandwagon. The ice cubes! Even though no one but me thought they were important.

As CJ wiped her tears away, Ocean asked her, 'So you admit you're responsible for those web searches?'

'Yeah. Yes, but not—'

'How good are you with computers?'

'I'm okay. I've designed websites, I've fixed routers, I've turned everything off and on again.'

Ocean's eyes smiled, though the intensity didn't leave her face. 'In that case, you know that browsing websites leaves traces.'

'Of course.'

'Yet you made no effort to hide your incriminating searches?'

'Oh!' CJ brightened despite her tear-streaked cheeks. 'That's so true.'

'Yeah,' I agreed. 'Everyone knows better than to leave a homicidal search history on your work computer.'

'Exactly! Yes. If I'd been planning murder, I would've used an anonymizer or – or what're those called?'

'No idea,' Ocean said.

'A VPN! Or one of those things . . . proxy servers?'

'That's them.' Hamilton turned to Mrs B. 'A virtual proxy network conceals traffic from your computer, even at the ISP level, which private browsing doesn't hide.'

Mrs B blinked owlishly. 'Oh, of course, the ISP level.'

'That's such a great point.' CJ wiped her tears with her palm. 'If I'd planned to kill Frank, why would I leave a search like that behind? I wouldn't. Nobody would.'

'So you *do* think you're being framed?' I asked, watching her more closely.

'I . . .' She pushed her auburn hair behind her ear. 'I don't know. Do people really get framed in the real world?'

'I doubt it,' Nicholas said. 'I mean, c'mon, that's like falling into quicksand.'

'Of course she's being framed,' Mrs B said. 'That's the only thing that makes sense. This is clear to an experienced investigator.'

'Do tell,' Ocean said.

'Karina was in a rush to inherit, to spend the money and—'

'Why?'

'Because life is short! She didn't want to wait around while the doctors kept Frank alive for fifteen years, at the cost of several small fortunes. Or maybe she wanted the money for a more specific reason.'

'Like what?'

'Like remodeling. Or she wants to invest in krypton currency.'

'Krypton currency?' I asked.

'Cryptocurrency,' Ocean translated.

'Like I said.' Mrs B snorted.

I turned to CJ. 'Is Karina interested in investments?'

'Not even a little,' she said. 'She tells Frank – she used to say, "Screw careful accumulation, it's time for conspicuous consumption."'

'The reason doesn't matter,' Mrs B said. 'But at the very

end of dinner at the Hope Ranch house – do you remember what always happened then?'

Ocean said, 'What?'

'They said goodbye for ten minutes at the stairs,' I reminded her.

'Every time,' CJ agreed.

Mrs B pointed a bejeweled hand at her in triumph. 'Exactly! So this is what happened. Karina slipped a handful of Frank's pills into his wineglass during dinner. He already had trouble with balance! You missed that, didn't you? Well, to the trained detective, it is a very red flag. Positively scarlet.'

'Now you're a *trained* detective?' Ocean asked.

Mrs B ignored her. 'After a little over-medication, Karina followed him upstairs, knowing he'd pause there for a bit. Then she waited for the inevitable.'

'If you're correct,' Lily-Ann said, 'she at best waited for the *probable*.'

'Well, she's probably tried this a half dozen times,' Mrs B told her. 'And now it finally worked.'

I squinted at her. 'What about the liquor bottle smashing?'

'Oh, I've no idea. CJ?'

She chewed her lip. 'I'm not sure.'

'Maybe that *was* a coincidence,' Nicholas said, 'and when Frank turned toward the noise, that's what unbalanced him?'

'Because he was already over-medicated,' Mrs B said.

'Or maybe Karina drugged the Amaretto,' Ocean said. 'Instead of putting the medication directly in Frank's glass. Then she left it balanced precariously, planning to break it and hide the evidence after he died, but it fell early.'

Mrs B beamed at her. 'Oh, perfect! You have all the makings of a diabolical murderess!'

'So you're a detective and I'm a murderess?'

'Naturally,' Mrs B said, then a flash of alarm crossed her face. 'Wait!'

My pulse jumped again. 'What's wrong?'

'Do we say "murderess" anymore, or just "murderer"? Like "actor" instead of "actress"?'

'Perhaps we don't care about the feelings of people who commit homicide,' Lily-Ann suggested.

'Well, a little politeness never hurts!' Mrs B huffed. 'Where was I? Oh! Karina arranged for a dizzy spell, then claimed she saw CJ push Frank. Why? To divert attention from herself, and because she was jealous of his extremely appropriate affection for her.'

The room grew silent until Nicholas said, 'I mean, that doesn't *not* make sense.'

'Except Karina wouldn't hurt Frank,' CJ said.

'Not for all the money in the world?' Nicholas asked.

'You never can tell,' I said. 'What do you think, Lily-Ann?'

'It strikes me as not impossible,' she said. 'Though we still need evidence.'

'"Not impossible!"' Mrs B crowed. 'As for evidence . . . well, that's what Sunny Wheeler is for.'

'How's he going to help?' I asked.

'Isn't that obvious?' Mrs B said, radiating somehow inoffensive smugness. 'Karina saw that her testimony wasn't enough to close the case, to fully frame CJ. So she convinced Sunny Wheeler to play along. Which means he *knows* she convinced him.'

'How did she convince him?' Ocean asked.

'Maybe they're lovers!'

CJ sniffed a laugh. 'They aren't.'

'Ah, but they used to be.'

'They didn't,' CJ said.

'Well, well, Sunny hates you!' Mrs B brightly suggested.

'Why on earth would Sunny hate me?'

'You're young? Believe me, dear, that's more offensive than you know.'

'I'd be shocked if he ever even thought about me.'

Lily-Ann cleared her throat. 'The best thing about Mrs B's theory is what she already mentioned. If Karina asked Sunny to fake his testimony, then her request condemns her. That gives us a way forward. By questioning him.'

'QED,' Mrs B said.

'You have no idea what QED means,' Ocean said.

Mrs B sniffed. 'Of course I do.'

I shared a look with Nicholas, eager to hear her definition. Sadly, Lily-Ann turned her hazel gaze on CJ before we dove into that particular rabbit hole. 'What do you know about this scandal of his?'

'Of Sunny's? Mostly whispers. He's obsessed with life extension. Obviously. He invested millions, maybe tens of millions, in various businesses and start-ups.'

'Like cryogenics?' I asked.

'They prefer the term "cryonics,"' Hamilton told me.

'And the scandal?' Lily-Ann repeated.

'Either Sunny lost so much money that he needed Frank to bail him out or . . .' CJ trailed off briefly. 'Well, one way to extend your life is by using blood transfusions. I heard maybe Sunny was paying teenagers for not-quite-legal plasma donations.'

'Oh, my goodness.' Mrs B fanned her face with her hand,

setting her bracelets jangling. 'Human experimentation is even better than illicit affairs!'

'For a very specific definition of "better,"' Hamilton said. 'That does sound like a good juicy scandal though.'

CJ gave a wan smile. 'The rumor is that Frank helped Sunny clear things up without facing legal charges.'

'And you know it's not *just* a rumor,' Lily-Ann announced with absolute confidence. 'Because Frank would've told you if it was untrue.'

'Exactly. If he hadn't promised Sunny he'd keep quiet?' CJ smiled in forlorn remembrance. 'Then he would've teased me for believing such a bizarre conspiracy.'

And that's how I knew CJ hadn't killed him. I could imagine passion turning into murder. I could imagine gratitude or dependence or lust turning into murder. But fondness? No. That smile of warm, uncomplicated memory? No.

CJ hadn't pushed Frank DeYoung. Now we just needed to find out who had.

54

CJ

Listening to the other tenants brainstorm on her behalf felt to CJ like cuddling under a quilt in front of a fire. All warm and soul-happy, even when they'd pushed her to admit to those terrible online searches. When Ocean had put her arm around her, she couldn't help but cry.

Then they'd started wondering if Karina arranged for Frank to have a dizzy spell that killed him. Mrs B suggested that Karina had drugged Frank, and Ocean thought maybe she'd doped the liquor bottle. CJ hadn't argued at the time because – well, because she'd felt completely out of it, after days in jail. And the entire pack of Marigolders could be a bit intimidating.

So after the meeting ended, she waited outside for Ocean to clear things up. However, Sophie emerged first. She stepped into the evening, a few stray strands of her hair wafting across her face, then gave CJ a quizzical smile.

'Hey, Sophie,' she said. 'Do you have a second?'

'Of course.'

'I just wanted to thank you.' CJ cleared her throat, an embarrassing nervous tic. 'I, uh, I know I slammed into Mrs B's life like a car crash, but you've been so kind.'

'No, no. You were kind first! And, uh, don't judge everyone for being blunt in there. We're so close we don't always bother with politeness.'

'It reminds me of Frank. He was, uh, he was well-named. Sometimes a little *too* frank.'

Sophie smiled. 'It's like once you hit seventy, you can say anything.'

'Okay, right, so I have a favor to ask. I was going to ask Ocean, but I don't want to add to her burden.'

'Oh. Sure.'

'Do you think it's possible to prove that I *didn't* kill Frank without suggesting that Karina *did*?'

Sophie tilted her head. 'You don't want to get her in trouble?'

'Yeah.'

'Not even if she's setting you up?'

CJ cleared her throat again. 'Here's the thing. The way Frank showed his love for Karina was by trying to protect her. He would've done anything to keep from hurting her. That was the most important thing to him.'

'Did Karina need a lot of protection?'

'Emotionally? Yes.'

'Then why didn't he let her remodel the house?'

'What?'

'If he was so concerned with pleasing her, why did he stop her from remodeling?'

CJ forced herself to take a breath. 'It – it was mostly me who stopped that. Frank was going to sign off but it would've been so disruptive for him. He'd been feeling poorly, so I kind of . . . sabotaged her plans?'

To her surprise, Sophie said, 'That's sweet. How?'

'I slow-walked everything. The contractors, the city. Plus, I confronted Karina about how a massive disruption would affect Frank when he was already so fragile. She hated me for that. She thought I was showing off how much more I cared.'

'She sounds selfish.'

'She is. And Frank knew that, though he never said it aloud.'

'Not even to you?'

'Especially not to me. He would *never* bad-mouth her to me. And, I mean, that's why he refused to write his charities into his will. He didn't want to hurt Karina's feelings, even though I told him he needed to lock in his support.'

Sophie's pretty eyes clouded with confusion. 'I don't understand how that'd hurt her feelings.'

'If he'd made the bequests mandatory, Karina would've felt that he didn't trust her to follow his wishes. Which he shouldn't have. The bequests are listed in his will, but only as requests . . . and she's refusing them.'

'Why? Why refuse them?'

'Karina's not a bad person,' CJ admitted, a little begrudgingly. 'She's just so insecure. Frank lavished too much money and attention on World of Goods instead of her. She's not going to reward that.'

'That's a little crazy.'

'Yeah, but Frank loved her. And whatever happened to him, he wouldn't want her to suffer.'

'So you're asking us what, exactly? Not to tell the cops even if we think she's framing you?' Sophie clicked her tongue. 'What if that's the only way to prove your innocence?'

CJ almost started crying again when she remembered her days behind bars. 'I won't go to jail for her! But she didn't hurt him. I know she didn't.'

'It's lovely that you care so much about what he would've wanted,' Sophie said, as a door opened in the darkness behind her. 'Even now, you're still looking after him.'

'Say what you want about me.' CJ sniffled, smiling and tearful at the same time. 'I always put Frank first.'

55

OCEAN

After the Murder Collective meeting ended, Ocean nipped into the kitchen for the box of leftover chocolates from the previous meeting.

She worried they weren't getting anywhere with the investigation. None of the current suspects struck her as particularly suspicious. At least not more than any random group of rich people. Jane had buried two husbands, and based her self-worth on getting fancy national awards at World of Goods. So what? George and Helene owed Frank for turning them into windshield wiper tycoons, and Sunny Wheeler was three kinds of weirdo. Who cared? The caterer was a no-drama local business, the masseuse was a sensitive new age guy specializing in geriatrics. Karina disliked CJ, and resented Frank's donations, but apparently did everything she could to keep him alive.

CJ was Frank's devoted assistant. And Frank, in his elderly brain fog, had started hoarding cash from ATMs.

To Ocean, that just sounded like people being people.

In Hamilton's kitchen, she picked through the half-empty See's Candies box for Miles and Riley. She wasn't sure which ones Riley preferred these days, and didn't want to give her milk chocolate if she only ate dark. Forget CJ, forget romance. Forget investigations. Those were the big questions in Ocean's life. The only ones that really mattered.

By the time she decided to nab the entire box, everyone was gone. Well, other than Lily-Ann, who'd stuck around to help Hamilton clean up – and look at cats on the animal shelter website.

She left the cottage through the kitchen door. She'd use the chocolates as an excuse to check in with Riley. She liked to periodically remind her daughter that she had access to a mother who loved her, who'd listen. However, before she took two steps, she heard Sophie's voice drift toward her in the darkness. Talking to CJ, which made her smile. When Lily-Ann had texted earlier, telling everyone to accuse CJ of lying, she hadn't expected anything from Sophie. Sophie was too sweet to convincingly convey callous suspicion.

On the other hand, after Ocean listened for a minute, Sophie said, 'She sounds selfish.'

She almost laughed. Sometimes she forgot how sharp she was. The girl could cut when she chose to. She almost backed away to let the private conversation remain private, but . . . well, there was too much Mrs B in her for that. So instead, she peeked around the side of Hamilton's cottage and listened until the kitchen door opened a few feet behind her.

She jerked in surprise, and Lily-Ann stepped beside her, a quizzical cast to her face, wondering why she was lurking. So Ocean spoke loudly, as if she'd just stepped outside, too. 'I'm taking the leftover See's candy for the kids!'

'Okay,' Lily-Ann said, and nobody who didn't know her would've heard her amusement.

Ocean continued toward her own cottage, the loose chocolates sliding around inside the box. She felt a little like she was stepping offstage after a scene in one of Sophie's plays. People popping in and out of the spotlight, eavesdropping and being discovered – and clumsily covering for themselves.

Then a whisper sounded from the hedge outside Sophie's old cottage: 'Oma!'

'Miles?' Ocean said.

'Jesus, Mother,' Riley rage-whispered. 'I do not sound like Miles!'

'Sorry, sorry!' she whispered back. 'What're you doing?'

'Shhh!' Riley said, and slipped toward her from the shadows.

She took Ocean's elbow and frog-marched her across the

courtyard to their cottage. Once they were inside, Ocean offered her the See's. She riffled through them with fingernails painted with Chanel Vamp polish, saying, 'Yum, gross. Yum, yum, gross.'

'What's up?' Ocean asked, meaning *Why were you lurking in the shadows*?

'What is up?' Mrs B asked, wandering in from the kitchen, holding two oven mitts.

'Well, you're in the kitchen, for one,' Ocean said, as Riley stepped to the window.

Mrs B flapped an oven mitt behind herself. 'I baked a kugel.'

'Not the sweet kind,' Riley said.

'Yes, the sweet kind!'

'Ugh.'

Miles poked his head out from his bedroom. 'I like the sweet kind.'

'Typical,' Riley grumbled, as she watched the courtyard through the window.

Ocean leaned against the kitchen counter. 'What are you doing?'

'I'm wondering why your oven seems to be working,' Mrs B said, a note of triumph in her voice. 'Even though you keep claiming you need to use mine.'

'It's finicky,' she lied, exactly like she'd been lying about it being busted so she could cook meals for Mrs B at her house while pretending Mrs B was doing *her* a favor. 'But I didn't mean you, I meant Riley.'

'She's hoping for a Pax sighting!' Miles mimicked his sister's voice. '"Look at those *arms* . . ."'

'No, I'm not, dummy,' Riley said, still at the window. 'I'm spying on CJ.'

'Why?'

'Because she's guilty and dating my mother.'

'Don't be silly.' Mrs B pursed her lips. 'She's a lovely young woman going through a terrible rough patch.'

'Also, I don't think we're dating anymore,' Ocean said.

Riley snorted. 'As if *you'd* know.'

'I mean, we haven't gone out since the arrest.'

''Cause you haven't asked her. She talks to her birds.'

Ocean blinked at her daughter. 'What? Am I supposed to—*what*?'

'I was outside her window and I heard her chatting away. Mouse this, Mona that. I couldn't make out the words, but I bet she was confessing.'

'To her birds?' Miles said.

'Okay, first,' Ocean told Riley, 'stop hiding outside people's windows. How did you even think of that?'

'Gee, I don't know. It's not like I was raised by you and Mrs B.'

Shame warmed Ocean's chest and Mrs B said, 'Oh, a hit! A palpable hit!'

'Not helping, Golda.'

'It's like being raised by wolves,' Miles helpfully explained. 'Except with less teeth and more nosing around.'

'And *second*,' Ocean said, pretending that the previous ten seconds hadn't happened, 'why do you think she was confessing?'

'Just a feeling.' Riley bit into a chocolate. 'Her tone of voice, I guess.'

Ocean didn't know what to believe. 'Well, please, *please*, as a favor to me, stop lurking in bushes.'

'At the very least,' Mrs B advised Riley, 'make sure you have a lie prepared. Like you were looking for the fuse box.'

'You two deserve each other,' Ocean groaned.

Mrs B beamed. 'We do! We *all* deserve each other! Now! Who's ready for kugel?'

56

LILY-ANN

The scent of cinnamon swirled from Lily-Ann's cappuccino as she settled on the sofa in front of her laptop. The cup warmed her in the chilly morning, though not as well as sharing a bed with Anthony had the previous night. He'd crawled in at two in the morning, freshly showered after work, smelling of rosemary-mint shampoo.

She'd climbed on top of him. She liked putting her palms on his broad chest and feeling his solidness. She liked that he thrilled to the fullness of her, the weight of her. In fact, she'd slept so well that she was almost late for her morning schedule. So she ignored the texts buzzing from the Marigold Cottages Murder Collective chat for a few hours, then made herself a second cappuccino and picked up her phone.

Ocean

Riley's convinced CJ is guilty. She's doing her own investigational services

Nicholas

Investigational? Is that a word? Not investigatory?

Sophie

Focus, Nico! Trying to solve a murder.

Hamilton

Are we calling Nicholas Nico now?

Nicholas

No.

Lily-Ann wrinkled her nose at the tangent.

Lily-Ann

Did Riley find any evidence?

Ocean

No. She just doesn't think she's being framed

Nicholas

Also she's protective of her mother

Sophie

Stop or you'll make Ocean blush

Nicholas

Also that is ridiculous.

Nobody gets framed. C'mon

Lily-Ann jumped in to agree before anyone mentioned how they'd successfully framed her ex.

Lily-Ann

True. Highly ridiculous.

Though even ridiculous things happen very very rarely.

Nicholas

Maybe Riley should question Karina. She might talk to a kid?

Ocean

No. Fucking. Way.

Nicholas

Okay, okay! Sorry, Mama Bear

Anthony

That rems

Hamilton

Are we calling Ocean Mama Bear now?

Sophie

What do you mean 'now?'

Anthony

The reminds me. You qsked

If lawn flowing is same as bochy

Sophie

So true, I did qsk that.

Nicholas

Lawn flowing would totally be your sport, Soph

Anthony

Bowing

Blowing

Fuck

BLOWLING

Hamilton

I just googled. They are similar though lawn bowling uses ovoid balls and a longer green.

Bocce spherical balls and shorter.

Anthony

Yes.

Sophie

Thanks, Anthony! Sweet that you remembered.

Anthony

Happy to hop.

Hop

Help

Nicholas

Is anyone else concerned that Lily-Ann broke Anthony?

Anthony responded with a shockingly fast middle-finger emoji.

Lily-Ann laughed and went into her bedroom where she found Anthony sitting against her headboard, her duvet bunched around his waist.

'Did I break you?' she asked.

'Into a thousand pieces,' he told her.

She simply stood there, because the tone of his voice or the gleam in his eyes almost made her blush. He kissed her goodbye, then headed to his studio for his weights.

Lily-Ann reapplied her makeup. She used sharp contour under her cheekbones and along her chin line. She didn't want to look good; she wanted to look intense. Well, more intense. She was aware that most people wouldn't call her easy, but she still liked to reinforce that impression on the days she worked at the office. That way, her boss was happier to let her work remotely.

She left her cottage and got halfway to her car before she caught sight of CJ standing in the shade of the hedge. She only noticed because that was the one place on the property that every other resident avoided: the spot where Sophie had found James Dedrick's body.

CJ was hunched over her phone, listening intently. She looked so tense that Lily-Ann wanted to imagine that she'd stumbled into a vital clue, though she knew CJ was probably just struggling to hear the automated voice of a utility company.

As CJ looked toward the street, her gaze swept past Lily-Ann, then returned with jagged surprise.

'Are you okay?' Lily-Ann asked, digging into her store of small talk.

'Yeah, thanks.' CJ showed her tight smile. 'I just, uh . . .'

She gestured vaguely, then bustled down the front steps without another word.

57

VERNON

Loose ends never surprised Vernon, but they didn't reflect well on him either. Especially not in a high-profile case like the DeYoung murder. That was why he kept thinking about the Marigold Cottages: Who better to tidy up loose ends than a pack of loose cannons?

The evidence had looked watertight. The grieving widow had immediately and decisively pointed her finger at CJ Moore. Then a second eyewitness emerged, along with a bag of cash and that incriminating laptop search history.

Watertight . . . until CJ Moore moved into the Marigold Cottages.

That made Vernon uneasy. He nurtured a furtive, unprofessional admiration for the Marigold mob. At the very least, for their ability to stumble upon bizarre events. If they were involved, there might be more to this.

So he visited the Cottages again, to check that he hadn't missed anything that could cast a shadow on his closure rate.

He knocked on CJ Moore's door, following up after she'd posted bail – though mostly using her as an excuse. He wasn't disappointed when nobody answered; he just crossed the courtyard toward Anthony Lambert's studio apartment. Vernon figured he understood Anthony. Was he an ex-con with the expressive range of a brick wall? Sure, but while Anthony only cared about protecting his neighbors, those same neighbors had changed him. Softened him with community spirit, with a sense of caring and responsibility.

Halfway to the apartment, Vernon heard voices behind Ocean's cottage. Huh. He wandered toward the high, sun-bleached wooden fence that bordered her outdoor art studio. An awning covered a quarter of the area, across from the shed where she must've kept her finished paintings and art material.

Vernon unfastened the latch. When the gate swung open, the first thing he saw was Anthony sitting on a stool, one foot on the lower slat, his forearms crossed on his raised knee. Also, he was bare-ass naked, the sun shining on him like a spotlight.

Anthony glanced briefly at Vernon, then looked forward again. Not even a flicker of an expression, which made Vernon give a snort of amusement.

Ocean stood in front of Anthony, looking about half his size. She wore a white smock covered with a rainbow of paint smears, and didn't seem to notice Vernon. She dug her hands into a plastic bag of clay and plopped a slab on the wheeled platform in front of her.

'Ocean,' Anthony said.

She blinked at him, then stiffened in surprise when she noticed Vernon. 'You don't knock?'

'C'mon, Ocean, we're old friends by now.'

'You're half right,' she said.

He acknowledged that with a smile. 'I'll accept surprisingly youthful acquaintances.'

'Can we help you?' Ocean asked, though he detected a slight smile of her own.

'Nah, I'm just passing through. What're you sculpting Anthony for?'

'Art.'

'Right. Yeah, that follows.'

'Let's take a break,' she told Anthony.

Anthony wrapped himself in a cotton robe that reached the top of his thighs and stretched meatily, rolling his shoulders and cracking his neck.

'I'm looking for CJ Moore,' Vernon said. 'Any idea where I might find her?'

'Nope,' Ocean said.

'I hear you went out.'

'A few times, yeah.'

'I'm sorry about, uh . . .' He gestured toward the courtyard. 'The whole arrest thing. Didn't know you were dating.'

Ocean eyed him warily. 'Why are you being so friendly?'

'This is my natural state, Ocean. Also, we are acquainted. You didn't kill anyone, I know that, and you aren't aiding and abetting either. So I'm hoping you'll tell me how on earth another murder suspect moved into the Marigold Cottages.'

'Oh. Yeah. Well, because Mrs B is like – what's that quote? "While there is a lower class, I am in it, and while there is a criminal element, I am of it."'

'You happen to have that memorized?'

She finally smiled. 'My mother painted it on my bedroom wall as a kid. My father painted, "If I can't dance, it's not my revolution."'

'I had Charlie Brown wallpaper,' Vernon told her. 'How about you, Anthony?'

'I didn't have wallpaper.'

'Uh-huh,' Vernon said. 'So is there anything either of you want to tell me about CJ Moore?'

Ocean wiped her hands on her apron again. 'I'm sorry to tell you she's exactly what she looks like. I know that doesn't help, but she's one of the good ones, Detective. She loved Frank. She devoted her entire adult life to him. There just isn't more to her than that. I like her.'

'Fair enough.' Vernon sidestepped the studio clutter toward Ocean's sculpture platform. As he got closer, the mound of gritty brown clay resolved into shapes. Its surface was choppy, roughed by one of her tools, but the planes and curves of a man's back emerged from the chaos.

'Damn, you're good,' he said.

Ocean spritzed the clay with a spray bottle. 'I didn't take you for an art lover.'

'No, but I can appreciate skill.' He touched a dab of gritty clay on the corner of the platform. 'From where I'm sitting, the investigation looks done. But you and your friends have a gift for un-finishing things. So ask around, would you? See what Lily-Ann Novak knows, what Mrs B feels in her bones.

You're the only one here with any common sense.'

She tilted her head in surprise. 'Me?'

'You'd make a good cop.'

'Jesus, Enible.'

'Talk about a low blow,' Anthony added.

That made Vernon laugh. 'Just ask around, would you?'

'Sure.'

'Thanks.'

'Break's over,' Ocean said. 'You can let yourself out, Detective.'

'You're not going to ask me to model?' he said.

Her gaze sharpened on him as she seemed to consider the suggestion.

'Okay, okay!' he said, heading for the gate. 'I'm going!'

58

OCEAN

'Anybody home?' Mrs B asked, opening the front door of Ocean's cottage.

'In the kitchen!' Ocean called back.

With a jingle of silver bracelets, Mrs B appeared in the doorway. 'So, nu?'

'Nu what?' she asked, scrubbing the clay from under her fingernails at the sink. She'd spent twenty years thinking that Mrs B was saying 'new' before she realized she was saying the Yiddish 'nu,' which she still couldn't quite translate. Something like *what's up*?

'I heard the detective talking to you,' Mrs B said.

'Where were you?'

'In your living room. The window was open.'

Ocean didn't bother asking why she was in her cottage. 'What did you hear?'

'That he asked for our help.'

'He's afraid he's missed something that will bite him on the ass.'

'He said he wants to know what I'm feeling in my old bones!'

'He did not say that.'

Mrs B straightened one of Miles's paintings on the fridge. 'Close enough. So now that we've been deputized, I need a favor.'

Ocean threw her rag aside. 'Is that right?'

'A lift to Hope Ranch.'

'You want to talk to Karina DeYoung?'

'I'm an old lady,' Mrs B said, in a dramatically wavering voice. 'I don't understand. Why is she so mean to my friend CJ?'

'That'll never work.'

'It never *fails*,' Mrs B announced, and Ocean belatedly realized that she was wearing one of her more elegant caftans, a minimalist design of red silk that highlighted her silver-blonde pixie cut.

'Is that what you're dressed up for? Hope Ranch?'

'These are my Karina-friendly clothes. I came over before I knew the detective was here. Because Lily-Ann can't drive me.'

'You asked her first?' Ocean asked, not at all sulkily.

'I thought they could bond about wealth. It's why I'm so glamorous. Speaking of which, you look like you've been mud-wrestling again.'

Ocean changed into dark jeans, a black tank, and the linen blazer she wore to gallery openings. She ran product through her hair, which she'd started doing after CJ had called Jane a 'knock-out.' That had shaken her so badly she'd almost considered wearing lipstick. Instead, she started using the hair serum Lily-Ann gave her. Not that she was trying to appeal to CJ anymore. At least, not now. When this was all over, she might try again.

Ten minutes later, she found herself driving Mrs B to Hope Ranch. She hadn't even agreed to give the meddlesome old woman a lift. Well, she'd always had a hard time saying no to Mrs B. And she hated to admit it, but the detective's request actually flattered her.

'What did Lily-Ann say about visiting Karina?' she asked.

'That I shouldn't expect her to answer any of the really important questions. About the cash, or being desperate to remodel, or how she convinced Sunny Wheeler to back up her testimony.'

'So what *are* you going to ask her?'

'All of that!' Mrs B said, cheerily. 'Lily-Ann is good at logic, but I'm better at—'

'Getting under people's skin?'

'Emotion. Though we both agree that Anthony is one big slab of cheesecake.'

Ocean slammed the brakes at a stoplight. 'Please don't spy on my models.'

'I don't spy,' Mrs B informed her. 'I merely ogle. Are you sure this is the way?'

'Yes,' she said.

She'd spent a good amount of time in Hope Ranch over the years. First when a high school friend hosted parties in his fancy house, then after college she'd offered art classes to Hope Ranch women who, despite their wealth, she'd found charming and down to earth. Still, she'd never been to a mansion like the DeYoungs'. The manicured lawns unfurled around rose gardens and outbuildings, stretching to the wildflower-embossed cliff top. Then the earth vanished and the ocean began, the gently rolling Pacific tossing glimmers of sunlight around like Mother Earth's own disco ball.

She parked in the drive and trotted around the car to open the door for Mrs B. She offered her arm, because Mrs B sometimes struggled to stand from low chairs, and said, 'So what's our game plan?'

'You know what they say about plans,' Mrs B told her, as they headed for the front door.

'What do they say?'

'Oh, *I* don't know. I thought you did.'

'Hoo boy,' Ocean muttered, before she pressed the bell. 'We could tell her a version of the truth – you spent all your money bailing out CJ, and now you're worried she'll run.'

Mrs B scrunched up her nose. 'The truth is so drab.'

'This is going to go super well,' Ocean said.

To her surprise Karina DeYoung opened the door herself. She was prettier than Ocean had expected, with short hair, a strong nose, striking light brown eyes, and the build of a sixty-year-old woman who played tennis three times a week. On the other hand, she was dressed fairly sloppily, in an oversized T-shirt and leggings, though Ocean could hardly throw stones.

'You must be Karina DeYoung,' Mrs B said, offering a jangling hand to shake. 'I'm Golda, I called a little earlier?'

'Of course,' Karina said, with a quick smile. 'Please come in.'

'And this is my driver and dogsbody.' Mrs B nodded to Ocean as she swanned into the big foyer. 'Oh, goodness! What a beautiful home.'

'It could be,' Karina said, her smile fading. 'With a little love and a lot of effort.'

Ocean missed a few words of their conversation, too busy contending with 'dogsbody.'

'Glad you could come on such short notice,' Karina was saying.

'Think nothing of it,' Mrs B assured her. 'Now, as I mentioned on the phone, my stepson works for the city. Nicholas Perez, did you goggle him as I suggested?'

Ocean gritted her teeth. First dogsbody and now goggle. Mrs B absolutely knew the word was 'Google,' which meant she was amusing herself by acting like a dotty old woman. But for what nefarious reason had she called ahead and roped Nicholas into her lies?

'I did, yes,' Karina said. 'Would you like a drink? Iced tea?'

'Please,' Mrs B said. 'And a light beer for Ocean, if you have one.'

She didn't bother saying she didn't like light beer – or any beer, this early. Instead, she studied the bottom of the wide staircase leading to the second floor. So that was where Frank DeYoung had died. There was no sign now, of course. She didn't know what she'd expected, a chalk outline?

Karina didn't seem to notice her inspection of the floor. She just led them to a sparsely furnished room on the far side of the house, with French doors and brown carpeting and chunky built-in bookshelves, then gestured unhappily. 'As you can see, nothing's been updated in thirty years.'

'Oh, dear,' Mrs B said.

'Just passing through,' Karina assured her, then opened the doors to the patio.

Sunlight poured into the drab room, which made it look even drabber. Karina narrowed her lips as she gestured for them to step outside. Ocean followed Mrs B onto a flagstone patio where two round tables stood in the shade of fancy market umbrellas, and flowers ruffled in the ocean breeze.

Karina invited them to sit, then returned inside for the drinks.

'A dogsbody?' Ocean asked, flopping into a wrought iron chair.

'I meant to say factotum,' Mrs B confided.

She wasn't sure what that was, either, so she said, 'You told her Nicholas would help with her building permits?'

'Well, I mean – a little, yes.'

'Did you ask him about this?'

Mrs B scoffed. 'And incriminate him? What do you take me for?'

'A Ferris wheel in human form.'

'You know I don't like heights,' Mrs B told her.

Karina reappeared with the drinks. She set them on the table, then sat opposite Mrs B and said, 'So you mentioned that Nicholas has been in his current job for seven years?'

'Almost eight now. He didn't mention his work when you met?'

Karina blinked at her. 'We met?'

'Oh, yes! I didn't know if I should say anything, but I am twice-widowed myself.'

Ocean almost snorted in disbelief. Now the old lady was inventing a dead husband? She'd seen her get this way before, reveling in her own outrageousness, but it still took her by surprise.

'Don't choke, darling!' Mrs B patted her arm before telling Karina, 'Nicholas was here on the night of your husband's death. That's how I know about the potential of the property.'

Karina frowned. 'I don't remember. Oh, he came with the pretty Asian girl?'

'Sophie, yes.'

'So . . . so he knows CJ? She invited him?'

'CJ?' Mrs B asked. 'Your husband's secretary? Well, I suppose—'

'Wait!' Karina's mouth turned down. 'One second.'

'Yes, dear?'

Karina didn't speak for a moment. The muscles in her neck strained and she clenched one of her fists, then she stood abruptly from her chair. 'You're the old woman from the YMCA.'

'Why, thank you!' Mrs B pressed her hand to her chest as if thrilled. 'I am, indeed!'

'What are you doing here?'

'Well! Nicholas tells me that zoning permission isn't—'

'You're CJ's friend,' Karina spat.

'I'm *everyone's* friend, dear. And it sounds like you need one. Also, I may have accidentally used my home as collateral for CJ's release from jail.' Mrs B blinked as if suddenly teary-eyed. 'Now I'm afraid she'll flee and leave me homeless, so please, really, we're on the same side—'

Karina pointed toward the driveway. 'It's time for you to leave.'

'I'm so sorry!' Mrs B wailed. 'But won't you just listen for a moment, I'm sure we—'

'Get off my property this instant.'

'C'mon.' Ocean tugged Mrs B up from her chair. 'We're leaving.'

Mrs B stopped wailing and glared at Karina. 'Why aren't you honoring Frank's last wishes?'

'What?'

'You cut off his donations. He trusted you with his legacy, and you betrayed him.'

'Screw you.'

'That's a good point, dear, but I'm worried you'll regret not supporting his—'

Karina took a sharp breath. 'Do you want me to call the police?'

'And why blame *CJ*?' Mrs B asked.

'Because she fucking pushed him!'

'You know they weren't sleeping together or any such nonsense.'

'Out!' she screamed. 'Get out!'

Ocean made placating noises as she ushered Mrs B around the side of the house. She opened the passenger door for her, then took her place behind the wheel and said, 'I hope you enjoyed yourself.'

'Well, of course. Though I'm not sure we learned anything.'

'You think?' she said.

'Except that it's terribly easy to upset her.' Mrs B clicked her seat belt. 'Which means she might blurt an uncomfortable truth the next time we chat.'

Ocean didn't bother responding to 'the next time.' Too busy checking for the flash of police lights on the road ahead.

59

SOPHIE

When Lily-Ann came to see me at work, I met her in the break room because I didn't want her to reorganize my office. She took the wooden chair and crossed her legs. Her block-heel sandals were handmade, and probably cost more than my monthly rent, so I looked them straight in the eye as I said, 'So what do you think about going easy on Karina?'

'Because CJ asked you to?'

'Yeah, she doesn't want to get her in trouble.'

Lily-Ann smoothed her skirt on her knee. 'Despite the fact that she blames CJ for Frank's death?'

'Despite everything. I guess CJ thinks it's disloyal to Frank to stir up more trouble for Karina while she's in mourning.'

'Mm. We'll see. However, the reason I stopped by was to ask you to learn more about Jane Sheffield.'

'Oh, sure. I didn't even know we still considered her a suspect. What do you want me to find out?'

'Nothing in particular, you're just well-placed to make the inquiries.'

'Okay, but what about my ice cube theory?' I'd been meaning to ask her.

'I wasn't entirely aware you had one. You mean the ice you spotted on the stairs after Frank died?'

'Yes! Yes, Lily-Ann. Sherlock would take one look at that ice and crack the case.'

'Or he'd conclude that Frank dropped his drink when he fell.'

'Maybe,' I admitted. 'But he'd still find some crucial detail that we're overlooking, that's all I'm saying. Like why was the cash in a Trader Joe's bag? Do rich people even shop there?'

'We have enough trouble focusing on the most mundane facts, Sophie. We don't need to speculate.'

'Everything seemed to fall into place last time.'

'Last time.' Lily-Ann straightened on her chair. 'Yes, well, Piotr's sister has been calling me again. And making insinuations. She thinks he's innocent.'

My stomach knotted. 'Wh-why?'

'Because that's what he tells her.'

'There's no, like, evidence, though?'

'No.'

'Then screw them, Lily-Ann. He tried to murder you.'

'And you saved my life.'

'Nah, I just . . .'

'Burst from your cottage wielding a bottle of wine like a barbarian queen wields a battle-axe.'

I felt myself flush with pride. 'Yeah, just *that*.'

'And now his family is making noise. And given Detective Enible's reappearance, we have to make extra sure we don't talk about the previous murders. You in particular.'

My cheeks flushed with offense. 'Why me in particular? You don't trust me?'

'You're far too honest.'

'No, I'm not.'

'Also, too kind.'

'I'm a barbarian queen! I wasn't too kind when I kicked my stalker in the balls.'

'Well, he deserved it, but I'm not sure Detective Enible does. So if he approaches you, just stay silent.' Lily-Ann leaned forward. 'Oh, and when you meet Jane, ask her about that award she wanted. The Millerbrandt, I believe it's called.'

I blinked at her in confusion. 'Am I meeting her?'

'Yes. Anthony insists that disrespect is a major motivation for murder.'

'Yeah, but that's *men.*'

'Well, find out what you can. You can ask her during your informational interview.'

'My what, now? What did you do, Lily-Ann?'

'I arranged a meeting for you to pick Jane's brain. I spoke to her assistant, and pretended I was you.'

'*Lily-Ann.*'

'"Hello, this is Sophie Gilman!"' she said in a high-pitched voice and flashed a smile that was, for her, positively impish.

I immediately forgave her. 'That's a terrible impression of me.'

'In any case, flatter her, then remind her you were at the DeYoungs' and appeal to her ego by saying she must have some insight into the guests.'

'You've thought this through.'

'I have a list.'

'Of course you do. What's everyone else doing?'

'Hamilton is trying to get more police reports. Apparently the "raid" is over in his game, so his leverage is weaker.'

'That's such a weird reason for a cop to share information,' I said. 'To beat a video game.'

'Yes, well, as you said . . . men.' Lily-Ann glanced at her phone. 'Hmm. Mrs B wants an address.'

'Whose?'

'She hasn't gotten there yet. Still typing.' She looked back to me. 'I asked friends of my family for information on the Hope Ranch guests and learned that Helene and George

Kagant are lovely and Sunny Wheeler is a kick. That's what they called him. A kick. They say Frank DeYoung was sweet, and Karina is a good hostess.'

'So they hated Karina.'

'What's wrong with being a good hostess?'

'It's damning with faint praise.'

'Hmm.' Lily-Ann tapped on her phone again. 'Also, Mrs B wants me to introduce you to my family friends with an eye toward fundraising.'

'Oh, god, no! I don't want to ask you for favors like that. That's just . . . no. Ignore her, please.'

'If I offer to help, Sophie, that's my choice and cannot cause obligation on your part.'

'That's great in theory, Lily-Ann, but I feel beholden to a waiter for refilling my bread basket.'

'We'll work on that later,' she assured me. 'Does Nicholas have any news?'

'Not since he dug up that bankrupt property Sunny Wheeler owns.'

'Speaking of which, one moment.' She paused to finish texting Mrs B. 'There we go. Now Hamilton is doing his best, but keep an eye on CJ, would you?'

'You think she's going to run?'

'No,' Lily-Ann said, as she stood to leave. 'But if I'm wrong, it will be a catastrophe.'

60

OCEAN

'Well, that was a disaster,' Ocean said, driving away from the DeYoung house.

'An invigorating disaster!' Mrs B checked her lipstick in the sun visor mirror. 'And look on the bright side.'

'What's the bright side?'

'There's plenty of daylight left.'

Ocean tapped the brake at the end of the drive. 'For what?'

'For the massage therapist.'

'What, Pax? *Now* you want to talk to him? You ignored him when he was hanging around the Cottages.'

'Well, I didn't want to interfere.'

She gave a bark of laughter. 'Didn't want to interfere? You've never seen a chance to meddle that you didn't want to kiss behind the bleachers.'

'I have no idea what you're talking about. I want to speak with Pax, that's all.' Mrs B flashed a sudden, mischievous smile. 'I'm telling you, Ocean, I feel younger than I have in years. Having a hobby is positively rejuvenating.'

'Poor Karina,' she said, following the winding road past the golf course. 'She just lost her husband and then you show up.'

'She's handling her grief by planning a renovation so extensive that she needs permission from the Coastal Commission.'

'People mourn in different ways, Golda. You told me that once.'

'What a tedious cliché. She's trying to frame CJ!'

Ocean side-eyed her. 'Now framing people is wrong?'

'Framing *innocent* people is wrong. Are you . . . How are you?'

'I'm fine.'

'With CJ.'

'I know what you meant. I'm fine, I promise. We went out a few times, we weren't even dating.'

'Yes, but aren't lesbians known for yoohooing?'

'What?'

'Yoohooing. You told me about it! Getting too serious too soon.'

'First, let's never say that again. Second, you mean U-Hauling, and don't say that either.'

'Well, I'm glad you're not upset. I know after your ex-wife . . .' She trailed off. 'Well! In any case, I doubt *Pax* is grieving, though I never really got a sense of him. We'll stop at his house on the way home.'

'What are you going to do? Pretend you're a city planning consultant?'

'I'm an old person who needs a massage. That's what he *does*.'

'Oh, true. We don't have his address, though.'

'Lily-Ann does.' After a few silent minutes of pecking at her phone, Mrs B announced, 'He lives back behind the Riviera, Mission Canyon, around there. She gave me a link to click for directions.'

'So we're definitely going, are we?'

Mrs B showed her a smug smile. 'I knew I could count on you.'

She grumbled, but Mrs B was happy, and frankly that was

all that mattered. Nothing like bullying a rich widow to put a spring in one's step.

The Mission Canyon area confused Ocean. Too many long windy roads, too many hillsides with looming eucalyptuses and live oaks. Still, she followed the directions on Mrs B's phone past the reservoir toward the outer fringes of Montecito. The homes tucked into the foothills probably cost three or four million, which raised the question of how a bodyworker, even one who charged three hundred bucks an hour, could afford to live there.

The question was answered when she discovered Pax's residence was a mobile home on a property that must've burned during the Tea Fire. The building's remaining walls were a smudged blue, and flowering hibiscuses in large clay pots flanked the drive as if to compensate for the fire damage. To the right of the mobile home, a semicircle of Adirondack chairs faced downhill, and Ocean caught sight of a trampoline around the corner.

'That's got to be his,' she said. 'I've never seen a place that looked more like a massage therapist's house. Who else could live here?'

'A palm reader,' Mrs B said.

She parked on the road and escorted Mrs B to the front door. She knew better than to ask about a plan, so she just knocked and waited.

'We should look inside,' Mrs B said, when nobody answered.

'Why?'

'Maybe he's got a Trader Joe's bag of cash on the kitchen counter.'

'Or a client on a massage table. Golda, you've seen enough nudes today.'

'You're such a prude.' She stepped backward to eye the mobile home, either looking for the best place to peek inside or the best place to break a window.

'Well, this was a waste of time,' Ocean said, as they returned to the car.

'Only because you're afraid to break and enter.'

'You've spent enough time in jail, Golda. Maybe we should ask Pax to meet for coffee, like normal humans?'

'That sounds boring,' she said, 'but effective.'

Ocean drove them past one of the entrances to Parma Park, freshly planted with native grasses and shrubs, and got halfway to the reservoir before Mrs B's phone buzzed.

'Oh!' she said. 'Lily-Ann wants us to make a stop on the way home.'

'Where?'

Mrs B squinted at her phone. 'A mile from here. Two miles? Hold on, where's the . . . three minutes away. At VivX. Sunny Wheeler's bankrupt business.'

'His life-extension place is back here?'

'Three minutes away.' She shuddered. 'Can you imagine wanting to live forever?'

'Don't you?'

'Goodness, no. On the other hand, I can imagine never wanting to die.'

'Let's focus on doing that, then.' Ocean followed the road around a gentle curve. 'Hamilton told me the life-extension people get organ transplants and inject blood proteins. Or, like, spinal fluid? I don't know. What does Lily-Ann think we're going to find at a defunct lab?'

'I've no idea. Maybe we can interview the grizzled caretaker and he'll tell us all about Sunny's scandal. Or there's a real estate motive? Like there was with poor Gregory Ybarra.'

'*Poor* Gregory Ybarra tried to blackmail you and steal the Cottages,' Ocean reminded her.

'Which is how he ended up dead,' she said. 'It's okay to feel remorse, Ocean.'

'Fine, but do it silently,' she said. 'We can't keep talking about how we covered up two murders.'

Mrs B checked her phone. 'It's up here on the right.'

Ocean pulled into a graded clearing outside a building with white walls and a red roof, which reminded her of a prefab house with four bedrooms and a two-car garage. Even though it was five times the size of her cottage, it was humbler than she'd expected from VivX Life Extension Incorporated. It was clearly out of business, with mounds of dried leaves in the lot and dusty windows. The only sign of recent activity was a car with a fancy front grille in the corner of the lot. No doubt a day hiker taking advantage of free parking for access to the Santa Ynez Mountains.

'No grizzled caretaker,' Mrs B said, as she climbed out of the car and peered at the clearly vacant building.

'Does that mean we can go?'

'Let's look in the windows first.'

'That'll crack the case,' Ocean said.

Still, she led Mrs B in a slow circuit around the building. They looked in the windows and discovered a waiting room with a counter and vaguely inspirational prints on the walls. Like a not-quite-doctor's office. The windows on the side of the building were blocked by blinds, though Ocean got the impression of empty offices within. Around back a flagstone deck was strewn with wind-blown leaves and empty beer cans and chip packages.

'Feh,' Mrs B said. 'What?'

'I'd hoped immortality would look more glamorous.'

Ocean laughed. 'All done here?'

'All done,' Mrs B agreed.

She walked her back to the car and opened the passenger door. When she headed around to the driver's side, her gaze brushed the parked car in the corner of the lot. From this angle, she saw dust and pollen on the hood, which made her think it wasn't a day hiker. Also, the shadows in the window on the driver's side looked wrong. Too dark. Was someone sitting inside?

She walked closer, gravel crunching under her sneakers. The air smelled of sunbaked sage. The sun warmed the back of her neck, and yeah, the shadows definitely looked wrong.

They weren't shadows.

They were splotches, like fluid had splattered across the inside of the window. Ocean's first thought was that someone had spilled a milkshake, because when Riley was five, she'd decided to *shake* her milkshake from Chubbies and a chocolate mess had erupted across the car.

Except that was just Ocean's brain trying to make sense of what she was seeing, before her body tensed with horror.

Someone was inside. Motionless. The air no longer smelled of sage. The windows were sealed but something stank, so rancid that Ocean covered her mouth and nose. She edged sideways, trying to see through the rear windows of the car. The logo on the back said GENESIS. She felt a hiccup of hysterical amusement – a 'genesis' in the parking lot of a life-extension business – until she recognized shapes inside.

She saw an arm in a sleeve, a bent elbow and a white hand. Not titanium white, a white with more blue. Streaked or marbled. The fingers reminded her of knotted twists of paper and that's when she realized.

'Gah!' she said, and scrambled toward her own car.

'What's wrong?' Mrs B asked through the window.

She licked her lips. 'There's a body in that car.'

'Why didn't you ask them any questions?'

'A *body*, Golda. Behind the steering wheel. A corpse.'

61

VERNON

When the receptionist directed Ocean Mistral's call to Vernon's desk, he felt a spark of excitement. She'd actually listened to him. She'd spoken with the other tenants and cobbled together some information. Of course, that could mean anything from a vital clue to Mrs B's carrot cake recipe, but still.

He lifted the receiver. 'Detective Enible.'

'This is Ocean. Mistral. Yeah. I found a body.'

He felt himself still. 'Where?'

'Mrs B and I. We found a body. Stabbed or— There's a lot of blood. In a car.'

'At the Cottages?'

'No, no. No, outside a place called VivX, way out by Parma Park? Um, wait a second. What's the address? It's on your phone.' He heard Mrs B in the background, then Ocean rattled off an address. 'It's inside a car. A Genesis G something. In the parking lot. I have a license number if you want.'

'Yes please,' he said.

'Oh! Shit, shit.' An edge of panic tightened in her voice. 'It's sun weel, S-U-N-W-E-E-L. It's – it's Sunny Wheeler, that's got to be . . .'

'Take a breath,' he told her, speaking softly. 'Good, that's good. Now stay put and don't touch anything and . . . don't let *her* touch anything.'

'Believe me, I won't.'

He did believe her. 'A patrol unit will join you in two minutes. I'm already on the way.'

'There's so much blood,' she told him.

Vernon submitted a verbal report and grabbed a few water bottles on his way to his car. He expanded his verbal on the radio, to officially note the possible connection to an ongoing case, and he was still only halfway to the scene when the Genesis tag returned an ID. Sure enough: Jonathan 'Sunny' Wheeler.

'Well, damn,' he said.

So Mrs B and Ocean, both friends of CJ Moore, had found Sunny Wheeler, a friend of Frank DeYoung, murdered in a parking lot. Two men from the same social circle died violently within a month of each other. Two men from the same *party*. Plus, Wheeler had provided testimony implicating Moore. That turned Vernon's simple case, his easy conviction, into something far more complex – and uncertain.

'Damn,' he said again.

When he arrived at the address, a patrol car had already taped off the area, and two more had preceded him into the lot. Everyone loved a murder. To his surprise and relief, only one of the officers had parked too close to the Genesis, undermining the integrity of the scene with new tire tracks and a billow of dust. He decided to show the kids how a veteran acted. He drove slowly to the far end of the lot, keeping his expression unimpressed, barely glancing at the murder car.

Then he stepped into the sunlight, in absolutely no rush, and offered Ocean Mistral and Mrs Bakofsky his water bottles. You prioritized the *living*. At this point, despite TV crime lab bullshit, the dead barely mattered.

'Thanks,' Ocean said, after taking a gulp.

'She wouldn't let me within twenty feet,' Mrs B complained. 'I've never seen a stab victim before.'

'I'll show you the pictures later,' Vernon said.

The old woman perked up. 'Really?'

'No,' he told her, before asking Ocean, 'Are you going to need a lawyer to talk to me?'

'Not if you agree to never tell Anthony,' she said.

'Hah. That's a deal.' He pulled out his notebook. 'So you're a ways from home.'

'Because you deputized us to investigate Frank DeYoung's death,' Mrs B explained.

'Uh. . .' That took him a second. 'Oh, right. My mistake.'

She nodded happily. 'You know Sunny Wheeler was a good friend of Frank's, yes? Well, apparently, years ago, Frank helped him out of trouble. Maybe legal trouble? Something to do with a failed business. With *this* failed business.'

Vernon peered at the abandoned-looking house. 'That's not a residence?'

'It's VivX,' Ocean explained. 'A life-extension company Wheeler owned. Now closed.'

'Life extension like freezing your brain?'

She shrugged. 'As far as we know.'

'Okay, so you drove out here . . . why?'

'Because we're thorough,' Mrs B told him.

He considered her wrinkled face. 'Are you thorough, or are you bored?'

'Oh, I'm never bored! Especially not now. Ocean went entirely eggshell when she found the body, yet she wouldn't even let me peek, which for the record I am *not* claiming qualifies as elder abuse. Why haven't you inspected the car? Aren't you supposed to march over there and look soulful?'

'The officer confirmed there's a body,' Vernon told her. 'Now we wait for forensics, they're the experts.'

'*Ocean* confirmed there's a body,' Mrs B said.

He shook his head. 'I once got called to investigate a murder behind a dumpster that turned out to be four rotisserie chickens.'

'Is the body Sunny Wheeler?' Ocean asked. 'Or it's just his car?'

'We haven't established the decedent's identity,' he said, looking toward the Genesis. 'Though yeah, I suppose I should take a stroll around.'

'I don't suppose you'd escort a harmless old woman?' Mrs B asked.

'I'd love to,' he told her. 'If there were any around.'

She hooted a laugh. 'Oh, good point! Point to you, Officer.'

Vernon felt himself smile along. God help him, he needed more irreverent, joyful energy in his life. Everything felt fresher in the company of the nutjobs of the Marigold Cottages. Still, he dropped the smile as he crossed the lot to talk with the officer who'd arrived first, a short steroidal guy who said he'd 'secured the zone' by checking there was no ingress or egress from the building.

'Egress,' Vernon said. 'Good job.'

Halfway to the Genesis, the scent struck him. Yeah, that

wasn't rotisserie chicken. His stomach bubbled so he secured a surgical mask over his nose, then walked in slow spirals around the car. After he documented the surroundings, he placed a gloved hand against the passenger window to block the glare of sunlight. The stench seeped through the scent of eucalyptus oil in his mask, and he felt his lips turn down.

He forced himself to catalog what he saw inside the car: an elderly man in a button-down shirt, now stiff with blood, slumped in the driver's seat. Sure enough, he matched the description of Sunny Wheeler. Dried fluids made ugly shapes on his sunken, purple-white face. A dark slash on his neck was oriented more vertically than horizontally.

'Huh,' Vernon said too softly for anyone to hear.

That was rare, an up-and-down cut to the throat. He took a few pictures, even though the CSI officer would take better ones. He wondered what cutting up and down meant in terms of positioning. The cut seemed to follow the jugular, which maybe explained the quantity of blood. And possibly implied a perpetrator who knew how to kill.

Okay, so *did* this relate to Frank DeYoung's death?

Vernon hoped not, for the sake of his current case. Still, two old men had died violently after attending the same party. Two long-time friends. Which meant, first, he needed to check in with CJ Moore, establish her whereabouts. She'd already killed one old guy.

62

SOPHIE

As I walked home from work, I kept my back straight and my chin up. I refused to hunch despite the news. Despite the murder. Despite hearing that Mrs B and Ocean had found Sunny Wheeler butchered in his car.

A cold body in a blood-splattered car.

I was okay. I was fine. Maybe not as completely fine as I'd pretended, though. The knowledge that bright, safe, sweet Santa Barbara concealed such brutality disturbed me. So when I reached the Cottages, I didn't even bother stopping at home: I knew Nicholas was still at work.

Instead, I knocked on Hamilton's door. Anthony greeted me, his expression as flat as ever, except for the faintest twinkle in his eyes. Which surprised me, given the news.

'What're you happy about?' I demanded.

'Camping next weekend.'

That lifted my spirits. 'Oh! You and Lily-Ann?'

'Me and Miles and his friends. Lil does not camp.'

I squeezed his bicep in a friendly, man-to-man sort of way. 'That sounds like fun.'

'You're welcome to join us,' he said, as I stepped inside. 'You and Nicholas.'

Which was tempting, though not as tempting as the romantic weekend in Portland that Nicholas kept talking about. So I made noncommittal noises, saying hey to Hamilton and Lily-Ann as I flopped onto the cushioned chair beside the reading lamp. I kicked off my shoes, dropped my bag, and stretched away the tension of the day, the dread of the murder.

'Bail doesn't exist in California,' Hamilton was saying to nobody in particular. 'Mrs B didn't pay bail. We only call it bail because of linguistic inertia.'

'Drink?' Anthony asked me.

'Anything cold and normal,' I told him.

His lip twitched, and he headed into the kitchen while Hamilton paced in front of the whiteboard continuing his seminar to nobody. 'Bail infrastructure is wrapped around a process called RAIs. Which is an upgrade. Bail forced people to spend months in jail if they couldn't scrape up a few hundred dollars. However, now an RAI algorithm decides how likely you are to flee or cause harm to the community, and I know what you're going to say, Lily-Ann.'

'Do you?' Lily-Ann asked, not looking up from her laptop. She was dressed elegantly, as usual, in an eggplant short-sleeve knit dress so perfectly simple it had to be Max Mara or something.

'That studies show judges assign bail based on things like the temperature, football results, and racism. However, the algorithm data uses those same decisions to—'

The door crashed open, and Ocean and Mrs B stepped inside, looking shaken. I bustled across the room and hugged each of them in turn. Anthony set my lemonade down, then pulled them into hugs, too. Mrs B claimed she was okay but she looked tired – especially after Hamilton started nattering about RAIs again.

'Hamilton,' I interrupted. 'Let's talk about the, uh, dead guy in the parking lot.'

'Nicholas isn't here yet,' he told me, as if I hadn't noticed.

'We can start without him.'

'Oh! Okay. Sure. No problem. Um, but does anyone want a prune?'

I blinked at him. 'What?'

'I have both pitted and non-.' He furrowed his brow. 'Or do I mean un-?'

'Three questions immediately present themselves,' Lily-Ann said, ignoring Hamilton. 'That is, other than, who killed Sunny Wheeler and why?'

'Do we know it was Sunny Wheeler?' I asked.

'Hamilton's police contact confirmed that,' Lily-Ann told me. 'But they can't explain the killer's presence in the back seat of Wheeler's car. We don't know if they intended to shed so much blood or—'

'We need to stop this investigation bullshit.' Ocean scrubbed her hair with her fingers. 'We found a man slaughtered in a parking lot. A man who Sophie and Nicholas met at the party where another man died. We are in so far over our heads.'

'Okay, but what about—' Hamilton started.

'You're the only one *guaranteed* not to find a body, Hamilton!' Ocean snapped.

He ducked his head and fell silent.

'I'm going to have nightmares for a year. I can't stop seeing him. The stains on the window, the way his sleeve was . . .' Ocean shuddered. 'We're in too deep.'

'You're right,' I said.

'Yes,' Anthony said.

I turned to him. 'You agree?'

'Someone's out there with a knife.'

'It's true that this is easy for me to say,' Hamilton said, with an uneven note in his voice. 'We all know *I'm* not going to leave the house. But walking away means leaving CJ to the tender mercies of the justice system.'

'We can't stop investigating,' Lily-Ann said. 'There are too many unanswered questions.'

'We were doing this for Mrs B's weird sense of friendship,' Ocean told her. 'Not for your weird need for resolution.'

'And for you, Ocean,' Lily-Ann said. 'Your feelings for CJ.'

'Are you okay with dropping it?' I asked Mrs B.

She looked up from digging in her purse. 'I am. CJ's not in danger anymore. The murderer struck again, and this time the police will establish a time of death that clears her name.'

'Are you sure she has an alibi?' Hamilton asked.

'Of course! Modern life provides so many. If she was on her phone, she can prove her whereabouts at the time of the crime.'

'Oh, *now* you understand how phones work,' Ocean muttered.

'That's a good point,' Lily-Ann said. 'However, even if she didn't kill Sunny—'

Mrs B pulled an emery board from her purse. 'Which she didn't!'

'Then two wealthy men, good friends, both died violently in the past few weeks. That is not a coincidence.'

'You mean the same person killed them both?' I asked.

'Or one death led to the other, somehow. They're almost certainly related.'

'Why is that almost certainly?' Ocean demanded. 'Because it's too messy otherwise, and you can't stand mess?'

'Yes,' Lily-Ann said.

'What the hell, Lily-Ann? Maybe you should stop with crimes and focus on your Wordle.'

Her hazel gaze settled steadily on Ocean. 'I didn't see the body, but—'

'I did! I did, and now I can't unsee it. Let the cops handle the killing. Let them handle both deaths.'

'You want to trust the police?' Mrs B murmured, starting to file her nails.

'We haven't unearthed a single clue, Golda. We're not one inch closer to proving CJ's innocence – much less who the knife murderer is.'

'I didn't see the body,' Lily-Ann repeated, 'but I know what it feels like to find a man standing over you with a weapon in his hand.'

That stopped Ocean. It stopped me, too. She was talking about how her ex-husband had attacked her with a claw hammer. Not thirty feet from where she was sitting right now. I hadn't realized that Piotr's attack still affected Lily-Ann, which was horrible of me. Of course she hadn't shrugged off a murderous assault from a man she'd thought she loved.

Yet I'd simply thought, *Oh, Lily-Ann is so tough and cold and impenetrable, she's probably fine*. That wasn't okay. I needed to be a better friend to her, and I saw the same realization in Ocean's face. Hamilton, on the other hand, focused on pouring himself another kombucha. At least Anthony shifted on the couch until his knee touched Lily-Ann's thigh.

She didn't flinch away.

'So we need to talk to CJ,' I said. 'And ask about her alibi.'

Ocean nodded. 'Okay, fine. If this stabbing gives her, um, reasonable doubt because she was elsewhere? Then our job is done.'

'If her alibi is strong,' Lily-Ann said, 'the police will still claim she pushed Frank DeYoung. They'll just say that, in an unrelated incident, another assailant stabbed Sunny Wheeler.'

Ocean hesitated. 'You think?'

'Yes,' Anthony said.

'Well, there's nothing we can do about that.'

Lily-Ann closed her laptop. 'If the police want to disentangle the two investigations, we should attempt to braid them more tightly together. Like you said, reasonable doubt about CJ's guilt is easy to raise if there's a murderer running around, targeting another guy at the same party.'

'For all we know,' I said, 'the killer was after Sunny, and Frank just got in the way.'

'Excellent point.' Lily-Ann opened her laptop again. 'I'll add that to the—'

The door burst open and Nicholas strode inside, his eyes wild. 'She's gone.'

'Oh, no!' Hamilton said. 'That's terrible! Who?'

'CJ! She didn't check in with the cops, she's supposed to check in every—' He turned to focus on Mrs B. 'They can't find her. She didn't come home. She's gone.'

'Fuck,' Mrs B said.

63

OCEAN

Now there was no choice. Not anymore. Forget about Ocean's personal feelings, the Murder Collective had to find CJ before the kids lost their home.

After Nicholas shared what he'd heard from the cops outside CJ's cottage, Ocean tried to believe that she was simply away from home, not missing. Surely, people sometimes blew off a little too much steam, given the stress of the legal system. Not that CJ was given to binges, but a missed check-in was no reason to panic.

Except she'd spent her entire adult life organizing calendars and scheduling appointments. There was no way she'd forgotten her legal obligations in the bottom of a bottle. Especially because she cared about the Cottages. She cared about Mrs B and . . . and about Ocean, too. She wouldn't simply vanish.

Ocean almost managed to reassure herself, but for Mrs B's faltering voice and trembling lips. She couldn't lose the Marigold Cottages. They were her life. Frankly, Ocean worried she wouldn't survive it.

So she settled Mrs B onto her couch and draped the rainbow crocheted blanket over her lap. She poured her an overly sweet old-fashioned, then went into the kitchen to make buttered noodles with Parmesan – Mrs B's comfort food.

After she set the plates on the dining room table, Mrs B clutched her wrist. 'I'm sorry. I should've listened to you.'

'Now *that* is an evergreen lesson,' Ocean said, and kissed the top of her white head.

'How could I be so stupid?'

'You're not stupid, Golda. Your fatal flaw is that you're so good you expect everyone else to be the same. You're the best person I know.'

Mrs B showed her a sniffling smile. 'Well, there's Miles.'

'True, but he's still young. He has decades to disappoint me.'

Her smile crumpled. 'Just like I have. What if you need to move? Oh, Ocean. What about *Hamilton*? Nicholas and Sophie just moved in together! I need to make this right.'

'You need to eat your noodles,' Ocean told her. 'And let the rest of us handle this.'

'Oma?' Riley called from the front door. 'Mrs B?'

'In here!' Ocean said.

'Karina knows more than she told us.' Mrs B frowned at her food. 'We should sneak into her house and—'

'We're not breaking into her house, Golda. We'll figure this out. I promise.'

'Break into whose house?' Riley asked, entering from the foyer. 'CJ's? You don't need to break in, you have the key. Just unlock the door.'

'Not helping,' Ocean snapped.

'God!' Riley huffed, and stormed out.

'My fatal flaw, on the other hand,' Ocean said, '*isn't* that I'm too good.'

64

NICHOLAS

CJ's disappearance upset Nicholas more than he expected. He felt sick at the prospect of losing the property. Mrs B loved every inch of the place. Ocean would never find a place half as good for her family, Lily-Ann needed the Cottages for a community, and God only knew what would happen to Hamilton.

Nicholas, however, would be okay. He and Sophie would be fine. At least that's what he told himself as they indulged in the comfort of burritos from their favorite hole-in-the-wall. But later that night, he couldn't fall asleep. And when he finally understood why, he was ashamed.

He'd never cared about inheriting the Cottages. He'd told Mrs B a dozen times that she didn't owe him anything just because his father had been her cheating husband. Hell, she should've resented him for that. And intellectually, he still meant that. Of *course* she didn't owe him anything.

Yet apparently he'd started to count on inheriting a valuable, income-producing property a few blocks from State Street. He'd begun to take for granted that money would never be a problem – and then he'd started to believe that he deserved it.

That was the twist in his gut: selfishness.

What if CJ's disappearance made him lose *his* property? He was ashamed of himself for thinking that way. For caring more about money than his friends' happiness. He almost told Sophie, but he didn't want her to know how petty he was. So instead, he drifted off to sleep, dreaming of ways to help. Ways to address Hamilton's issues, to find housing for Mrs B, to convince one of Sophie's philanthropists to cover a single mother / local artist's rent . . .

65

SOPHIE

I felt Nicholas's mind racing as he lay beside me, unable to sleep. Poor guy. He'd tried so hard, for so long, to stay out of the Marigold Cottages drama. For years, he'd barely spoken to anyone on the property. Yet look at him now. Living with me and deeply entangled with everyone else.

He was probably obsessing about the murders. I didn't

know what to make of this second one, Sunny Wheeler's stabbing, but my playwright senses were still tingling about Frank DeYoung's death. My mind's eye kept zooming in on details nobody else seemed to notice. The ice cubes, for example. They changed everything. Somehow.

Well, say the killer planted ice at the top of the stairs, knowing that's where Frank lingered while saying goodbye? In that case, they wouldn't need to be present when he fell, widening the field of suspects!

I almost shared that with Nicholas, but kept quiet when I heard his unhappy sigh.

On second thought, he probably wasn't obsessing about the murders. He was probably worrying about the other residents. And about Mrs B. He considered her family. We all did, but his relationship with her was deeper. If Ocean was her daughter, Nicholas was her son.

'We'll figure it out,' I murmured, in the dim light of the bedroom.

'There's just so much to lose,' he said.

I knew what he meant. I wanted to cry at the thought of Marigold Cottages breaking apart, of the community fracturing and fading. Of losing these connections. I hated the chance that he'd lose the property, too. I treasured the weird, beautiful home we'd made together, and I felt it slipping away.

66

HAMILTON

A forest path unfurled in front of Hamilton. Light seeped through the canopy and strange birds called in the distance. Trees with impossibly glossy leaves flanked him as he ran with a cheetah swiftness toward the elven village.

In *Realm of Rangers*, every horizon beckoned to Hamilton. How ironic that he embraced danger in this treacherous imaginary world while the mundane town outside his door terrified him.

Maybe more pathetic than ironic.

Yet, he'd built a life despite his limitations. Surely, that counted for something. He held a steady job, doing IT and database management. He managed an online guild of a thousand people who shared a hobby and a passion. And for the first time in decades, he was part of a friend group in real life, too. A community. Nicholas texted him from grocery stores, asking if he needed anything. Miles burst inside after school, to play games and get homework help. Sophie and Lily-Ann competed with him on the *New York Times* puzzles, while Mrs B brought rugelach and told him in painful detail the plots of TV series she'd watched. Ocean scolded and encouraged him in equal measure, and he enjoyed that, too.

At the moment Anthony was in the other room listening to a book on tape. Choosing to spend time in Hamilton's space. Hamilton rarely clicked with other men, and never with guys like Anthony. Until now. He felt a flush of gratification as he opened a chat window in his game.

There was still nothing from PB Cyntria, the 'player behind' the *Realm of Rangers* character, the cop he'd asked for information about Sunny Wheeler's murder. Nothing *yet*, but once he secured the map from the Elf Queen's alchemist, Cyntria would send him every scrap of evidence from the police servers. Hamilton was doing everything he could to help.

67

LILY-ANN

Every one of Lily-Ann's therapists had agreed that scouring the house was a coping mechanism. Of course it was, she knew that; it's why she did it. Coping mechanisms helped her cope, hence the name. Also, she ended up with a cleaner house.

She knelt in the shower, sprinkling baking soda on a rust stain she'd dampened with vinegar. When she started scrubbing, a lock of her hair dangled in front of her face, and she felt a too-sharp stab of annoyance. She took a slow breath. Her irritation wasn't about her hair. Her irritation wasn't even about CJ's disappearance. What infuriated her was that she'd spent weeks sketching mental pictures of this shifting, cluttered puzzle of a crime. Then Sunny Wheeler showed up dead and CJ stepped completely off the board, leaving everything newly unresolved.

'Fine,' she said.

When she finished wiping down the baseboards, she poured herself a glass of local rosé from Cote of Paint, then settled on the couch and opened her laptop. Better to focus on the possible. She didn't know how to track a missing person, and she expected that was one of the few things the police did well. So instead, she'd put together the edges of the puzzle by disentangling the deaths of Frank DeYoung and Sunny Wheeler.

From there she'd work her way inward.

She'd keep the others busy, too, so they'd stop focusing on Mrs B losing the Marigold Cottages. Once the puzzle's full picture took shape, she'd know why CJ had fled.

And that would reveal how to find her.

68

VERNON

The police station seemed to quiet around Vernon as he gazed in horror at his phone. He couldn't believe the words that had just come out of his mouth. He'd mentioned to his wife that he 'knew someone' at the New Vic Theatre Company, and now found himself tasked with buying tickets and attending a play.

Goddamn, the Marigold mob was really getting under his skin. He 'knew someone' because Sophie Gilman worked there? Sure, maybe he'd ask her for front-row seats.

He slumped at his desk, gazing absently at his houseplant as he focused on the murder investigation. Okay, now he had a second body that didn't fit anywhere. And CJ Moore had gone missing, yet there was no physical evidence that she'd killed Sunny Wheeler. Hell, there was barely any evidence that she'd killed Frank DeYoung.

So what did he have? An eyewitness claimed CJ had pushed Frank DeYoung, a second witness – now murdered – submitted a signed statement making the same claim. And the fact that she'd jumped bail implicated her almost as well as a confession.

Except *had* she run? If she'd taken off for good, would she have left everything behind? If she was savvy, yes, but he didn't see CJ Moore as a competent criminal.

Vernon poured a sip of water at his houseplant's roots. There was a killer running around with a knife. Most murders, you knew the killer immediately because they 'loved' the victim, and weepingly admitted everything when you asked. Most murders, despite the Hollywood nonsense, were one-offs. Crimes of passion and stupidity. But this felt different.

This felt planned.

This didn't feel like the *end* of something.

And that was exactly why Vernon needed to ensure it went no further. Okay, so assume the two deaths were related. CJ had killed Frank DeYoung, but she hadn't killed Sunny Wheeler. A young woman dating Ocean Mistral? No. Mistral had more sense than to fall for a killer. Plus, nobody with a big sweet smile and silly eyeliner had sliced into a guy's neck like that.

Who did? A killer with some knowledge of anatomy, judging by the cuts. So who, in all this mess, also understood the human body at that level?

Artists studied anatomy. Ocean Mistral had found the body, and Vernon didn't doubt that she *would* kill for her family. On the other hand, she wouldn't kill a man like slaughtering a pig. She had too much respect for human life. Hell, she wouldn't kill a *pig* like slaughtering a pig.

What about George Kagant? He'd worked for a medical instruments company as an engineer. He probably knew his way around an anatomical drawing. As did Jane Sheffield, who'd spent half her time moving surgical equipment to disaster zones.

None of that called out to Vernon, so he needed to assume the cases were completely unrelated. Except that struck him as wildly coincidental. Still, the most bizarre coincidence of all would be if strange flukes never happened. So was there another killer, an unrelated killer, stalking the foothills of Santa Barbara?

He thought about that as he shuffled through the paperwork on his desk. Nah. The murders were definitely connected. And if CJ Moore had killed Frank DeYoung, then she must've arranged Sunny Wheeler's death, too, if only to lose the second witness.

And how were Mrs B and her tenants involved? He didn't know, but for the first time that struck him as more of an opportunity than a curiosity. There were people who didn't talk to the cops, but everyone opened up to the Marigolders.

69

SOPHIE

'Explain this one more time,' Nicholas said, a teasing note in his voice. 'I'm taking off work for what exactly?'

'Not for what,' I said. 'For *whom*.'

'For you.'

'No. For Lily-Ann.'

He shifted his hands on the steering wheel as he drove away from Old Town Goleta. 'Lily-Ann is fine. She's got all the money in the world.'

'She's not fine, Nicholas.' I steadied the pastry box in my lap. 'This whole thing is a mess, and you know how she feels about messes. None of us are fine.'

'But you know *we'll* be okay, right?' He glanced at me. 'You and me. Even if Mrs B loses the Cottages?'

'Don't even say that.'

'I know, but . . .' He turned in to the World of Goods parking lot. 'We have each other.'

I ignored the catch of emotion in my throat and unbuckled my seat belt. 'We do. I— we do. But if we lose the Cottages everything falls apart for everyone else. So we're doing whatever Lily-Ann asks, to keep that from happening.'

'And that's why we're bringing mini-cupcakes to Cougar Jane Sheffield?'

'For an informational meeting,' I said. 'About working in development.'

'And I'm here because—'

'Eye candy,' I said, which I enjoyed maybe a little too much.

When I'd mentioned in the Givemore Girls chat that I was visiting World of Goods, Angela warned me that Jane didn't warm easily to younger women. She claimed that if I brought Nicholas, Jane might open up a little, show off her wisdom and expertise. 'Also, her legs.' Which sounded ridiculous, but I found myself amused at the thought of Nicholas getting ogled.

World of Goods was housed in a lofty space with offices around the margins and a warehouse in the center, complete with pallets and forklifts. When the receptionist brought us to

Jane's office, she was all smiles . . . until she caught me gazing at her shelf of awards. Most were thick black plaques, though a few were of the clunky cut-glass variety. What stood out, though, was that she'd arranged them in a semicircle, with an empty place of honor in the middle.

Where clearly that big national prize, the Millerbrandt Award, should've gone. But hadn't – possibly because of Frank DeYoung's lack of support.

'I, uh, promise we won't take much of your time,' I said, looking away from the display, 'but I'm new to the field and would love to hear your advice.'

'You're the one from Frank's party,' she told Nicholas, as if I hadn't spoken. 'I remember you standing with Pax.'

'I went as Sophie's plus-one.'

Her gaze flicked to me. 'Such a tragedy.'

I couldn't tell if she meant Frank's death, or that Nicholas was my plus-one, so I blurted, 'Wow, that's a lot of awards.'

'Yes.' She bared her teeth. 'All of them except the one that matters.'

'Well, er . . .' I offered the mini-cupcakes. 'Consolation prize?'

Her eyes turned to ice. 'Refined sugar is poison.'

Oops. Time to change the subject with a little ass-kissing. 'No wonder you're so skinny!'

'One's body is a temple,' she said. 'Not a trash can.'

'Oh, Angela shared that quote with me just the other day.'

'Did she?' Jane asked, clearly pleased.

'Yeah, with our whole fundraising group. She, uh, says that you're among the most successful development directors in World of Goods history.'

Jane adjusted the neckline of her blue leopard-patterned

wrap dress. 'The Millerbrandt Award notwithstanding, I can confidently say that I'm among the top two most successful development directors, and I'm not in second place.'

'Ha!' Nicholas leaned forward. 'Sophie says she doesn't know what Frank was thinking, not making sure you got that award.'

'He was weak about that kind of thing. Too persuadable. And with his failing health . . .'

'You don't think Karina influenced him?' I asked.

'Karina didn't care enough to interfere.' Jane's plump lips turned down. 'And now she's cut us off completely. Not just us, either. She threw a dozen organizations under the bus – against Frank's will – though sadly, not against his actual *will*.'

When I kicked Nicholas, he chuckled at the wordplay. 'Well said! Uh, but why did she do that?'

'She resented anything that attracted Frank's attention. Charities, causes . . . beautiful women.'

Nicholas ignored my next kick so I was forced to say, 'That must've been tough on your friendship.'

She granted me a tolerant smile. 'It was, a little.'

'Do you think she really saw CJ push Frank?' I asked. 'Or, I mean, would she point the finger at CJ just because she was jealous?'

'Jealous of that girl with her silly makeup? Her hair is exceptional, obviously, but if Karina were jealous of anyone . . .' Jane stared at Nicholas soulfully. 'Don't you think she'd have targeted *me*?'

Nicholas squeezed the back of his neck. 'Right, yes. Of course.'

'Are you stiff?' Jane asked him.

I gaped at her.

Nicholas said, 'P-pardon?'

'Rubbing your neck like that.' Jane rummaged in her desk for a business card. 'You should give Pax a call, his hands are divine. His client list is a who's who of Santa Barbara. Well, most are elderly, but he made an exception for me. I'm sure he will for you.'

Nicholas reached for the card. 'Oh, thanks.'

'No need to thank me.' She held on to the card for a moment too long before she let Nicholas take it. 'I'm happy to help.'

'Are they sleeping together?' Nicholas asked. 'Karina and Pax?'

She shot him a naughty look. 'No, Pax refuses to sleep with clients. Ask me how I know.'

'How do you know?' I asked.

'I'll never tell.'

Okay, then. That was more than I wanted to hear about the cougar life of Jane. I leaned forward like I was confiding a dirty secret. 'Did you hear that CJ disappeared?'

'She's such a nonentity, how can you tell?' Jane gave a tinkling laugh, then stood behind her desk. 'Well! My best tip for you is that this business is built upon personality. We're not selling a concrete benefit, we're selling a *feeling*. Pride, altruism, vanity. So one's personal appeal is key, which is one more reason you should learn to sparkle. At least try. Here, I'll walk you to your car.'

Well, this was a waste of time. My phone buzzed again as we followed her from the office, so I glanced at the messages piling up.

Hamilton

Initial police exam revealed ligature around Sunny W's neck. Not sufficient to kill him.

Lily-Ann

Someone strangled him, but not to death?

Hamilton

Yes. They confirmed from behind. Inside the car.

The screen dimmed when he didn't continue, so I refocused on Jane, who was telling Nicholas about positive self-talk and the power of yes.

Lily-Ann

What else, Hamilton?

Hamilton

Sorry, back now. The assailant slit his throat. Lengthwise. Which is rare and bloody.

Lily-Ann

Clearly.

Hamilton

Though I don't know if bloodier than normal throat slitting.

Lily-Ann

Why stop strangling him, and slit his throat instead?

Hamilton

And takes some degree of skill. The police don't know.

Lily-Ann

I didn't expect them to. But the question strikes me as a key one.

Hamilton

Oh, and they found CJ's cell phone.

On an unhoused guy outside the Art Museum.

Ocean

Oh. No.

Anthony

Not sure that that means.

What

Hamilton

Some homeless guy found her phone.

Anthony

What what means

WHAT THAT MEANS

Lily-Ann

She abandoned her phone.

Or someone abandoned it for her.

'Mostly people don't know what they want,' Jane was telling Nicholas. 'Especially rich men. George Kagant wants whatever his wife, Helene, tells him to want. Sunny Wheeler thinks he wants eternal life but he really wants meaning in his meaningless life.'

I grimaced, but didn't tell her that his meaningless life was over.

'What about Frank?' I asked.

She shook her head sadly, her first hint of real emotion. 'He was as lost as the rest of them.'

70

OCEAN

Ocean stood in front of her unfinished painting, trying to focus on it instead of on CJ's disappearance – but all she saw were flaws. She liked the excessive glossiness and specificity of the hedge, yet her attempt to suggest what the hedge concealed still escaped her.

'I mean, it's just a *shrub*,' she told Riley, whom she'd dragged from her lair for a second opinion.

Riley wrinkled her nose. 'You're trying to show what the viewer *can't* see?'

'Yeah. To evoke a feeling that is sort of subtextual.'

'What do *you* think is behind the hedge?'

'I don't know,' she admitted.

'Maybe that's the problem.' Riley tilted her head. 'How come you're painting on metal?'

'I want the option of displaying this outside. I'm using mural paint, too.'

'So you're painting a super-realistic hedge to go outside where the real hedge lives.'

'Mm,' Ocean said, as her phone dinged.

'Huh. That sounds *very* arty.'

She was surprised by the note of approval in Riley's voice. 'What?'

'Yeah, I love it.' Riley grabbed Ocean's phone and read her text. 'Ooh! Hamilton says the police found CJ's phone. Some unhoused guy fished it out of a trash can at the train station.'

'Oh, no,' Ocean said, feeling herself deflate.

Riley tapped on her phone instead of responding, sending a text.

'What're you saying?' she asked.

'"Oh, no," obviously.'

She grabbed her phone back. 'Did Hamilton really say "unhoused"?'

'No, because he's a thousand years old.' Riley squinted at her. 'So are you . . . y'know. Heartbroken?'

Ocean scrolled back to read the conversation. 'No, we weren't even . . . what do you say? "Talking"? Or we were talking, but we weren't a thing?'

'Sure, Oma. What else does Ham say?'

She read aloud. '"Sunny – guy from the parking lot – bought plasma from college students for his life-extension thing. Their blood solids. For research into longevity, according to his business model, but to inject himself according to the rumors."'

Riley made a face. 'Like a vampire?'

'Yeah, and not the sparkly kind.'

'Great reference.'

'Really?'

'No. I *do* like that the vampire's name is Sunny, though. That's deep.'

Ocean turned back to the phone. 'Right. So apparently Frank – he's the first dead guy – helped Sunny keep a lid on the scandal. Or the criminal charges.'

'So if the first dead guy was part of the cover-up, maybe the same person really did kill them both.'

'Huh. Yeah. How do you know so much?'

'I'm a natural,' Riley said, and headed inside without another word.

Ocean kept reading about the police report, thinking about

all that blood. So Wheeler was strangled from behind, from inside the car. That meant he was half-dead before the guy slit his throat. Slit his throat *vertically*. Why?

Ocean

The killer was trying to Maximize blood loss.

Hamilton

Do the police know what happened to the college kids Wheeler hired?

Lily-Ann

Which blood loss?

Hamilton

Because maybe someone's brother or mother is out for revenge.
After transfusion gone terribly wrong.

Ocean

Sunny Wheeler's blood loss.
The killer wanted as much blood as possible.
That explains the vertical cuts

Sophie

You know what else?
Oh, that makes sense Ocean

Lily-Ann

Yes, good point. That's why the killer stopped strangling and started cutting. More blood.

Hamilton

What else?

Sophie

Who is most concerned with aging? Other than Sunny Wheeler?

Hint: Nicholas is stuck talking to her right now while I text.

Hamilton

Oh! Jane Sheffield. She'd pay for blood solids to stay young-looking?

Ocean

Focus. Sunny's killer slit his throat to draw attention to his business. The amount of blood is a MESSAGE.

Sophie

Oh. Yes. True.

Hamilton

So next we need to decipher what that message means.

Anthony texted a thumbs-up and Miles shouted, 'Oma! I'm home!' from the front of the cottage.

By the time Ocean got inside, he was lying on the couch with the iPad eating a bag of cheese puffs.

'You want a tangerine?' she asked.

'Yes please!'

She handed him a tangerine and removed the bag of cheese puffs. 'How was school?'

He started telling her, but she wasn't listening. Too distracted by the murder, by the blood. She regretted sharing any of that with Riley. A photorealistic painting of a hedge was one thing, but talking about 'blood solids'? Badly done. Plus, she kept thinking about CJ's phone. That she'd abandoned her phone . . . or someone had abandoned it for her. She kept thinking about that.

So the second time she missed what Miles was saying, she said, 'Oh! I almost forgot. Why don't you run and ask Lily-Ann to take you to the shelter to look at cats for Hamilton?'

'Really really?'

'Really really.'

'Kitty time!' Miles sang out, as he shoved through the front door.

Ocean smiled at his excitement, but only until the screen door slammed shut. Finding the corpse was bad enough. She shuddered at the memory. But CJ's disappearance hit even harder. What if she was responsible for Sunny's death? Ocean had introduced CJ to her kids. Could she and Mrs B really have been so fooled by CJ? There was only one way to find out. The Marigold Murder Collective needed to finish this investigation for good.

71

LILY-ANN

Lily-Ann felt a spark of satisfaction every time she introduced Anthony to something new. She'd never shared her enthusiasms with Piotr, her ex-husband, because he'd mocked or belittled them, but Anthony thrilled to every discovery. And he'd missed a shocking number of basic experiences. He'd never eaten lamb or sushi or gazpacho. He'd never ridden a horse – or been on a plane – and he'd never even left California.

So she bought a rack of lamb home for dinner. She placed it on the cutting board, and when she reached for her boning knife, an idea occurred to her. Using butcher's twine, she tied the rack into a loose cylinder, which she balanced vertically on the board.

Then she slid a chef's knife from the block and imagined herself in the rear seat of a car. Holding the knife, reaching around the headrest to slice the rack like a neck. Aiming for the jugular. A vertical stroke? Would that really increase the amount of blood?

She brought the knife thoughtfully forward, then switched her grip and tried again. The rack was nothing like a neck. She couldn't even picture the killing blow, yet she felt confident that it would require precision or experience. Perhaps not *surgical* precision, but basic knowledge. She certainly wouldn't know how to cause a wound like that. So who would? Hunters might, if they field-dressed deer or—

Her phone rang and she answered hands-free.

'Hey, Lily-Ann!' Sophie said, her voice filling the kitchen. 'You saw we had the meeting with Jane?'

She untied her rack of lamb. 'You think she's involved with Sunny Wheeler's life-extension business.'

'It's possible, I don't know. Just a thought. I called to tell you what she said before we forget.'

Sophie relayed the conversation almost verbatim. Her memory for dialogue was close to perfect, possibly because of her passion for playwriting. She even gave Nicholas and Jane different intonations. As Lily-Ann listened she thought about awards and marriages and murders. What connected Frank to Sunny besides friendship? What could lead a killer to target them both?

'Losing the Millerbrandt Award pissed Jane off,' Sophie said. 'But it's not a motive for anything.'

Lily-Ann started stripping thyme leaves from the stalks. 'Why not?'

'She's too full of herself. *She* knows she deserved the award, so there's . . .' She paused. 'Riley just texted me. Shit. She sent a photo. She stole a key and searched CJ's cottage. She found a note CJ wrote. I'll forward the file, hold on. The note says, "I'm so sorry. Guilt is a nightmare. I can't continue."'

'Well, that sounds incriminating,' Lily-Ann said, and her phone buzzed. 'Wait, I just got it.'

'Riley's afraid to tell her mom.'

Pinch-zooming her screen, she inspected the handwritten note. Ten words on a sliver of awkwardly ripped notebook paper. 'Huh. Brief.'

'I'm not sure there's a minimum length for suicide notes, Lily-Ann.'

'Messy, too.'

'Riley is freaking out. Hold on. Uh, she says she went downtown to avoid her mom. She wants us to tell her.'

'Hm,' Lily-Ann said, then finished stripping the thyme.

After ten or fifteen seconds of silence, Sophie said, 'Lily-Ann?'

'Text her that I'll take care of it. Then call her, don't text, and tell her that she was actually in CJ's cottage to feed the birds. That's when she happened to see the note.'

'Oh, okay. And what are you going to do?'

'Think.'

'Shouldn't we tell the cops?'

'I'll handle that. Wait a moment.' Lily-Ann texted, *Tell Riley she doesn't need to do anything. You don't either. I'll pass this along to the police.* 'There.'

'Okay, uh. And are you going to pass it along?'

'That depends on what I think.'

Sophie wheedled for more assurances, but she didn't give them. She said goodbye, then trimmed the rack into chops. She started dry-brining them with thyme, rosemary, and garlic, as she considered CJ's note. It struck her as sloppy, though you probably shouldn't judge the literary merits of suicide notes.

The handwriting looked like CJ's, but the notepaper was torn at an ungainly angle. That offended Lily-Ann's sense of propriety. On the other hand, one might tremble while writing a suicide note, or—

A knock sounded at the front door. Not a normal knock, a childish *rat-a-tat-tat-tat-rat-a-tat*. For a moment, Lily-Ann expected that Riley wanted to talk about snooping in CJ's cottage, then she recalled that particular knock belonged to Ocean's *other* kid.

She called for Miles to enter, and he burst into the kitchen and said, 'Are you ready?'

'Why aren't you in school?'

'School's been out for like an hour, Lily-Ann! Oma said you were waiting for me.'

'Did she?'

Miles hopped happily. 'So can we go now? Please? Please please please?'

'Where exactly are we going?'

His little face glowed with hope. 'You said you'd take me to the animal shelter to look at cats for Hamilton.'

Ah. She'd planned on bringing both Miles and Anthony, because watching them together pleased her. Of course, she hadn't planned on visiting the shelter *today*. Still, she needed time to think, and this felt like the perfect opportunity to keep her body busy as her mind worked.

'Then that's exactly what I'll do,' she assured Miles.

'How come you're not a vegetarian?' he asked, then peered at the counter. 'What is that? Is that oregano?'

'It's thyme.'

'That's a lot of garlic. Oma says you can't have too much garlic but Riley says that depends on your breath. She once told me a story about a dragon with garlic breath instead of fire breath.'

He didn't stop chattering as she shepherded him into her Volvo and then merged onto 101 North. His voice receded into white noise while she considered the investigation. Sometimes you needed to look at the big picture without focusing on individual pieces. Miles was describing cat videos and she was considering George Kagant's background in medical equipment when she finally parked at the cat shelter.

She escorted Miles inside. The shelter smelled of disinfectant, which Lily-Ann found reassuring. She signed in, sanitized her hands, sanitized Miles's hands, then stepped into a warm room with rows of neat wire cages and the occasional meow.

Miles swept his phone along the cages as he FaceTimed Hamilton, showing him the cats. 'How about a kitten? Oh, there are two in this one. The lady said you should think about adopting two; it's no more work than one and it's a . . . What does Mrs B call it, when you do something good?'

'A good deed?' Hamilton asked from the phone.

'No, like a matzoh.' Miles panned to the next cage. 'Ooh, look at these two gray girls!'

As Lily-Ann trailed after him, a volunteer with long, untidy hair pointed her to another cage. 'That's Cali Berry. She's nine, I'd love to find her a home.'

Lily-Ann considered the skinny tabby half-covered by a fleece baby blanket. 'What happens if you don't?'

'We'll keep her until we do.'

'You never resort to euthanasia?'

'We're a no-kill shelter. We only put a cat to sleep if they're in distress.' The volunteer adjusted her glasses. 'And they know when it's time. I like to think that *they* tell *us*. When there's nothing left for them but discomfort, we—'

Miles popped around the corner and asked the volunteer, 'Are the gray girls sisters?'

'Hm? Oh, no, they're not. They do look like twins, though, don't they?'

'Identical twins!' Miles said. 'What do you think, Lily-Ann?'

'I'd expect cats of the same color to look similar.'

'No, I mean do you think one of them is right for Hamilton?'

Lily-Ann's breath caught. Ideas slotted together like figures in a spreadsheet and she said, 'I know who killed them – and why.'

'Not the cats!' Miles assured the volunteer. 'She doesn't mean the cats.' He resolutely ushered Lily-Ann toward the door. 'We'll come back another time, thanks.'

72

ANTHONY

Anthony set his audiobook aside. He watched Lil pace in her living room while she spoke on the phone, barefoot in a white knit dress that highlighted her red toenails and all those curves. She'd been on the phone for an hour, searching local obituaries and calling strangers.

He liked her voice. Smooth and steady as she contacted the family of the deceased, expressed her condolences, then asked intrusive questions, which, to Anthony's surprise, most of the people answered.

When she ended her latest call, she turned to him with a flush of success in her cheeks. 'Ashley!'

'Who's she?' he asked.

'She's not a she.' Lily-Ann plopped onto the couch. 'Okay, that's one. Not a pattern, but still a confirmation.'

'Of what, Lil?'

'Shh,' she said, and stared at him.

Or maybe she stared *through* him, her mind working on a problem he didn't understand. She didn't move, so he didn't move either. He didn't mind stillness. Time passed, then her phone dinged. She didn't look at the screen, so when his dinged a moment later, he read the message aloud. 'Ocean says Sunny Wheeler's scandal was an off-the-books blood transfusion operation at VivX.'

Lily-Ann's gaze didn't falter. 'Mm.'

'For life extension.' He continued to read. 'Ocean thinks that's why the killer cut his throat. To shed his blood. She thinks his "vampire blood business" hurt someone, that's why they murdered him. Revenge.'

Lily-Ann finally focused on him. 'Hamilton mentioned that earlier. They're wrong. I'm almost certain I know who killed them.'

'*Them*? Both of them?'

'Yes, both of them.'

'Are you going to tell me?'

She frowned. 'I'm not completely certain.'

'Was it one person?'

'There are two killers,' she said. 'I think.'

'Two killers and two bodies.'

'No,' she said. 'Two killers and *three* bodies, at the very least.'

Anthony cracked his knuckles as he considered. Three bodies? Who else was dead? Nobody. Except maybe CJ, given that note. And she was the only suspect who made sense. She'd inherited over a hundred grand. Nobody else seemed to care about that, but plenty of people would kill for a couple hundred. Plus, she'd disappeared without saying goodbye to Mrs B. So maybe she'd killed herself out of guilt. That would've been easier to believe if she weren't clearly still carrying a torch for Ocean.

He grabbed two beers from the fridge, poured one into a glass with a wedge of lime, and returned to the living room. When he set Lil's beer on the coaster, she looked at the glass for a few seconds, then her expression changed, blossoming into something softer.

'What?' he said.

'You didn't forget my lime.'

''Course not.'

She said, 'I think I'm falling in love with you.'

'It's about time. I've loved you for months.'

She nodded briskly, then turned away to hide the flush of pleasure on her cheeks, which made him love her even more. 'Good!' she said. 'Good. So, uh, where were we?'

'You think you know who killed them, but you're not sure.'

'Right. Yes.'

'What do you need to be certain?'

'Evidence.'

'Where can we find it?'

She sipped her beer. 'Do you know how to pick a lock?'

'No.'

'I thought criminals learned that in prison.'

'No.'

'Pity,' she said.

Anthony finished his beer and brought the empty to the kitchen. Lily-Ann wasn't fond of his cooking, but she liked how he prepped. She'd assigned him to start the Mexican slaw, which she said paired well with the lamb, so he started slicing the cabbage thin, with a couple onions and carrots waiting their turn. He'd never eaten so many vegetables in his life.

Lily-Ann slipped behind him, putting one hand on his waist. 'I'll make a few more phone calls.'

'What would proof look like?'

'The murder weapon. Footprints, I guess. Fingerprints or – cut the carrots into matchsticks. Though I suppose we don't need proof, not if we're only trying to raise reasonable doubt for CJ.'

'You think she's alive?'

'Oh!' A worried V appeared on Lily-Ann's forehead. 'Oh, you're right. Is she already dead?'

'Well, she vanished, tossed her cell phone – and left that note.'

Lily-Ann frowned at the cutting board. 'She didn't kill herself.'

'What did you tell Ocean?'

'Nothing yet.'

'Why not?'

'Because I like her.' She kept frowning at the cutting board. 'If she's dead, why haven't they found her? Why leave the note and not a body? Was she a threat to him?'

'To who?'

'No. She wasn't, not really. But he needed to control the timeline.'

Anthony wiped his hands on the dish towel. 'Tell me what you're thinking, Lil.'

'I'm not sure.'

'Well, what do you need from me?'

She gave her head a little shake. 'Could you run to the store and pick up Cointreau for margaritas?'

73

OCEAN

Ocean returned home after teaching her adult ed art class, parked on the street, and turned off the car. She didn't leave the driver's seat, though. She checked nobody was looking, then played a voicemail from CJ that she'd saved, talking about an Etsy shop that sold handmade felt monsters: 'One is part mermaid and part fox. There's a frog with starfish hands – oh! Oh, one is a sexy polka-dotted cyclops. That one looks a little like you.'

Then she'd giggled, which made Ocean even more embarrassed to be sitting there mooning about her. She hoped she was okay. Despite everything, she hoped she was okay.

As she headed for her cottage, she noticed Mrs B's front curtains were closed. Huh. Mrs B never closed her curtains during the day. So she tried the door, and it was locked. She fished in her bag for the key and went inside, her mouth suddenly dry, afraid of what she might find. What she found was a half-empty box of Entenmann's apple cider donuts on the kitchen table beside Mrs B's collection of pills.

'Golda?' she called. 'Golda!'

She checked all the rooms, then went back outside. Mrs B's car was still parked in its place, thank god, so at least she hadn't driven off again. She started for Hamilton's cottage, to see if he knew anything, when a text dinged on her phone.

She read the message, then ran back to her car.

74

SOPHIE

I slunk away from the office, trying to remain unseen. I felt bad about leaving before five. Of course, nobody else cared. I didn't have to clock in. I was salaried. Still, I stayed quiet and furtive, eager to return home to contribute something, *anything*, to the effort of saving the Cottages.

I didn't know what to make of CJ's suicide note. Lily-Ann had told me not to worry, but I couldn't tell if she was just saying that because she found worry inefficient. Still, I tried to put it out of my mind, except for texting Riley and trying to assure her, not entirely honestly, that the note definitely meant nothing.

When I got home, I discovered that Nicholas must've left his office even earlier than I had because I found a bottle of sparkling pear cider – my favorite – in the living room, along with a bouquet of dahlias and zinnias.

'What is the meaning of this?' I called, as if I'd caught him cheating. 'I come home early and *this* is what I find?'

Nicholas stepped in from the kitchen. 'It isn't what it looks like!'

'What's the occasion?'

'There's no occasion, I'm just that good a boyfriend.'

I eyed him suspiciously. 'There's sparkling pear cider. You hate pear.'

'It's the apple's mushy cousin.' He shuddered. 'Okay, fine, there is an occasion.'

'I hate occasions.'

'You'll like this one.' He poured my cider into a champagne glass. 'Helene and George love your script.'

'What? No. They read my play? Oh, god.' I felt sick at the thought. I barely knew Helene and George! I hated the idea of strangers reading my play – or, even worse, watching it onstage. Which I knew defeated the entire purpose of playwriting, but still. 'Wait, back up. They told you that? What did they say exactly?'

'That they love it, Sophie.'

'*They* said that or *you're* saying that?'

'They said—'

'And you believed them?'

'Sophie. Sweetie. Why would they lie?'

'Because they're liars!'

'They're not liars. They love it because it's wonderful.' He took my hand. 'The same reason I love you.'

I tried to catch my breath. 'What exactly did they say?'

'That they're excited to know such a talented playwright. That they cannot wait to see it performed. I told you so! I knew they'd love it.'

'Shut up.' I couldn't believe this was happening.

He grinned. 'So we're having dinner with them next week.'

'What? Nicholas! What is wrong with your boundaries? You're not my manager, you're my boyfriend. You can't just go around forcing innocent strangers to—'

My phone rang, and I *knew* it was George and Helene. I almost started hyperventilating before I saw the caller was Mrs B. Which was weird. Usually she'd just stop by, like a character in an eighties sitcom – or a person from ye olden times.

I answered and switched to speaker. 'Hey, Mrs B.'

'Sophie, there you are!' she said, sounding almost querulous. 'Thank goodness you answered. Oh, thank goodness. I'm in a bit of a . . . what's the word?'

I didn't like the frightened tone in her voice. 'Is everything okay?'

'A kerfuffle! That's what I'm in. Oh, I'm fine, don't worry, I'm perfectly fine. Only could you come get me?'

'Of course,' I said.

'Don't tell anyone! Promise you won't.'

'You're on speakerphone,' Nicholas said.

'Oh, Nicholas! That's fine. You come, too. I'm at the DeYoungs' house.'

'In Hope Ranch?' I asked. 'What are you doing there?'

'I'm hiding on the deck around back. So the sooner the better!'

Nicholas shot me a disbelieving look. 'Why are you hiding?'

'Because my ride isn't here yet!' Mrs B said, and ended the call.

* * *

I made Nicholas drive, because he didn't mind speeding. My contribution was grinding my teeth and asking unanswerable questions: 'What is she doing there? How did she get there? Oh, god, is she trespassing? Do you think she broke in? Are *we* going to break in?'

Nicholas accelerated through the iron gates of Hope Ranch and past the lagoon.

'Maybe CJ is back at the house,' I said, trying to cheer myself up. 'Maybe that's why she called!'

'Why would—' He shook his head. 'That doesn't explain anything.'

I told him to stop picking on me, then chattered nervously until we arrived at the property. Nicholas followed the drive toward the house and parked beside a car that reminded me of Ocean's.

Because it was.

'That's Ocean's car,' I said. 'What's she doing here?'

'Maybe Mrs B drove it over.'

I blinked at the house. 'Uh, should we ring the doorbell?'

'Yes?'

'No, Mrs B said she's around back, let's look for her first. Oh, god, what if Karina catches us creeping around?'

'At the very worst, she'll yell at us.'

'I don't *like* when people yell at me! And at the very worst, she'll call the cops. All we need is another run-in with Detective Enible. Lily-Ann told me I can't speak to him.'

Nicholas started around the side of the mansion. 'C'mon.'

I hated breaking the rules, but Mrs B had sounded so worried that I followed Nicholas along the flagstone path to the rear of the house. The air smelled different here, as the sea breeze welled up the cliffs from the beach.

I stopped and didn't see Mrs B.

But a moment later, we heard her. 'Sophie! Nicholas! Up here!'

75

LILY-ANN

After Anthony left for the store, Lily-Ann spent a minute staring out the window. She didn't know why she'd sent him away. Well, no, that was a lie. She'd sent him away because she'd finally admitted that she loved him. That frightened her. Needing him frightened her. After Piotr, needing anyone frightened her. Though perhaps that was a lie, blaming it on Piotr. She'd never been comfortable needing people. She'd always suspected that she did it wrong.

She was thinking about that when Mrs B texted. She read the message and frowned. Mrs B's motivations made sense, but her logic rarely did. She was an odd combination of good intentions and terrible ideas.

As Lily-Ann considered her next step, she caught sight of Ocean jogging across the courtyard. Heading for her car. Which meant that Mrs B hadn't only texted Lily-Ann. She'd probably texted the entire Murder Collective, and sworn them all, individually, to secrecy. Oh! This was the perfect opportunity to check for evidence. So she slipped into her mules, grabbed her phone, and bustled out the door.

She caught Ocean entering her car and called, 'Will you drive me?'

'Uh,' Ocean said.

'I presume we got the same message from Mrs B.' She trotted closer, trying to catch her breath. '"Hurry to the DeYoungs' house and don't tell anyone."'

Ocean's worry turned to irritation. 'Treacherous old woman.'

'And Anthony's got my car, so . . .'

'Oh, yeah. Of course. Let's go.'

Ocean muttered during the drive, working out her anxiety, but Lily-Ann didn't listen. She was too busy considering this opportunity to search the DeYoung property. Not inside, naturally. No, she knew better than that. She needed to check the outbuildings. Well, one in particular.

As they entered Hope Ranch, Lily-Ann texted Anthony to explain her absence, and Ocean parked on the beach-facing side of the driveway.

'Wait until I get my hands on her,' she grumbled, as she stomped around the DeYoungs' property.

Lily-Ann lagged behind. She eyed the low, sprawling mansion, then followed a path in the other direction, scanning the opposite edge of the estate for outbuildings until her phone rang.

'Lil,' Anthony said, when she answered. 'Just got your message. You're in Hope Ranch?'

'Yes.'

He grunted. 'I'm already in the car.'

'Don't bother coming. If only you'd learned how to pick locks.'

'Next time I'm incarcerated,' he promised.

She headed toward the sunken garden. 'What do you need for meditation?'

'Um, I don't know . . . a comfortable place to sit. Incense? Quiet music?'

'Exactly,' she said. 'Quiet.'

He fell silent, like that had been a request.

'I don't know if I'll find anything,' she told him. 'But this is a perfect time to look. I'll see you later.'

'Are you sure you don't need me?'

'Yes,' she said, but she didn't end the call.

'Do you want me anyway?' he asked.

She felt herself flush. She felt her heart pound, and she said, 'Yes.'

'I'm on the way,' he told her.

She cut the connection and crossed the sunken garden, appreciating the geometrical paths far more than the overblown flower beds. The gravel crunched under her black mules and the cool air felt clean on her face. The ocean spread spectacularly below her, a great expanse of blue. She knew it wasn't whale season, because Anthony watched them when it was, but she still lingered a moment trying to spot dolphins before returning to her task. Because Miles had once announced that he'd decided that seeing them gave you good luck.

On the far side of the flower garden, a gravel track followed the perimeter of the property past a brick building tucked among the trees. She went to the building, peered through a window, and saw two riding mowers. Dozens of hand tools were arranged on hooks on a pegboard with silhouettes that showed which tool went where.

Nobody was inside, so she opened the door. The scent of mown grass and gasoline wafted around her. She gazed at a corner dedicated to what looked like irrigation equipment. The interior was cleaner than she'd expected – no spiderwebs, no scattered dirt. She admired the tidiness of the pegboard. She wondered how that basic organizational model – shapes that indicated proper placement of items – might work in other contexts.

Then she returned outside. She poked around for a few minutes before she caught sight of a building flanked by yellow urns planted with young citrus and olive trees. There were no windows, which made sense for a backyard music studio, though she noted a row of skylights along the Spanish tile roof.

She checked the front door, then the back door. Both were locked, which wasn't suspicious.

Still, she finally admitted to herself that she really did know what happened to Frank DeYoung. She knew who'd killed him and why. She was confident in most of her theory, but not this part, so she simply stood there, not dialing 911.

76

SOPHIE

When I heard Mrs B calling from above, I felt almost faint with relief. She was okay, everything was okay.

Nicholas and I climbed a set of exterior stairs to a second-floor deck that stretched halfway across the house. Chairs clustered around a faux firepit that must've provided heat on cold evenings, and a bunch of furled umbrellas rested against a tiki bar. From the deck, the ocean view was even more spectacular, and Mrs B seemed to be enjoying the vista as she stood with Ocean and Helene and George Kagant, in all their Beard and Bird glory.

Though what the hell were they doing here? What was going on?

'Sophie!' Helene chirped. 'Your play is wonderful!'

George's beard shifted when he smiled. 'Oh, this is perfect. We wanted to meet the entire Marigold crew.'

'Yeah, uh, perfect,' I said, trying to sound more cheerful than panicked.

Mrs B rattled her bracelets happily. 'You may be wondering why I asked you all here.'

'The old bat reached out to each of us separately,' Ocean told me, 'pretending she was stranded here. This is her big idea. Gather everyone together, like in a goddamn movie, and get to the bottom of things.'

'You called George and Helene?' I asked. 'Oh, god, I'm so sorry.'

'I didn't have their number.' Mrs B had clearly dressed for the denouement, in a black-and-silver art deco caftan. She might as well have had a cigarette holder in one hand. 'They dropped in to see Karina, but she's busy getting a massage. Every day at four-thirty since Frank died, that's what Jane told you, remember?'

'We mentioned that to you?' I asked.

'Nicholas did, and I filed it away. Say what you will, I still have a mind like a steel colander. Oh! Then George and Helene spotted me skulking, though I don't know how. I was fully enskulked at the time.'

'You were napping on the lounge chair,' George said.

'In any case!' Mrs B gestured toward the house. 'If we speak to Karina together, as a group, I'm sure we can figure this out.

We need to find CJ. Lily-Ann will know what to – Where *is* Lily-Ann?'

Ocean looked behind herself. 'Huh. No idea.'

'Well! We can brainstorm without her. Sophie?'

I blinked at Mrs B. 'Yes?'

'You start. You're the creative one.'

'Uh . . .' I wanted to slink away, but George and Helene seemed happy to chat, which made this feel less like trespassing. Also, I wanted to impress them. 'Well, we're still struggling with the same problem, right? Which is that Karina says she saw CJ push Frank. So there's an eyewitness. Two eyewitnesses, with Sunny Wheeler. And, um, uh . . .'

Nicholas saved me. 'How would you analyze this in terms of a dramatic narrative?'

'Oh!' Helene tilted her head, looking even more birdlike. 'Is that part of your process? We know your previous project was based on true crime.'

George stroked his beard. 'If you were writing this, which facts would you focus on?'

'The trivial ones,' I told him. 'Like, uh, the bruises on Frank's back, the Trader Joe's bag. Hmm. For a play I might turn Jane into Karina's older sister.'

Helene gave a little laugh. 'Oh, she'd hate that.'

'What else?' George asked me.

I almost launched into my suspicions about ice cubes, but Mrs B spoke first: 'There's that broken liquor bottle, providing a distraction.'

Nicholas prompted me again. 'What about Sunny Wheeler's murder? Is that related, or sheer unsatisfying coincidence?'

'Well, it definitely can't be a coincidence in my play,' I told him, suddenly considering writing an outline.

'In real life,' Ocean said, her mouth turning down, 'Sunny was murdered because of his company. That's why he was killed so bloodily.'

'That sounds plausibly dramatic,' George said, getting into it. 'I wonder if we need more characters.'

'What about Karina?' Mrs B asked. 'That's why I invited you all here. We need to confront her.'

'How exactly is that supposed to work?' Ocean demanded.

Mrs B made a face. 'With Lily-Ann. She's the—'

Then the French door slammed open and Karina stormed onto the deck.

77

LILY-ANN

Lily-Ann turned away from Frank DeYoung's music studio to watch a flock of pelicans glide along the cliff top. She smelled eucalyptus and the tang of fertilizer, and considered trying to force the door.

She couldn't decide if she should call the cops – well, the *cop*. She didn't trust Detective Enible with justice, but she trusted him not to burst onto the scene with guns blazing. Upon reflection, that felt like a remarkable amount of trust. Still, she felt comfortable with the decision. Enible wasn't the sort of fearful, macho cop who reached for a gun. Also, he was willing to be persuaded if you presented the right argument.

However, what if her theory about the murderers was wrong? She considered that as the wind shifted and the fertilizer stink turned sour and visceral and rank.

Oh. Oh, no. What if she was *right*?

She crept around the side of the building, then almost gagged when the stench curdled in the air. It wasn't like fertilizer at all. More like an outhouse. The smell seeping from under the music studio door.

Lily-Ann felt her throat clench in disgust but she made herself try the door.

The handle didn't move. She banged with the heel of her hand and the door still didn't budge. She heard nothing from inside, yet a sense of urgency rose in her chest, almost like panic. What if it was a matter of life and death?

She tugged the handle once more, then crunched across a carpet of fallen eucalyptus leaves to a pile of branches the gardeners must've left behind. Her pulse rushed in her ears. She grabbed a branch that looked right – two feet long, as wide around as her wrist – and jammed it behind the door handle to use as a lever.

Then she pulled and pulled, but nothing happened except the smell got worse. So she wrenched with all her might and tore the handle from the door. However, the door itself remained closed. Shit. Using her fingernails, she tugged at the splintered mechanism. The door still didn't open. She'd torn the handle away but the door remained locked.

She swore and reached for her phone again. Her hands were shaking so hard that she dropped it. She took a calming breath, then regretted taking any kind of breath, and caught sight of her Volvo pulling to a stop in the driveway.

She grabbed her phone and texted Anthony to look to his

left. She watched as he stepped from the car and didn't glance at his phone. So she shouted his name and waved until he came toward her across the grounds.

'You okay?' he said.

'Break this down,' she told him. 'We need . . . You need to look inside.'

He didn't ask why. He simply looked at her face for a moment, then kicked the door away from the frame and, as the stench billowed forth, he went inside.

Lily-Ann waited until he reappeared with CJ in his arms. Her head lolled and her feet dangled. She was caked in filth, lumps of sick in her hair, but her face wasn't the white of a corpse. She was alive. Barely alive.

The smell shoved Lily-Ann back a few paces. She said, 'Don't move her too much.'

'Four empty pill bottles,' he said.

'You're not supposed to move injured people. Stay here with her, I'm calling an ambulance.'

As Anthony set CJ gently on the ground, Lily-Ann headed for the main house.

78

OCEAN

When Karina stepped onto the deck, Ocean's stomach clenched. She heard Sophie gasp and saw Nicholas grimace, while George Kagant muttered, 'Hoo boy.'

However, Mrs B brightened as she waved her hands in an

overdramatic greeting. The ridiculous old lady loved a rousing argument.

So Ocean took her elbow while Karina snapped, 'What the hell?'

Helene strode forward to intercept her. 'There you are! Let's talk inside.'

'What is everyone . . .'

Helene was a tiny woman but she managed to halt Karina's scowling advance. She peered at her with inquisitive, gentle eyes, and Karina trailed off and tightened her grip on her shoes, which she was holding in one hand. She must have just gotten a massage, but her jaw was clenched so tight that it looked like she'd never relaxed in her life. And her eyes were worse.

'Oh, god,' Sophie whispered, after Helene ushered Karina inside. 'Let's go before she calls the cops.'

'We'll say you're here as our guests,' George told her. 'There's nothing illegal about it.'

'You're not the owners!'

'No, but we have long-standing permission to treat the house as our own.'

'And isn't this *exciting*,' Mrs B exclaimed. 'I only wish we knew what happened to CJ.'

'I only wish you hadn't gambled the Cottages on her,' Ocean said.

Mrs B sighed. 'She was so lovely in the locker room.'

Ocean couldn't even respond to that. She couldn't think about CJ. Happily, she didn't need to because George started telling a story about how he'd once spotted the actor Simon Callow in an airport and greeted him with a heartfelt 'Maestro!'

She couldn't believe that Mrs B had tried to assemble the suspects like a TV detective – except without any suspects.

And where the hell was Lily-Ann? She'd disappeared two seconds after they'd arrived.

The French doors opened again and Karina returned onto the deck, still carrying her shoes. Her hair was stringy from massage oil and her shirt was only half-buttoned, which made her look a little deranged. Pax stood behind her, his tight white T-shirt bright in the gloom of the house, while Helene looked on nervously from one side. If everything hadn't felt so fraught, Ocean would've appreciated the composition of the scene.

'What the *fuck* is going on?' Karina demanded.

From behind her, Helene said, 'I told you! The Marigold Cottages Murder Col—'

'You think *I* killed him?' Karina demanded, her gaze narrowing on Mrs B.

'Let's all take a breath,' Pax said, his voice deep and mellow. 'And remember our better angels.'

'Stuff your angels up your ass,' Karina snapped at him. 'This wrinkled sea hag thinks I killed my husband.'

'Oh, no, dear, that's not at all what I think,' Mrs B assured her, while Ocean squeezed her arm in a show of silent support. 'However, it's also true that I don't *not* think that.'

'Who the hell asked you?'

'You did! Just a moment ago, you asked if I—'

Karina's lips thinned. 'I loved Frank. You think I killed him?'

'Well! I think if we all put our heads together, we might answer some lingering questions.'

'Maybe we should sit down,' Helene suggested.

'With a nice cup of chamomile,' Pax said.

Karina narrowed her eyes at Mrs B. 'I know who killed him, you bitch. I saw her do it.'

'Then there's no reason not to chat with us! Betwee—'

'Shut your mouth! Why would I kill Frank?'

'I'll tell you why.' Sophie stepped closer, and Ocean saw flashes of her anger at how Karina was speaking to Mrs B. '*And* how. You hated whenever Frank spent time on anything that wasn't you. Charities, CJ, anything.'

'That's not—'

'Your turn to shut up! Your jealousy was enough reason to kill him. Maybe you had other reasons, I don't know, but what you did was, you rigged the Amaretto bottle to fall, then you ran upstairs to your husband and CJ, knowing he always lingered on the landing as everyone said goodbye, and—'

'That's a lie!' Karina snarled.

Still, Sophie didn't back down. Apparently you didn't call Mrs B an old bitch without the sweetest of the Marigold Cottages tenants going for your throat. 'And when the bottle broke, you spilled ice on the floor at Frank's feet. I don't know, maybe you nudged the cubes into place. You're a gifted bocce player, aren't you? Either way your husband stepped on an ice cube, you know how unsteady he was, and—'

Karina screamed and threw one of her shoes at Sophie. It went flinging past her, off the deck. A woman yelped, then Lily-Ann emerged at the top of the stairs, uncharacteristically flushed and untidy.

'Someone almost beaned me with a slingback pump,' she said, stepping onto the deck. 'I believe it was a Jimmy Choo.'

79

SOPHIE

Nicholas looked like he wanted to punch Karina for throwing her shoe at me, which would've been romantic if she weren't a middle-aged woman. When I laid my hand on his arm, he contented himself with glaring at her.

Lily-Ann said, 'We found CJ.'

And just like that, my anger melted away. I'd hated how Karina spoke to Mrs B, but the wash of relief left me lightheaded. Thank God. Thank God. Mrs B muttered a few words in Yiddish and clung to Ocean's arm. They'd found CJ. That meant she was safe, the Marigold Cottages were safe, we were all safe.

'She's alive?' Pax said. 'Thank God.'

'Wait,' Nicholas said. 'You thought she was dead?'

'Where was she?' Helene asked.

'In Frank's music studio.' Lily-Ann brushed dirt from her hands. 'She's in bad shape. Unconscious. Drugged, Anthony said. He found pill bottles.'

Ocean's breath caught. 'Where is she now?'

'She was *here*?' Karina's cheeks flushed furiously. 'Hiding on my property?'

'She must've tried to commit suicide,' Pax said.

'I wish she'd succeeded,' Karina said.

'Guilty conscience.' Pax turned somberly to Lily-Ann. 'Was there a note?'

'You think she killed Frank?' I asked him.

'I *know* she killed him.' Karina pointed her remaining shoe at me. 'I saw her!'

'Where is she now?' Ocean demanded, more loudly.

Lily-Ann pointed across the property with her chin. 'The music studio.'

'Do we need to call an ambulance?'

'I already did,' Lily-Ann told her. 'And Anthony's with her.'

'I'll help,' Ocean said.

Mrs B didn't release her arm. 'She's unconscious – stay with me.'

'I don't know if—'

'We'll go,' Helene interrupted, starting down the stairs. 'George was an EMT in college.'

'We're going to miss the big reveal,' George complained, but he followed Helene away.

'I haven't the slightest clue what's going on,' Mrs B announced. 'But I knew we'd figure this all out once we put our heads together.'

Karina looked ready to start yelling again, so I said, 'What have we figured out?'

'Well, I mean . . .' Mrs B tilted her head at me. 'What *haven't* we figured out?'

'We don't know anything about Sunny's murder,' Ocean told her. 'There's no way that wasn't revenge for a botched blood-infusion procedure.'

'Right?' I said. 'And what about the ice cubes?'

Karina took a step forward, like she wanted to slap me. 'Shut up about the ice cubes.'

'You're the one who withdrew the funding from Frank's charities! People are going to die because of you. How can you have so much and give so little?'

'It's my money.'

'Because of Frank,' Nicholas told her. 'It's not like you earned it.'

Karina scowled. 'Get off my property before I call the police.'

'They'll arrive with the ambulance anyway,' Lily-Ann told her, picking a eucalyptus leaf from her sleeve. 'Frank loved you, Karina. That is at the heart of this case. He loved you. He would've done anything to keep from hurting you.'

Karina seemed to deflate. She made a noise like a whimper and sat heavily on the cushioned bench. 'Yes. Yes, he would've.'

'And you didn't want him gone,' Lily-Ann continued. 'Maybe you're greedy, maybe you're jealous, but you wanted to enjoy his final years together.'

She gave a watery smile. 'More than anything.'

'Karina didn't hurt Frank,' Lily-Ann told the rest of us. 'And of course CJ didn't stab Sunny Wheeler.'

'Unless there's something we don't know,' Pax murmured, before raising his voice when we looked at him. 'Maybe CJ was getting revenge for something he'd done to her, or to someone she loved.'

Lily-Ann inclined her head as if she accepted his judgment. 'And she arranged to meet Sunny at VivX, his defunct company . . .'

'How did she sneak into the back seat of his car?' I asked.

'That's an excellent question,' Lily-Ann said, though she didn't answer. 'The murder of Sunny Wheeler certainly looked like a message, with all that blood. There's a good reason for that. It *was* one.'

I noticed Ocean give a shudder as Nicholas said, 'The message being that he was killed in revenge for illegal transfusions?'

'That was indeed the message,' Lily-Ann said.

'Loud and clear,' Pax said.

'And untrue,' Lily-Ann said. 'That was a distraction. His murder had nothing to do with VivX.'

'How do you know?' I asked.

Lily-Ann's gaze shifted past me to Karina. 'Frank was done with living. He was finished, he was ready to die. CJ told us that. His friends said the same. Everyone admits that except you, Karina. Frank wanted to die, but—'

'That's a lie,' Karina said, though she sounded more weary than convinced.

'But he didn't want to break your heart. He loved you. He didn't want you to know that he preferred dying to living with you.'

I almost gasped. Damn, Lily-Ann, that was cold. So cold that Karina simply gaped as Lily-Ann kept talking.

'That meant he couldn't resort to legal-assisted suicide. You would realize that he'd rather rest in peace than live with you in luxury. So he quietly contacted a specialist he'd heard whispers about. Someone who'd helped other wealthy people in the same situation.'

My breath caught and my mind raced. Okay, so Frank had wanted to die? We knew that. He'd wanted to die without Karina knowing? That made sense. So he'd hired someone to kill him? Well, that explained the cash . . . but what about Sunny?

'I'm not sure I get it,' I admitted.

'It's entirely clear!' Mrs B turned to Lily-Ann. 'Why don't *you* explain it, dear?'

'Imagine you're rich,' Ocean told her. 'You want to die painlessly, on your own schedule. So you hire someone. That's what rich people do.'

'And yes, Pax,' Lily-Ann said, answering a question I'd forgotten he'd asked, 'there *is* a suicide note.'

Mrs B whimpered, pressing a palm to her chest. 'Oh, that poor thing. So wait, Frank hired CJ? She killed him at his own request? If that's the case . . .' When she turned to Karina, the grooves in her face seemed to deepen. 'You really did see her push him. I'm so sorry, you were right all along.'

Her kindness seemed to loosen the anger in Karina, who began to cry. Sometimes you could face anything except gentleness.

'So the other clues are just the messiness of ordinary life?' Nicholas asked. 'The World of Goods award, the, um, ice cubes. The bag of cash and . . . oh, the cash was CJ's payment, huh?'

'No,' Lily-Ann said. 'Because CJ wasn't the killer.'

80

OCEAN

Ocean touched Mrs B's elbow to steady her, and to remind her that she wasn't facing this whirlwind of revelations alone. Especially the latest one. What was Lily-Ann talking about now? After finding CJ locked in a room with empty pill bottles and a suicide note, she *wasn't* the killer? Even her motivation made perfect sense: she'd never deviated in her loyalty to Frank, her caretaking of Frank. She'd given him what he wanted – his death – despite the danger to herself.

Except now Lily-Ann was saying she *wasn't* the killer?

Though of course she wasn't. Right? Maybe. For painfully

obvious reasons, Ocean didn't like to think about helping someone she loved – someone she treasured, someone who gave shape to her life – move on. So she didn't. Instead, she thought about CJ, drugged unconscious. She still thought she should go to her, except she needed to stay for Mrs B – and CJ wouldn't want her to see her like that. Better to let the ambulance handle things. Or was it? As she dithered, Lily-Ann continued to explain.

'Does the name Horace Ashley mean anything to anyone?' Lily-Ann asked.

'Not me,' Nicholas said.

'What kind of name is *Horace*?' Mrs B said.

'Um, actually . . .' Sophie chewed her lower lip. 'I think he's on my donor list? Isn't he a local philanthropist?'

'He was,' Lily-Ann told her.

'Oh, right! I crossed him off because he passed away.'

Lily-Ann nodded. 'He's one of three wealthy men who died in the past four years in Santa Barbara. All of whom worked with the same masseuse. A masseuse who specializes in elder care.'

There was a pause, then Pax gave a disbelieving snort. 'I specialize in end-of-life care, Lily-Ann. Death is hardly a surprise when one assists those on the brink of the great transition.'

'I searched the obituaries for the wealthiest families in Santa Barbara. I called and asked if they recommended your services. They knew you. That's when I figured that Frank withdrew cash to pay for your *true* end-of-life services. He hired you to kill him, at home, with no physician rigamarole. I have no problem with that.' Lily-Ann's gaze turned icier than usual. 'Except Frank tripped before you earned your money, and Karina thought CJ pushed him. Every single problem is a consequence of that. He tripped, yet the police began investigating, which was a threat to you. You couldn't allow the investigation to continue, in case the cops discovered your side gig – even though you'd done nothing this time.'

'All I've ever done is treat my patrons with the love and—'

'You were right to worry,' Lily-Ann cut in. 'Your previous clients weren't hard for *me* to find, the police will have no trouble once they start looking.'

'I wasn't anywhere near Frank when he fell!' Pax said.

'Of course not. He stumbled. It was an accident . . . this time. Still, you are a serial euthanizer. You've done this before. And I'd support your work, except you framed CJ to divert attention from yourself – and you murdered Sunny Wheeler.'

'Oh, bullshit!' Pax stood from the bench. 'That's bonkers. Sure, I worked for some of the wealthiest families, but I didn't kill them.'

'Three dead within months of working with you. All at home. All painless, private, with no doctors in sight.' Lily-Ann turned to address everyone else. 'Pax convinced Sunny Wheeler to support Karina's testimony about seeing CJ. He needed to frame CJ and end the investigation. Either he blackmailed Sunny, or he pretended that Karina wanted his support. Basically, he panicked when the investigation didn't go away.'

'I don't panic.' Pax exhaled slowly, like the massage therapist he was. 'I am calm. I am centered.'

'After he arranged for Sunny's testimony,' Lily-Ann continued. 'He realized that he'd made a terrible mistake. He'd created a witness. Now Sunny *knew* Pax was involved. So he needed to die. Perhaps Pax offered to give him a quick car massage, that's why he was in the back seat.'

'This is bullshit!' Pax gestured angrily toward the music studio. 'CJ swallowed bottles of pills! You said so yourself!'

Lily-Ann's gaze turned milder. 'You live near VivX, don't you? What is it, Ocean, a bike ride away?'

'A short one,' Ocean said, thinking back. 'And damn, a massage therapist would know enough about anatomy to slit a throat for maximum bloodiness.'

'Except why would Pax kidnap CJ?' Sophie asked. 'Why not just kill her?'

'I didn't!' Pax said.

Lily-Ann inclined her head to Sophie. 'He needed to keep the details vague. The time of death, CJ's movements. He had to ensure she wouldn't have an alibi for Sunny's murder, or everything would fall apart.'

'How'd you even know she was here?' Sophie asked.

'Because of the music studio,' Ocean said, as realization dawned. 'It's soundproofed, private, and makes sense for a faked suicide.'

Lily-Ann nodded. 'It fit the bill exactly. We know Pax has access to drugs from his elderly clients. I presume he forced CJ to overdose, then locked her in.'

'So he gave her what he thought was a lethal dose, then left,' Ocean said, still putting the pieces together. 'That way he wouldn't need an alibi for her time of death? He wouldn't even be sure when it happened.'

'I thought *Sophie* was the playwright.' Pax appealed to Karina. 'You saw what you saw. You saw CJ push him. Don't let them convince—'

'You left a paper trail,' Lily-Ann interrupted, her voice sharp, like she didn't want Pax to finish. 'How many of your clients withdrew cash shortly before they died? People dying during end-of-life care isn't a surprise, but the fact that they all withdrew cash?'

'That sounds like damning evidence to me,' Ocean said, to support Lily-Ann. 'And I'd bet the cops find a stack of cash when they search your house.'

Pax pressed his palms together. 'I didn't kill Frank.'

'No, but you killed the other ones,' Lily-Ann told him. 'The cops *will* find the evidence. And that gives you motive for killing Sunny.'

'I promise you . . .' Pax stepped closer to Karina, his voice soft. 'Frank asked me to ease his passing, that's true. That's the only thing that's true. This isn't about the money. Frank asked me, implored me, to guide him to the next stage, to the great beyond, and I—'

'He asked?' Karina blinked up at him. 'Frank asked you to . . . to do this?'

'He approached me, yes. He was ready to move on. I'm sorry, Karina. He was eager to move on. He'd lived a full, wonderful life, but he had nothing left to live for.'

'He had me.' Karina leapt from the bench. 'He had *me*!'

81

VERNON

Paramedics liked to claim that they didn't diagnose patients; they merely 'assessed and treated.' Still, Vernon rattled off a few questions to the ones moving the still-unconscious CJ Moore into the ambulance.

'Looks like an overdose,' the woman told him. 'No idea on what. Or when. Plus, severe dehydration.'

'Which takes days?' he asked.

'Right,' she said, and slammed the doors.

He watched the ambulance pull away, then strolled to the patrol car in which Anthony Lambert was cuffed. He opened the rear door and leaned in. 'So this keeps happening.'

'Seems like,' Anthony said.

'You must've pissed off the officers on scene. What'd you say?'

'Nothing.'

'Yep. That'd do it.' Vernon thumped the car roof with his palm. 'Why don't you head home? I know where to find you.'

'I'd rather wait for Lily-Ann.'

'You really are head over heels for her, aren't you?'

Anthony looked up at him. 'I really am.'

'You know what I say?'

'What's that?'

'I say good for you, Anthony. Most guys in your position never crawl out of the hole they dug. Look at you. A steady job, a fine woman. Marigold Cottages, huh?'

'Marigold Cottages,' Anthony agreed.

Vernon told the uniformed officers to uncuff Anthony and let him wait in the Volvo, which they did not appreciate. Then he returned to the active scene. Another staircase – this one outdoors – another body, the same property. What were the chances?

'The decedent is Pax Heron,' the crime scene officer told him. 'A local masseuse.'

'He specialized in seniors,' Vernon said, to prove he knew his case.

'Well, he's not getting any older himself.'

He circled the area, then stopped at the corpse. Pax Heron, dead at the bottom of the stairs. One arm folded beneath him, his neck angled too sharply. Vernon checked the area a second time, though he knew he'd find nothing, and ten minutes later, he headed inside to his favorite room in the mansion, the one with the big stereo and liquor bottles.

He settled himself on the gold leather couch and asked the officer to send Karina DeYoung to join him.

She looked rough when she entered – puffy eyes, a nervous twitch. When she sat across from him, the words came pouring out: 'Pax admitted everything. Lily-Ann already knew he'd helped other people with assisted suicide. Which, I mean, I support that, who doesn't? Except Pax says he didn't do anything to Frank, he never had the chance. But Frank wanted him to. Lily-Ann said that you, the police, would trace the cash Pax's other clients withdrew, you'd track the withdrawals, at which point . . .'

Vernon pretended to take notes as his phone recorded the conversation. 'At which point?'

'That's when Pax admitted what he'd done.' Karina swallowed. 'That he killed Sunny after he asked him – or blackmailed him to – to echo my testimony. Because he was terrified that if you didn't arrest CJ, if you kept investigating, you'd uncover his past. Except then he realized that now Sunny knew he was guilty and, um, so yeah, he killed him. And he did it there, I mean at that location, to make you look at Sunny's business.'

'That's all well and good, Mrs DeYoung, except you saw CJ push your husband.'

'No, I didn't.'

'You're changing your story.'

'I was wrong.' Karina shifted on the couch. 'She tried to steady Frank and it looked like she'd pushed him. I swear it looked like that, but I was wrong. Maybe Frank wanted to fall, I don't know. But Pax admitted everything.'

'Then he simply fell,' Vernon said.

'Frank? Yeah. Yes.'

'No, Pax. He happened to fall down the stairs and break his neck. How exactly did that unfold?'

'Oh, well, after he said – after Pax admitted that Frank hired him, I yelled at him.' She touched her face with a trembling hand. 'I shouted at him. I was so angry. I shouted and he took a step backward and tumbled down the stairs. He tumbled down.'

She looked away, her gaze shifting to the hardwood floor as Vernon talked her through the events twice more and learned nothing else. Hmm. What if he took this new information at face value? In that case, Pax Heron offered euthanasia services to wealthy clients. He'd agreed to kill Frank DeYoung, but Frank died before Pax did anything. Then Karina pointed the finger at CJ Moore. That sparked an investigation that threatened Pax, so he arranged Sunny Wheeler to offer testimony, at which point he realized he'd left himself exposed.

That was stupid, but in Vernon's experience murders usually were. Then Pax killed Wheeler in a way that implicated VivX.

That tied together well enough, except what did it mean for Vernon? That he'd been wrong about CJ Moore, true. But also that he'd close a handful of deaths at once, if the cash trail panned out on Pax's former clients. And more important, he'd get a repeat murderer off the streets. Not too shabby.

He asked the officer to send in Lily-Ann Novak, and she

told him the same story, more coherently. 'Once I realized Frank wanted to die, everything made sense. Frank was solicitous of Karina's feelings, so he kept this secret from her. The rest flows from there. You should interview the families of Pax's now-deceased clients and track the cash they withdrew to pay him.'

'Thanks for the guidance,' Vernon said, his voice heavy with sarcasm.

'You're welcome. Also, search the VivX area for bicycle treads or footprints that match Pax's bike or shoes. I suspect he left evidence in the Sunny Wheeler murder.'

'Walk me through Pax Heron's fall,' Vernon told her.

'Karina stepped forward like she was going to slap him. He jerked backwards and fell down the stairs.'

'Simple as that?' he said.

'Yes.'

'And CJ Moore's abduction and drugging?'

'I suspect Pax told CJ that he wanted to talk privately about something important to Frank. She couldn't have resisted that. He took her to the soundproofed music studio and fed her an overdose of drugs. He wanted it to look like she hid there, then killed herself – something like that. I doubt he was thinking clearly after he cut Wheeler's throat. That was the first time he'd committed a real murder. Especially one as bloody as that.'

Golda Bakofsky and Ocean Mistral told the same story, with the addition of a few elaborate and unhelpful tangents from the former. Sophie Gilman's tale didn't deviate from the narrative, and neither did Nicholas Perez's. Everything fit together neatly, yet Vernon found one fact jarring: the tenants of the Marigold Cottages all spoke to him without hesitation.

Nobody refused, nobody requested a lawyer. Which was normal, for normal people. But for these glorious weirdos? For them it was extremely suspect, especially considering how closely the stories matched.

There were no contradictions. The whole thing felt rehearsed, like one of Sophie Gilman's plays. Too pat, too tidy, too perfect.

They were hiding something – again.

Well, fine. He'd look into the cash withdrawals and he'd question the families of Pax's now-deceased clients. And if CJ lived, her statement would make Pax's behavior pretty damn clear. And Vernon would lock down another tricky case, and close some old files. He might even ask Sophie Gilman for the theatre tickets for his wife.

82

SOPHIE

I pushed through Hamilton's front door with my hip, holding the plate steady. I'd baked shortbread cookies again. Keeping things simple after my whole 'she killed him with ice cubes and bocce!' fiasco. That made theatrical sense, but maybe I'd leave the actual clues to Lily-Ann.

I stepped inside and glanced at the banner Miles painted, with HAPPY PARTY MRS B! in huge letters and a dozen stick figures prancing around colorful marigolds. At least three of the figures were Mrs B, with white hair and bracelets, which I thought really captured her ubiquity. The drawing of Anthony looked like the Michelin Tire Man, while I looked like a stick figure in a skirt with a ponytail. At least I'd gotten off easier than Nicholas, who was the most default stick man possible: five lines and a circle, which made me laugh. Poor Nicholas. For some reason Lily-Ann's stick figure was the only one with eyelashes, and Hamilton's was wrapped in a flowery shirt.

I smiled to Ocean and Mrs B, who were bickering about the best way to unwrap a present. Having a grand old time. Those two really enjoyed a good bicker.

As I brought the plate to the table, Lily-Ann called, 'Close the front door.'

'Hm?' Nicholas asked, entering behind me with an armload of drinks.

'We need to talk before CJ gets here.' Lily-Ann's sharp gaze swept across the room. 'And agree not to tell the whole truth.'

I glanced at Ocean, but she was focusing on fiddling with the presents so I couldn't see her face. According to Riley, she'd tried to talk to CJ in the hospital, and again after she returned home. Unsuccessfully, both times.

'She deserves to know,' Mrs B said.

'Does deserving matter?' Lily-Ann asked.

'She won't say anything to the police,' Nicholas assured her, setting the drinks down. 'She *can't*.'

'Telling her the truth is your birthday gift to me,' Mrs B told Lily-Ann, in a wheedling voice. 'Please?'

'It's not your birthday,' Ocean said, setting a present aside.

'*CJ* doesn't know that. She's still weak and uncertain. She needs a party, but she refused to let me throw a welcome-home-from-the-hospital bash, so here we are.'

'She said she's not ready.'

'Bah,' Mrs B said. 'Readiness is overrated. And just because she's not ready to talk to *you*, Ocean, doesn't mean she's not—'

'Telling her is a bad idea,' Lily-Ann interrupted.

Mrs B sniffed. 'Of course you think you know best.'

'That is correct.'

Hamilton interrupted by offering everyone his homemade fruit leather, in strawberry, strawberry-zucchini, and spicy strawberry-zucchini. He was explaining that he used a mix of habanero and jalapeño when a knock sounded and CJ stepped inside. She still looked wan, but she was getting better every day – and I was happy to see she'd recovered enough to do her full eye makeup for the pretend birthday party.

After Mrs B kissed everyone, we settled in for a feast: mounds of rice and mapo tofu and spicy green beans and orange chicken and plates of dumplings and spring rolls. We chatted about everything except murder . . . until CJ dinged her glass with a chopstick.

'I don't want to make the birthday all about me,' she said, after Hamilton stopped talking about how the word should actually be *reredundant*, 'but I need to thank you all again.'

'I wouldn't worry about the birthday,' Nicholas murmured.

'I can't even express how grateful I am,' CJ continued. 'I'm just so . . . grateful. Uh, maybe you'll understand how I feel if I say the word "grateful" another ten times.'

I laughed. 'We're just happy you're back.'

'Well, about that. That's the other thing.' She glanced at Ocean and then away. 'I, um, hate how much trouble I've been. To you all. How needy, I guess. So I'm leaving Santa Barbara for a while. I need a fresh start.'

'I adore fresh starts!' Mrs B told her. 'They're my second-favorite kind of start. But I hope you're not leaving because you're afraid we'll learn your secret.'

CJ blinked at her. 'My secret?'

'Oh, yes. We know all about that.' Mrs B peered across the table. 'Lily-Ann?'

Lily-Ann set her napkin aside. 'Frank DeYoung wanted to die. That is established. He told you that, he told you everything – except that he'd hired Pax. Which he didn't mention because he didn't want to make you an accessory.'

'Is that why he didn't tell me?' CJ asked faintly. 'That's so Frank.'

'He loved you like a daughter, and you loved him. You couldn't stand seeing him in pain.'

'He was so unhappy.' She twisted her napkin in her hands. 'He kept telling me that he was one lucky slip in the shower from painlessness and peace.'

'You wanted to help him end things quickly. However, unlike Frank, you had no plan. You simply saw him standing on the landing after the party – and you pushed him.'

'I pushed him?' CJ's teary gaze flickered to Ocean, then back to Lily-Ann. 'But you convinced that cop that he fell.'

'Enible is cannier than he looks, CJ,' Ocean said, her voice brusque but her eyes gentle. 'I don't know if we convinced him so much as gave him an acceptable alternative.'

'Still,' I said, 'you *did* push him.'

CJ wiped tears from her face. 'When I heard that liquor bottle shatter, it was like a starting gun. It startled me into action. He wanted to die, but Karina wouldn't let him so . . .' She took a hiccupping breath. 'So he suffered instead. I couldn't take it anymore. I didn't know he'd hired Pax. I didn't know anything.'

'You knew what he wanted,' Nicholas told her.

She didn't seem to hear him. 'All I know is that I deserve

what Pax did to me. For what I did. I don't deserve happiness and freedom and – and friendship. Not after what I did. I deserve worse than I got, worse than what Pax—'

'No,' I said. 'You absolutely do not.'

'Can you explain the supposed suicide note?' Lily-Ann asked, which was interesting because she hadn't told anyone else about the note until after Pax died.

CJ shuddered. 'Pax called me. He said we needed to meet about Frank. About what Frank would've wanted. He brought me to the music studio and gave me a drink and . . . I guess he'd gone through my journal when he was feeding the birds and tore out a section that looked bad.'

'And the search on the laptop?' Lily-Ann asked.

'That was me. I forgot I'd done that. I only – I wasn't serious, not at first. Oh, god.' Her shuddering grew more pronounced. 'I never meant this to happen, I only ever wanted what *Frank* wanted.'

Mrs B chirped, 'Well, I'm thrilled we proved your innocence!'

'I'm not sure that's what we proved,' Hamilton told her.

She waved his words away. 'Oh, pish! She was just trying to help. She *did* help! That poor man. At least, I know Ocean will carry me the last few steps, when the time comes.'

'When the time comes?' Ocean said. 'I'm ready right now.'

Mrs B cackled. 'I'm not ready yet, you horrible child! I only wish we'd stopped Pax before he hurt Sunny Wheeler.'

'I mean, Wheeler *did* illegally buy plasma from college kids,' Nicholas said.

'True, but I'm not sure he deserved—'

The front door banged open before she finished, and Ocean's kids burst inside. Miles swept his hand grandly toward his sister and said, 'Introducing the newest member of the family! The one, the only . . .'

Riley revealed a white kitten in her arms. 'Mr Betty!'

'We're changing his name to Mr Marigold,' Miles declared.

'We are not,' Riley said.

Ocean laughed. 'Maybe we should let Hamilton name his own cat?'

'He's not just his,' Miles insisted. 'He's all of ours.'

Hamilton gazed at the cat, his eyes misty with delight. For the first time since I'd met him, he didn't seem to know what to say. He looked for a long moment at the cat, then he looked around his crowded living room and blinked a few times and whispered, 'He's perfect.'

'He came with regards from Helene and George,' Nicholas told him.

'We could call him Beluga,' Miles said, peering at Anthony. 'Like the whale.'

'Or Moby 'cause he's white!' Riley said.

'Not Montevideo?' Anthony asked.

Everyone started suggesting names, though to my surprise Mrs B didn't say anything. She simply watched, a happy glimmer in her warm brown eyes.

So I asked, 'What do you think, Mrs B?'

'I think Miles is right,' she said. 'He's not just Hamilton's, he's all of ours. We *all* belong to all of us.'

And that was the end of that.

Except not really.

I left work early again, though this time with a spring in my step. I'd signed my very first Platinum Patron donor, which covered the cost of an entire production, from set design to bathroom soap. And I'd officially earned the theatre ten times my salary, which felt pretty good. I reported my triumph to the Givemore Girls as I walked home, then made self-deprecatory comments as I strolled along.

When I reached the courtyard, I paused to study my old cottage. It looked lonely now, with CJ gone.

Poor Ocean. She was taking CJ's departure as a personal romantic failure, even though Riley had reported that CJ left her with a long handwritten letter and a big bouquet of flowers. So naturally we were all rallying around Ocean. Well, Lily-Ann and I had taken her out a few times, Anthony brought six-packs to her studio, Nicholas talked to her about galleries in LA, Hamilton shared kitty videos, and Mrs B cornered Detective Enible to ask if 'that adorable policewoman' was perhaps single.

As I stood there, a breeze wafted across the property, bringing the sound of Miles chattering at Anthony and the whine of Ocean grinding marble behind her cottage. For a moment, the courtyard felt like a stage to me, with all these wonderful characters waiting in the wings. I smiled and thought about the new play I was working on, very loosely based on the death of Frank DeYoung. I was making Helene and George the villains – because they'd insisted. George even demanded that I switch his beard for what he called 'a glossy and luxuriant' mustache.

However, in real life, villains were a little harder to identify. And I found myself mentally drafting scenes that would never see the light of day:

ACT III
SCENE IV

Curtain opens on the same lovely deck overlooking the same shimmering ocean. LILY-ANN, OCEAN, MRS B, SOPHIE, NICHOLAS, PAX, and KARINA are frozen in place until . . .

PAX

(to Karina)

Frank had nothing to live for.

KARINA

(springing to her feet)

He had me!

(KARINA shoves PAX, who stumbles backward. OCEAN grabs for PAX but he windmills his arms, then tumbles backward offstage, to the sound of slamming, crashing, and a fatal crack. OCEAN follows him offstage.)

KARINA

Oh, no, oh, god!

LILY-ANN

An ambulance is already on the way.

OCEAN

(from offstage)

Too late for Pax. I really need to stop finding dead bodies.

KARINA

I killed him. I killed him.

MRS. B

Yes, dear. On the other hand – not to say the bright side – he did murder your old friend.

LILY-ANN

That won't impress the police.

MRS. B

Surely, they'll understand! We all make mistakes.

KARINA

I didn't mean to! It was an accident! I just shoved him and I . . . I'm going to be sick.

(A siren sounds in the distance, warbling closer.)

MRS. B

Oh my shit, as the kids say. Lily-Ann, think of something!

LILY-ANN

Yes. Well, we all witnessed Karina push Pax down the stairs to his death. After blaming CJ for doing the same to Frank.

KARINA

Because she did! I saw her!

LILY-ANN

Still, I'm not sure Karina deserves to spend the rest of her life locked in a cell. Alone, suffering, forgotten. So let's agree that she merely stood abruptly and shouted a few intemperate words. Pax took a step backward and fell accidentally. Karina didn't touch him. If we say that's what happened, then—

KARINA

Would you? Please, I never – I didn't mean . . . When I heard Frank went behind my back, to, to escape me, to—

LILY-ANN

We will need compensation.

(KARINA reacts in shock – as does everyone else, though LILY-ANN remains unruffled.)

We'll forget how Pax fell if you reinstate Frank's charitable donations.

KARINA

His donations?

LILY-ANN

All of them, yes.

SOPHIE

Plus, a one-time twenty-million-dollar gift to World of Goods!

MRS. B

What a lovely way to honor your husband's memory. Such a wonderful memorial.

(The sirens get louder, louder – red lights flash from offstage.)

KARINA

T-twenty million to World of Goods?

LILY-ANN

And reinstate Frank's donations for the rest of your

life – which you'll spend on an ostentatious Italian yacht instead of locked in a cell.

(The static of police radios sounds offstage.)

MRS. B
Oh, good! I knew we'd figure this out if we put our heads together.

Of course I knew that covering up *another* murder wasn't exactly ethical. Still, I felt a warm glow of satisfaction at the money I'd raised for World of Goods. Well, the money I'd *extorted.* That donation would save thousands of lives – tens of thousands. Though I guess I'd leave it off my résumé.

When a meow sounded at my feet, I knelt to scratch Mr Betty behind the ear, and noticed the camera on his collar. Typical Hamilton.

I tilted the lens toward me and made a funny face.

As I straightened, I caught sight of Ocean's latest painting propped against Mrs B's cottage. At first glance, it looked like an almost tropical bush, with lush leaves covering the entire surface. Yet if I looked longer, I felt a glow of happiness in my chest. I didn't know why. It didn't make sense. Still, the painting never failed to make me smile.

Something about that swath of berries and leaves felt . . . joyful. Hopeful. Like Hamilton's expression whenever he offered Anthony a strange beverage, or like Mrs B's when she gazed at Ocean. Like the way Lily-Ann leaned into Anthony when she thought nobody was looking.

Like how I felt now, heading home to Nicholas. Leaving my old cottage behind. Empty again, until Mrs B found another lost soul who needed our help.

ACKNOWLEDGMENTS

Many thanks to Caitlin Blasdell, Pete Wolverton, Claire Cheek, Ana Couto, Ryan Jenkins, and Laura Apperson. Also to Kelley Ragland, Catherine Richards, David Rotstein, John Morrone, Alisa Trager, Sara Eslami, Kayla Janas, Meryl Levavi, and Ally Demeter.

ABOUT THE AUTHORS

JO NICHOLS is the pseudonym for husband-and-wife team Joel Ross and Lee Nichols. They published over thirty books in five genres and wrote an animated series for Netflix before they sat down to write *The Marigold Cottages Murder Collective*, their first mystery.